STOLEN MATRIMONY

Tay Mo'Nae

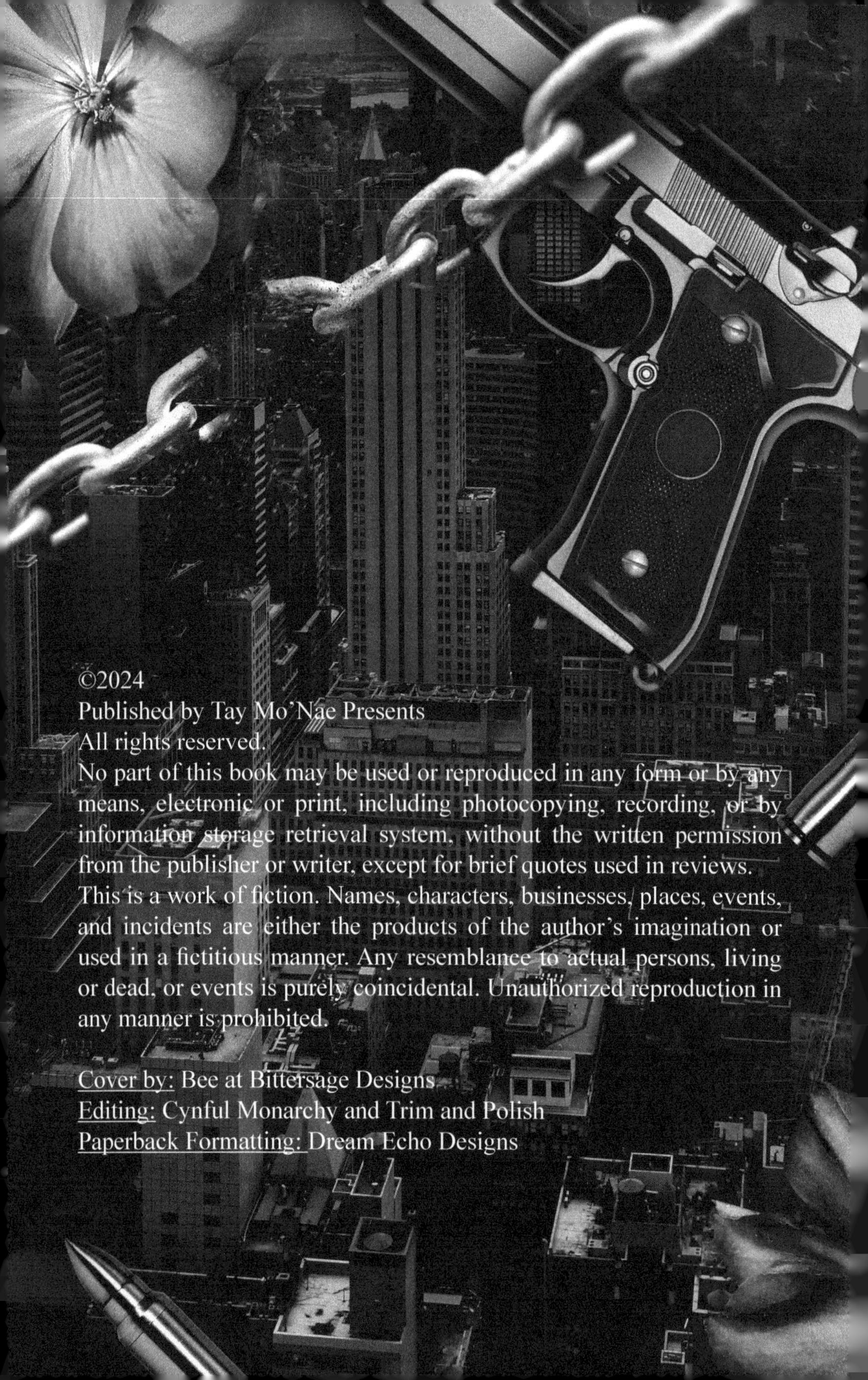

Cover by: Bee at Bittersage Designs
Editing: Cynful Monarchy and Trim and Polish
Paperback Formatting: Dream Echo Designs

AUTHOR'S NOTE

Stay up to date with Tay Mo'Nae
Want to stay up to date with my work? Be the first to get sneak peeks, release dates, cover reveals, character updates, and more?
Join my Facebook reading group: Tay's Book Baes, and like my like page: Tay Mo'Nae.

Make sure you check my website out for updates as well: Taymonaewrites.com

Also, join my **mailing list** for exclusive firsts by texting **AuthorTay** to **33777**

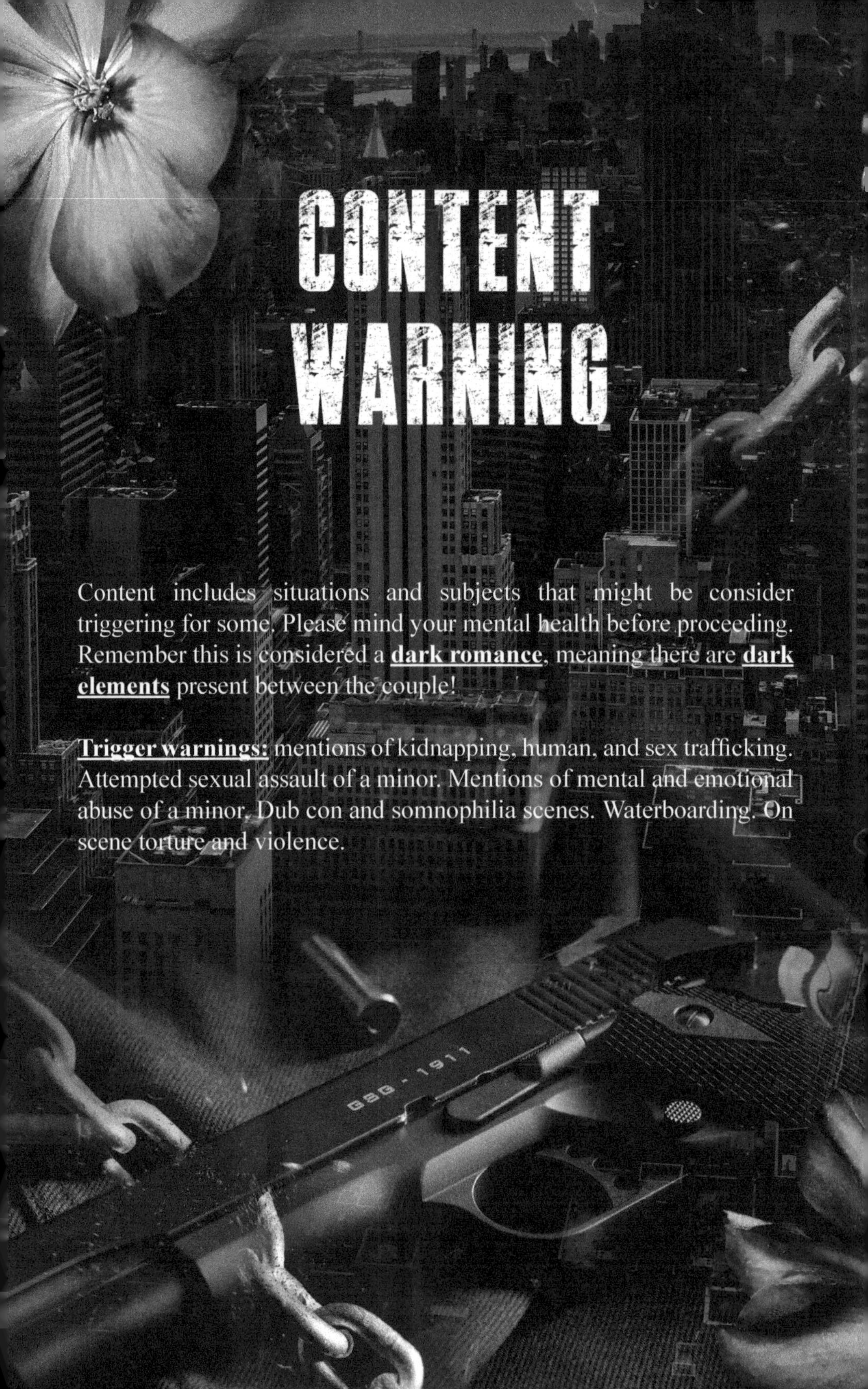

CONTENT WARNING

Content includes situations and subjects that might be consider triggering for some. Please mind your mental health before proceeding. Remember this is considered a **dark romance**, meaning there are **dark elements** present between the couple!

Trigger warnings: mentions of kidnapping, human, and sex trafficking. Attempted sexual assault of a minor. Mentions of mental and emotional abuse of a minor. Dub con and somnophilia scenes. Waterboarding. On scene torture and violence.

CONTENTS

PROLOGUE

"You have three months until your thirtieth birthday and instead of taking things seriously you've been fucking off." My dad scolded me while sitting behind his large, wooden desk.

"I haven't been fucking off. Just because I don't see the point in being forced into a marriage I don't want doesn't mean I'm fucking off," I countered.

Dad's jaw ticked and the vein on the side of his neck bulged, showing his irritation was growing. He leaned forward, folding his hands on his desk, cutting his eyes into slits.

"We've been through this, hijo. For you to take over the business, you need a solid foundation. Being a single unwedded man with no heir in sight is not a solid foundation. You're not getting any younger, it's time to take life more seriously."

I widened my legs and clenched my jaw while my hands balled into fists. This had been an ongoing argument between me and my father since I turned twenty-nine last year. For some reason, to be seen as the true head of The Bloodline, I had to have a wife and kid. I never understood what they had to do with each other. Not that I never wanted to get married and start a family, but that shit wasn't on my mind right now.

"You've been grooming me since I was old enough to talk to take over. Over the past couple months, you've been involved less and less, allowing me to take the reins and run things. *You* know I'm ready for this. Me not having a wife justifies nothing."

Dad's bronze face reddened. "Damnit, Nazai!" He slammed a balled fist on top of his desk but I didn't flinch. While I loved my dad, we often butted heads. My mom said it was because we were too alike, too stubborn for our own good. "You *will* find a wife if you want to take over. It's a tradition in the family that you will *not* tarnish. In this life, nothing is guaranteed, you know that. Making sure you have someone to pass your legacy down to is just part of it. Having a family to protect gives you drive, not to mention a king with no queen is nothing to take seriously. Do you think I would have gotten this far without your mother by my side to help keep me grounded?" He spent his childhood between The States and the Dominican Republic, where my paternal grandfather's family was from, settling in Silver Stone when he and my mom married. He barely had an accent, but it was present, mainly when he was upset.

My dad was in his mid-fifties. His Dominican and Black genes mixed well, causing him to still look like he was in his late thirties. Out of all my brothers, people said me and my second youngest brother favored him the most. My parents had been married since before I was born, meeting in their early twenties while my dad was finishing law school, having me shortly after, then the rest of my brothers. There were four of us altogether, my brothers were twenty-eight, twenty-six, and twenty-five.

What had made them want to give their lives up to one person so early was beyond me, but I never saw them show each other anything but love.

His bushy brows furrowed and his square jaw relaxed slightly. "Your mother is looking forward to my retirement. While I know you're more than capable of handling things, I cannot break tradition and officially retire until you get your shit together. I've let a lot of shit pass when it comes to you and your rebellion, but all that is over now." Dad pushed an exasperated breath out and sat up straighter. "Marco's daughter is single and she's had her eyes on you for some time now. She's a beautiful young lady, raised around the business, will make a good wife. She's loyal, trustworthy, and available. You two would look good together."

A deadpan expression formed on my face as I pressed my lips together. Marco was an associate of my dad's who worked under him at his law firm. I pictured Marco's daughter and scrunched my nose. Marco's daughter was far from anything he described. While in front of her dad she appeared to be the perfect wife, but behind closed doors she was a whore who opened her legs for anyone who batted their eyes at her. I chalked it up to not having enough attention from her old man. Still, little did my dad know, I'd already had her and it wasn't worth the headache to keep around for the rest of my life. Not to mention, my brother Lucas had fucked her too, and I was sure he still was.

I snorted. "Not happening. I don't need your help when it comes to finding a wife. Women line up for me to just breathe in their direction. The issue isn't finding a wife, I simply don't want one." I shrugged. It might have sounded cocky, but it was the truth. My access to women wasn't lacking. Women would love to say they'd trapped or locked down a Tavarez. It was one reason I never took any of the women I bedded seriously. The last thing I needed was to be trapped by some gold digger only after the money and power my last name brought.

The Tavarez family was one of the most prominent families on the East Coast. My dad built the Tavarez name by becoming the youngest black judge in the district, gaining the title at twenty-eight. He retired at fifty but still practiced law, running his own firm. This year he was due to pass the reins to my younger brother, Ezra. His brutalness was one reason they called him "The Shark" in the courtroom. Seeing how he argued and composed himself, you wouldn't bat an eye after learning that behind closed doors he was a killer with a lethal group alongside him. The plus side was we had so many city officials in our pockets that no one batted an eye at our dealings.

Me and my brothers were seen as successful businessmen, each contributing to our dad's success and adding to the Tavarez legacy. The business we did outside of that, only few knew about, and that was only if you knew how to find us. The Bloodline, as it was referred to among us, had been functioning for the past three generations and I planned on continuing that legacy with pride. Because me and my brothers had a range of different skills, each one of us contributed to how things were run. The connections built and the loyalty we showed was another reason we'd never had issues keeping business going.

My family got hired for a different variety of jobs. I was the eliminator. Whenever someone needed taking out, I was called. There were times my brothers accompanied me, but their skills often played a role for other things. Each role contributed to the wealth of the family. Multiple streams of income kept us in the upper echelon of the city. When I took over, my role would be to distribute those jobs and make sure they were executed correctly. The leader role would be something I'd take on with pride, but the directing I could do without. Still, my dad was putting faith in me and that wasn't something I took lightly. Finding a wife was the hard part in all this.

"Stop the bullshit and get serious!" my dad demanded sternly in Spanish before switching back to English. "You have three months to find a wife and get her pregnant by the end of the year. If you don't, then you *will* marry Marco's daughter and that isn't up for debate. I've been patient but you're testing me. Three months or we'll do it my way." With his tone, he left no room for argument. I tightened my jaw and bit the inside of my cheek. "You can go now. Be ready for a call tonight." He waved me off then reached for his phone, dismissing me.

Standing up, I turned and stalked out his office. Anyone who knew me knew I hated people attempting to tell me what to do. My dad was the only one who could get away with talking to me like he had. I passed one of the housekeepers, making my way to the front of the large house, thankful my mom wasn't home so I didn't have to stop and talk to her. Irritation flooded my body as I snatched the front door open and stepped outside in the heated summer air.

Once in my blackout Maserati, I checked the time. I had another meeting following this one before I headed to my nightclub. It was a separate business outside of what my family did. It was proof that I could build something on my own and make it successful. While I knew it was my birthright and I had no issues taking over, I wanted to prove I could make a name for myself outside of my family.

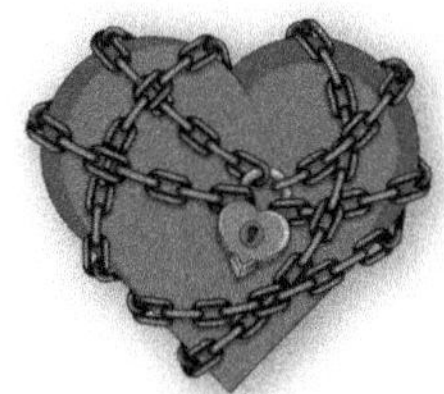

"I'm looking to up my intake," I told Major Montgomery as I sat across from him. He ran drugs through Silver Stone. Anything a person needed to get their hands on, he was the man to talk to. His family also ran a large pharmaceutical company that fronted their wealth. My family had done a few jobs for him, mainly my brother Lucas who was a surgeon and my brother Emmet who was a whiz with computers. He also had Ezra on retainer in case one of his guys ever got caught in some mess.

As for me, our business was simple. He supplied me with the pills I sold through my club. I had been doing so for the past year and people took to the idea quickly when the word got out. The pills were a secret menu thing and customers had to know what to order to get what they wanted, but it seemed like we were going through inventory faster than we could carry it.

"I had a feeling you were going to make this move. Business has been good then I take it," Major replied.

My grin grew. "Better than good. Adding the pills to the club only increased traffic."

Major chuckled and nodded. "When you first came to me and suggested we go into business together, I didn't think you would be able to fulfill what you wanted. Your family is known for the work they do, but drugs were never in the work. You proved me wrong."

I smirked.

"This has nothing to do with what my family has going on. The District is my thing. Whatever business I handle with it is mine alone."

Major nodded. "Understandable. When I first took over, I had to prove I could live up to the shoes left for me. My family isn't in the spotlight like yours, but I can understand wanting to build your own name outside of your dad's."

The Montgomery family had their own success in Silver Stone, but behind the scenes they ran the largest drug empire in the area. While they ran successful businesses to cover up their illegal dealings, the drugs they flooded through the city were what put their name on the map in the underground world. No one ran drugs around here without going through them and they weren't friendly to those who tried to undermine them. In Silver Stone, people were untouchable if you had wealth and connections. The Montgomery's were one of the high power families that matched mine which was why I respected them as much as I did.

Major was a couple of years older than me but had been in charge for a few years now. He was a hothead from what I was told. He hardly showed his enemies mercy and he never let someone cross him twice. Even with all that, he was a good businessman. I met with him once a month and hadn't had any issues.

Major grabbed the duffle bag off his desk and held it out. One of the men in the room came and grabbed it. "Take care of this."

"You're not gonna count it?" Normally when the money was brought in, he counted it while I was still there to make sure I wasn't short changing him. I never took it personal, knowing with what he did, he could never be too trusting.

Major lifted one corner of his mouth. "Nah, you do good business, Nazai. It's one reason I wasn't worried about working with you. It'll be counted, but I know it's all there. Your next delivery will be doubled. I take it you're sticking to just E and molly? Or are you finally adding the good stuff?" He raised a brow.

I shook my head. "Nah, I'm good on that. The pills are more than enough. When you start being greedy, that's when you start making mistakes." Although legal measures weren't what I was worried about, I cared about the reputation my club had. If harder drugs were brought in, the chances of overdoses and things increased and that wasn't something I wanted to deal with.

"I get it." Major nodded. "If you ever change your mind though."

"I'll let you know." I went to stand and held my hand out.

"As always it's a pleasure doing business with you."

"You as well." We shook on it.

Since that was out of the way, I could head to my club and make sure things were prepared for the weekend. Thursdays through Sundays were always the busiest and I was confident today would be no different.

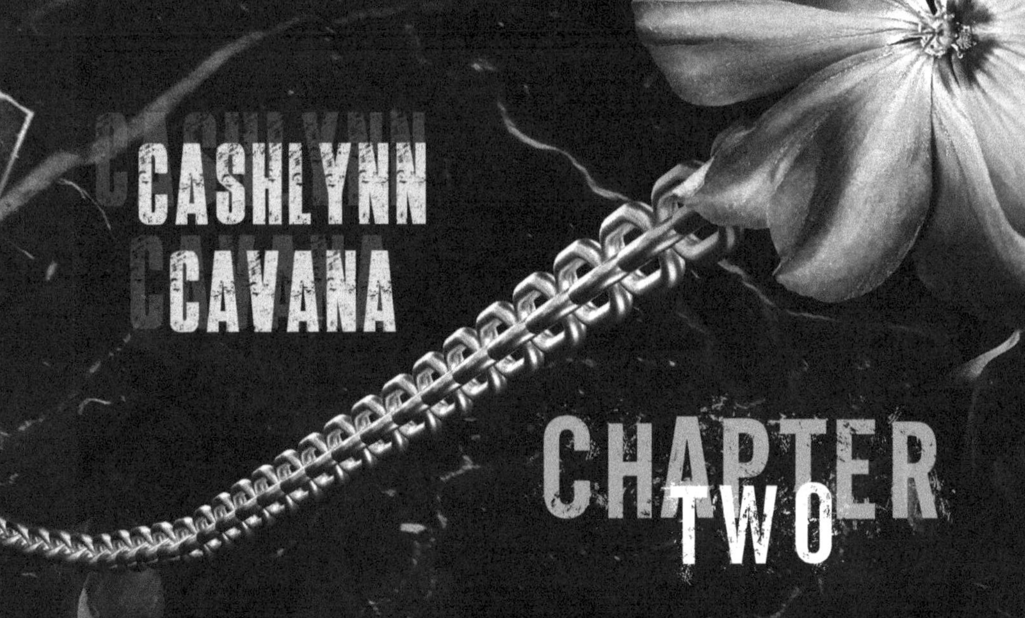

Adrenaline rushed through my veins as my hand tightened around my gun. My eyes narrowed as I peered through the dark closet I was in, watching the man laugh obnoxiously with someone on the phone. After watching him for three days, I had learned his routine. Knowing he would be home after six, I made sure to get to his house half an hour before him to scope the inside out. He stupidly didn't have any security measures in place, too cocky for his own good.

Steven Reynolds was a known doctor in the underground world, making money from those who couldn't get proper treatment in the hospitals for the fear of too many questions being asked. He was a man who would do anything for the right price, including gathering organs for the black market if asked. Turned out Dr. Reynolds not only was shady as shit but had hands that liked to touch underage girls. From the information I was sent about him, he'd been messing with a few teenage girls and had made some enemies that wanted to take him out. The why didn't really bother me. As long as the money cleared at the end of the kill, I was good.

"Those idiots don't know their heads from their asses. All they're good for is making my pockets fatter. He doesn't even know I'm skimming more money off him." The annoying laugh that fell from his mouth again caused me to cringe. It was like a hyena cackling, hurting my ears.

Making sure the safety was off my gun, I tightened my grip around the handle again. Slowly, I pushed the closet door open more.

"A'right, I'll see you at the convention next month," he told whoever was on the other line. They spoke for a little longer before hanging up.

Dr. Reynolds set the phone down and leaned back, stretching his back. He picked up the glass of brown liquor and brought it to his mouth just as I pushed the door open fully and stepped into the office, causing the doctor to sputter, spilling some of his drink. His eyes bucked, falling on my gun.

"Who, who are you?" he stuttered, slowly lowering his glass.

A smirk formed on my face and I crept closer. "Seems like you've met some enemies, Dr. Reynolds."

He blinked slowly and his mouth opened then snapped shut. His eyes darted wildly before landing back on me.

"If this is about money, I can give you money! It's in a bag in the closet you just came out of. Take it all!" he rushed out.

I snorted. "I don't give a damn about your money."

Sweat beaded on his forehead and his breathing sped up. "Then what? Did-did James send you?"

I shrugged. "I didn't get a name, turns out however, someone isn't a fan of you enjoying teenage girls." My nose scrunched in disgust. A surprised look formed on his face.

"I don't know what you're talking about." I sighed and lowered my shoulders, feeling my patience starting to dwindle.

Dr. Reynolds straightened in his seat and narrowed his eyes. "I don't know who hired you, but you need to go. I don't have time for this shit." The sudden bass in his voice humored me. His body was shaking but he tried to stand his ground.

"I agree. This is pointless." Wrapping my hand around the trigger, I pulled it. A whisper of a sound filled the room due to the silencer. The bullet went straight between the doctor's eyes. One thing I always prided myself on was my aim. Whether it was a gun or blade, I hardly ever missed my target.

Dr. Reynolds's head fell forward, hitting his desk with a hard thump and causing his glass to spill, the liquid scattering.

Walking toward him, I went into my pocket and pulled out a card that displayed the queen of hearts and tossed it on the table before grabbing my untraceable phone and taking a picture of the body, then stepping closer, grabbing his head and forcing it up to take one last picture. Once I was done, I quickly sent an encrypted message to my handler. His or her number was the only number this phone was able to receive and send texts. The line was secured and always erased after a certain amount of time. I never saw their face, only received my targets and an encrypted link that broke after the mission was completed, which gave details about the target.

A few seconds later a message of confirmation came through and I knew within the hour I would have the payout in my account.

Removing the silencer from the gun, I put the safety on before sliding both in my black hoodie pocket. I kept my black leather gloves on then headed out of the office, this time walking out of the front door, making sure to lift my hood over my face before leaving.

I was here longer than I would have liked and needed to hurry and get back to the motel room across town.

Once I was at my car, I removed my black leather gloves and quickly went to my trunk to put my things inside my duffle bag, keeping my gun on me.

I waited a couple of blocks to finally pull my main phone out of the glove compartment and turned it on, making sure I didn't have any messages. My nerves were shaky and running wild as I drove as quickly as I could to the motel without bringing too much attention to myself. With everything going on around me, I couldn't be too careless.

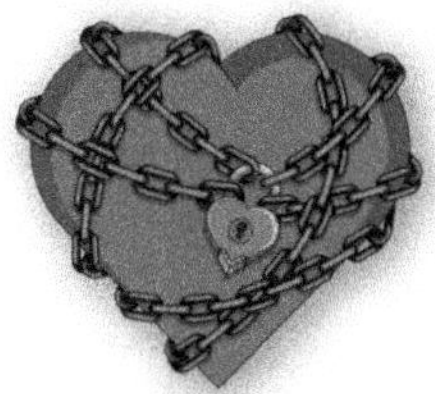

"Hey bud, I got you something to eat." I walked over to the double beds and placed a paper bag on the table between them along with the cup holder that held sweet tea.

My ten year old brother Carson sat up and set his Nintendo Switch on the bed, smiling at me. It wasn't as bright as I was used to and that made my heart ache. I hated that we had to hide out in this dingy motel, in the sketchy part of town. It was over the bridge in an area called The Sticks. A lot of shady shit went on here, so the front desk didn't care about proper ID and accepted cash without asking questions. It was hard to complete jobs at times, knowing I had to leave my brother completely unprotected to make money for us. While I made sure he knew not to open the door and always had a weapon close by in case he needed it, I still didn't feel right about leaving him. The past couple of weeks had been a shit show, but I was working on making everything better for us.

"Thank you," he said quietly, making me smile softly.

Carson was the only person in this world I gave a fuck about and I would do whatever I had to, to make sure he was protected and taken care of.

I kicked my shoes off then went to the bag, removing the burger and fries and handing them over.

"You eat while I shower, okay?" I told him and he nodded quietly, grabbing the food from me.

Making sure I had my phone, I went to the couch on the wall, grabbed my bookbag, and headed for the bathroom. As soon as I closed the door, I pressed my back against it and pushed out a deep breath. Too many eyes were looking for me right now for me to put us in a safer environment, but I had a plan.

I lifted my phone and rolled my eyes, looking at the basic smartphone. It was a burner, and unable to be tracked, but functional. The notification came through about my deposit for the job, which was bittersweet. The money from the few jobs I'd done was collecting but I couldn't use anything that would give my location away. So I had to be careful how I used and withdrew my money.

"Enough of this shit," I scolded myself after a while. I was never the one to engage in self-pity and I wasn't gonna start now. As soon as I took the threat against me out, I could go back to life as I knew it.

13

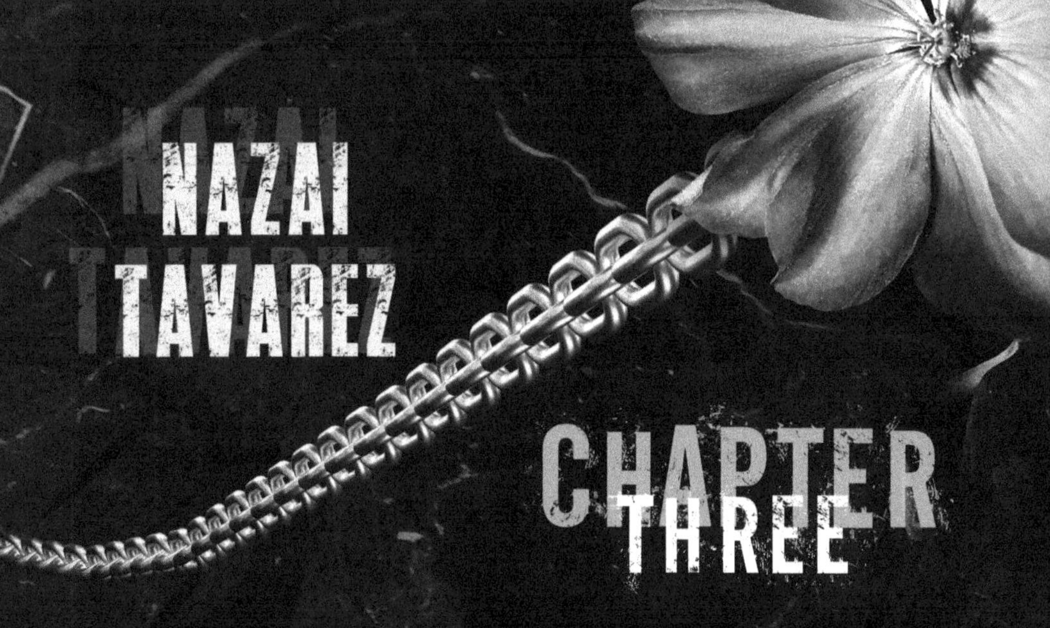

CHAPTER THREE

I stood in front of the man currently tied to the chair with my arms crossed, waiting for him to wake up. My brothers—Emmet, who was the youngest, and Ezra, who fell right before him—stood on the side of me. The latest target had been knocked out and gagged in his kitchen, currently waiting for his final resting.

"Can we get this over with now? I'm bored." Ezra yawned.

Cutting my eyes at him, I made eye contact with River, my best friend and the muscle in operation, and nodded.

River and I had been friends our whole lives. Our parents were close, his dad worked under mine. Unfortunately, his parents were murdered when he was fifteen and my family accepted him with open arms. Loyalty and family were big in the business; so taking in River was a no brainer.

Nodding back, he walked to where the guy was tied up with his head dropped and pulled a rag out of his pocket, putting it to the guy's nose. The man's head lifted and he blinked lazily before widening his eyes.

"What, what, what's going on?" he stammered, bouncing his eyes around.

I smirked, stepping forward. "You know one thing I hate more than anything in the world is a pedophile," I snarled.

"No, I was found innocent! I never touched that girl." He quickly shook his head and wiggled, attempting to get free.

"These pictures say differently," Emmet objected, tossing the pictures at him. They slapped against him before falling to the ground around him. They were pictures of kids; some had him in them, others were the kids dressed and posed in ways no kid should be.

"Those aren't mine!" he blurted out with a bewildered look on his face.

Ezra snorted behind me. "Can we just kill him already?. Wilma wants some action." He stepped closer to me with his custom steel mallet he had personalized in hand.

Marvin's, the guy tied to the chair, eyes widened.

"You thought you hid your kiddie porn, and to an amateur you did, but unfortunately for you, my brother isn't an amateur," Ezra boasted, causing Emmet to grunt.

Marvin's eyes slowly lifted from the pictures on the ground and he swallowed heavily. "Look, I beat those charges. They didn't have enough evidence on me. Those pictures are photoshopped."

Glancing over my shoulder at Ezra, I nodded, giving him the go ahead. He grinned and light filled his eyes. He swaggered over to Marvin, whose eyes bulged larger.

"Wait, wait-ah!" he cried when Ezra sent Wilma slamming into his kneecap. The crack of his bones filled my ears faintly, his screams drowning it out. Ezra hit him in the other kneecap, making sure to put extra force in it.

"Please," Marvin sputtered, with tears and snot running down his face. "I won't look at another kid, please."

Disgust filled me. "Your promises mean nothing to the kids you've already hurt," River said, sending his fist across Marvin's face. He and Ezra got off on this type of thing. For the next twenty minutes I let them work Marvin over as they pleased. River and Ezra took turns, throwing punches his way.

Marvin coughed out blood and his head sagged more. I went into the small of my back for my gun. While I got a thrill out of killing, torture wasn't really my thing. I preferred to get the job over with and move on. People like Marvin, however, didn't deserve easy deaths though. People like him were special cases that got handled accordingly.

Marvin, and many others who the justice system failed, were the reasons me and my family did what we did. While we got hired for some jobs, the ones like tonight I preferred. Taking out trash like Marvin would always be my guilty pleasure.

A smile formed on my face as I stared out of the two-way mirror, looking down into the strip club floor. The rush of last night's kill still had me on a high. Business was booming, which wasn't shocking. Since I'd opened The District it'd been a cash cow that only continued growing in revenue. It was two clubs in one. The bottom level was a nightclub always maxed to capacity and the top half was a strip club, Euphoria, that employed only the baddest fantasies a man could want. Anyone who came to The District knew it was a high-class establishment that was strict when it came to dress code and conduct. People couldn't walk through the doors wearing everyday street clothes. My girls were all vetted and knew to keep their hair, nails, and clothes up to par always or they wouldn't step foot on the floor. Same with my waitstaff. People waited in line for hours to get into The District for a reason, it was a high class experience.

I brought the glass of liquor to my mouth and watched as Majesty worked the pole. All the girls who worked for me made good money, but Majesty was one who made more than others each night. She dropped down into a split and made her ass cheeks clap. Bills flew on the stage.

Taking my eyes off the glass, I shifted them to the screens on the wall. They gave a visual of the bottom half of the club and different angles of the strip club.

The District was my first big investment. It was a way to show my dad I was able to make money and be in control of my own shit without him. While he wanted me to have a profession that benefitted the family, more like my brothers, I chose a different path. Being in charge was something I was built for, but I wasn't meant to be in the courtroom or behind a desk all day. The District was my way to rebel against the plan he had for me and show him I determined my own future.

Happy with what I saw, I turned and faced the men on the other side of my desk. My brothers and River were all seated around me. River smoked a blunt, nodding at whatever Ezra was saying to him.

"Did Monty give you any trouble?" I asked as I walked to my desk, sitting down and setting my glass down. My eyes settled on River. I had sent him after Monty, a low-level criminal, after he ran up a large tab at the club then dipped out on us without paying. He thought he would get away with crossing me, but he should have known no one crossed a Tavarez and got away with it. When it came to certain jobs, River had no problem getting his hands dirty.

"I did." He smirked, stretching out on the couch.

"And?" I raised a brow.

"And we handled it," Ezra jumped in. "Let's just say, Monty's hand gon' be in a cast for a few weeks and your money is handled." He nodded toward the briefcase River brought in with him.

Lucas snorted and shook his head. We all knew that meant Ezra had used Wilma on Monty's hand. Whenever he needed to teach someone a lesson, Wilma came into play.

"Crazy fucker," River mumbled. "The situation is handled. And we got the money he skipped out on, plus interest."

Ezra smirked while Emmet laughed quietly not looking up from his Rubik Cube. Most people thought they were twins, but they were eleven months apart. The two had some screws loose too, that often came in handy. "As long as it's taken care of." I waved them off.

I focused on River. "How's your end looking?"

River would be my head enforcer when I took over. He would make sure security surrounding me and my family was tight. With my dad being who he was, he couldn't have built his name in the justice system without having enemies too. While we all hated having the extra people, we knew it was necessary in our line of work. We never knew when our enemies would attack. We listened as River went over the last couple of guys he had hired. He also handled security at my club so I never had to worry about major issues going on when I wasn't around.

The meeting wrapped up and everyone left except River.

"I heard your dad's on your ass about a wife again." He smirked and relit his blunt, blowing smoke out and leaning forward.

Sighing, I loosened the tie around my neck and leaned back. "It's a pain in the ass, but he isn't budging on it."

A week had passed since talking with my dad and I was still no closer to resolving the wife situation.

"What about Anastasia?" he suggested, blowing smoke out.

I scratched my cheek thinking about it. Anastasia was a girl I fucked off with from time to time. It was just sex between us, but occasionally I used her when I needed a date to an event. She was the perfect eye candy and hardly gave me any hassle.

"I thought about her." She would make the most sense. While she didn't know the ins and out of my family's business, she was quiet and stayed in her lane. I knew whoever I took as a wife would have to be trustworthy enough to be involved with certain things. A person couldn't be weak and be a part of this family. She would be chewed up and spit out easily. Anastasia *was* a better choice than my dad's suggestion.

River stayed around a little longer before dipping out to find some entertainment downstairs. A few minutes after he left, there was a knock on the door. I loosened my tie more and undid my suit jacket.

"Enter," I called out, lifting my glass and finishing my drink.

Majesty stepped inside the room and closed the door behind her with a grin on her face. "You called for me, boss?" Her head tilted slightly and she dragged her tongue across her lips. On his way out I had River tell one of the guards outside my door to page her to come up.

Standing, I walked around my desk and took a seat on the couch with my legs gapped. "You know why I called you up here." Her eyes lit up and she strutted over to me. She didn't hesitate to drop to her knees and reach for my pants.

As soon as she removed my dick and took me in her mouth, I closed my eyes and laid my head back. My hand went to her hair and I gripped it tightly, forcing her to take more. She moaned and gagged around my dick, always loving when I took her mouth roughly. Having the freedom to fuck who I wanted was one luxury I enjoyed while being single. There was no way I was looking forward to giving it up with marriage.

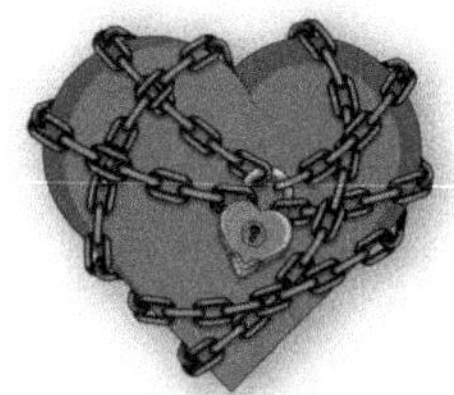

"I'll be looking forward to working with you more." I shook Zylus's hand while my dad stood next to me, observing quietly.

"Same here. Since I'm back in the city permanently for the time being, I hope to do more business with you." He turned to my dad. "As always Dominic, it's good doing business with you."

Dad stepped forward and shook his hand. "I heard about your brother. I hope everything pulls through."

Zylus stayed quiet but I didn't miss how his jaw flexed slightly at the mention of his brother, whose car was shot up recently.

"We'll be on the lookout for your call," I followed up.

Zylus ran a large shipping company and specialized in moving guns in and out of the city. He normally came into the city every couple of months but now he was back for family reasons, at least that was what the rumors said. If someone was ever in need of heavy artillery, he was the man they got with. He supplied our organization, and for that, we kept his pockets laced. My father had been doing business with him for years and was setting me up to be in communication with him going forward.

Jackson and Luke, my two guards, fell in step behind us along with my dad's guards when we headed for the exit. I didn't use them often unless I was out handling business and it was only because my dad insisted.

"Your mother told me to tell you to stop by soon. It's been too long since she saw you," Dad commented as we approached our cars. We came to meet Zylus separately, meeting here at his building down near the docks where his office was located.

Devin, my driver, was waiting outside the blacked-out Range Rover for me. When I got closer, he pulled the door open and waited for me to climb in.

"Let her know I'll be by this week."

We stopped in front of our cars. "Have you thought about what we spoke on?"

I bit the inside of my jaw and shook my head. I should have known I wouldn't leave here without him mentioning it. "I'm working on it."

His eyes narrowed. "I hope you are. Time's running out, hijo." He held his hand out. When I took it, he pulled me into a fatherly hug and patted my back. "Be sure to visit your mother soon," he called out on his way to his car where his driver was waiting.

Turning for my truck, I slid in the back seat with Jackson behind me and Luke taking the front. Devin closed the door and walked around to the driver seat.

I pulled my phone out and scanned the messages. "Headed home, sir?" Devin asked.

"Take me by the barn first." The Barn was where the family meetings took place. It was on the outskirts of town, toward the country, with no neighbors in sight. The country house we used as the central operating area, but the barn in the back was where we took people for their last moments. Me and River used it more than anyone.

I kept my eyes on my phone. I was in the middle of reading a text from Ian, the manager of my club, when an alert came across my phone. My brows furrowed when I clicked on it. Someone had triggered the silent alarm at my house on the outskirts of the city near the mountains. It wasn't one I stayed at often, mainly when I wanted to duck off and get off the grid.

I switched to my camera app and pulled up the grid, locating the culprit right away.

"Change of plans, head to my house on the east side," I told Devin.

"Yes, sir," Devin answered.

"Everything okay boss?" Jackson asked.

"I'm not sure yet." I watched a girl and young boy move through the house. Most of the time this house was left alone outside of the staff I hired to maintain it. It was in the suburbs and break-ins were hardly ever an issue. I didn't keep much security at the house unless I planned on being there.

I watched the pair move around the house without a care in the world. The girl seemed to be scoping it out. It was summer but she had on a hoodie and leggings. However, she must have felt comfortable because she removed the hood and turned to face the young boy. I switched to a different camera to get a better view of her light brown face. She had on large sunglasses so I couldn't see her eyes. Her jet-black hair was pulled into a ponytail at the top of her head.

I tried to think if I'd seen her before but came up blank. Most people weren't stupid enough to try me like this. She didn't look like a threat, but in my line of work I knew I could never be too sure.

Sitting back, I pressed my lips together and my trigger finger itched. It had been a minute since I'd had to punish someone for something outside of the job.

I made sure to let my guys know to keep quiet when I opened the front door to my mansion. It was a four-bedroom, four-and-a-half bathroom, two garage, two-story house. On my block were only three other houses and there was enough space between us that I had privacy. The high shrubs surrounding the property helped too.

With my gun in hand, I stepped behind Luke and Jackson. I knew where the woman was already and planned to head her way.

"Keep an eye on the boy. Don't hurt him," I told them when we got into the living room. He was laid out on my couch asleep. Looking at him, I noted he couldn't have been older than twelve.

"Do you want one of us to come with you?" Luke asked when I turned for my bedroom, where the girl was.

I shook my head. "Nah. Stay here." The master bedroom was across the hall from the living room. While I was sure there was no reason for me to have backup, I still kept alert.

I made a quick sweep of my bedroom, making sure nothing looked out of place. I had kept eyes on the girl on the drive here, but it never hurt to be on guard.

I could hear the shower running and it grew louder the closer I got to my ensuite bathroom. Steam filled the room and heat hit my face soon as I stepped over the threshold.

Through the foggy glass I could briefly see the girl washing her hair—her head thrown back and hands massaging her scalp. My eyes swept over the bathroom floor. Her clothes were scattered in a pile on the floor along with a purple backpack.

Walking over to it, I kneeled, keeping my eyes on the shower and picked up the bookbag. I searched through the contents inside, mostly clothes and toiletries. Buried at the bottom was a wallet. Grabbing it, I opened it and was happy to see an ID inside.

My eyes widened when I noticed the name on the license. Flickering my eyes up toward the shower, the corners of my mouth lifted. With my gun still in hand, I dropped the bag and stood before dragging my tongue over my top teeth and stepping around the small mess.

Cashlynn finally must have sensed me because her eyes snapped open and her head whipped in my direction. She pushed the glass door open and looked shocked to see me.

"Fuck!" she cursed. Her eyes went to the gun at my side then darted behind me. A frantic look switched onto her face.

"Don't move," I warned her.

Not listening, she reached for something and launched it at me.

"Shit!" I gritted when it hit me in the face. Water flicked in my direction as she rushed me, throwing hits. My gun fell from my hand, causing me to curse under my breath.

Cashlynn was like a wild animal, throwing hits my way left and right.

"Stop!" I bellowed, finally gaining my bearings and grabbing her wrists.

"Let me go! Where's my brother?" she shouted, attempting to wiggle free.

She was shorter than me, stopping at my chest. Water and soap dripped down her body, covering my arms and floor.

"Settle the fuck down before I shoot you," I warned her.

Her eyes lit up mockingly, then narrowed. "I'd like to see you try." She shot her head up and pain radiated through the bottom half of my face when she slammed the top of her head into my chin. I groaned and my knees gave out when her knee connected with my dick.

"Muthafucka!" I let her go. She rushed to grab her things and attempted to run. I could taste blood filling my mouth. It took me a second to recover, ignoring the slight pains from her attack.

"No you don't." I snatched her by her hair and pulled her back. My blood ran hot with fury.

"The fuck!" she shouted.

Sick and tired of fighting with her, I pulled her so she was pressed against my chest and secured my hold on her hands. It was time to get this shit under control. No way was I about to let some girl make a fool of me. Her fight was comical at first, but now I was growing annoyed.

I spit some of the blood that filled my mouth on the floor and seeing it only caused my mood to grow sourer.

Moving one of my hands to her neck, I pressed the pressure points and soon her body relaxed and sagged against mine. Breathing hard, I shook my head and lowered her to the ground.

"Jackson!" I called out, looking around my bathroom, noticing the shampoo bottle on the floor and realizing that's what she must have thrown at me. The liquid mess scattered around it pissed me off even more. I walked to the shower to turn the water off.

Jackson came rushing into the bathroom and paused with wide eyes seeing the naked woman on the floor.

"Look in my nightstand and grab the handcuffs," I demanded.

My eyes went to Cashlynn. I'd never met her, but I knew of her family. The rumors weren't pleasant. She was a feisty one, I could give her that. She'd caught me off guard, but she had to try a little harder to outdo me.

25

My eyes fluttered open and I had to blink a couple of times to get my eyes adjusted to the lowly-lit room. My brows furrowed and I went to move but noticed my hands were bound above my head. My body stretched vertically, with my legs shackled as well. Dull aches passed through my shoulders.

"What the fuck!" I attempted to move and glanced down, noticing I was naked. My heart slammed against my ribcage and my eyes darted around the room.

"Carson!" I whispered.

A low chuckle caught my attention. I whipped my eyes in that direction. A man sitting in a chair leaned forward. He had a notepad in hand and a thick, black pencil.

"Let me down! Where's my brother? Carson!" I shouted, struggling to break free. My stomach twisted in dread not knowing where Carson was. It looked like I was in a basement and us two seemed to be the only ones down here. My wrists ached from where the cuffs rubbed against my skin due to my struggle. My shoulder muscles pulled and strained.

He stood up and slowly made his way closer to me, blowing smoke out of his mahogany, cupid's bow lips.

Nazai Tavarez.

I swallowed hard and leered at him. I'd have to be living under a rock to not know who this man was, yet I refused to show any fear. My stomach flipped as his dark, almost black, upturned eyes peered into me.

Rumors of his dad being corrupt and ruthless in the courtroom were loud and hard to ignore, but that wasn't what bothered me. If someone was a part of the underworld, they knew them as the cleaners. If a person needed a problem to disappear or be taken care of, then they knew who to call. I remember my parents mentioning them a few times, apparently there was underlying beef there. Nazai was the oldest son and rumored to be next in line to run things.

If I would have known it was his house I was breaking into, I would have chosen differently. I expected someone like him to have higher security measures than he did. The only reason I needed to break into his house was because I'd ended up getting blood on me from a job a couple streets over and needed to shower. Somehow, someone had found out where I was staying and tried coming after me. Thankfully, I was able to get both me and Carson out safely. For the past two nights we had slept in my car. My goal was to get enough money to pay for a new identity. It was the reason I was taking jobs left and right. After my parents died a few months ago, we were left with nothing, so I was starting from the bottom.

"Cashlynn Cavana." He spoke in a deep baritone with a slight rasp to it, causing me to flinch slightly before I could catch myself. "You're a hot commodity right now." His head tilted to the side and his eyes ran down my body. I tried not to squirm under his scrutiny. My chest rose and fell a bit quicker. The way his eyes peered into me caused my nipples to harden.

"Where's my brother?" I asked, ignoring his comment.

He towered over me—his skin the color of a gingerbread cookie, beard thick, but low cut and shiny and hair faded on the sides with a low Caesar cut on top. He wore a dark red, short-sleeved button up with black dress pants that hugged his thick thighs.

"Oh, the boy?" One of his bushy brows rose. "He's around." One corner of his mouth ticked up.

My lips pressed together and I flared my nostrils. "If you hurt him I swear—"

"You swear what?" He stepped forward and brushed his hand across my bare breast.

"Don't touch me!" I attempted to yank out of his touch, ignoring the way it sparked heat in my stomach. He smirked and gripped my nipple, twisting it painfully, making me wince but become aroused at the same time.

"You're in no position to make demands right now. Now, who sent you?"

Breathing in, I spit, sending it into his face. "Fuck you, where's my brother?!"

His eyes narrowed and grew darker. His partially-crooked, medium-sized nose flared at the nostrils.

Stepping back and releasing my nipple, he wiped his hand down his face. "Now I get why your fiancé's family put a two hundred and fifty thousand dollar bounty on your head."

The blood running through my veins ran cold. My heart beat painfully against my chest as my stomach twisted in knots. Just the mere thought of Maddox caused my body to fill with rage.

The bounty on my head was my biggest issue right now. It wasn't hard to get news around in the underground world, so people knew there was money on my head. Thankfully my handler only knew me by my alias "Queen of Hearts". Either way, I didn't regret what I did to get the bounty; I only hated that my brother was affected by it too.

"That's not my fiancé," I said coldly, my words thick with malice.

"You're a wildfire, you know that?" He licked his lips, studying me for a second. "I think you need some time to yourself."

My eyes bucked when he turned and started to walk toward the steps. "Wait! Wait! Where's my brother? Where's Carson?" Panic exploded inside me. "Fuck! Nazai!"

I struggled against my restraints, still shouting at him but he ignored me. "Fuck! Fuck!" I yelled when the lights flickered off and I heard the door close.

Darkness surrounded me and my breathing was heavy. I tried to stay calm. In situations like this, I was trained to keep a level head, but my mind kept going back to my brother. While I could handle myself, he was innocent in all this. The rumors about the Tavarez family indicated they weren't the people to mess with. There were a handful of people in Silver Stone I never wanted to beef with and they were one of them. While it wasn't clear to most people, I knew they were well connected. My heart ached and my muscles twitched. I squeezed my eyes shut when I felt pressure built behind them.

Memories of my childhood flashed through my mind. This wasn't the first time I'd been restrained in a dark room alone.

I didn't cry, crying was a weakness. I had been conditioned to deal with situations like this.

Taking a couple of deep breaths, I tried to locate anything I could use to help me once my eyes became adjusted. I couldn't hear anything going on around me or above me. My mind raced as memories I wished I could forget flooded my mind.

# NAZAI TAVAREZ

CHAPTER FIVE

"What did you call me over here for?" Emmet sat on the couch and pulled his laptop out of its bag. Emmet took more after my mom but had my dad's bronze skin color. Most people thought he was a pretty boy, but he was the definition of looks could be deceiving. He kept his tight curly hair cut low. He was on the leaner side and the tallest out the four of us at six five. I had called him after finding out who Cashlynn was and demanded that he meet me here. My house was about twenty-five minutes outside the city, but the good thing about taking over was when I said come there was hardly any room for complaints or objection.

"I need you to run a name for me," I said, sitting next to him.

Opening my phone, I checked the camera in the hall upstairs. I had Luke stationed outside the bedroom to make sure the kid didn't come out. When he first woke up, he was confused and looked frightened seeing the three of us. He cried for his sister but he was a compliant kid and calmed down once I told him his sister would be okay as long as he listened.

"Who is it?" Emmet was a professional hacker in the family. He also owned his own P.I firm. There wasn't a shadow someone could hide in that he couldn't locate. He was overly intelligent when it came to computers and I hadn't seen a firewall or security system he couldn't hack.

"Cashlynn Cavana." Emmet looked confused.

"Why do you need to learn about her?" His brows squished together. "Wait, isn't she the girl with a bounty on her head? The Rhodes put a price on her head, right?"

Along with being intelligent, Emmet had a photographic memory. The little shit used to annoy the hell outta me with it too.

"Yeah, that's her."

Emmet shifted his attention to his computer and started tapping the keyboard. "What's she gotta do with anything?"

"She's hanging naked in my basement right now," I said calmly.

Emmet sputtered and stared at me wide eyed. "What the fuck? Why is she chained up in the basement? Wait, you're not about to try to tap into sex trafficking when you take over, are you?"

I frowned. "Don't play with me." I waved him off. "She broke into my house and now I need to know why. Her parents were trained assassins and rumor was they were training her to join the business."

My dad had issues with her parents over a job. I never knew the root of their issues, but my dad loathed the family.

"The last known info about her is her parents being murdered in a robbery at their house seven months ago. It's just her and her kid brother now."

"That's public knowledge. Dig deeper," I told him, cracking my knuckles. I glanced at my phone and switched to the cameras in my basement. Thankfully I had it soundproofed so I didn't have to hear her yells. The cameras installed had night vision so I was able to see Cashlynn. Her head was lowered and she had to be in pain since it had been a few hours that she'd been hanging. I smirked.

"A month ago, she took five thousand dollars out of the bank. After that, she went off the grid. She's gotten deposits in her bank account but no transactions have been made on her end. It's like she disappeared." Emmet tapped his keyboard a couple more times.

I pulled on my beard. That sounded about right. That was around the same time the bounty on her came out if I remembered correctly.

I stood up. "Stay here. Keep digging. I want whatever you can find on her and her parents and on the Rhodes too." Emmet looked confused again but nodded. Out of all of my brothers, he was the quietest but probably the deadliest.

"Are you planning on using her?"

I smirked at my youngest brother but didn't answer.

"Let's go, Jackson." I headed for my foyer then the front door. Cashlynn caught my eye and now I was intrigued to learn even more about her.

"Mr. Tavarez, this is so unexpected." I stared at Neil Rhodes who had a shocked expression on his face. He was the father of Cashlynn's ex-fiancé, Maddox, the man who'd put the bounty on her head. I knew little about him except he distributed drugs under Major. Apparently, they oversaw one of Major's larger territories. The family was loud and flashy, however.

Neil fidgeted under my gaze. "Are you gonna invite me in?" I raised a brow.

His brows shot to his hairline and his eyes bucked. "Oh yes, sorry sir, please come in." He stepped back and opened his door wider.

I stepped in the house with Jackson at my side and followed Neil. He had a nice size home with a large, open entryway.

"We can talk in here." He opened a door that led to an office. "Miranda, get our guest something to drink!" he called out to the lady approaching us.

"No need, I won't be here long," I assured him.

Stepping inside I looked around the office then headed for the chair closest to me. Jackson stood alert at the door, his arms crossed and eyes focused on Neil.

Neil walked around his desk and took a seat, clearing his throat. "What can I do for you, sir?" The reputation of my family wasn't one to take lightly. While we might not be as sinister as some others, we had built the reputation of taking care of problems.

I lifted a brow. "You look uncomfortable? Is there a reason why?"

He swallowed visibly hard and shifted, clearing his throat again. "No, sir. It's just neither you nor your father have ever made a call that you were coming to my home; so I'm not sure what's going on."

"Cashlynn Cavana. You know the name, correct?"

Neil's eyes darkened and his face hardened. "I do," he answered stiffly. His back straightened as he sneered through gritted teeth.

One corner of my mouth lifted. "What's your issue with her exactly? Last I heard she was engaged to your son."

It was clear there was more to Cashlynn than what met the eye. Knowing who her parents were and seeing how she handled herself with me had me more intrigued about her. She was a beautiful woman, but it was clear that beauty shouldn't be mistaken for weakness.

"That bitch almost killed my son. Stabbed him and nipped his spine. He's currently in a rehabilitation center trying to recover from the mobility issues she caused. We welcomed her and her brother into our house after her parents died and she tried to take my boy out!" His face reddened and twisted in anger. Veins bulged from his forehead. Neil was a couple inches shorter than me, his body held muscle. He reminded me of a body builder that skipped leg days one too many times and were top heavy.

I stayed silent for a second. "And what made her suddenly want to kill her fiancé?"

His eyes grew sharp. "She's a rabid bitch that needs to be put down. A psycho just like her damn parents."

I stroked my beard. "I see."

"You wouldn't happen to know where she is, do you?"

A smile crossed my face. "I do." Leaving it at that, I stood. "Cashlynn is currently under my protection, meaning she's off limits to touch."

An astonished look formed on his face. "But Mr. Tavarez! My son." I shot him a glare, causing his mouth to snap shut.

Truthfully I didn't know much about The Rhodes, but they were ass kissers, that was clear. Neil was known to blow smoke up peoples' asses to get ahead and Maddox wasn't much better.

"If anything changes, you'll be the first to know." I turned to leave, nodding at Jackson who opened the door for me.

Coming here gave me a little more clarity about the girl who was chained in my basement, but it wasn't enough to get a full picture. Cashlynn was a firecracker and obviously not afraid to use force if need be. She was a wild card and I still wasn't sure why she'd broken into my house or what she wanted. Maybe it was time to have another conversation with Ms. Cavana.

Stepping on the last step, I laid eyes on Cashlynn who looked like it was a struggle to even keep her head up. She was still naked and while she wasn't the shapeliest woman, she had a nice figure on her. Slim waist, nice childbearing hips, toned thighs. Her medium-sized breast looked like two melons. She had a couple of scars on her light brown skin that looked a couple years old, but still her skin was smooth like whipped butter.

I approached her slowly. My nose twitched at the smell of urine coming from her. I glanced down, seeing the puddle under her, causing my mouth to twitch.

"If you're here to kill me…" she started in a raspy, strained tone but I cut her off.

"I'm not here to kill you." I grabbed the chair and placed it in front of her, taking a seat. "I spoke with Neil Rhodes."

Her eyes were emotionless and her face was blank as she stared at me. I almost missed the small twitch of her mouth.

"You stabbed his son."

"Fuck him and his son." I had to give it to her, Cashlynn was tough. She hadn't cried or begged for mercy since she'd been here. Outside of worrying about her brother, she hadn't shown any emotions.

I licked my lips and straightened my spine. "If I were to give you up to the Rhodes, they'll kill you and your brother would be forced into the foster system alone, correct?" Fire lit in her eyes, causing me to smirk.

"I'll blow that damn house up before I allow that. This one too." Her fiery spirit was one reason I chose her.

Normally I had a meek woman on my arm, someone to shut up and look good when I needed her to. Cashlynn was far from that. She had a burning personality, smart mouth, and was good to look at. Taking her in made my dick jump. Whenever she spit her malicious words my way or narrowed those honey-colored, doe-shaped eyes as if they could cut me in half, I had the urge to force her to her knees and stuff her mouth with my length and fuck her throat until she was a crying mess, begging me to stop.

A chuckle left my mouth and I narrowed my eyes, adjusting myself and clearing my throat. "Most people who are being held prisoner wouldn't toss out threats. I could kill you and chop your body up right now and no one would know or miss you, but your brother." My voice came out as a low growl.

Her nostrils flared. "Good thing I'm not like most people."

"A wildfire, indeed." I shook my head. My eyes ran over her body. "I have a proposition for you." I changed the subject. Maybe I was losing my mind. Maybe the pressure of having to give up my life as a single man was getting to me, but it seemed like fate dropped Cashlynn in my lap and I was answering it.

She didn't reply right away, instead she tried to tug on the cuffs holding her. Her strength wasn't as strong as before which made sense. She had been tied up for almost six hours.

"Marry me and the threat against you will go away. You'll be under my protection and I'll make sure you and your brother are taken care of."

"Marry you?" she choked out after a couple seconds. Her face still and eyes unwavering.

"Yes. I need a wife and you need that bounty gone. It's a win-win."

She licked her dry lips and inhaled a deep breath, causing her chest to rise. Her eyes burned into me and as she tucked her lips into her mouth "Why me? How do I know I can trust you'll keep your word? For how long?"

The smile on my face grew and my head tilted an inch. "You don't." I scraped my bottom lip with my teeth. "But becoming a part of my family means you'll be protected and looked after. The Tavarezes look after their own and once in, it's *for life*."

"And if I say no?" My jaw clenched. No wasn't a word I heard often, especially from a woman. If I'd offered this to anyone else, they would have jumped at it before I could finish my sentence.

Pushing off the chair, I approached her and gripped her chin roughly, making sure she saw how serious I was.

"If you say no then I hand you over to the Rhodes and you'll be killed, leaving your brother with no one but himself to look after him if I don't toss him to the wolves too, that is." A crude smile formed on my face.

The idea came from left field but it worked. Cashlynn was on the run and needed help, even if she didn't want to admit it. I needed a wife and was running out of time. While I didn't want to get married, something about the fire in her caught my eye and intrigued me. On the outside, she was beautiful and tempting. If the circumstances were different, I wouldn't hesitate to bed her. On the inside, it was clear she was a spitfire ready to set anyone she saw as a threat ablaze. She was indeed a flame that needed to be tamed.

Hatred penetrated her glare.

I shoved her head back and stepped back. "I'll give you some time to think it over. But tick tock, Ms. Cavana. I'm not a very patient man."

Spinning around, I headed for the door. Cashlynn was strong spirited; that was clear to see. Having more time to herself in the dark should be enough to break her and have her bending to my request.

I wasn't sure how many hours I'd been down in this basement but the closed in room was starting to get to me. Nazai sent a couple men to untie me the same day he requested I marry him. I wanted to try and fight and get away but I was too weak and my bones ached from being tied in the air for so long. They refused to give me my clothes, leaving me naked and exposed. He kept the room slightly dimmed, gave me a single thin mattress to sleep on with a thin blanket to sleep under. The air had been running, leaving the stone-built room freezing. I hadn't laid eyes on Nazai since he last left, but his men did bring me two meals a day and a single bottle of water. Based on my meal arrivals, I believe I'd been down here two days now.

I could deal with all that, growing up I learned breaking someone mentally was one of the easiest ways to get them to submit to your will. My issue was not knowing where my brother was and if he was okay. Whenever I asked one of the men about him, they ignored me. My brother had been through enough and it left me unsettled and infuriated not knowing the status of his wellbeing. I vowed to slit everyone's throat in this house once I figured out how to get out of here.

My body was weak and I couldn't stop shaking from the coldness. My muscles were sore and tight, even my toes had grown numb. I hadn't been able to bathe since the day I broke in and I had a bucket in the corner for the bathroom. I was being treated worse than a dog and the thought left my blood boiling.

Currently I was laying on the mattress when the door to the basement opened. I kept my eyes closed. The cover was wrapped tightly around me as I attempted to find some warmth as my teeth chattered together.

"I think I've given you enough time to decide about my proposal." My eyes snapped open at the sound of Nazai's voice. I glared at him through tight eyes and slowly pushed the blanket off me and sat up.

Nazai stood above me with a smug expression on his handsome face. He looked clean, freshly oiled beard and cut hair. Today he wore an orange dress shirt with brown dress pants. He wasn't overly built, but between thin and bulky. His body showed he took care of it and worked out frequently. His arms were slender but toned under his short sleeve shirt that hugged them securely. He towered over me like he was a God or something.

A heavy breath pushed out my nose and I bit the inside of my jaw. *Marriage.*

I still couldn't believe Nazai had made such a proposal to me. If anything he was lucky I didn't have my butterfly knife or gun in hand because he would be laying in his own blood right now.

My jaw clenched and heartbeat roughly inside me while my hands balled and unballed in my lap.

He spoke again and turned to leave. "If you need more time to think, then so be it."

As much as I wanted to hold onto my pride, I knew I couldn't tolerate being down here anymore, not without laying eyes on my brother and making sure he was okay.

"Wait," I called out. My voice came out strained and my throat hurt from the lack of usage in the past couple of days. I attempted to swallow my spit and cleared my throat. "I'll do it," I uttered.

A cocky, crooked grin formed on his face. "I thought you would see things my way. You just needed some time to yourself."

I gritted my teeth and sank my nails into my palms. "I want to see my brother," I demanded tightly.

Nazai tapped away on his phone, ignoring me. "Hello! Did you hear me?!"

He finished his text then lifted his eyes to me. A few seconds later the man who had been serving me my food and another one I only saw when they removed me from the ceiling appeared at his side. Neither of them spoke, but one handed him a box then the two started toward me. My heart slammed into my ribcage and my eyes bounced between the two.

The first time they came down here and saw me, I wasn't sure how to react. Looking weak wasn't something I was used to and being seen naked by strangers was foreign as well. I didn't know their intentions with me and I refused to be used and raped by two silent brutes. To my surprise they barely batted an eye, even now it was as if I wasn't sitting there with everything visible.

"What are you doing?" I asked, my voice heightening as my body tensed. I pushed back toward the wall behind me. My hands balled tighter with anticipation of swinging.

The two looked unbothered as they launched toward me. I attempted to kick and punch but my body was too weak for any real impact.

"Get off me!" I shouted, flailing in their hold. My breathing grew heavier.

Nazai walked toward me with a calm expression on his face. "I said I'd marry you, what the fuck is this?!" I shouted at him.

Ignoring me, he stepped around me. They now had me on my feet, holding me securely.

Something wrapped around my neck, causing my eyes to widen. It was leather and cool against my now warm neck. A faint click filled my ears.

Nazai soon walked back in front of me and ran his eyes down my frame. That smug grin formed on his face.

"What did you just put on me?" The guards let me go and I snatched away and brought my hand to my neck.

"A tracker." Nazai answered.

"A what?" I shrieked.

"I don't trust you not to try and run before the wedding, so this is my insurance. The only way to get that off your neck is a special key only I have. If you try anything funny, not only will you not have to worry about the Rhodes being after you, but I'll cut your brother's body up in front of you before slitting your throat." His smirk caused my stomach to churn. Ice crept through my veins and my jaw clenched painfully hard. "Now the smell of you is making my nose hairs burn. Luke is gonna lead you upstairs to a bathroom where your clothes are waiting for you. Go get yourself together then he'll lead you to the living room where we'll talk more."

Nazai didn't wait for me to answer. I glowered at the back of his head. Hatred filled my body and visions of blowing his brains out filled my head.

"Don't touch me!" I snatched away from the guy when he attempted to grab my arm. I didn't care what Nazai said, I didn't care who his family was. I would figure out how to get this thing from around my neck and when I did, I would kill him in the most painful way possible.

"Cash!" Carson rushed toward me once I stepped into the living room. Relief filled my body and I dropped down to hug him, squeezing him tightly.

Laying eyes on my brother lifted a weight off me. I felt better now that I had showered and brushed my teeth. The hot water and heavy pressure felt amazing against my aching muscles. My wrists and ankles were still raw, bruised, and swollen from being tied up for so long. My book bag was waiting for me when I got out of the shower with everything in it, minus my weapons.

"Are you okay?" I asked my brother, searching him over. He looked clean and healthy. I didn't notice any marks or wounds on him.

He nodded. "Yeah. Nazai told me you weren't feeling good. Are you still sick?"

I glanced behind him at Nazai who was sitting on the couch, observing the two of us, then looked back at my brother.

"Yeah, I'm good."

"Nazai told me we're going to live with him and we'll be safe now. Is that true?" Hesitation filled his face.

My brother had been through a lot of shit to be ten years old. While I tried to protect him from a lot of things, there were some that slipped through the cracks. He was often jumpy and didn't like to be away from me for too long; I was happy to see he seemed to be managed well while I was locked away.

"Yeah, bud," I said thickly.

Nazai spoke. "Carson, I need to talk to your sister. Why don't you go grab your Switch and give us a minute."

A worried expression formed on my brother's face and he eyed me, waiting for my confirmation. A forced smile formed on my face.

"Go ahead, bud." I nodded to assure him.

He didn't move right away but eventually walked off.

Standing up, I scowled in Nazai's direction and stomped toward the chair on the side of him.

"You look better," he noted.

"Fuck you."

He chuckled. "Don't worry we'll get to that." His face suddenly turned serious. "I hope you'll play nice and I don't have to go forward with my threat."

Blinking blankly at him, I crossed my arms over my chest. My brother was the only reason I was keeping my composure right now.

"The wedding will happen at the end of the month. You need to be pregnant within a month following that."

My eyes grew and my brows shot up. "Hold up a second. Pregnant? You didn't say anything about getting pregnant! I don't want to have any damn kids," I rushed out, sitting forward.

"Neither do I but here we are. The agreement is us getting married and me getting you pregnant by the end of the year. That gives us five months, the sooner the better."

"I don't want kids. So if that's the deal; then you're shit out of luck." I shrugged.

A dark look blanketed Nazai's face. "You'll agree to these terms or I can have Jackson go put a bullet through your brother's head right now."

One of the men standing behind the couch, Jackson I assumed, moved to leave the room.

"Fine," I gritted stiffly. "Whatever, just leave my fucking brother alone." My skin was too tight. Every atom inside me was jittery. My nerves were twitchy and unsettled. Being backed into a corner wasn't an ideal situation for me. Feeling helpless wasn't something I took to well and the fighter in me wanted to push back.

One corner of Nazai's mouth lifted. "I thought you would see it my way. Now, as I was saying. There's a lot of responsibilities that come with being married to a Tavarez that I'll go over later, for now you're just meant to look pretty on my arm. Just know you better not try anything funny and don't make me regret this."

I was confused why Nazai even needed to force me into this marriage. He was an attractive guy and I'd seen multiple photos of him with different women on his arm. He had money, power, and looks.

"Just keep your end of the bargain and handle Maddox and his family and leave my brother alone and we'll be fine." My voice was toneless and void of emotion. Once again I was forced to play someone's puppet, and if Nazai wasn't careful, then the outcome would become as deadly as the first time.

"Where are we?" Cashlynn questioned, following me with Carson close at her side. She looked around the lobby as I ignored her.

"Charles." I nodded at the doorman.

"Mr. Tavarez," he greeted. "You got a package delivered earlier today, sir." He went behind the desk and picked up the brown box.

Going into my pocket, I grabbed my wallet and pulled out a fifty-dollar bill. "Thank you, Charles." I handed him the money and grabbed the package. "Also, I would like to introduce you to my fiancée Cashlynn and her brother Carson. Familiarize yourself with them. You'll be seeing them a lot."

I could tell he was caught off guard but he quickly fixed his face and nodded. "Yes, sir. Nice to meet you two."

Charles was an older black man and had been working here as a doorman longer than I'd been living here, which was three years now. I purchased the penthouse for the privacy it offered, not to mention the twenty-four hour attendants at the door and security was never an issue I had to deal with. The luxury building housed a lot of elite people throughout, and it was a pretty penny, but worth the buy.

"Anything else?" I asked Charles.

He shook his head. "No, sir."

Nodding, I started for the elevator that led to the penthouse. I had my own private entrance, which was another bonus. Using my key fob, I scanned the tag that opened the elevator door. Once inside, I typed in my access code on the keypad by the PH button for the doors to close and the car to move.

"I'll have key fobs made for you and get your code set up so you can get inside." I said, looking down at Cashlynn.

The fob was needed to get inside and the doors wouldn't open without the code. If entered wrong too many times, it would send a security alert to my phone. The only other way to get up here was if I buzzed the person in from the top. The doormen had fobs to get visitors up here as well.

"Where are we?" she asked again with hardened eyes.

"My house. Well… *our* house, I guess now." I chuckled bitterly. I still couldn't believe I had been forced into this situation.

"I thought we were at your house already?" Carson asked.

Once we had everything settled, I had them collect their things and Devin brought us to my actual house. Carson wasn't that bad of a kid. He was quiet, to himself, almost like he was used to making himself small and invisible. While I had Cashlynn in my basement, he stayed in the room I'd placed him in for the most part, only coming out to eat, then going right back.

"That was my other house. I only use it when I need to get away. This is my main residence."

I also had cameras set up in the elevator so I always knew who was trying to access my place. Emmet made sure the security was foolproof. Only a couple of people outside of my staff had a code, but every code was different so I always knew who was entering and when. The elevator opened into a hallway that housed a single door. We walked to the door and I used my key to unlock it.

It was a four-bedroom, four-and-half bath, three-story apartment with a chef's kitchen, breakfast bar, and top of the line stainless steel appliances used daily by my chef. Off from the kitchen was a fully-stocked wine cellar. The floors were black and gray marble.

The first level also housed the living room, den, laundry room, my office, dining room, and a bedroom, and one and a half baths. It was an open floor plan on this level. A large gas fireplace was set on the wall in the living room and den. My favorite feature was the four large, tall windows that showed the city from the living room. Often I drew the automatic blinds to bring in natural light and the city's skyline.

To the left between the kitchen and living room held the door that led to the private balcony. On it was a private pool and jacuzzi, deck, changing area, as well as a terrace with a grill and seating.

The second floor had the second and third bedrooms and two bathrooms, a gym with a built in sauna, another office, and the media room.

The final floor was where the master bedroom and bath were. It came with two walk-in closets, a sitting area, more large, tall windows, another fireplace, and a skylight.

"Shit," Cashlynn gasped. Both her and Carson's eyes widened as they took in the high ceilings. The second floor could be seen from the first, but I made sure the third was closed off. Even if I lived alone, I still valued my privacy when I was entertaining. When I did bring women home, I rarely took them to the third floor, usually using the bedroom on the first floor.

"Wow, look at the fish, Cash!" Carson gushed, rushing over to the built in fish tank full of exotic, imported fish.

"Neither of you are to touch it either. Those fish cost more than your lives combined."

Cashlynn turned and glared at me. "No one wants to touch your damn fish." She grabbed Carson, pulling him away.

Pulling my phone out, I tapped the screen a couple times, assuring my brother was on his way, then slid my phone into my pocket.

"I'll give you two a tour later, for now we'll get you set up in your rooms. You two stay down here," I told Jackson and Luke who were with us. I nodded for Cashlynn and Carson to follow me, heading to the second elevator.

"Are they always gonna be around?" Cashlynn asked.

My gaze narrowed on her. I wasn't sure if she was asking because she wanted to try some slick shit or because she was genuinely curious. "For now, they are."

She rolled her eyes as I hit the button for the elevator.

"Why not just take the steps?" Cashlynn asked. "Kind of lazy if you ask me."

Smirking, I stepped inside and hit the second floor button. One thing that sold me when I bought the penthouse was the inside of the elevator being glass. I enjoyed being able to see the floors when inside.

"This floor is where your room will be, Carson. There are two bedrooms, pick whichever you want." We stepped out of the elevator into the hallway. He looked around, still in shock, then faced his sister. It was clear he was waiting for her direction.

"Go ahead, bud," she encouraged.

He gave her a faint smile before moving down the hall.

"That boy needs to toughen up," I mentioned, causing her to spin and face me with a spiteful glare.

"He's fine and if you do anything to him or say anything, I swear—"

"Relax, Wildfire." I waved her off. "It's just an observation. With a sister like you, I just expected him to be more tough." I shrugged. Her eyes darkened and her jaw clenched.

"I'll take this one," Carson called down the hall, hanging out the doorway. The room he chose was the biggest on this floor.

"Good. Set your bags down and get comfortable. There's a media room at the end of the hall with games and shit, feel free to make use of it." His eyes lit up and he nodded. I made a note to call my personal shopper to go shopping for him. Carson only had two bags with him and Cashlynn had one large bag, a book bag, and a duffle bag. I didn't know the full story with them but I figured they had to travel lightly being on the run.

"I'll take the other room." Cashlynn went to walk forward but I grabbed her arm. "Uh uhn." I shook my head with a crooked grin. "You'll be staying upstairs in my room."

Her eyes widened. "No. The agreement was that I marry you, not stay in your room."

My grip tightened on her arm. "The agreement is whatever the hell I say it is. You're staying in my room. Now let's go." I yanked her, causing her to stumble. Her eyes flared with anger and her cheeks grew red.

When we were back in the elevator, I hit the button to the third floor and Cashlynn snatched away from me.

We stopped on the final floor and it opened to a small hall with my bedroom door directly in front. Stepping to the door, I pushed it open. "This is the master suite. The second closet will be cleared for your things."

"Yeah, like I have tons of things to fill it with," she said sarcastically.

"I'll have my personal shopper get clothes and whatever else you need. You'll also have a credit card tied to one of my accounts to get what you want." While I wasn't keen on the idea of taking a wife, I had to make sure she looked the part to stand by my side. While she was beautiful in looks, it was clear she had seen better days. It was now my job to make sure she was taken care of.

"Must be nice to just throw money at people and they do what you want, huh?" She stared at me blankly.

"It is." I nodded and stepped forward. My California king bed was in the middle of the room. On the right side was the sitting room, to the left was the door to the small, private balcony. "The bathroom is through there. There's a double sink, feel free to use the side my things aren't on."

Cashlynn ignored me, set her bag down, and began exploring the room. My phone vibrated in my pocket.

"Yeah?" I answered, watching her. I had taken the two weapons she had on her, so I knew she was unarmed. Still, I couldn't be too sure she wouldn't try to use something else to take me out if she wanted. Not that she would make it far, Jackson and Luke would end her before she fully got off the elevator.

"Mr. Tavarez, your brother is here to see you."

"Send him up." I hung up and locked my phone. My brother was one person with an access code to get to my floor. "C'mon, you can look around later. We have more important things to handle."

Cashlynn turned and faced me, confused. "Like what?"

"You'll see." I turned and hit the button to open the elevator.

Rolling her eyes, she sighed and walked toward me. "You would think you'd be less snappy with someone who's saving your life."

"I didn't ask you for shit," she snapped, glaring at me. "And you seem to need me as much as I need you." We stepped into the elevator and I crowded her as soon as the doors closed.

"Make no mistake, I don't need you for shit. I saw an opportunity and took it. The moment I feel like you're more of a hassle to keep than marry, you're done. Don't take my generosity as weakness, because I promise you, you won't like how I react then."

Her nostrils flared.

"Are you gonna tell me what was so important that I come here?" Lucas questioned after I opened the door for him.

"Follow me and I will," I said and faced Cashlynn. "C'mon, Wildfire."

Cashlynn muttered something under her breath and followed us. "You can get set up in here. I want a full health screening done." I pushed the door open.

"What's going on?" Cashlynn asked. She looked around the room hesitantly. Her eyes were guarded.

"You know I'm not a primary care doctor, right?" he complained but set his bag down and opened it up anyway. He pushed his glasses up and his eyes circled the room.

Lucas was the perfect blend of my parents. His skin the same golden brown as our mom's. He was the shortest of the four of us, at six foot even. He kept his face clean outside of a mustache and chin hair. He was medium built. My brother didn't care for the gym much, but body didn't reflect it.

"Lucas is here to give you an examination," I declared, then faced my brother. "I'm sure you know how to do the basics though, correct?"

Lucas shifted his eyes to Cashlynn. I could see the questions bouncing around them.

"Examination?" Cashlynn asked.

"Yes. Full STD panel. As well as an overall health screening."

"Excuse me! Wait a minute," Cashlynn protested.

"Make sure you don't half ass this either, Lucas. I want everything tested and brought back to me." I went to leave the room.

"Hold on!" Cashlynn stepped in front of me. "Who said I approved of this? You never asked for my permission."

I snorted. "If you believe I'ma put my dick in you raw and not have you thoroughly examined, you're outta your mind. You were engaged before I met you and who knows what or who you've been with besides him."

She inhaled deeply and blew a heavy breath out of her nose. "What are you trying to say?" She balled her hands at her side.

"That you're gonna go sit on that bed and let my brother take your blood and do whatever the fuck else he needs to."

Her eyes narrowed. "And what about you?"

"What about me?"

"If I'm forced to do this, then you should be too! Don't think I don't know you're a manwhore! I've seen the pictures." I smirked. Her right eye twitched. Even with her face twisted in anger, she was still attractive.

"Fair," I agreed. I was clean, one thing I always made sure to do was wrap my dick up when I had sex. The last thing I needed was an unwanted leech attached to me.

"Let me know when you're finished with her. I'll come in for my turn." I waved my hand dismissively and went to leave. I could feel Cashlynn shooting lasers in my back but I paid it no mind. For now, I needed to get things settled for this marriage that would be happening soon. The sooner I said "I do", the sooner I could take my rightful position.

"I'll have the results to you within three hours," Lucas assured me.

"Make it two," I told him.

He gave me a deadpan look. "Care to tell me what all this is about in the first place?" He hiked a brow.

"In due time, little brother. For now, just get those results to me and I'll see you at Mom and Dad's." He pressed his lips together tightly, but he didn't object.

"You owe me for this shit," he mumbled, heading for the door.

Cashlynn was sitting on the couch in the living room with her arms crossed. I checked the security cameras a little bit ago and Carson was locked in the media room playing the PS5.

"You need to go get ready," I told her.

"What now?" she groaned, rolling her eyes to the ceiling. My eyes locked on the leather band around her neck. A sense of ownership passed through me. It was made to look like a necklace and had a steel band between the material so it couldn't be cut off easily.

"We're having dinner at my parents' house."

She sputtered. "Your parents' house?"

"Yes. We'll be announcing our engagement as well."

"It hasn't even been twenty-four hours yet."

"Your point?" I stared at her blankly.

Cashlynn hopped up and stormed my way. "My point is, you've demanded I wear this fucking collar, I had to get pricked and prodded, now you're forcing me to meet your parents. I'm not gonna keep jumping like your fucking lapdog."

My mouth curled into a tight sneer. Reaching out, I grabbed the top of the "collar", as she put it, and yanked her forward.

"Your life is in my hands. So if I tell you to jump, you'll say how fucking high with a smile. Now take your pretty ass upstairs and change into something more suitable. I had some clothes dropped off for both you and your brother. I'll be waiting for you down here. Don't take all day either." I pushed her away.

While she was getting examined, I made a call to my personal shopper to have a couple of outfits for both her and Carson delivered.

"You better hide every knife you have in here tonight," she threatened, causing me to smirk.

"Some have tried to take me out, Wildfire, and I'm still here." I tilted my head and ran my eyes over her. I could see it in her eyes, she wanted to fight me. Her right eye twitched and her nostrils flared. Swiping her full, heart-shaped lips with her tongue, she turned and stalked toward the steps that led upstairs.

I would break Cashlynn one way or another. That fighter in her would keep me on my toes. I already could see it. But even the hardest stone could be broken with the right amount of force.

Cashlynn and Carson were quiet on the ride to my parents' house. Instead of letting Devin take us, I decided to drive my car. My custom, matte black Lamborghini with black and gray interior and tinted windows was one of my most prized possessions. It had been adjusted and customized to my liking from the moment I purchased it.

The large driveway was filled with cars. A couple belonged to my parents, the others my brothers.

"Are we gonna be here long?" Cashlynn asked as we walked up the stone path to my parents' front door.

"Long enough." I rang the doorbell.

It took a few seconds before the door was opened. Macy, the main house attendant, stood in front of us. Her hair was in a tight bun, just like it'd been since I was a kid. She had overseen the house upkeep for as long as I could remember.

"Hello, Macy."

She gave me a light smile. "Mr. Nazai. Welcome. Everyone is waiting in the dining room." She stepped out of the way, allowing us in.

My parents' house made the house Cashlynn broke into look like a one-bedroom cottage. It was massive with several bedrooms and bathrooms. There were basketball and tennis courts as well, out back along with an indoor and outdoor pool. A bowling alley, gym, and many other rooms my parents probably never touched. They had lived here since me and my brothers were kids. My dad had it built from the ground up and added onto it as the years went on.

"Shit. Your family truly is as loaded as the people say," Cashlynn muttered, causing a half grin to form on my face. A lot of articles came out about my family, most were rumors reporters pulled out their asses. In the eyes of the public we were a respectable family with respectable jobs. Those jobs also helped what we did behind the scenes. My dad's judicial ties helped us have many city officials in our pockets and kept us in the clear too.

"Guess you lucked up, huh?" A crooked grin split my face.

She huffed and continued looking around. I took a second to look her over. My stylist did well. Cashlynn was dressed in a black Alexander McQueen mini jacket dress with a pair of Givenchy G Cube sandals in leather.

I licked my lips. My money looked good on her.

We continued down the hallway until we got to the dining room where the rest of my family was already waiting.

"Seriously Nazai, are you ever on time to anything?" my mom huffed, laying eyes on me.

Going over to her, I leaned down and kissed her cheek. "Nice to see you too, beautiful."

"Yeah, yeah. It's a shame a family dinner must be called for me to see my firstborn."

"I'm a busy man, Mama."

Standing, I turned and nodded at my dad but his eyes were locked on Cashlynn and Carson.

Sighing, I knew it would be better to jump right into things before the night started.

"Everyone, this is my fiancée Cashlynn and her brother Carson." I walked back to Cashlynn's side.

"Fiancée!" Mom gasped before switching to Spanish. "Wait a minute! I didn't even know you were dating seriously."

"Dating is a stretch," Lucas muttered with a smirk on his face. I cut my eyes at him.

"Dad said I needed to get married, so here I am." I shrugged.

Mom eyed Cashlynn and turned her mouth upside down. "Well act like we raised you right. Finish the introductions, hijo." My mom was fully Black with golden brown skin but being with my dad had her speaking Spanish just as fluently as the rest of us. They made sure we all were fluent in both languages.

"Right. That's my mom Nora, father Dominic, and my brothers Ezra and Emmet. You already met Lucas." I pointed to each brother as I spoke.

"Hi." Cashlynn gave a faint wave and Carson stayed tucked at her side.

"Well don't be shy, take a seat," Mom encouraged. "Ezra, move so they can sit together," she demanded.

He muttered something but did as she said.

"Macy, let the cook know we're ready for dinner," Mom announced as we took our seats. I turned to my dad, noticing he still hadn't commented. His eyes were still locked on Cashlynn. He always had a great poker face, so I couldn't decipher what he was thinking.

A few seconds later, platters of food were brought out to the table.

The dinner table was silent, which wasn't common. Usually one of my brothers would be talking shit, but everyone seemed to be studying Cashlynn.

"What did you say your full name was?" Dad finally asked.

Cashlynn tensed at my side briefly, but quickly straightened up. "Cashlynn Cavana."

Dad's eyes hardened. "I knew you looked familiar. I'm usually good with faces. Your parents were Joe and Brandy, correct?"

"They were," Cashlynn replied stoically.

Dad turned to me with hard eyes and his lips pinched.

"¿Estás loco, carajo?"

"What do you mean, Dad?" Nazai questioned his father in Spanish.

"Do you know who her family is? The Cavanas are blackballed disgraces. They're untrustworthy bastards that deserved what they got," Dominic ranted in Spanish. "I'm sure they raised their daughter to be just like them!"

"I'm confused, Dad. You demanded me to find a wife and I did, yet you're still unhappy?"

"Not to a Cavana."

My eyes bounced between the two as they continued arguing in Spanish. Irritation rose inside me. I could feel my brother's tension radiating off him as he shifted closer to me. Although I'd heard of Dominic Tavarez, this was the first time I had laid eyes on him in the flesh. He was said to be a cruel and calculated man. He started a law firm shortly after retiring from being a judge and built it from the ground up to what it was today. He was a smart man to question my motives after learning who my parents were. When most people heard my last name, a negative reaction followed. Turns out Mom and Dad had burned a lot of people before they died. However, I would not allow him to talk about me as if I wasn't sitting here.

I broke into their exchange, also speaking Spanish. "Excuse me, Dominic, knowing what you and your family are into, I would be the last to judge anyone," I started. Nazai looked at me surprised and Dominic's face hardened further. "And for the record, your son came to me and demanded I marry him. I didn't ask for this. Who my parents were has nothing to do with who I am." I picked up the glass of water in front of me and brought it to my lips.

"Damn," one of the brothers muttered under a laugh, but my eyes were too focused on Dominic to tell which one.

"You speak Spanish?" Nazai asked, still shocked.

Setting my glass down, I twisted my neck to face him. "I actually speak four different languages. Spanish being one, yes."

Dominic cleared his throat. "Offending you wasn't my objective, but you must understand where I'm coming from. My family has a lot to lose and your parents were shady bastards." My brother flinched at the mention of my parents.

My eyes narrowed at Dominic. "You're right, they were, but they're no longer here or a problem, now are they?" I blinked at him blankly.

"Oh she's feisty. I think Dad's about to blow a gasket too," Ezra said with a chuckle.

My parents might not have been the best people but they raised me to stand on my own. While my heart pounded wildly inside me, not knowing how Dominic would react, I refused to show any fear. He could shoot me dead right here and no one in this room but my brother would bat an eye. Yet I sat straight and stared him in the eyes.

He truly was a handsome man. His genes passed on perfectly to his sons and blended well with his wife's. The main indicator of his aging was the gray speckling his goatee.

"A'right, that's enough!" Nora spoke up. "Dinner is on the table and I for one refuse to eat cold food. You also know I don't like business talk at the table. Dom, you two can discuss this after dinner. Now let's bless the food."

Dominic clenched his jaw but didn't argue with his wife. We lowered our heads and Nora blessed the food before everyone dug in.

"Cashlynn, Carson, go ahead and get whatever you want," Nora encouraged.

I looked down at my brother who was eyeing the fried chicken in front of him. "Do you want some, bud?"

He looked up at me and nodded. I gave him a small smile. "Okay," I started preparing his plate. This was the first homecooked meal we'd had in ages. Even when we were staying at Maddox's house, we rarely got homecooked meals, always forced to fend for ourselves.

Tension was still high but the conversation seemed like no one knew how to proceed after Dominic's rant. All that could be heard was the forks hitting the plates as we ate.

"Cashlynn, what is it that you do?" Dominic questioned.

"Dominic," Nora warned.

"I'm just curious, Miel. From what I heard, your parents were training you to join the family business, sí?"

Wiping my mouth, I gave Dominic my attention. He didn't try to hide the disdain as he stared at me with cold eyes.

"I hear a lot of things about you too but that doesn't make it all true."

His jaw clenched. "You disrespectful little pu—"

"Dominic!"

"Padre!"

Nora and Nazai shouted simultaneously. Dominic's face reddened as veins bulged from his forehead. Nazai glowered in my direction. "Have some more respect!" He faced his dad. "You need to respect my choice and my fiancée."

My nostrils flared and my brows furrowed. "Respect is earned and since I sat down he's lacked it for me!" The man in front of me wasn't the same Dominic I'd heard rumors about. From what I was told, he was normally calm and levelheaded. He was intelligent too. Whatever issues he had with my parents must be bad if he was this upset just by my last name.

"Oh shit." The brother I learned to be Ezra laughed. "Big bro, looks like you got your hands full with your fiancée."

Nazai shot his brother a look. I was learning Ezra was the brother that lacked a filter. He favored Nazai the most. His body less bulky, but it was clear he worked out. His arms were decorated with colorful ink as if it were a mural. His goatee surrounded his square jaw perfectly.

I rolled my eyes and caught Emmet's eye. He had a wary aura around him. I didn't know much about him. Out of all the brothers he seemed to be the one that stayed out of the public eye the most. He had been staring at me all evening, like he was watching me. His face gave nothing away. It was creepy honestly.

"Cash." Carson tapped my arm, gaining my attention.

I glanced down at him. "What's wrong?"

"I need to use the bathroom," he whispered.

I nodded and looked toward Nazai and got his attention. "My brother needs to use the restroom."

Nora spoke up. "Oh, Macy can show you. Macy!" she called out.

Before I could protest Macy had appeared.

"Can you show Carson the bathroom?"

"Of course." Macy smiled down at Carson. "Follow me."

Carson looked hesitant but I gave him a nod of assurance. He stood up and followed Macy, looking over his shoulder at me and nibbling on his bottom lip.

"Why little dude look like he be ready to jump out his skin?" Lucas asked.

My eyes cut to him. "He just doesn't trust people easily," I defended. No one would understand Carson's behavior because they didn't go through what he did growing up.

"You would think the boogeyman was about to jump out at him," Ezra joked, but I didn't see anything funny. My grip on the knife in my hand tightened. My body grew hot. Nazai must've noticed because his large hand covered mine and clenched it tightly. Shooting a tight glare up at him, I bit the inside of my cheek.

"When do you plan on having the wedding?" Nora asked.

"In two weeks," Nazai answered.

I bit the inside of my jaw again, this time harder. I still wasn't happy about being forced into this marriage. "That quick?" Ezra asked.

Nazai shrugged. "I only got two months left, why wait?"

"What about the bounty?" Emmet asked. Those were the first words I heard him say all night.

"What bounty?" Nora asked.

"Ah yes. I do recall there's a two hundred and fifty thousand dollar bounty on your fiancée's head. What do you plan to do about that?"

Dominic jumped in questioning with a smug expression plastered on his face.

"Once word is out Cashlynn is my wife, everyone will know not to lay a hand on her or they'll be killed. The bounty is non-factor at this point." I couldn't deny the confidence in Nazai's tone was attractive as hell. He spoke so sure of himself and with authority in his voice. If only his personality wasn't so shitty, maybe this marriage thing wouldn't be so bad.

A few minutes of silence passed between us. Carson returned and took his seat, going right back to eating. I hated how invisible my brother always made himself. When he was younger, he was such a vibrant kid, but my parents made sure to kill that light quickly.

Dinner wrapped up after a while and I couldn't be happier. Nazai's mom wasn't bad, and even his brothers, but the longer I sat at the table with his dad, feeling his judging stare, the more I wanted to react.

"Cashlynn, I know dinner started off rocky, but don't mind my husband. He's just protective of his kids. We want to welcome you both to the family." Nora caught me off guard when she pulled me into a hug. "Try anything funny with my son and I'll slit your throat myself," she whispered and released me with a smile on her face. Her husband stood at her side. The brothers had already left, leaving just us three here still.

My body stilled at her threat. I blinked slowly at her.

"Son." Dominic held his hand out for Nazai. "Come to my office tomorrow. We need to discuss a few things and how we're going to announce all the changes happening." He shifted his eyes to me but didn't speak further.

When we finally left the house and got back into Nazai's car, I turned to say something to Nazai but he was already facing me with cold, darkened eyes. He grabbed the collar around my neck and yanked me forward. "If you ever disrespect either of my parents again, I'll hang your naked ass from the ceiling for a week and use you for target practice. If you're gonna be my wife, then you need to learn some fucking respect." He shoved me away and pressed the button to start the car.

A heavy breath pushed through my nose and fire raced through my veins. Who the hell did he think he was throwing out threats and demands? Nazai was getting too comfortable with how he handled me.

It was time to show him I wasn't gonna be some meek wife he could control.

Later that night I changed into black leggings and a black hoodie, put my hair into two braids and pinned the bottom so none was hanging before covering them with a black cap.

I grimaced looking in the mirror. The black collar on my neck could be seen as a fashion statement. It had a heart metal lock in the front, but that wasn't what bothered me. It was the tracker inside. I attempted to pick the lock when Nazai dropped me and Carson off to go handle business, but it seemed to need a special tool to unlock it.

I shook my head, not bothering to think about it right now. I had more important matters to tend to. I checked my phone, making sure I had the location of my next kill. A rideshare was on the way to take me to my car. Thankfully, both my favorite gun and butterfly knife were in the truck of my car. I didn't want to leave Carson here alone, but it wasn't the first time and the security in this place was top notch so I knew he would be safe.

Leaving the bedroom next to Carson's, I went to his door and knocked. Nazai thought we were about to share a bed and I refused. I didn't trust him and wouldn't be able to sleep next to someone I didn't trust. As soon as he left, I took my bags out of his bedroom and moved them downstairs to the second floor. I wasn't his child for him to demand anything from me.

Pushing Carson's door open, I stepped inside and closed the door behind me. "Hey, bud. I'm going out for a bit. Will you be okay here?" I asked. He lifted his eyes from his Switch and faced me.

"Do you still need to go? We're safe now."

I sighed and looked around the bedroom. It was a nice size, but empty. I made a mental note to take him shopping to get some things to fill it. Since Nazai was gonna take care of my Rhodes situation, I was free to use my debit card without fear of being tracked. There was over thirty-five thousand in my account. It wasn't a lot but enough to get Carson comfortably set up here.

"I know you don't get it, but we're still not safe, Carson. We don't know Nazai and he can kick us out at any time or things could go wrong. I wanna make sure we're always prepared for anything. I won't be gone long, okay? Don't leave this floor and I have my phone if you need me. Do you have yours?"

He nodded. "It's in my bag."

"Okay, good. Call me if you need me. I'll be back." I stood and leaned over the bed to kiss his forehead then stood straight.

My only issue with leaving was that I would have to be buzzed in when I got back since I didn't have a key fob or code to the elevator. It was a nuisance to think about, but I would worry about that later.

I wiped my brow and tapped my foot, waiting for the elevator to get to the top floor. The kill was simple and went easy enough. The guy was a wife beater whose wife got fed up. He deserved worse than what I did if you asked me, but it was handled and I had another five thousand in my account.

Nazai had beat me home, which was good since I didn't have a code to get into the house. The new doorman had to call up to get permission to let me up, not believing when I told him I lived in the penthouse now.

I stepped off the elevator and walked to the door. I had made sure to purposely leave it unlocked so I could get inside. When I stepped inside, Nazai was standing in front of it with a hard expression on his face. His arms were crossed over his chest and he was dressed in a wife beater and basketball shorts. This was the first time I'd seen him dressed down since I'd been with him.

"Did you enjoy yourself tonight?" he asked.

My eyes swiped across the room before settling back on him. "You can say that."

"What were you doing by the docks?"

Defiance filled me. "That's none of your business. I had business to handle; that's all you need to know." I needed to shower. I enjoyed what I did, loved it even. It always caused a thrill to shoot through me, but that didn't mean I didn't feel nasty after. I also wanted to check on my brother.

Walking through the foyer, I stepped by Nazai so I could get to the elevator when he grabbed me. His hold on my upper arm was painfully tight, but I refused to show any fear. Before I could blink he had a gun pointed under my chin. My jaw clenched.

"If I find out you're on any funny shit, I *will* blow your fucking brains out. Do you understand me?" He pushed the gun further into my chin. His eyes were as dark as coal and his jaw twitched violently.

My hand balled but I didn't react. My brother was upstairs and the last thing I needed was for him to think something was wrong or for something to happen to him.

"We have an agreement," I reminded him calmly. "As long as you keep your word, I'll keep mine." Rage filed through my veins, swarming my body. My right eye twitched but I kept calm.

Nazai narrowed his stare on me. His face suddenly twisted and his mouth curled into a crude smile. "Make sure you remember that and we won't have any problems." He ran his eyes down my body and licked his lips. Flashbacks of the training my parents put me through when I was younger flooded my head. My jaw clenched tighter and my body stilled. He inched to reach behind me and grab the gun I had tucked in the small of my back before releasing me.

Shooting lasers his way, I turned and stalked to the stairs, not even caring about the elevator.

My heart pounded behind my breasts. My pulse was elevated and a pounding grew in my ears. My body felt like a volcano exploded in my stomach as heat flooded my body. Typically when a gun was pointed at me, that person didn't make it out alive.

I peeked in on Carson when I got upstairs then went to the room I was staying in and shut the door behind me.

I was too wired to get ready for bed now. At first I was willing to give

Nazai peace, but he wanted to choose violence, so violence was what he'd get.

"This is Bruce and James; they'll be your new guards," I told Cashlynn.

Her eyes traveled to the two men standing at the entrance of the kitchen. They had been hired and vetted by River. They knew my wife's life was in their hands and if anything happened to her they would be signing their death certificates.

Her face balled up.

"My guards? I don't need guards." She waved me off. I nodded for Bruce and James to leave the kitchen so I could explain some things to Cashlynn.

"You do and you will have them. Being a part of my family puts a target on your back. You never know when an enemy will try something; not to mention it's clear from last night that you can't be trusted to be left alone. So they'll keep an eye on you too."

I finished my coffee and put the cup in the sink then turned to face her at the breakfast bar. I always got up at six a.m. to take a swim in my pool to get my mind ready for the day. It seemed my fiancée was an early riser too. By the time I showered and got dressed for the day, she was downstairs at the breakfast bar drinking apple juice and eating toast with grape jelly.

The night before when I got home, I realized Cashlynn was nowhere in sight. Her brother was still here so I knew she hadn't attempted to run off, but still it made me wonder where she could be so late. When I saw Cashlynn was near the docks it really piqued my interest. Most dealings after dark around there were shady and corrupt. Since my soon-to-be wife was still a mystery to me, I couldn't put anything past her or pinpoint why she would be down there or who she was dealing with. Instead of going down there, I waited and confronted her at home. Cashlynn was smart, I was sure about that. She wouldn't do anything that would threaten her brother. Still, whatever she had going on would eventually come to light.

"I'm not a little kid. I don't need a babysitter and I'm capable of looking after myself."

My temple throbbed. I didn't have the patience to argue with her this morning.

Going into my suit pocket, I grabbed my wallet and took out my black card.

"I'm not going to argue with you on the matter. Here." I walked to her and set the card down. "I'll get you one with your name after the wedding, for now use this. Get some stuff for you and your brother. I have a personal shopper; I'll send her your number and she'll help you when it comes to clothes." Last night I'd found the phone she had in her bag when I looked through it and called myself when I saw she didn't have a lock on it.

Cashlynn looked down at the card but didn't reach for it. "What's wrong with my clothes?" She shot me an annoyed look.

"You're going to be a Tavarez, meaning you'll be held to a certain standard. What you have in your bag is fine around the house, but not when we're out."

"You went through my bag!" She puffed her cheeks out.

"Of course I did. You broke in my house." I checked the watch on my wrist. "I need to get going. Your driver's name is Dante. He will be available and waiting downstairs for you whenever you want to leave."

"I got my car last night."

"Just let James or Bruce know when you're ready to leave and they'll page him to be ready," I told her, ignoring her last statement. "I'll program you into the system today so you won't have to be buzzed in."

I stopped and looked at her. She wore a large T-shirt that made me wonder if she had anything under it. Her nipples were visible through the material. Her hair was in two straight back braids and her face glowed.

"Do you have shorts on under that?" I questioned, narrowing my eyes.

She glanced down. "No, why would I?" Her face scrunched.

Reaching out, I grabbed one of her nipples and twisted it. "What the fuck," she groaned out, but it came out as more of a moan. Memories of how she came in my basement when I pinched her nipples came to mind. I smirked. "I would hate to kill one of my guys because they see something they're not supposed to."

She blinked a few times to focus herself. "It's not like they didn't already see everything."

I twisted harder. She reached for my wrist and dug her nails into the small part of my skin showing from my suit arm pushing up.

My tone hardened. "That was before. Now you're about to be my wife and only I will see your body from now on." I watched her eyes dilate. Her breathing picked up, bringing my attention to her lips. They were full and wet from her drink. "You like this, huh? Your nipples are overly sensitive it seems. Tell me, Wildfire, is nipple stimulation one of your kinks?"

Her honey orbs flashed. "Fuck you," she gritted out.

"All in a matter of time. Don't worry." My brother had sent the results back and we both came back clean. Now it was only a matter of time before I had her. I released her nipple and smirked. "Now, be a good girl while I'm gone. And put some damn clothes on if you're gonna be on this floor."

I adjusted my suit jacket and turned to leave the kitchen but paused.

"Oh, before I forget, my mother is putting together a party to announce our engagement, you have two days to prepare for it." One thing my mom didn't play about was events. I didn't know anyone who could put one together as quickly as she did. When she texted me after dinner and let me know about the engagement party, I wasn't even shocked. I went into the pocket of my pants and pulled out the newest iPhone.

"Also, this is yours. It's already turned on and you have a new number too." I set the phone in front of her.

"I have a phone already."

"I know you do. I saw it in your bag and also saw it was a burner that wasn't worth shit."

"No one asked you to get me a new phone. No one asked you for guards. Stop trying to control me!" The lustful haze she was in quickly disappeared and switched to annoyance.

I was pushing Cashlynn's buttons mostly because I wanted to know how far I could push until she snapped. I saw some of her fight when she was locked in my basement, now I wanted to see how hot that fire could burn.

"You needed a new phone. I got you a new phone. The guards are for your own safety. Feel how you want about them, but they're staying." I left without letting her say anything else. James, Bruce, Jackson, and Luke were all standing in the foyer when I stepped foot in it.

"You two are not to leave her or her brother's side. One of you is always with one of them if they leave the house. You are not to leave the first floor either. The second and third are off limits unless absolutely necessary." My eyes bounced between James and Bruce. River was my best friend and I trusted his judgment. I wouldn't have anything to worry about if he thought these two were the best fit for my wife.

"Yes, sir," they answered.

I nodded at Jackson and Luke so we could leave. I wasn't sure how the meeting with my dad was going to go. He wasn't happy about my union with Cashlynn and I was sure he was going to make it more known when I saw him.

I wasn't shocked when I stepped foot in my dad's office and saw he was already waiting for me. He as working out his law firm today. I shut the door behind me and walked to the desk to take a seat.

"Padre." I acknowledged him. "You summoned me here. I can't only guess why." It had only been two days since breaking the news of my engagement and I knew I couldn't avoid my dad forever.

He stared at me with eyes that matched mine, but they were hard. His face still, lacking any emotions.

"We need to talk." On cue, his office door opened and Emmet stepped inside. He approached the vacant seat next to me and took a seat. Dad looked toward him. "Did you bring the files?"

"Yeah." He pulled his book bag in front of him and handed it over. Dad grabbed it and opened the folders. He searched the files silently, with me watching him curiously. I turned to Emmet but he gave nothing away. My brother had inherited our dad's poker face.

Dad soon placed the folder on the desk and pushed it toward me. "Here. Emmet, what else did you find?" he asked.

"Well, outside of what's in the folders, there's speculation about her parents' death." My brow rose. I reached for the folder so I could look inside. It was obvious this was about Cashlynn. "While it was deemed as a robbery gone wrong, at one point they thought it was murder and Cashlynn was the main suspect."

I scanned the documents. There was information about her parents and Cashlynn, including her bank statements and phone records before she got her burner. There were health records, showing a few broken bones she had as a kid, and other visits, one being a gunshot wound at sixteen.

What the fuck did she have going on then?

"Why was she looked at?" I lifted my attention to my brother.

He went into his book bag again and pulled out another folder. "There was no forced entry, no struggle or evidence that anyone else was inside the house. The only reason they ruled it a robbery was because some things were missing in the house, the window downstairs was open, and it wasn't when everyone went to sleep. After further investigation, they ruled her out and deemed it a break in homicide. There's been no arrest so far though."

"Something about that situation doesn't sound right to me." Dad's eyes landed on me with intensity as he rubbed his chin. "How did the two of you meet?"

"She broke in my house. I demanded she marry me." I shrugged.

Emmet released a small chuckle while my dad looked like he was about to blow a gasket. "Do you understand the risk our family could be in if she's on some shady shit? Her parents were snakes! They couldn't be trusted, why do you think I never worked with them. A lot of people wanted their heads."

"What does that have to do with Cashlynn?"

"Are you an idiot?" he asked in Spanish. "For all you know the apple doesn't fall far from the tree!" I shook my head. While my dad made some valid points, I didn't get traitorous vibes from Cashlynn. Dangerous maybe, but she didn't seem untrustworthy if she didn't see you as a threat. "Did you find out why there was a bounty on her head in the first place?"

"She stabbed Neil's son and he wanted revenge."

"Even more of a reason you need to reconsider marrying her. She could be the downfall of everything! From what I saw last night, she's irrational and disrespectful. Is that someone you want to bring into the family?"

My dad rarely lost his cool. It was one reason things ran so smoothly so he must have really disdained the Cavanas for him to act like this.

My jaw clenched. Not only did I not like my judgment being questioned, but my dad having some of the same thoughts as me didn't sit well with me, but I refused to give him the satisfaction. Since he was still technically in charge of The Bloodline and my dad it was his right to voice his concerns. Straightening my spine, I set the folders on the desk and stared him in the eye.

"I can handle Cashlynn. There's no need to worry."

"And how do you know that?"

"Because I know what I'm doing. When you demanded I get married, you never said my wife had to meet a certain criterion. I found someone that I saw would match me and just because you don't approve doesn't mean I'm going to get rid of her."

Dad's eyes hardened and narrowed. "You better know what you're doing, Nazai. I'm not passing my legacy down to you just for you to fuck it all up because you chose a piss poor bride."

"I never wanted a bride in the first place." My voice elevated. "So now you have to deal with the one I chose. She will become a Tavarez and you will respect it and her," I made clear.

There was no one on this Earth I respected more than my father, but at the same time he needed to learn to trust my judgment and allow me to lead how I saw fit.

"Careful, hijo. I'm still the head of this family and your father. Until I officially hand things over. So I advise you to fix your tone." His voice was laced with warning.

It took a few seconds for the tension in the room to settle. I had to take a couple of breaths and remind myself that soon everything would be mine and I wouldn't have to answer to anyone else.

"Now tell me it's time to talk business. There are some things I want you to be aware of once you become in charge."

Emmet ended up leaving during the sit down. His part of being called here was taken care of anyway. I was still on edge about my dad's accusations. They were nagging me in the back of my mind.

I had taken my phone out of my suit pocket and set it on the desk next to me. It was vibrating wildly and hadn't stopped, halting the conversation. I glanced at it on the desk and saw it was flooded with notifications.

"Do you need to get that?" my dad asked, irritation laced on his face and in his voice.

"Nah." I set the phone back down. "Just my fiancée doing some payback." I chuckled. When I gave Cashlynn my black card, I half expected her not to use it. It seemed like I was wrong. She had been going crazy with purchases and they weren't small ones either.

"I see," he said tightly. "Anyway."

The discussion continued and my phone kept vibrating. If spending my money made Cashlynn feel better, then who was I to stop her.

"I plan on increasing the number of pills distributed in the club, meaning traffic is bound to increase. Make sure your men are prepared for that,"

I told River. After meeting with my dad, I headed to The District to handle some club business.

My phone vibrated in my pocket as he answered.

Taking it out, I checked the screen, seeing it was one of the guys guarding Cashlynn.

"Yeah?" I answered.

"Uh, boss, we have a problem." My brows furrowed.

"Did something happen to my fiancée?" I made eye contact with River who didn't look happy either. We were in the middle of discussing he switch up for security concerning the club. Since I would be adding more product I wanted more men available for unseeable issues.

"No, but uh, you might want to check your messages."

Pulling my phone from my face, I opened my messages.

"What's going on?" Lucas asked.

My eyes ballooned and my nostrils expanded as I stared at the picture of my destroyed Lamborghini.

"Who did that?" I'd taken my Maserati today instead of having Devin take me or the Lambo.

"Your fiancée." I shot up. "And where were you fucking idiots when she was doing it?" I bellowed.

Quickly, I hit the Facetime option and waited for a few seconds before James answered.

"Where is she?" I gritted, gripping the pen in my hand tightly. I could feel my brother and best friend's eyes on me, but I paid them no mind.

Without saying anything further, he flipped the camera and Cashlynn came into view. The crowbar she must have used on my car hung over her shoulder while she stood in the center of the penthouse.

"Cashlynn!"

She turned and faced the phone with a deadpan look. "Must be nice to be a snitch."

"Are you out of your fucking mind? Do you know how much that car cost?"

Her shoulders lifted and her eyes cut into slits. "Does it look like I give a damn?"

My jaw clenched so tightly I was surprised I didn't crack my back molars. "You think this is funny? That car was customized to perfection!"

Bringing the crowbar to her front, she waved it around. "I bet you'll think twice about holding a gun to my head." Her eyes scanned the room before lighting up. Her brows shot to her hairline and a crude grin formed on her face. "In case you need another lesson on why you shouldn't fuck with me…"

My heart hammered in my chest as I watched her waltz over to where my built-in fish tank was. My eyes ballooned and my body ran hot.

"Don't you fucking dare!" My words were slow and my muscles grew taut.

Those fish were specially imported and cost millions of dollars. They were rare and from all around the world.

Mirth danced in her eyes before she pulled the crowbar back and swung it forcefully toward the tank. The bar connecting with the glass was like nails to a chalkboard. The glass crashed and water gushed out. The fish flooded the floor, flopping all over. Water spilled out, pooling at her feet. Blood rushed through my veins. My temples throbbed.

"Fucking bitch! Where the hell is Bruce? Why are you just standing there?" My heart raced as the blood pumped wildly through it.

"We didn't think it was wise to touch her, sir," James stammered.

A satisfied look formed on Cashlynn's face. "Don't fuck with me, Nazai, or your car and fish will be the least of your worries." She pointed the crowbar toward me before tossing it on the ground next to my flapping fish and walking off.

"Cashlynn!" I shouted.

Instead of listening, she turned to walk away, but not before tossing her hand up and flashing me her middle finger.

River and Lucas muttered to each other behind me but I was too hyper focused right now to take in what they were saying. I was already on edge from the meeting with my dad earlier, then I had a meeting in a couple hours with Zylus. This was the last thing I needed on my plate.

"I'm about to ring her fucking neck," I gritted, hanging up the phone. Cashlynn thought her little act was cute, but all she did was poke the bear and now it was ready to attack.

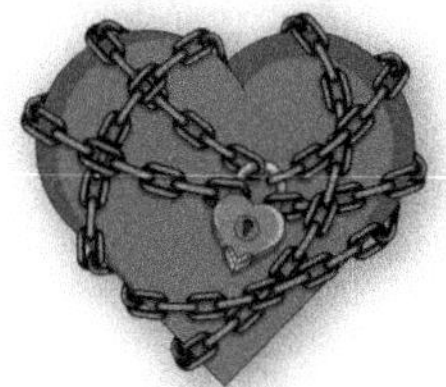

"Oh damn." Lucas whistled as I walked around my car with my mouth hanging open.

"What the hell did you do to make her do this?" River asked, holding back a laugh.

Clenching my jaw I examined the car, wondering what the hell was going through her head. She had busted out my windows, including the windshield. On the driver side it looked like she dragged her key from the front bumper to the back and on the passenger side she spray painted 'Limp Dick' in red paint.

"You got ED, big bro?" Lucas questioned. "I can recommend someone if you need some help."

Turning, I shot him a glare.

"Shut the fuck up. Ain't nothing wrong with my dick." I dragged my hand down my face and pushed out a heavy breath.

"And you sure you want to marry this girl?" River asked. "She doesn't seem like she's gonna be easy to deal with."

My Wildfire was a handful indeed. Turned out her silence shouldn't have been taken lightly. I wanted to see that same fight I saw in the basement when I had her hanging from the ceiling, but I hadn't expected her to fuck with my car.

Ignoring both Lucas and River as they continued making jokes, I stormed inside the building, ignoring Charles and heading straight to the elevator with my brother and River behind me.

"I knew she was gonna be a handful when she tried to buck at Dad."

"She did what?" River asked.

"At dinner you missed it…" Lucas started explaining how Cashlynn didn't back down yesterday at dinner and River thought it was the funniest thing in the world.

My hands balled at my sides. I hurried and put in my access code. As the cart rose, my foot tapped rapidly and my jaw ached from how hard

I was clenching it.

Briefly, I glanced at where my now destroyed fish tank was once in my foyer. The fish had been cleaned up and put in a tub, but it didn't matter. They had specific living conditions; so they most likely were done for.

Just the thought of it had my nostrils flaring and hands balling into tight fists. Thankfully I had hardwood floors in that area. The floor had been cleaned of water, the shattered glass, rocks, sand, and the decorations inside of the tank.

My breath sped up and I tasted blood as I bit the inside of my cheek.

"Where is she?" I asked James, swinging my eyes back to him.

He avoided my eyes. "Upstairs. She said she was taking a bath."

Making my way to the elevator, I undid my suit jacket when I stepped on. Since she ignored my request and slept on the second floor anyway, I figured that was where she was. I didn't put up a fight when she didn't come to my room. For now I would let her have her way, but once we were married all that was changing.

Cashlynn was lying peacefully in her bed, in nothing but a towel, with headphones over her ears. The smell of her body wash filled my nostrils. Seeing her so relaxed after she destroyed my car and fish tank caused my blood to boil and my hands to twitch at my sides. Not only had she done damage to my car that would more than likely cost me thousands to fix and destroyed a tank worth millions, but she'd disrespected me as well. It seemed I was taking it too easy on her. She saw my threats as a joke. It was time to show her what happened to those who angered me.

Pulling my phone out of my pocket, I sent a quick text before removing my suit jacket. I turned and hung it on the doorknob.

Luke and Jackson soon came into view with my brother and River following behind them.

"All this over a car and some fish?" River asked with amusement, handing me the bucket from the utility closet.

"It's more than just the car and fish. She's gotta be taught a lesson about respect." I cracked my knuckles. "My future wife is about to learn an important lesson."

I nodded at Luke and Jackson and they headed for the bed with zip ties in hand while I turned for the bathroom to turn on the water. The room smelled like something fruity, residue of bubbles remained in the tub when I walked over to fill the bucket. I could hear Cashlynn's curses and yells over the running water, causing my mouth to turn upward.

I went into the cabinet on the wall, grabbing a towel once the bucket was filled and heading back into the bedroom.

"What the fuck is going on!" Cashlynn snarled when I walked back into the room. She was fighting to break free of the zip ties.

"You wanted my attention fucking up my car and my fish tank, well now you got it. Do you know how much money I invested in both of them?" I placed the bucket down near the bed and took a seat.

She glared at me with fire burning in her eyes. "Fuck you, your car, and those fish!"

I chuckled darkly. "You look beautiful when you're at my mercy." I brought my hand to her face and ran it over her skin lightly.

She bit her teeth at me and yanked away from my touch. "Don't fucking touch me!"

Ignoring her, I ran my hand to the collar around her neck. I loved that my ownership was present. While to some it might look like a normal necklace, I knew better. It showed that Cashlynn was *mine*. That she belonged to me, my wife-to-be.

I cleared my throat and stood. "You thought it would be funny to fuck with my shit, huh?" I rolled my shirt sleeves up.

"You put a fucking gun to my head. You're lucky it was the tires I slit and not your damn throat."

"Shit." River chuckled behind me.

My face fell and I bit the inside of my cheek. I grabbed her cheeks, squeezing them tightly, causing her lips to pucker. "That's cute, Wildfire, but I'ma let you know a little secret. You might think you're a threat, but you ain't seen shit yet."

Standing up, I released her face and placed the towel I had over it. "What the hell are you doing?" she shrieked. I admired her will to still fight, even while being tied up.

Ice crept through my veins. My heart beat pounded loudly in my ears. Everyone stood around me, anticipating my next move. "Leave us," I demanded. An audience normally didn't bother me when I needed to teach a lesson, but for this I wanted only me and my wife to be present.

"Lucas, stay close."

My brother mumbled something under his breath as everyone left the room, giving me privacy.

"I'm going to show you why you should stay in your place," I said, grabbing the bucket. My pounding heart grew wilder and my blood hummed in my veins. Endorphins exploded inside me and my dick hardened with anticipation. Cashlynn was still pitching a fit under the rag. I enjoyed hearing how pissed off she was. Her anger fueled my desire to teach her a lesson even more. My knees pressed against the bed as I lifted the bucket and poured it directly over Cashlynn's face.

Muffled, gurgling noises replaced her screams. She fought against the restraints. My dick grew harder, pushing against my slacks.

CHAPTER TEN

When I decided to fuck with Nazai's car it was supposed to be a big fuck you to him. I knew he might be upset since that was the most expensive car he owned, but I couldn't have expected this reaction. I hadn't even planned on destroying the fish tank until he called.

I was in the middle of meditating when I felt my hands and feet being bound to the metal head and footboard. By the time I realized what was going on it was too late.

The anger I saw in Nazai's eyes when I laid eyes on him caused my stomach to recoil but I refused to show fear. When he placed the towel over my face, my heart sped up but I still refused to submit to him.

Now my lungs were on fire and it was hard to breathe. Panic shot through my body as I attempted to take in large gulps of air between him pouring the water, but it was useless. I fought against the restraints again, clenching my hands as I began to choke. For a brief second the cloth was lifted and through my blurry eyes Nazai came into view with a taunting expression on his face.

"Had enough?" He smirked. "Ready to apologize?"

"Fu-fuck you," I coughed out, gasping for air. My body quivered uncontrollably.

"Tsk, tsk. Guess not."

"No!" I strained to get out when he lowered the towel again. Soon, the water hit it. My mind raced and I coughed harder as water slid down my throat. I kept telling myself to keep calm and tried to ease my racing heart, but it was hard. It felt as if I was drowning with no life jacket in sight.

"You'll learn to respect me and obey or you'll suffer daily," he said tonelessly.

I wasn't sure how long it went on, but it felt like forever. I wondered how much water he had left. Every so often he'd tease me with air by lifting the towel, but it was never long enough.

CHAPTER ELEVEN

"**S**he's fine, from what I can tell," Lucas commented, pulling his stethoscope from Cashlynn's chest. She was hunched over, breathing heavily while rubbing her bruised wrists.

Once I figured she got the point, I ended her suffering and freed her. She broke out in a fit of coughs instantly, gasping for air. Her skin was flushed and her breathing staggered.

"You're lucky no fluid got trapped in her lungs." He glared at me before standing up. I waved him off, leveling my eyes on Cashlynn.

Her head drooped forward and slowly lifted. Her tired, red eyes met mine.

A lopsided grin suddenly split my face. I stepped closer and reached for her collar, running my hand over it. "You're gonna pay off however much it's gonna cost to get my car fixed. That was a custom job."

"I'm not doing shit." She slapped my hand away, wheezing slightly.

I reached for her nipple, pinching it, causing her eyes to flutter.

"Don't fucking touch me! You almost drowned me."

"If I wanted to drown you, you would be dead." I hooked a finger under the collar and yanked her forward. "Just remember that next time. I'll let you know how you can pay for the damages." I ran my eyes over her body. My dick took notice of her naked form and stiffened.

"Kiss my ass," she spat through clenched teeth.

A lopsided smile formed on my face. "In due time, Cashlynn, I will. I plan on tasting every inch of you in fact."

"On that note, I'm out. I'll see you at the party." Lucas headed for the door.

Cashlynn blinked a few times. Creases formed in her forehead. "You're insane. You just tried to drown me and now you're acting normal." Smirking, I released her and stepped back.

"You're lucky I don't force you to your knees and fuck that pretty little mouth, show you what this 'limp dick' can do." Her eyes flashed and her cheeks reddened more. "Get dressed. It's almost time for the party and we can't be late. You'll ride with me," I let her know. Maybe my actions were confusing, but I couldn't help it. One moment I wanted to wring Cashlynn's neck, the next I wanted her under me moaning while I fucked her mercilessly. Either way, playing with her was becoming the most entertainment I'd had in a while.

"As you know, me and my beautiful wife just celebrated our twenty-fifth anniversary." Mom blushed as Dad lovingly gazed into her eyes. "While I'm enjoying my retirement, I'm happy to announce my son has finally found someone to settle down and start his future with. I pray you two have a fruitful marriage as me and your mother have. I see nothing but more success in your future, my son." Dad turned and looked at me while everyone around us started clapping. Mom had insisted on throwing an engagement party, and how she'd gotten everything together so quickly I did not know, but I'd learned not to question her madness. The event was filled with many people, a few close associates and business partners, and a few press members. I had been trained for the press since I was a kid because of the spotlight Dad always had on him. It only got worse once he published his case studies, using his psychology minor to his advantage.

My brothers stood at my side, along with Cashlynn, Carson, and River. Cashlynn protested coming up here with me at first, not wanting to be in the spotlight, but I didn't give her much choice. After what happened back at the house yesterday, she had stayed out my way. It was a fight to get her to even agree to come tonight. So far she had refused to let me touch her. I ignored that too, of course.

Grabbing Cashlynn's hand, I pulled her up to the podium. Reporters threw questions and took pictures as I shook hands with my dad then took the mic.

"Growing up I always watched my dad and admired the kind of husband and father he was. I saw how strong my mom was and how she held my dad down even when things got tough. The two of them were a power couple that I always knew I wanted to be like when my time came." My words weren't a complete lie. My smile broadened. "He was always a fair man and hardworking, making me want to be just like him when I grew up. When I first started my nightclub, The District, it was to honor my padre and the legacy he's been building." I turned to my dad and he stared at me with pride in his eyes. Sometimes things got rocky with us but I knew, no matter what, he always had my back. "I won't let you down, Pops. You built this family on your back with hard work, blood, and sacrifices and I plan on doing the same with my own family."

"I'm proud of you, hijo." He stepped forward, pulling me into a fatherly hug and patting my back. More claps exploded around us.

"Mr. Tavarez, rumor is you're retiring from law soon. Is that correct?" a reporter asked.

I stepped to the side so Dad could take the mic. Better him than me.

"Yes, that's true. I've served my time in the justice field and now I'm handing my reins over."

"Nazai, are you taking over?"

My dad's eyes flashed momentarily when he turned to look at me before facing the crowd again.

"No, as you all know, my son Ezra has been working at my firm for some time now. He will take over once I officially step down." I know it still upset my dad that I refused to step up and follow his lead with a law degree, but being in a courtroom all day was never something I saw for myself. We fought about it often when I first graduated high school.

Ezra, although he didn't seem like it from the outside looking in, always admired that part of my dad's life. So it only made sense he was the one who took over.

"That's not why we're here. Tonight is about my oldest and his celebration in union."

"Nazai, what's your fiancée's name?" one of the members of the press called out.

"Ms., what's your name?" another one shouted.

Releasing my dad, I turned to face Cashlynn who had a blank face but her body screamed that she was uncomfortable.

I wrapped an arm around her shoulder and tucked her into my side. "I would like to announce my engagement. This is my lovely fiancée, Cashlynn Cavana!"

Murmurs spread and more pictures went off. "Is she related to the same Cavanas that were murdered in their homes recently?"

"Wasn't she seen as the primary suspect?"

"Is it true her parents were murderers for hire?"

Again, Cashlynn stilled briefly in my arms. My face fell and my mouth thinned. "My soon-to-be daughter in law had nothing to do with the murder of her parents. It was an unfortunate, traumatic event that she and her brother are still grieving and trying to get over. If anyone is seen harassing or printing false information, legal actions will be taken," Dad said, cutting in.

Part of me expected the questions regarding her family. It was no secret about the murders. The Cavanas weren't exactly the people to stay off the radar with things. While my family was always in the limelight, our business was mere secondhand rumors among the public. The Cavanas had no code, so the speculation with them was frequent if someone knew what to ask and what to look for.

"When's the wedding?" someone asked, breaking the silence.

"In two weeks."

"Why so soon?"

"Are you two marrying in order to combine the illegal activities your families have been rumored to be involved with?"

I narrowed my eyes at the reporter. She had on sunglasses and a hat low over her eyes. She was the main one spitting things out about

Cashlynn's parents.

"I have no clue what illegal dealings you speak of, but I can't wait to make her my wife. Now, if you all will excuse me, I have other business to handle." I turned to Cashlynn. She was staring at me with a mixed expression on her face, somewhere between perplexed and amused. It was different from her normal scowl when she looked at me.

My dad stepped up again and spoke. "We are excited to welcome Cashlynn and her brother into the family. She will be a great addition to the family." His words shocked me. It made me wonder if he was starting to accept my proposal. I could never tell with my dad. He was the master of putting on for the public.

To pull them in more, I reached up, grabbing her by the chin and tilting her head upward. Suddenly, she looked like a deer caught in headlights. I lowered my mouth, ignoring how her body froze, and placed my lips on top of hers. A small gasp fell from her mouth, giving me an in. I wrapped an arm around her waist and pulled her body closer, pushing my tongue inside her mouth and exploring.

"Kiss me back," I muttered against her lips.

She grabbed my suit jacket and gripped it tightly, then suddenly a metallic taste filled my mouth as she bit down on my tongue, causing it to bleed. It caught me off guard but turned me on at the same time.

My mom's voice broke in. "Okay, that's enough, that's enough. God, son, save it for home."

"Yeah, hijo. Not too much in public," my dad said with a hint of warning in his voice.

I pulled away from Cashlynn whose eyes were a bit bewildered, the lip gloss on her mouth slightly smeared. I licked my lips, tasting the blood from my tongue and smirked. That scowl returned to Cashlynn's face.

Chuckling, I turned back to the mic. "As y'all can see, my fiancée causes me to lose my composure sometimes. You folks enjoy the rest of the party." I grabbed Cashlynn's hand and turned to leave.

When we passed her brother, she made sure to grab his hand and pulled him off the stage into a hallway. Once we were in the hall, Cashlynn snatched out of my hold.

"What was that?" she hissed. Her cheeks were still flushed.

With a crooked grin, I scanned her. "Is it a crime to show my fiancée some love?" I cocked my head to the side.

She pressed her lips together tightly and narrowed her eyes. "Don't do that again." She turned to her brother. "Are you okay? Was that too much?"

He shook his head. "I'm fine."

Cashlynn was usually cold and guarded, except with her brother. I didn't know what made her so protective and soft with him, but I was curious if she would be the same way with our child. I dropped my attention to her flat stomach, trying to picture her round with my seed.

I blinked a couple times, snapping myself out of the thought. I still wasn't happy about the marriage and pregnancy ultimatum I was given, but Cashlynn was keeping things interesting.

"That went well." My dad's voice broke me out of thought.

I turned to him and he along with my siblings and River were standing around us. He stared at Cashlynn for a long minute without speaking then glanced down at her brother.

"Attention is gonna be on you a lot more now. While I hoped people wouldn't put it together, your parents weren't the most upstanding people in the public eye so they are probably waiting for you to show those characteristics too." He cleared his throat and rolled his shoulders back then turned to me. "Make sure the publicist is on standby just in case. I'm still not crazy about this union but I've spoken my piece."

"Yeah, it's official now. Welcome to the family, sis. I never wanted a sister, but something tells me you'll fit right in." Ezra walked to her and put his arm around her shoulders.

She cut her eyes at him and nudged him off her, making him laugh.

"Can me and Carson go back home now?" she asked with impatience.

"Yeah, Devin will drive you today."

"Cashlynn, tomorrow I'll be by to get you. We must get you fitted for your dress," Mom piped up.

Cashlynn looked caught off guard. "A dress? Isn't this just gonna be a courthouse wedding?"

Mom laughed. "Oh heavens no, honey. You're having a real wedding. It'll cost a little extra since it was short notice but my planner is the best in the business and always on call for me. She's getting things in order now. I'll show you what she came up with tomorrow."

Cashlynn looked between me and my mom. "Right," she mumbled, shifting on her feet.

Eventually everyone scattered. Before he could leave, I called Emmet over. "That reporter, the woman throwing out things about Cashlynn, find out who she is for me then let me know what you can find on her."

He nodded. "Gotchu, bro."

Now that it was out in the public, the engagement just became that much realer.

My hand moved back and forth across the sketchpad, shading in the section of Cashlynn's face I was working on currently with my charcoal pencil. I paused, eyeing my phone, looking at the picture of reference. It was one from the party tonight that one reporter had captured. It was a picture of her side profile and I also found one of her from the front with a blank expression on her face I planned to draw next.

As I sat out on my private balcony, I stared at the small ruffles in the pool's water and admired how the moon reflected off it. The weather was comfortable, and I always enjoy sitting out here and taking the peace it brought me.

Dropping my eyes back to my pad, I studied it carefully. Drawing had always been something I was into, but recently I'd been into more lifelike pictures, with Cashlynn being my current muse.

Halting from my shading, I flipped back a couple pages and admired the drawing I'd finished recently. It was her hanging from the ceiling in my basement in nothing. Since then I'd drawn her three other times before this.

Going back to my current page, I stared at the drawing. Since proposing the marriage idea to Cashlynn, she'd consumed my thoughts more than she should. Drawing her was a way to help release her from my mind, but it seemed to only make things worse. Whenever I tried to draw my next inspirations, it was her face that popped up.

My hand brushed over the paper. With any hope I would move past this. This marriage wasn't something I wanted, but *had* to do. The issue was I was becoming infatuated with my wife.

STOLEN MATRIMONY

Currently, I was lying in bed with the lights off, staring at the ceiling, headphones on, and listening to a random meditation playlist I found on YouTube. Normally I would close my eyes to meditate and center myself, but after what happened last time, I needed to be alert.

Carson was in the game room, which seemed to be his favorite room in the house. He had adjusted to living at Nazai's house a lot quicker than I expected him to.

My nerves were rattled from earlier when Nazai kissed me. It caught me off guard for many reasons. Mainly because that was the first time anyone had kissed me. It was embarrassing and pissed me off at the same time. I just froze, eventually biting his tongue, not sure how else to react.

I sighed. It had been a while since I'd meditated. My mind cleared and my body relaxed the most it had been in months. I hated that the Tavarezes were so in the public eye. I never cared for attention and wished they just would be a normal crime family and leave the spotlight to the upstanding citizens.

My calmness was interrupted when the lights were turned on and my headphones were snatched off my ears.

"What the hell!" I hissed.

Nazai stood above me with that annoying, cocky, crooked grin he often wore on his face. He was still in the same suit he'd worn to the party. It was unsettling how arrogant he was. It would be better if he was ugly, but Nazai was far from that. He was extremely attractive and always well put together.

When I logged onto social media today, for the first time in ages, I went to his Instagram and saw it was flooded with women gushing and lusting over him. He didn't have much on it, mainly a couple of selfies and pictures with his brothers. Those pictures got double the comments with women wishing they could land one of the brothers. Both his personal and business pages had thousands of followers.

Yesterday I hadn't expected his reaction when it came to his car or fish tank. I was still seething about the gun situation and wanted to get a reaction out of him and show him I wasn't a pushover. Blowing thousands of dollars on whatever wasn't enough. Feeling that water rush against my face and the towel blocking my airwaves caused a fear I hadn't felt in a long time to come crashing into me. I was furious, but I also felt a rush I hadn't felt before either. It was confusing to me.

"What do you want? I was busy!" I squinted at him, sitting up on the bed.

"You were sleeping," he noted.

"I wasn't sleeping! I was meditating and you interrupted me…again." He stared at me curiously, as if he couldn't understand what I meant. It caused me to roll my eyes and grab my phone, pausing the playlist.

"What do you want, Nazai?"

"Get dressed. We're going to my club tonight."

My brows bunched and my mouth turned upside down. "Pass. Can I have my headphones?" I held my hand out.

"There is no passing. We need to make an appearance at my club. My brothers and River are meeting us there. Get dressed. Put something tempting on that snatches people's eyes but doesn't give away too much. If you don't have anything like that, I had my stylist get you something." He nodded at the dress that wasn't on my bed when I'd first lay down. Another unsettling thing was my awareness when it came to Nazai. Normally I was very aware of my surroundings. It was critical with what I did, but with him I never seemed to be able to detect him.

"I don't like clubs and I'm not leaving my brother."

"Your brother will be fine. I called the lady who used to watch me and my siblings to come keep an eye on him."

"No." I shut him down. "I'm not leaving my brother with some stranger I don't know."

"Mrs. Rosebud has been in my family since I was a kid. She's more than qualified to watch him. He'll be in good hands."

A standoff happened between us, neither willing to back down. "Why do I have to go? You can just go by yourself." I had never been to The District nightclub but I'd heard about it, of course. It was always packed with people, both it and Euphoria, the strip club attached.

He tossed the headphones on the bed. "I've announced you as my fiancée, now we need to sell it. You're gonna be my wife and we need to show you stand by your husband."

I rolled my eyes, feeling a headache rise. "Now hurry up, we're leaving in two hours." He turned to leave. I turned to look at my phone; it was eight o clock. I wanted to fight him and stand on not going, but eventually I sucked it up. Leaving my brother alone with a stranger still made me uneasy, but I was going to go against my better judgment and trust Nazai's word. I would talk with Carson before I left to make sure he was okay though.

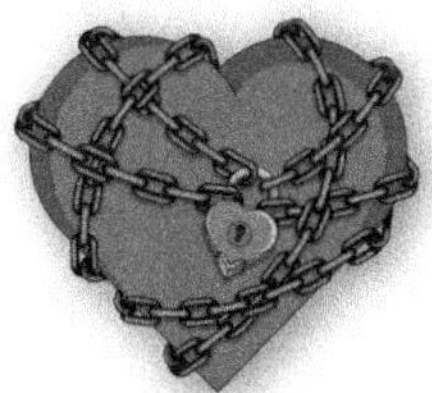

The music was loud, lights flashed, and people talked loudly, having a good time around us. A woman dressed in nothing but a skimpy thong was on stage getting a bunch of bills thrown at her. The District was packed and when we got here the line was wrapped around the corner. When customers first stepped inside, there was a small area where they could either go into the nightclub or go up the stairs that led to Euphoria.

The first hour we were at The District, we were downstairs in the nightclub. Nazai had a private section close to the entrance for him and close friends only. Eventually, we headed upstairs to the strip club. It was a little less chaotic up here than downstairs. Again, we were in the owner's section, as he called it. His brothers, along with River, all seemed to be having a good time. Lucas and River had been making it rain since they'd gotten here. Emmet had been sitting back nursing a drink, observing his surroundings and Ezra had left to get a private dance in one of the back rooms.

"This must not be your scene." I jumped when River sat next to me. Nazai had gone to the bar to handle some matter they needed him for. A few girls were in the section entertaining.

"It's not," I told him, sipping my drink. I didn't know what it was but it was fruity and good.

Where we were gave us a full view of the rest of the club. "Me and Nazai been best friends our whole lives. You're the first woman I've seen give him a run for his money though," he mentioned.

This time I turned to face River. He was an attractive man—smooth chocolate skin, bulky frame, five o' clock shadow that highlighted his chin.

"Do you have a point?"

He smirked. "Nah, just making an observation."

I ran my eyes over him. "You're considered his enforcer, right? The one that takes care of issues?"

His face straightened. "I'm his head of security, yeah."

I tilted my head. "Mhm. For both businesses?"

River eyed me curiously but I made sure to give nothing away. Since I would be marrying into the Tavarez family, I wanted to play a part in the business, but it hadn't come up yet. If I had to guess, River was the one who carried out the killings when they were needed. So I figured he was who I should talk to.

Before I could say anything more, Nazai returned. "Back off my wife. She's off limits," he joked, sitting next to me and pulling into his side.

River eyed me a little longer before a crooked grin formed on his face. "She's not your wife yet."

"In less than two weeks she will be." I glanced up at Nazai and he stared down at me, licking his lips.

I hated the flutters that filled my belly. Snatching my eyes from him, I watched one of the girls in the section lean down and whisper something to Emmet. He shook his head and brought his drink to his mouth. Usually I could read people well, but Emmet was hard. He seemed like a blank slate, never giving away how he was feeling, but always watching.

"You glad you came now?" Nazai asked, leaning down.

"I would rather be at home."

He chuckled and brought his cup to his mouth.

Eventually, Ezra returned with a wide grin on his face.

I had my phone out, checking on Carson. Nazai ended up upgrading his phone at the same time he did mine.

"You the only person I know who comes to a strip club and looks mad at the world." I glanced up at Ezra. "You ever smile?" He grinned and cocked his head to the side.

Finishing my message to my brother, I tucked my phone in my crossbody purse. It was small enough for essentials, but big enough for my butterfly knife and gun. Thankfully no one bothered to search us at the door.

"When I have something to smile about." He chuckled and took a seat next to me.

"Lucas sent us a picture of Nazai's car. I knew you would be the one to give him hell."

"Your brother needs to be humbled."

He smirked. "And you're the one to do it."

My shoulders lifted. "Maybe."

He tossed his arm around me. "I'm gonna enjoy you being around. You're gonna keep shit entertaining for sure."

Snorting, I finished my drink and shook my head. Out of all the brothers, Ezra seemed the most welcoming.

As the night continued, Ezra eventually disappeared again. I heard him mention something about the basement. Not sure what he had going on, but Emmet left with him.

Nazai had spent most of the night being the boss. He disappeared a couple of times but I didn't question it, happy to be left alone. A few times Lucas or River remembered I was there and briefly entertained me, but I seemed to be an afterthought to my fiancé. His presence was demanding and it was clear everyone respected him. We had been here for three hours now and I was ready to call it a night.

I was in the middle of ordering a ride share when Nazai finally appeared next to me. He had a cool expression on his face with a lazy grin.

"Why you look so tense?" Nazai asked, leaning into me. His warm breath against my ear smelled of alcohol and cinnamon.

I tilted my head so I was looking him in the eyes. "You forced me to come here and then just left me alone. I'm ready to go."

He tossed an arm around the back of my seat. "Nah, not yet. You just need to relax some."

A girl approached us, her eyes bouncing between me and Nazai. I narrowed my gaze, not feeling how she was watching us.

"Hey, boss. Lindsay told me to bring you this. You ordered a Blood Lust on the rocks." My brows furrowed.

"Yeah, thanks Majesty." She licked her lips and gave him a flirty grin.

"*Anything* for you." The suggestion in her words caused a foreign feeling to twist in my stomach. She lowered the tray in her hand. I noticed a small, clear bag taped to the glass. "Did you two want a dance too?" She fluttered her eyelids.

"No." I shut her down, clenching my purse.

This thing with Nazai was unorthodox, but the disrespect wasn't something I would tolerate either way.

He nodded at her. "You heard my fiancée. We're good. Go ahead and work the floor. Next time let the bottle girls do their job."

The smile on her face fell. "Yes, sir." She shot me a glance then turned and stalked away. Her ass cheeks bounced as she strutted away in the tall heels.

"Now back to you. What's it gonna take to get a smile out of you?"

Facing Nazai, I ignored the way my heart raced as his dark orbs peered into me.

"I don't like large crowds," I stated.

My eyes kept darting to the exit all night. In case of danger, I needed to make sure I had a getaway route. Security was tight here, Jackson and Luke stood guard outside the section too, but still. I didn't like how open this place was.

For a moment Nazai's face fell, then that lopsided grin appeared. He brushed my arms with his hands, causing goosebumps to form and the hairs to raise.

"I got you. I didn't mean to leave you alone most of the night." He tossed back the drink then took the baggie off it. I noticed a white pill inside. He placed it in his mouth then leaned in. Like earlier, his mouth crashed into mine, catching me off guard.

I opened my mouth to object to the kiss when I felt the pill he'd just put in his mouth enter mine. He pulled back and watched me. "Swallow it."

My heart thumped at the raspy demand. My breathing picked up. I didn't know what it was he had given me and the kiss caught me so off guard that I listened. Swallowing the pill, I grabbed the outstretched glass he gave me.

"What did I just take?" I asked.

"Ecstasy." My brows shot to my hairline.

"Why the fuck would you give me that?"

"I've been keeping an eye on you the whole night and you've been tense. This will help chill you out." My heart slammed against my ribcage.

My eyes darted around the section. I didn't notice it had cleared out, outside of us two. I'd never taken drugs before. I wasn't sure what to expect either. His hand went to my thigh. The dress I wore rested right above my thigh. Goosebumps scattered across my body. I still wasn't over what Nazai did to me, but my body didn't seem to care.

"Because I want to see you relaxed. While I enjoy you being my Wildfire, I want to see how you are when you're relaxed too."

Wildfire.

It was a name he used frequently with me. No one had ever given me a pet name before.

"Stop calling me that." I shifted in my seat. The back of my neck grew warm.

Nazai leaned in and cuffed the back of my neck, causing a shockwave to shoot up my spine. "But you are my Wildfire. Your mouth is reckless, your personality bold and wild. I think the name fits." Nazai leaned in and brushed the tip of his nose against my jawline. I inhaled a sharp breath.

"Stop that," I said on a shaky breath.

A couple of employees came over to speak with Nazai and I found myself more relaxed. The drug must have started to take effect. My body felt lighter. A throbbing formed between my legs.

"How you feeling?" Nazai whispered.

My stomach skittered. "Nazai, I—" My words got lodged in my throat. Was this what it felt like to be high? I felt like my body was floating and my skin felt sensitive.

Pulling back, he observed me, tucking his bottom lip into his mouth. "C'mon." He stood and held his hand out.

I grabbed it and he pulled me up. My legs felt like jello. He must have known because he dipped down and picked me up bridal style.

"My purse!" I rushed out.

"I got it." He started out of the section.

Suddenly my body felt like a furnace. I had too many clothes on. "I want this dress off," I stated.

A pounding formed in my ears. My heart was beating too fast inside me.

Nazai moved through the club until we were walking down a dark hall then upstairs. He opened a door to a well-lit room. When I looked around, I saw it was an office. He moved to the couch and lay me down with my purse next to me.

"Hot," I moaned, pulling on the bottom of my dress. It hugged my small frame and currently felt suffocating.

"Let me help you." He pulled me up and unzipped the dress. I didn't have a bra on. My breasts were perky enough to sit up high on their own. They weren't the largest but looked good either way.

"I'm not having sex with you," I said breathlessly as he helped me out of my dress, pushing it down my body.

"Don't worry Wildfire, when I fuck you, you're gonna be sober and coherent."

His hands pushed over the collar on my neck and he tugged on the heart. A wave of possession passed through his eyes.

He dipped his head so he was eye level with my breasts. A loud, embarrassing moan left my mouth when he ran his tongue over one. My already sensitive nipples seemed to be even more alive than normal. As

I arched into his mouth, he used his teeth to pull and tease my hardened nubs.

"I never met a woman whose nipples were as sensitive as yours. I could just blow on them and you're ready to cum." To prove his point he blew on my breast and my body shivered. "You're usually talking shit, but I don't hear anything now. Where's that smart ass mouth at?" His hand went between my legs and he pressed on my pussy.

I whimpered and ground against his touch, needing more. His hand on my skin made my body ache with yearning desire.

His mouth bounced between my breasts—teasing, sucking, and licking my nipples. A tsunami formed between my legs, drenching my panties. I had come once already just from the stimulation to my hardened nubs. My body felt more alive than ever. It was a feeling I never wanted to lose.

"I love when you fight me, but I think I love seeing you turned on more. The blissful look on your face is captivating," he uttered against my skin, kissing down the valley between my breasts to my stomach. His tongue swirled around my belly button. Butterflies fluttered wildly in my belly.

My eyes closed, my breathing grew heavy, and my chest rose and fell quickly. I felt him pull my panties down. My skin was still extra sensitive. A shiver raced through me when he got to my mound. He pushed my legs wider and kissed the inside of my thighs.

"I'ma write my name on this pussy so it only knows me," he rasped, sinking his teeth into my skin and sucking hard.

I moaned in response, unable to form a proper word.

What the hell was he doing to me?

I shouldn't be allowing him to touch me. I should be fighting him and pushing him off. My blame went to the drug; that was the only explanation. Foolishly, I'd taken it, not knowing what it was. Now I was at Nazai's mercy.

"Oh fuck!" I cried out when his tongue swiped across my pussy. My clit throbbed as my pussy grew wetter.

"You taste good as hell." He sucked my lower lips into his mouth. My hands balled tightly at my sides as an overwhelming sensation filled me.

"When I finally have this pussy wrapped around my dick, I know I'ma be hooked. Look how fucking wet it's getting for me and I barely touched her."

I tuned him out, getting lost in the sensation his mouth was bringing me. I had never felt like this before. The pleasure was almost overwhelming.

I squeezed my eyes shut, fighting to keep my moans to myself until Nazai slapped my pussy. "I like to hear the outcome of my work. Let me hear you," he grunted, pushing a finger inside of me. I winced and pushed out a shaky breath. "Fuck, how long has it been? You've got a vice-like grip on my finger." He pushed another finger in, moving them back and forth. It was painful but the pleasure overshadowed it.

"Nazai," I whimpered as my body trembled.

"There you go, Wildfire. Cum for me. Show me what this pussy can do. Just like that. Fuck!" he growled, covering my clit with his mouth and sucking it roughly.

I didn't know how long we stayed in that office or how many times I came. Eventually I passed out, feeling exhausted and overstimulated.

I had to blink a couple times to focus my eyes as I listened to Nora speak with the lady at the dress shop. I brought the glass bottle of apple juice to my mouth, appreciating the cool liquid as it ran down my parched throat.

Last night was a slight blur to me. I remember bits and pieces like going into Nazai's office before passing out. The main thing that kept playing over in my mind was the multiple orgasms he brought me and the way his eyes burned into me whenever I caught his stare. Heat flooded in my stomach and I downed the apple juice faster. This morning he was gone before his mom popped up at the house. I had forgotten she'd mentioned coming to take me to dress shop.

I wasn't enthusiastic about going with her. My guard was up, not forgetting her threat toward me. I had my gun and knife in my small, book bag purse. Hopefully this lady wouldn't make me use it. Carson was with us too. He seemed fine this morning when I checked in on him. He was currently sitting against the wall, playing his Switch, lost in his own world.

"Cashlynn, did you hear me?" I snapped out my thoughts and peeked up at my future mother-in-law. She was a beautiful woman. Almost too beautiful, made me wonder if she had any work done. Her face showed minimal signs of aging, although I was sure she was in her fifties. Her makeup was done to perfection, hair done in soft locs. She had the same gingerbread skin color as Nazai and penny-colored eyes as well.

"What did you say?" I asked, looking between her and the worker.

Nora's lips pressed together. "For your dress, would you rather go strapless or strapped?"

My face balled in confusion. "Doesn't matter to me." It wasn't like I was the most girly girl, so dresses weren't my specialty or preference. I could barely walk in heels without breaking my neck. Getting dressed up for a wedding I was being forced into wasn't ideal either; so I couldn't care less what I wore.

Nora blew a frustrated breath out and irritation passed on her face. Apparently this shop was a big deal and it took months to even get an appointment. Once again I was shown being a Tavarez came with certain privileges because I was able to get an appointment right away.

"Stand up," Nora demanded. We hadn't spoken much. She was locked into her phone and iPad the entire drive here. When we got to the dress shop, she immediately took over, talking with the lady servicing us.

Sighing, I set my bottle down next to my book bag and did as she said.

The worker circled me. "You have a wonderful neckline and shoulders. While you're not very tall, you still have a delicate figure. I believe a halter mermaid style would do you justice." She stopped in front of me and gave me a onceover. Her head tipped to the side slightly as her hand went under her chin and she squinted.

After a few seconds of observing me, I felt myself getting antsy and was about to speak when she snapped and smiled.

"I got it!" She clapped happily while her eyes lit up in excitement. "Just leave it all to me."

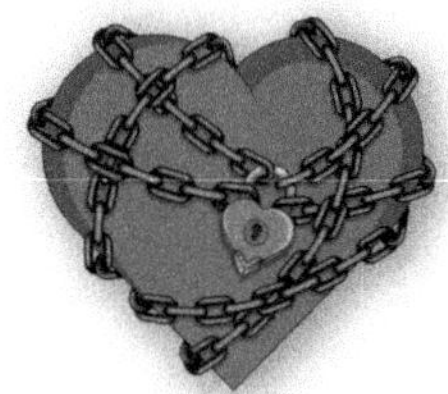

It felt like we had been at this shop for hours. I went through six different dresses before finding one even I loved.

"That's it! This is the one," Nora gushed with a bright smile on her face.

Shifting my eyes, I gazed at myself in the full body mirror. The white halter sweetheart top dress hugged my frame perfectly. It was overlayed in lace, backless, and mermaid style. With a court train at the bottom. As much as I hated to admit it, it looked like it made for me.

I spun around to face my brother. "What do you think, bud?"

His eyes lifted from his game. A smile split his face. "You look really pretty!"

I ran my hand down the front then looked at the worker. "I'll go with this one."

She clapped happily. "Great. The chest area needs to be altered a tad, and the waist, but those are simple modifications. I have your measurements and it'll be ready in time for your big day."

I twisted my lips to the side and turned back to the mirror. Typically, I dressed simply and homely. In the short time I'd been around Nazai, I'd been more dressed up than in my whole twenty-three years of life. I'd be lying if I said I didn't feel good either. My mom was far from motherly and didn't really care to show me femininity, so this was new territory for me to explore.

There was a lot of movement going on around me but I couldn't focus on anything except that in a few short minutes I would be tied to someone for the rest of my life. While to most marriage was a beautiful thing, to me it felt like chains were being wrapped around me, locking me in place. My soon-to-be wife was a mystery to me too. All I knew about her was what my brother was able to dig up. A few red flags rose with some of the information, like her being looked at for her parents' murder, who her parents were, even how she reacted to certain things, but call me foolish, none of those made me want to call off the wedding.

"You ready to be locked down?" Lucas asked as he approached, patting me on the shoulder.

Adjusting my tie, I made eye contact with him in the mirror. He had a taunting smirk on his face.

"Of course he's not. He's about to turn in his player card for a girl he doesn't even know," Ezra said, coming up.

Lucas winced. "That's true. I couldn't imagine. Is being the head of the family worth it?"

I twisted my head so I was looking him in the face. "You think I've been through all I've been through to not cross the finish line. Padre's been preparing me for this my whole life, it's my birthright."

"You got that right, hijo!" Dad said out of nowhere. "I might not agree with your choice, but I'm glad you did what needed to be done."

I turned and eyed my dad and brother. Emmet was sitting on the couch near the wall, messy with his Rubik Cube, looking in deep thought. I wasn't sure what his fascination with the thing was, but he's been into them since we were kids.

"It is weird though, right? She doesn't have anyone here but her brother. Does she have no family at all?" Lucas questioned.

"No she doesn't. I checked," Emmet commented.

I hated when he popped in a conversation after looking like he wasn't paying attention. One thing about my brother was that he was always watching and listening even if he didn't seem like it.

"Them the ones you got to watch. The ones with little to lose be reckless," River commented.

We made eye contact. He had expressed his concerns about me marrying Cashlynn. Being my best friend and head of security, I typically took his opinion to heart but this wasn't one of those times.

There was a knock on the door and Mom popped inside. "Let's get this show on the road, boys." She stepped inside. "Look at my handsome son." Mom approached me with admiration in her eyes. Smiling, she lifted her hands and adjusted my tie. "There." She grinned and stepped back, giving me a onceover.

"It's now or never," Dad said, stepping next to my mom, studying me as well.

My chest tightened and my tie suddenly felt tighter. The room filled with chatter but I zoned them out. In the blink of an eye my life was about to change. Not to mention I was expected to get Cashlynn pregnant soon too. My birthday was in a month and a half, and I was bringing my thirtieth in a married man starting a different life from what I was accustomed to.

I stood at the end of the altar waiting. Time seemed to tick by slowly as the ceremony went on. It was the most traditional wedding yet there was no love in the air; it was full of associates and close family. Cashlynn had no one but her brother, who was due to walk her down the aisle. We didn't go through the typical things one would when it came to getting married.

The doors opened when it was time for Cashlynn to make herself present. I was lost in my head until I laid eyes on her. For the first time since she came into my life, I felt my chest grow tight and my heart exploded. My stomach dipped and my mouth grew dry.

Cashlynn had always been attractive, but since meeting her I'd only seen her in normal everyday clothes, besides the few times my personal shopper dressed her. This was the first time I saw her done up like this though. The dress she wore looked as if it was specifically made for only her. Cashlynn was small and petite and the dress complemented her size well. Her jet-black tresses were parted down the middle in spiral curls, framing her heart-shaped face. The closer she got, I saw she had makeup on too. It wasn't anything too dramatic, but the colors were bold yet tasteful. Her lashes looked longer than normal, bringing more attention to her eyes. Her walk was slow and a bit unsteady. I was sure it was because of the heels I knew my mom forced her into.

"Damn, she cleans up nice," Ezra muttered next to me, causing me to smirk.

A small wave of satisfaction passed through me knowing from this moment on she was mine. Possession filled me as all eyes stayed trained on her. Low whispers filled the background. It was a shock to everyone that I had chosen to take a Cavana as a wife, but the potential I saw in Cashlynn being by my side was endless. Her fiery spirit and toughness was made to be tamed by me.

Once she approached me, I saw she wasn't happy about today in her eyes, but I ignored the daggers being shot at me.

Carson took his place next to her. The kid was obedient and quiet. He never complained and did what he was told. I wondered if he would object to this marriage but so far he hadn't said anything.

A crooked grin formed on my mouth when I grabbed her hand. She narrowed her glare and pressed her lips tightly together.

I turned us to face the minister and nodded for him to start.

The ceremony went off without a hitch. I felt Cashlynn tense next to me a couple times but she didn't object. She mumbled when it was her turn to speak but that didn't bother me.

When it came down to the end and time for the kiss, I turned her to face me and she looked resistant to the gesture.

Wrapping my arm around her waist, I pulled her into me and lowered my head, connecting my lips with hers. Just like always, she was stiff and unwilling at first, but slowly fell in line.

Grinning against her lips, I nipped the bottom one and pulled back. Swiping my tongue across my lips, I winked at her then faced the crowd.

"Mrs. Tavarez, everyone!" I called out, lifting our united hands in the air.

Cheers spread through the room. There was some press inside we had on payroll to make sure nothing that wasn't supposed to get out didn't. They captured pictures that would more than likely get printed for tomorrow.

Leaning down, I brought my mouth to her ear. "Now you're really mine, wife."

She cut a look at me and snatched her hand out of mine.

Grabbing her brother's hand she walked down the aisle swiftly, dragging him along, causing me to chuckle.

"Now it's official. Good job, hijo." Dad said as he approached me.

"I told you I would do what I needed to do for the family."

"Nazai," a deep voice called out. I looked up and saw three men approaching me, one being Zylus. Wise and Major were with him. Zylus Moran handled guns, but we also used his shipment services when it came to importing different things through his shipping company. Wise Benson oversaw the biggest gambling ring and casino in the city. All three played a large hand in the underground world and coexisted together, benefiting each other in some way.

"Zylus." I stepped forward, shaking hands with him. I moved to the other two, also shaking hands with them. They were all around my age, already having taken over from the elders before them. My dad was the last to retire from the game, too stubborn to give up.

"When your dad said you were taking over and he was stepping up, I thought it was a lie. My pops said he'd never step down," Wise mentioned.

Dad chuckled next to me. "All good things must come to an end. Now it's time for the next generation to take over." It had been over a year since the other guys stepped down and my dad refused to until I drew closer to thirty. Even though I was the youngest of us, I was more than capable of filling his shoes.

"Congrats on your marriage. I will say I'm shocked you married Cashlynn Cavana. I've been told she was being trained by her parents and started taking jobs. Rumor has it, she is just as, if not even more, vicious as they were," Major informed me.

Dad grunted next to me.

"Really?" I pulled on my beard, getting lost in thought.

His news was new to me, not shocking but new. Even Emmet hadn't gotten that info. It would explain the fearlessness she had and the fight inside her.

"I'm not worried about that. It just goes to show she's better equipped to be my wife than anyone else," I said, waving the warning off. The last thing I wanted to show was a potential weakness in my marriage and it just started.

"I agree." Zylus nodded. "In this work you can't have anyone who'll fold under pressure and can't hold their own."

We all nodded in agreement. They stuck around a little longer before departing.

"Tonight you'll consummate your marriage, create a baby, and get ready because in a few more weeks, you'll be the head of the family." My dad patted my shoulder just as the rest of the family walked up.

"I didn't think you would go through it, but you fucking did." Ezra laughed. "Damn." He dug into his pocket and slapped money into both Lucas' and River's hands.

"We're in church! Watch your mouth." Mom slapped the back of his head.

"Sorry, Mama." He grinned at her, causing her to roll her eyes.

A couple of other people in attendance came over congratulating me and speaking. Some reporters wanted an official statement from me as well.

"Nazai, what's the rush with getting married? You two just recently announced your engagement and now here you are married. Are there alternative motives?" My eyes cut at the woman in front of me. I noticed it was the same reporter who gave us issues at the engagement. Dressed like she was before, in large sunglasses and a hat covering her face.

"Who the fuck let you in here?" I waved for Jackson. "Escort her ass out!" She protested and fought against Jackson's hold when he came over to drag her out.

"I know there's some shady business going on! I'm gonna get to the bottom of it!" she called out.

"The hell was that about?" Lucas questioned.

I kept my eyes locked forward. "I don't know but I plan on finding out." Making eye contact with Emmet, he gave me a subtle bob of the head, already knowing to get on it. I wanted this to be moved up in priority. Something about the woman didn't sit right with me.

"My guys are scanning the rest of the church and perimeter," River said as he stepped up. "She slipped in with the rest of the press."

"I'm going to get Cashlynn; we need pictures," my mom expressed, dashing out of the room.

"This might be a fake wedding but to mama it's real." Ezra laughed.

I shook my head. He wasn't lying. She had made sure everything was done up as if we were two people really in love committing to each other.

A couple of seconds later, Cashlynn was dragged back in with a frown on her face. Mom waved the photographer she had hired over and forced all of us to pose for pictures.

Soon, everything was wrapped up and we all prepared to leave.

"My parents are gonna take Carson with them for the night," I informed Cashlynn.

Confusion and defiance filled her face. "No. I didn't approve of that."

"You don't have anything to worry about Cashlynn; your brother is in good hands," Mom told her.

"With all due respect, I don't know you two and your husband isn't a fan of me and vice versa. I'm not letting my brother go to his house alone." She cut her eyes at my dad who stared at her blankly.

"We have plans this evening. Nothing is going to happen to your brother, you both are family now."

"I said no," she gritted, stepping into me.

"And I said he's going." My eyes narrowed.

"Oh shit," Ezra mumbled behind us with a chuckle.

"It's okay." Carson spoke up, stepping to his sister and staring up at her. His voice was small.

"Carson."

"I don't want to cause trouble Cash. Please," he begged.

Confliction passed through her eyes. "You have your phone?"

He nodded. Her eyes bounced between everyone. "Nothing better happen to my brother. He's the only thing in this world I care about and there's no length I won't go to protect him." Her words and tone were deadly.

"Careful, girl. I don't take threats well," Dad snarled in Spanish.

"It wasn't a threat," Cashlynn told him unblinkingly.

While I loved that my wife refused to back down, I didn't have the patience for this shit right now.

"Enough. Nothing is gonna happen to your brother. We're going to have the night to ourselves and he's gonna go with my parents."

Her honey orbs found mine, small nostrils slightly flared.

Finally, the tension was broken. Carson assured his sister he would be fine. It took a couple of minutes but she finally agreed for him to go.

I ignored the way my heart hammered in my chest and my hands shook as I dried my body. Goosebumps covered my skin. I stared at myself in the mirror, running my eyes down my naked frame. Today I had officially become Cashlynn Tavarez.

Tavarez.

I huffed. It hit me that I was now a Tavarez. I bit the inside of my cheek and gripped my towel tighter. My muscles were rigid and my stomach was queasy. As soon as we got to his house outside of the city, I ignored Nazai and went straight to the same bathroom he'd first caught me in, which I learned was the master bath. Knowing what Nazai expected of me once I left the bathroom caused me to bite the inside of my cheek harder. A copper taste fell on my tongue.

I eyed the collar around my neck. It seemed to have become a part of me to the point I didn't even feel it on me anymore. It was the constant reminder that I had signed my soul over to the devil.

Standing straight I pushed a heavy breath out of my nose. I wrapped my towel around my body, cursing myself for not bringing my duffle bag with my clothes inside.

Realizing I couldn't stay in the bathroom all night, I finally pushed out another deep breath and turned to leave. When I stepped into the bedroom, Nazai was sitting on the edge of the bed with his phone to his ear. My brain suddenly stopped working as I watched his mouth move but couldn't hear exactly what he was saying. His orbs penetrated me, causing my skin to grow hot. He scanned me over, his eyes growing darker.

I swallowed hard and pressed my lips together tightly. He was shirtless, giving a full display of his tattoo covered chest and torso. His pecs were cut to perfection—broad and defined. My stomach rolled and a balloon of tension expanded in my chest.

Nazai hung the phone up, reaching over and setting it on the table before he stood. My eyes dropped to the towel wrapped around his waist. His long, muscular legs showcasing from under it. My throat constricted laying eyes on the noticeable outline of a bulge under the thin fabric. Nazai made a sound, causing my eyes to snap up and my cheeks to flood with heat. A crooked grin was on his face.

Rolling my eyes, I swallowed hard and went to where my bag was on the end of the bed.

My body stilled when he got behind me and pressed up against me. He reached over and grabbed my wrist just as I was picking the bag up.

"You don't need anything in there right now." Straightening my spine, I snatched away from him and spun around, glaring at him.

"Don't touch me!"

He smirked. "You're *my wife* now. I can touch you whenever I want." To prove his point he reached out and brushed his hands from my collarbone over to my arms.

"No you can't," I gritted, pulling out of his touch and ignoring the goosebumps that formed and the way my skin hummed with awareness.

Nazai narrowed his eyes and reached out again. He gripped my arm and yanked me closer to him. "The more you fight me, the more I want to break you." His voice came out in a low, husky timbre, sending a ripple through my belly.

My breathing sped up and I willed my face to stay still. The last thing I wanted was for Nazai to think he affected me in any way.

He leaned in and his nose brushed against my collarbone, his beard tickling my skin. His lips grazed my flesh. My breath hitched as my heart slammed against my too tight ribcage. I squeezed my eyes shut, reaching out and grabbing his wrist, digging my nails into his skin. My jaw tightened.

"I can't wait to have you under me and begging."

"I'll never beg you for shit," I rushed out in a strained and thick voice.

I jumped and my lips parted when his teeth sank into where my shoulder and neck met. My nails dug deeper into his wrist. The night was still fuzzy, but faint pictures of us in his office flashed through my mind. The way my body felt alive and on fire as he kissed and touched me. How my pussy cried when his lips made love to it as if it were his last meal.

Nazai's hand moved to the front of my towel again and he tugged it, causing it to come undone and fall to my feet. His dick tented his towel, pushing against my thigh. His tongue swiped up my neck up to my ear where he nipped the lobe. My hand not gripping his wrist balled tightly. Pulling back, he licked his lips and examined the front of my body. Blinking slowly, I bit down on my back molars. My body trembled. I hated how my nipples hardened under his eyes and touch. Between my legs seeped with wetness.

Spinning us around, Nazai smirked as he pushed me backward, causing me to fall on the bed.

"Normally you have more mouth on you. You're mighty quiet right now."

My nostrils flared and my chest rose and fell slowly. "Fuck you!"

That smirk ticked back onto his face. "Nah, I'm about to *fuck you* though." Snatching the towel off his waist, he hovered over me on the bed and lowered his face to my breasts. His tongue flickered over my nipple and his teeth sank into it. A moan left my mouth and my back lifted off the bed. I squeezed my eyes shut, trying to mentally distract myself from the euphoric sensation rushing through my body. He moved his hand between my legs and pressed my clit. I gasped and my breathing picked up.

"Get off me," I gritted, attempting to push him. He grabbed me and moved his hands up, keeping me hostage with one and moving the other back between my legs.

My body and mind were currently at odds. While my body melted into the touch, vibrating with desire, my mind fought against it, begging me to fight.

I wiggled under him and attempted to break out of his tight hold.

"That's right, fight me, Wildfire." He teased my bud with his tongue. Two of his fingers pushed into my pussy, causing me to hiss. My walls locked around them. I hated how sensitive my nipples were and that he knew it. The more he teased and played with them, the hornier I felt myself getting. My pussy became wetter. My skin prickled with need.

"Mhm, so fucking tight," he growled, moving to the valley between my breasts, biting the side of one.

"No," I moaned when he pushed deeper into me. My stomach quivered. I wriggled more under him, my mind going into fight or flight. My body craved his touch. My pussy clenched around his digits. His dick poked me, precum wetting the top of my mound.

"Can't wait to feel you stretch around my dick. This pussy's already soaked for me." He released my hands and lifted. His eyes burned into me.

"My collar looks good on you." He went to reach for it but I moved out his touch. He snatched his fingers out of me and I winced and flinched when he slapped my pussy and quickly grabbed the collar. He yanked my body up and leaned forward until his face was just inches from mine. "Originally I only put it on you to track you but seeing it now, along with my ring on your finger, proves you belong to me." His eyes dropped to the pear-shaped, three point five carat diamond and fourteen karat white gold ring on my finger.

His hands lightly brushed my neck under the collar. Jolts of electricity shot through my veins. "You might act like you don't want it, but your body tells me differently. I can see it in your eyes, you want me to fuck you, don't you? You want me to stretch that pussy until it's weeping around my dick."

My cheeks flushed as my nostrils flared and my breathing was still heavy. Anger burrowed in my chest, partly because of his taunting, partly because my body refused to agree with my head. Lifting my hand, I sent it across his face before I could think. "That's what I think of you and your dick. And I don't belong to anyone!"

His head whipped sideways then slowly turned back to me. His eyes flashed and darkened as his nostrils expanded. Nazai's jaw ticked before his mouth slowly lifted in a crude smile.

"That's the fight I was looking for."

I went to strike him again, but this time he caught my hand and squeezed. My eyes tightened but I fought not to show the pain.

Nazai's hand went to my cheeks. He squeezed them tightly, then leaned forward and licked my lips. I inhaled a deep breath. My eyes fluttered.

Releasing me, Nazai moved off me and flipped me so I was on my front. He spread my thighs and positioned himself behind me. My heart thudded when he grabbed me by my sweated-out tresses and gripped them tightly, yanking my head back.

He leaned over my body and whispered in my ear. "Say sorry and I'll take it easy on you."

"Fuck you! I'm not apologizing for shit," I gritted and my scalp screamed when he pulled my hair tighter. Tears pooled in my eyes.

"Have it your way." He pulled my hips up and pushed the small of my back down, creating an arch.

My stomach fluttered when his lips went to my shoulder and his teeth nipped my skin. I clenched the comforter tightly. My teeth sank into my bottom lip. *I didn't want* to want this. I tried to tell myself to fight but my sense froze when I felt his dick brush over my pussy from behind.

His lips were back to my ear. His warm breath brushed across it. "You act like you don't want me, but why is your pussy so wet?" The hairs on the back of my neck rose, creeping with heat.

"I don't." I attempted to move out of his hold. "I hate you!"

I bit back the moan that desperately wanted to escape as he ran his dick up and down my entrance.

He chuckled darkly. "Good. Hate sex is hot as fuck." He pushed forward. The tip of his dick teased my entrance. "By the time I'm done with you, your pussy will only remember me."

"I heard men who talk a lot are making up for something. You probably don't even know how to fuck good—ah!" I cried when he slammed into me. My body froze and my breath got caught in my throat. Pain rippled from my pussy up my spine.

"Don't get quiet on me now, Wildfire. Keeping talking shit." He tightened his hand on my hair. My neck strained and ached. My body tensed and more tears pooled in my eyes, slowly streaming down my face.

Nothing about the way Nazai was fucking me was gentle. I attempted to speak but my words refused to form. Pleasure and pain twisted through my body in a way I'd never felt before.

CHAPTER FIFTEEN

I knew from the moment Cashlynn broke into my house she was going to be a problem. From her spitfire mouth to her fighting spirit. Sex was nothing new to me. I'd been fucking since I was fourteen and had bedded a plethora of women since, but nothing could prepare me for Cashlynn's pussy. She surrounded me with a vice-like grip around my dick. It felt like I'd taken a dip in a lake the way she soaked me. She held some resistance at first, but the more I moved in and out of her, the more she opened for me.

My dick grew harder as she took me. The fight that was once in her seemed to die out. I knew all she needed was a good fucking to straighten her out. My eyes dropped to where my dick moved in and out of her. A flash of red caused my strokes to slow and my brows to furrow.

I blinked slowly, flicking my eyes up to where her head was dropped. My stomach twisted as the realization slammed into me. When I'd fingered her, her walls had been tight, *too tight*, but I just thought it had been a while or her ex hadn't been getting the job done. But as I watched the blood mix with her cum, I knew that wasn't the case at all. A wave of possession that shot through me.

I paused for a second. Slowly, Cashlynn lifted her head and looked over her shoulder.

Tears. My tongue craved to taste them.

"You're a virgin?" I asked, raising a brow.

"Not anymore," she sneered with tight, blurry eyes.

Fuck.

Scraping my bottom lip with my teeth, I glanced down again. Knowing I was the only one who had been inside her and would be the *only one* excited me. I hadn't touched a virgin since I was a teenager. They became too clingy and wanted too much from me, but this was different. Cashlynn was my wife. I owned her. Her body was mine to pleasure how I pleased. I wanted her obsessed and needy for me, wanted to bring her to her knees until she was begging me to please her.

"Seems not," I mused. Flicking my eyes back up, I watched her as I started moving again unhurriedly. In reality I was torturing myself dragging out the pleasure between us. My plan tonight was to tease and get to know Cashlynn's body before claiming her and marking her with my seeds. I knew she wouldn't make it easy and would fight me. My goal was to make her bend to me in every way, to break past that hard exterior she kept up.

She inhaled sharply. "Don't pussy out now. I thought you said you'd make me beg." She pushed back into me. Logic told me I should stop and take it easy on her, but I loved a challenge.

Chortling, I grabbed her hips, shifted mine, and quickly moved in and out of her. "As you please, wife." With each thrust pushing deeper, her eyes glazed and her lips parted. Her head dropped again. My teeth sank into my bottom lip.

"Oh my god," she gasped.

"That's right, wife. Let me hear you. This pussy loves how my dick is stretching it right now, doesn't it?" Her knuckles were turning white from how hard she gripped the covers. Reaching for her hair again, I pulled her head back and leaned over her body so my mouth was against her ear.

"You wanna cum?" My strokes slowed. I eased in and out of her teasingly. My teeth scraped over her ear. "I wanna hear you say my name and I'll let you cum," I rasped in Spanish.

"Gotta give me a reason to."

I wrapped my arm around her front, finding her clit and thumbing it.

Sweat beaded on her forehead and her eyes dilated.

I kissed the shell of her ear. "I should feel bad right now. Instead of being gentle and taking your virginity like a gentleman, I'm fucking you like a worthless slut." I pinched her clit, causing her to hiss. "Seeing your virgin blood covering my dick and my collar on your neck proves you belong to me now. Tell me, wife, tell me you're mine." I kissed my way to the side of her face.

Her body jerked and a whimper fell from her mouth. My nose dragged along her skin. She still smelled like the body wash she'd used a few minutes prior.

"Say it."

"No," she moaned.

Smirking, I knew the perfect way to make her break. Leaving her clit, I moved my hand up until I was at her breasts. I swiped her nipples with my fingers at first before fondling them and finally twisting them.

"Wait," she cried.

My hips swung faster. Her sex grew wetter. I continued to switch between her nipples. When I felt she was about to cum, I'd stop.

She released a frustrated sound, breathing heavy.

"You know what I want, Wildfire. Give it to me and I'll let you come." I kissed her shoulder. Pressing my body against her back, I forced her to lay flat. I grabbed her neck from the front, the collar pressing against my palm. My balls begged for relief, but I fought it.

"Stop doing that!" she begged the last time I stopped.

Chuckling, I kissed her shoulder again. My hold on her neck tightened. "You know what I want."

"Fuck, Nazai there, please!" she cried.

"Tell me."

"I'm yours!" Something between a moan and whimper fell from her sweet lips.

My smile widened. This time when she was about to cum, I didn't stop. I continued fucking her through the orgasm. A loud moan escaped her lips.

"That's right, wife. Give me your pleasure," I growled, sucking her earlobe.

Inaudible sounds fell from her mouth. "I'm about to fill this pussy now," I muttered in Spanish. "Can't wait to see my cum leaking out of you." She inhaled sharply.

"You want my cum, wife?"

"Yes," she whimpered.

"As you wish." Lifting her hips slightly, I moved my hand around her front, causing it to lift off the bed, and grabbed her breasts. I quickened my strokes and pinched her nipples as I released inside of her.

A roaring shot of pleasure exploded through me. My seeds filled her tunnel. She tightened around me.

"Fuck," I grunted.

Cashlynn might hate me, but it was clear her pussy didn't agree.

Cashlynn ended up falling asleep shortly after we finished last night and I was sure that was the only reason she slept next to me all night. She woke up before me, but I noticed the moment she did. When we fell asleep, she was across the bed. When morning came she was curled into me and jumped when she realized where she was.

Now I watched her pop one of her birth control pills. "You might as well throw that shit away," I said, causing her to jump and spin to face me. I didn't immediately open my eyes when she got up so she must not have noticed I was watching her.

"Why would I have to do that?" She narrowed her eyes, tossing the pill into her mouth and swallowing it dry.

I smirked and sat up. "How you gon' have my baby when you poppin' that shit?" My eyes dropped to her stomach. She was no longer naked and had pajamas on.

She rolled her eyes. "I told you I agreed to get married, but I'm not having kids anytime soon."

"If you say so, Wildfire." I licked my lips, remembering last night.

"Come back over here so we can go another round." I grabbed my morning wood, itching to feel her wrapped around me again.

She scoffed. "You're not touching me again."

My tongue went across my top teeth. "Answer me this. You ever kissed someone before me?" Some things were starting to make sense to me now. I thought the reason Cashlynn tensed when I kissed her was because she didn't want me touching her. Her kisses were always uncoordinated, if she even participated at all. After learning she was a virgin, it made me think about if she'd even kissed a guy before. Cashlynn was guarded and unwelcoming. It was clear outside of her brother she didn't let people close to her.

Cashlynn opened her mouth then snapped it shut. Her cheeks flushed. "That's none of your business." Spinning around, she started for the bathroom. One corner of my mouth lifted seeing the slight limp in her walk.

I chuckled and shook my head. She gave in last night and eventually submitted to me, but that hard exterior was back. I should have known it would take more to crack her fully.

"What is this? I thought we were going to get my brother," Cashlynn complained, looking around the abandoned area. We weren't at the meeting place the family used for obvious reasons, but this one was just as secluded.

"We'll go grab him after this." I looked over at Jackson and nodded when we got to the door. With his gun drawn, he stepped in the door first and looked around. Turning toward me, he nodded. I made sure him, Luke, Bruce, and James met us here and were on guard.

"I didn't agree to any detours."

"This one is necessary. Let's go."

Cashlynn mugged me and stomped forward.

"What the fuck is this?" she shouted.

Shit.

I rushed into the building and saw Jackson restraining Cashlynn who had a gun in hand and struggled to break loose.

Anger traveled up into my chest. "Get your hands off my wife," I demanded with narrowed eyes.

Jackson quickly released her. Cashlynn spun around with fire burning in her eyes. "Why the hell is he here?" I eyed the gun.

I wasn't sure where she'd gotten it from. I had taken the one from the night she snuck in the house. Also, I remembered the day I found her in my bathroom she also had a gun in her bag. I had confiscated it and hadn't given it back, so it made me wonder how many she had in her possession.

Stepping toward her, I didn't flinch as she held the gun out. The barrel pressed against my chest as I stared down at her. She glared at me with burning, stormy eyes. Her jaw clenched.

"Do you think this is a joke?" Her finger twitched on the trigger. By the look in her eyes, I could tell she was seconds from pulling the trigger. That caused my dick to twitch behind my slacks.

Reaching up, I grabbed a hold of her wrist and gripped it tightly. "I'm giving you two seconds to pull the trigger and you better make it count," I said calmly. All eyes were locked on us, but I only saw her.

Her mouth twitched and her nostrils flared.

Twisting her arm, I de-armed her, causing her to yelp and the gun to drop before pulling her into me and slamming my mouth into hers, kissing her savagely.

For a second her body relaxed and a moan fell into my mouth. "Now, be a good girl and let me handle this," I mumbled against her lips, then nipped her bottom lip.

She snapped her head back and glared at me.

Winking at her, I released her. Her cheeks puffed out and she released a heavy breath. She leaned down and snatched her gun back up resting it at her side.

"Now let's go." I adjusted my tie.

We headed for the table where the Rhodes sat. Both Maddox and Neil sat there shooting daggers at Cashlynn. On her face was a deadpan expression. Tension was high in the room. Jackson and Luke stood to the side of us while Bruce and James stood behind.

"Don't look at my wife," I sneered at the Rhodes. "This is between us," I snarled, causing both of their eyes to snap to me. All of the playfulness left me. Now it was time to handle business. "This won't take long." I stood straight, making sure I had their attention.

"You see this?" I reached over and grabbed Cashlynn's hand. "This rock on her finger shows she's mine. Which means she's a Tavarez. Which means any threat on her life is null and void. I don't give a fuck what issues you had with her before, she's mine and I don't play about mine."

"She tried to kill my son!" Neil gritted. Jackson and Luke's hands went to their sides where their guns were and they stepped forward. I lifted my hand. These two were a joke. They might be known because they pushed drugs widely across the city, but they put no fear in my heart. When I set this meeting up, it held one purpose, to make it clear Cashlynn was off limits now.

"You're lucky I failed because I don't miss. I should put a bullet through your sick ass head now." Cashlynn still had the gun in her hand and went to step forward, but I held her in place. She glanced up at me, scowling.

"Now, now Wildfire. No need for all that. Neil and Maddox here understand that if they try to harm you in any way, I'll make sure their whole bloodline is erased from existence. Your son having to relearn to walk will be nothing compared to what I do to you. Unless you want your bodies chopped up and scattered around the city, I advise you to make it known to everyone that the hit on my wife is no more. Understood?"

Maddox's face paled; Neil's still held a scowl.

I released her hand and turned to leave. Cashlynn had other plans. She lifted her gun and pulled the trigger.

"Ah fuck! The bitch shot me!" Maddox cried, holding his arm.

"I don't care what was said here. I *will* kill you, Maddox, and I'm going to make it slow and painful too. So sleep with one eye open." A taunting grin formed on Cashlynn's face before she spat on the ground then turned and stormed out.

Neil was yelling violently while applying pressure to his son's wound. I should be pissed off but all I was thinking about was burying my dick in Cashlynn until she was a crying mess, calling my name out over and over. I pictured filling her walls with my cum and watching it drip out of her.

Not bothering to say any more, I turned and followed Cashlynn with my men behind me. I wasn't worried about the Rhodes doing anything. They'd be dead before they could even lift a finger. I didn't see her, but I guessed she was in the back of the truck already.

Devin nodded at me and opened the car door when I approached. I climbed inside and Cashlynn sat there seething, her foot tapping rapidly and arms crossed.

Both front doors opened and Devin got behind the wheel while Jackson climbed in the passenger seat.

"To my parents' house," I said, then hit a button when the car was on. I had this truck modified for when I wanted privacy. A dark window lifted, separating us from the front.

Cashlynn spun to face me. "If you ever blindside me like that again and put me in the same room as that man, I'll—"

I moved over, crowding her, causing her words to halt.

"You'll what?" I asked in a low, sultry tone. Reaching forward, I brushed my hand over her collar. I traced the front of her body, moving my hand down until I was cuffing her breast.

"I'll make sure he isn't the only one with a bullet in him."

One corner of my mouth kicked up.

"Oh Wildfire, out of all the things in the world, that's the last thing I'm worried about." I moved my face closer to hers. Her breathing picked up and her eyes faltered.

I massaged her breast and moved in, lightly brushing my lips against hers. It was hot as fuck seeing her with the gun and how fearless had been when she pulled the trigger. It made me realize though, there were deeper issues between her and Maddox.

"I wanna know what's the beef between you two." I pecked her lips again. It didn't sit right with me that my wife had an enemy and I had no idea why.

My wife.

Inwardly, I snorted. The comfort I had with that term so soon amazed me.

"It's none of your concern." Her voice was breathy and her chest rose and fell quickly.

She gasped when my hold on her breast grew rougher. My other hand went to the metal heart hanging from her collar.

"That's where you're wrong, Wildfire. Everything about you is my concern." I leaned in and brushed my nose against her face. Her body froze. "Any enemy you have becomes mine." It also bothered me that she had such high emotions toward someone who wasn't me. It didn't matter that it was hatred, it was strong enough for her to *feel* something for him. That didn't sit right with me. "So tell me why you hate that man so bad. Did he cheat on you?" I kissed her cheek. "I know it wasn't because he didn't fuck you right. Were you upset because of that?"

She grabbed my wrist and dug her nails into it. "No."

Pulling back, I studied her face, blank with underlying coldness in her eyes. I released her breast, but kept my hand on the collar.

"So tell me what happened. What did he do?"

"He tried to sexually assault my brother," she blurted out, causing me to freeze.

"What?" This time I released her completely.

Her hands balled into fists and her body straightened. She stared forward at the glass privacy window. "After everything that happened with my parents, me and my brother went to stay with Maddox until I could figure out our next move." Her tone was emotionless, almost robotic. "I was on my way to my brother's room when I heard a slap, then the sound of crying and someone murmuring. I rushed into the room and saw Maddox cornering my brother with his pants down. Carson was on his knees, holding his face and crying. I blacked out and saw red. I pulled my knife out and next thing I knew we were rushing out of the house."

Slowly Cashlynn turned to face me. Her eyes were cold and lifeless. "My brother is the most important person in my life, Nazai. He's the only person I give a fuck about. If anyone tries to harm him, I *will* eliminate them and not think of the consequences."

That was the last thing I expected Cashlynn to confess. Nothing in the world disgusted me more than child predators. Now it made sense why Cashlynn wanted Maddox's head. He deserved way worse than gunshot and knife wounds.

"Hey bud, want to go in there?" I pointed to the video game store. With everything going on, I felt like I'd been neglecting him. After seeing Maddox and rehashing the memory of him trying to assault my brother, I knew Carson and I needed to spend time together one on one. We ignored the fact that Bruce and James were trailing in the rear and went in and out of stores. My brother was into computers and coding so I made sure to grab him a new laptop while we were out too.

He looked up at me with a subtle nod while giving me a small smile. My heart squeezed knowing my brother seemed like a shell of himself. He became a quiet kid growing up because my parents were always so hard on him, but now it seemed he was even more withdrawn. We moved around the store and I allowed Carson to get what he wanted. I had another job tonight. It had been a few days since my wedding but a week since my last job and I needed to release some building frustration. Not much had changed between us since we married. Nazai always was on the go since taking over. I didn't know the ins and outs of what their family did, but I did know they made people disappear and were connected to some powerful people.

My parents always used to complain about them stealing business from them. They hated the Tavarez family and getting married to the new leader was the ultimate smack in the face. That fact alone brought a smile to my face. It was my final fuck you to them and I hoped they were rolling in their graves.

Once Carson got what he wanted, on Nazai's dime, we left the mall and went to grab something to eat at a hole in the wall seafood place. Silver Stone, since it was by the water, had some of the best seafood.

"Carson," I called out after we were seated and our drinks were ordered. The two of us had been here enough times to know what we wanted without menus.

His eyes lifted and he gave me his attention. "I know a lot of changes have happened to us lately and we haven't had the chance to talk about everything. How do you feel about living with Nazai now?"

One of his shoulders lifted. "It's fine I guess. I like his game room." He gave a shy smile.

My back straightened. "And Nazai, how is he toward you?" I leaned into the table. After what happened with Maddox, I was on edge about living with someone other than us two. We had been at Nazai's house for a month and my brother hadn't complained, but most of the time he didn't. He was taught it was better to not be seen or heard.

"He's nice." Again, he shrugged and avoided my eyes.

"He hasn't tried anything, has he?" My throat was tight as I asked.

Quickly, he shook his head. "No."

For a second I studied my brother to gauge if he was lying to me. Satisfied that he was telling the truth, I nodded.

"Good, good." My hand raked through my hair. "I know I dropped the ball with Maddox." He tensed at the name. "But it won't happen again. I plan on making him pay, painfully, for what he tried to do to you." A dark haze covered me. My body grew tight and my muscles tensed.

"Cash," he called out, his eyes locked on the table.

I didn't realize I had blanked out until I looked down and realized I had grabbed the knife on the table and held it tightly. My knuckles were white.

Blinking slowly, the fog started to lift and I looked up at him. "Mom and Dad were pieces of shit, but they made sure I was always able to protect myself and handle business. My point is, I'm going to make Maddox pay and anyone else who fucks with you, okay?"

He nodded with a slight smile forming on his face. "I'm glad we don't have to run anymore."

Sighing, I didn't disagree with that. I looked away, watching as our waiter spoke to the table not far from us. "I hate to admit it but Nazai's to thank for that. One good thing has come out of this marriage."

"Do you like him?"

I gave my brother my attention back. Nazai's touch was like a ghost haunting my mind. I tried to brush it off, but anytime I thought about his hands on me my skin flushed and my nerves became jittery. I always felt itchy, as if ants were crawling under my skin. My heart raced uncomfortably. I didn't know how to handle the feelings forming inside of me.

"I tolerate him," I answered thickly, rolling my shoulders back. My fingers tapped on the table.

The waiter came back for our food order. The two of us got a seafood boil. My stomach rumbled soon as the order left my mouth. It felt good not having to be on edge and look over my shoulder. Not to mention, I could openly go to places I was used to and not worry about being bothered.

"We need to get you in school soon," I stated. Now that we were stable, I wanted some stability in his life, wanted him to live a normal life.

Your life isn't normal.

I pushed that thought away. What I did I was born to do, literally. Since I had been able to walk and talk properly, I was trained to be a killer, both physically and mentally. I endured it all so Carson wouldn't have to. He wasn't meant for this life, but I breathed it, craved the rush taking a life and watching it drain from someone's eyes brought. No matter what it took, I would always be my brother's keeper too.

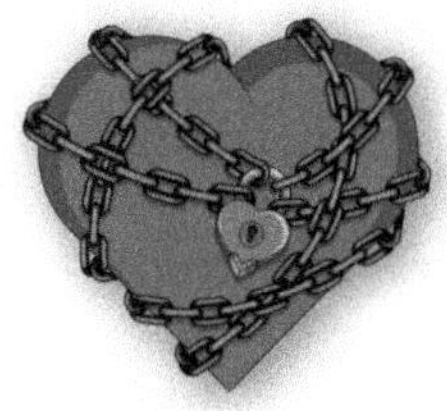

The door to my bedroom opened, causing my face to ball up.

"You don't know how to knock?" I finished pulling my black leggings up. I was about to leave for a job and hoped to be gone before Nazai got back from wherever he was. Outside of when I first moved here, he didn't question when I would disappear. I knew he could see my movements from this collar on me, but I paid that no mind. Part of me hoped he would chase me and learn my secret. I had grown to love the high I felt when I pushed him.

One corner of his mouth kicked up. My body heated as he scanned me with mirth in his eyes.

"Why should I have to knock in my house?" He cocked his head, narrowing his eyes. He dragged his tongue slowly across his heavy bottom lip. My body shuddered.

"What do you want?"

He smirked and walked toward me. Standing in front of me, he studied me intensely.

"Get on your knees."

My eyes widened. "What?" I sputtered.

The smile on his face turned crude and his eyes lit with mischief.

"On your knees. I've had a long day and need some relief." My eyes dropped when he fumbled with his slacks and pushed his boxers down. His dick popped out semi hard. He gripped it and stroked it slowly. It matched the color of his skin, the head fat, on the right side was a large bulging vein. The hair at the base was groomed and cut low.

Flicking my eyes up, I watched his darken and droop. Something in me flipped. Lust flooded my stomach seeing the passion gushing from his orbs.

My heart stuttered. A slow warmth spread through my body starting at my chest and radiating outward. I licked my suddenly dry lips. My cheeks grew hot.

"You're out of your mind," I breathed in an airy tone. "Get out."

The smirk returned to his face. He stepped closer to me, his dick brushed across my mound. I inhaled a deep breath. My blood hummed. I'd never been interested in sex with another person. My life was built on survival, sex wasn't important. After sleeping with Nazai, I felt something I never had before. For the first time, I was attracted to someone. I craved his hands on me. Enjoyed feeling the way his lips brushed against my flesh. And when he took me roughly, with no remorse, my body felt like fireworks went off inside me.

"When you get on your knees and handle this, I will." He nodded toward his dick that had grown harder.

My mind screamed for me to knee him in the dick or take it in my hand and squeeze until he begged me to stop, but another part of me wondered how it would taste in my mouth. Would the weight of it feel good against my tongue? My cheeks grew warmer under his gaze.

My hands clenched and unclenched at my sides. We stood in a stare off. I tried not to think of the sinful sensations he brought to my body.

"I'm not doing shit!" My words had more bite than I felt.

The darkness in his gaze increased. He reached out and grabbed me by the hair, wrapping it in his hand, causing me to wince.

"You wanna try that again?" His low husky growl made my stomach do a somersault. The room felt stiffly warm. The back of my neck filled with heat. My skin tingled with each passing second.

I sneered at him and swallowed around the lump in my throat. The room felt smaller.

"If you want me on my knees, then you better make me."

His eyes flashed and his nostrils expanded.

Suddenly I was forced to my knees, eye level with his dick. Beads of precum leaked from the fat tip. I'd never tasted a man before, never had the urge either, until now.

"Open up, Wildfire." He pushed his dick against his mouth. The precum spread against my lips. It was warm and thick. When he pulled away, I couldn't help but lick the salty substance.

"Fuck you!" Again his eyes flashed and mirth filled his face.

He clenched his jaw before reaching down with the hand not holding my hair and squeezing my jaw. I tried to fight it, but the harder he squeezed, the more turned on I felt. Between my legs grew wet and throbbed.

When he pried my jaw apart, he shoved his dick in my mouth. I widened it to accommodate his size.

"Thatta girl," he groaned.

I gagged when he pushed my head down completely until his hairs brushed across my nose. I gripped his thighs and attempted to pull back, but he didn't let up, thrusting forward. Tears clouded my eyes. Drool spilled out of the sides of my mouth.

My head spun and blood rushed through my veins. His scent was captivating.

"Fuck, this mouth. I knew it was good for more than talking shit." He pulled my head back and I attempted to breathe through my nose, but it didn't last long. His thrusts became more forceful. The more he fucked my face, the more turned on I found myself getting. To my horror, I moaned around his length when I felt myself growing lightheaded from the lack of oxygen. I felt like I was high and floating.

"Look at me!" He yanked on my head.

My eyes fluttered up. He stared down at me with hard, hunger-filled orbs. "You like when I fuck your throat, huh? You like when I use your mouth as just another hole on your body?"

My eyes rolled to the back of my head and I swiped my tongue around his dick. He grunted. I knew when I thought about it I was going to be pissed at how he was treating me, but right now all I could think about was how turned on I was.

"You don't know how sexy you are, blurry eyed with your cheeks flushed. You look like you belong on your knees, sucking my dick until I'm bored of you. I bet you never sucked dick before, huh? Little virgin wife. This'll be the only dick you ever suck." His nostrils flared and goosebumps filled my arms seeing the fire that blazed in his eyes.

I gagged again when he sped up. His dick tapped the back of my throat over and over. My eyes bucked when he exploded in my mouth. He held my head still, pushing deep, causing me to choke. Cum spilled out of my mouth.

"Fuck, you look good as fuck just like that," he gritted.

Nazai pulled out of my mouth and stroked his dick. Cum splattered on my face, dripping down my chin.

I blinked and my vision cleared when he pulled my head back and tilted my chin up to face him.

"Fuck I wish I had my phone. I like you with my cum scattered on your face and running over my collar." He bounced his eyes around my face. "Now I can go to the club with a clear head."

A heavy breath pushed out my nose as my eyes tightened, my body tensed, and my jaw ached. My throat felt sore.

Nazai released me and stepped back, tucking himself back in his pants. "Maybe next time you'll follow directions then you can get off too." He winked at me.

My hands balled on my thighs as I watched him leave. My body was stuck in place. It wasn't until the door shut that I seemed to snap out the trance.

Subconsciously, my tongue swiped over my lips, tasting Nazai's intoxicating flavor. I couldn't decide if I hated what he just did to me or craved it so much I wanted him to do it again.

The kill today was simple. The mark sat in his car for fifteen minutes, drunk, talking on the phone. I was able to finish him without going inside. Since it was an in and out mission, I had some time to spare. Typically, I would go back to the penthouse, but the babysitter Nazai hired to keep an eye on Carson wasn't that bad. He seemed to enjoy when she was over and she did a good job with him.

I blinked slowly as I stared up the building. I was driving and without thinking I'd ended up at The District. I'd been sitting across the street, watching the line grow longer and longer. I chewed the inside of my cheek. Crowds weren't my thing and I hadn't been back to The District since that first time. My thighs pressed together tightly thinking of what had happened in Nazai's office.

I looked down. I wasn't dressed to go to the club but my husband owned the place so I couldn't care less.

My husband.

I stopped mid grab for the door handle. We had only been married a few days and listen to me.

Shaking my head, I grabbed my phone and climbed out of the car. Checking the street, I walked across, not bothering to get in line. The security guards eyed me warily. Yells from the crowd of people in line didn't bother me.

"Back of the line," the bulky guy told me, barely giving me a glance.

"I don't think so." I went to step past him, but he grabbed my upper arm.

"You're not getting in. Now back of the line."

My eyes went to where his hand was on my arm then up to his face. My eyes narrowed.

"Unless you want me to slit your throat, I advise you to let me go." My knife was in my jacket pocket. It would take me less than a second to whip it out and leave him bleeding on the ground. Just as I was about to reach for the knife, my name was called.

"Mrs. Tavarez." I glanced up, seeing Bruce stepping up to me. "What's going on? Ted, why is your hand on the boss's wife?" he growled with his face pinched. Usually I was annoyed with him and James since I was able to handle myself, but at this moment him being here worked out.

"Shit!" Ted's eyes widened and he quickly released me as if I was on fire. With a frown, I eyed him up and down, imagining him bleeding out on the ground.

I stalked past him, bumping him in the process. The bottom sections were filled to capacity. The music was loud and the lights were bright. People were scattered around the floor and lined up at the bar. My nerves grew twitchy seeing the large crowd.

I didn't think Nazai would be down here so I turned for the steps that led to Euphoria.

"The boss wants me to bring you to him." I glanced over, seeing Bruce at my side.

Ignoring him, I headed to the steps, skipping past the people waiting for the bouncers to let them in. The man standing in front of the door moved to the side instantly. I started to feel like this was a bad idea seeing how filled Euphoria was too. I bit the inside of my cheek and scanned the area. My gun was tucked safely in the small of my back under my jacket. Sticking my hands in my pockets, I gripped my pocketknife.

"This way." Bruce nodded, guiding me.

Naked women moved around the room, lap dances were being given. A girl was on stage bent over and shaking her ass toward the crowd.

When we got to the section, I saw Ezra grinning with a girl bent over in his lap. River stood close by, eyeing the crowd. I knew it was his men that guarded the club. I was prepared to go to him and let him know his man downstairs' time was limited when something caught my eye. Walking toward us was Nazai, but what caught my eye was the topless girl walking next to him. He wasn't paying her any attention. His eyes were locked on me as if I was his prey and he was a lion. The way the girl grinned and ran her hand down his arm caused my eye to twitch. My eyes narrowed, remembering her from the first time I was here. She was all over Nazai then too. The two looked familiar. A feeling I'd never felt before twisted in my stomach. My grip on the knife tightened.

"This is a surprise." He paused in front of me.

I pressed my lips together tightly and my gaze shifted to the girl whose face was balled up. She eyed me as if I was gum stuck on the bottom of her shoe.

"I was in the area." My eyes narrowed. "Unless you want to lose that hand, I advise you to remove it from my husband's arm."

Nazai's mouth ticked up in amusement. The girl's eyes widened and she opened her mouth to speak.

"Go ahead and get ready for your set, Majesty. I'll handle it," he told her without taking his eyes off me.

Her face balled up and she rolled her eyes before turning and storming off in her six-inch, clear heels.

"I got it from here, Bruce." Nazai dismissed him and stepped to me. His arm went around my waist. I flinched slightly and my breathing staggered. He leaned down so his mouth was close to my ear. "You aren't dressed to come out. Does that mean you missed me?" He kissed the shell of my ear. For a second I closed my eyes and embraced the gesture, realizing I liked it.

"No." I pulled away from him, realizing what I was doing. He chuckled lowly then pulled up.

Nazai held me and turned us to guide me inside the section. "Sis!" Ezra called out. The girl was still in his lap entertaining him. I paused and turned to River.

He noticed me and raised a brow. I pulled away from Nazai and leaned toward River. "You should warn your guys about putting their hands on the wrong people."

I was snatched back and Nazai's arm wrapped protectively around me. "The only man's ear you should be whispering in is mine," he whispered before he kissed the shell of my ear.

My stomach fluttered. I turned to him. "You and River need to vet your guys better. One downstairs grabbed me and—"

"Someone grabbed you?" The playfulness in his voice left and his face straightened.

"That guy Ted." His eyes turned deadly. My stomach swirled and blood rushed in my veins. He lifted his attention to River and stepped to him, leaning over and speaking to him quietly. River glanced at me, nodding every so often.

Finally they broke apart and River pulled his phone out of his pocket and tapped the screen before leaving the section.

"Did he hurt you?" Nazai's eyes leveled on me and he scanned me. I had on black leggings and a black jacket so none of my skin was visible.

I scoffed and rolled my eyes. "No." I waved him off.

The loud music caused a thumping in my chest. I turned and moved closer to Nazai, realizing the crowd had grown bigger. I wasn't even sure what made me come here. Tension filed through me and I clenched my fists.

"Here you go, sis." I jumped, not realizing Ezra had come over to us. "Have a drink."

I side-eyed him then the drink. Nazai played interference before I could think about grabbing it.

"If anyone's offering my wife a drink, it's me."

Mirth formed on Ezra's face. "You're taking this marriage seriously, huh big bro?" He grinned, downing the drink he'd just offered me.

"As long as my ring's on her finger and my collar's on her neck, it is serious." Subconsciously I reached up and touched the leather on my neck. I hated the way heat flooded my stomach at the possessiveness dripping from Nazai's tone.

"Stop treating me like I'm your property!" I protested.

Nazai stared down at me and smirked. "You *are* my property, Wildfire." He licked his lips, eyeing me.

My cheeks flushed and I snatched my eyes from him.

"I got some work I need to get back to, but stay here with Ezra. I'll have a drink brought over to you and Bruce is gonna stand on guard outside," Nazai told me after a few minutes. He and Ezra made eye contact, having a silent conversation.

Nazai leaned down. I held my breath when he moved in, pressing a kiss to the shell of my ear, then moving to peck my lips. "Be good and I might have them bring you something extra." He winked at me. My cheeks grew redder seeing Ezra grinning at us.

Nazai turned and left the section.

"C'mon, sis." Ezra wrapped his arm around my shoulder, causing me to flinch. He either didn't notice or didn't care. We walked to the couch and took a seat.

My fingers tapped my thighs as my eyes bounced around the room. Now that Nazai was gone, I felt back on edge. I darted my eyes to the exit.

"You really need to learn to relax," Ezra said, leaning back. "You look like someone's gonna jump out the dark at you. Ain't no one gonna bother you here."

I cut my eyes at him. Ezra was a lawyer, apparently taking after his father, but he was the least serious.

"You never know. It's always best to stay alert."

Ezra chuckled. "Damn, you and my brother are so alike, yet so different." I studied my brother-in-law. From what I heard, he was unhinged when it came down to business and someone that attacked in the courtroom with no remorse.

"Why are you the only brother here?"

"The club isn't Emmet's thing and Lucas is at his clinic." My eyes narrowed. Lucas worked as a surgeon a couple times a week at the hospital, but I knew he also ran his own underground clinic for those who had injuries they wanted to keep under the radar.

"Mrs. Tavarez," a female voice called out, causing my eyes to snap to her. "From your husband." She held the drink out.

I eyed it for a second then grabbed it. "Thanks." She nodded and turned to leave.

"Drink and live a little, sis. You're good here."

"You know… for you to have such a serious job, you're the least serious person I know." I brought the drink to my mouth and took a drink. My nose instantly scrunched at the strong taste.

"I get serious when it matters." Ezra shrugged.

Slowly I drank my drink, continuing to scan the floor. I took my phone out of my other jacket pocket to check on my brother. Nazai was in and out of the section, checking on me. Being here showed me I was not like most people. While everyone else was here to have a good time, I was wired up, twitchy, and uncomfortable. Growing up, I was secluded. My parents homeschooled me until I was in seventh grade, and even then, I didn't socialize much.

I stood up and Ezra grabbed me, causing me to tense. "Where you going?"

I pulled away from him. "Bathroom," I said stiffly.

When I walked to the entrance of the section, Bruce stopped me. "Boss doesn't want you leaving the section."

I rolled my eyes. "I'm going to the bathroom." He leveled his stare on me. He pulled his phone out and tapped the screen.

"C'mon."

Bruce led me through the club. I wilted every so often into myself when we got too close to a group. My hand was inside my jacket again, wrapped around my knife.

Bruce nodded at the man standing guard in front of a cut out part of the room. "The boss wants you to use the bathroom in his office. Straight up the stairs, the door's unlocked."

I furrowed my brows and bounced my eyes between the two before pushing past them and heading up the stairs. Last time I was in the office I was high on ecstasy so I didn't get a good look at it. It was a nice size, with a large desk toward the back and glass windows that oversaw the club behind it. On the wall were video monitors. I noticed he had a built-in fish tank, like at his house but smaller, on the opposite wall. My cheeks flushed when I eyed the couch against the wall, remembering what had happened on that couch. Shaking my head, I located the other door in the room and headed to the bathroom.

When I was done, I washed my hands and left the room. I walked to the windows behind Nazai's desk. They gave a full view of the club floor. It was lit up, making it easy to see everything. I scanned the floor, and like my eyes were drawn to him, I spotted Nazai at the bar, signing something and nodding at whatever was being said to him. I clenched my jaw when Majesty walked up to him.

I glanced at the screens on the wall. The first screen showed the downstairs club, which wasn't as lit up as the strip club. The second screen showed the strip club. I focused on the square showing the bar. Majesty leaned up and whispered something in Nazai's ear. Her hand went to his arm. I might not have ever been in a relationship, but I knew how to read people and it was clear by the way Majesty looked at Nazai she had a thing for him. A possessiveness I'd never experienced before grabbed me. I remembered how just hours ago I was on my knees for Nazai and how calm my mind felt as he fucked my face, then I thought of Majesty feeling the same thing.

Pushing a heavy breath out of my nose, I turned and stormed to the door. I hurried down the steps, not bothering to wait for Bruce as I passed him heading for the bar. I pushed people out of the way, not caring about their protests.

Majesty was leaving the bar by the time I got close. I redirected myself and followed her. She went down a dimly-lit hallway. I crept behind her. The hall was empty. After waiting a couple of seconds, I stepped into the room Majesty had gone in.

We were in the dressing room. A couple of girls walked out and stared at me curiously. I didn't pay them any mind as I walked to where Majesty sat on a bench, kneeled over and looking through a bag. Pulling my pocketknife out of my jacket pocket, I flicked it open and grabbed her by the hair, yanking her head back. The rush I got during a kill filled my body.

She yelped. I pressed the blade against her neck. "I'm only gonna tell you one time. Touch my husband again and it'll be the last thing you ever do." I quickly swiped the knife and it cut into her flesh on her cheek. She cried out and grabbed her face.

Smoothly I turned, went to one of the vanities, and grabbed a towel to wipe my blade before closing it and tucking it back in my pocket.

I left the dressing room, leaving Majesty crying and complaining about her face.

I was startled briefly seeing Nazai mid-reach for the door. "What were you doing in there?" He shifted his attention to the door, then back to me, cutting his eyes into slits.

I smirked. "Showing your employee she should learn to keep her hands to herself," I told him calmly.

It had been a while since I'd done something irrational like that, but I couldn't lie and say it didn't feel good.

CHAPTER SEVENTEEN

I stepped in the dressing room and Majesty's cries filled my ears. When I caught sight of her heading toward the dressing rooms, I instantly followed her. She was staring in the mirror holding her face. Blood covered her fingers. When she noticed me, she spun around.

"Look what your crazy ass wife did to my face!" she shrieked.

My teeth sank into my bottom lip as I took in the wound on her cheek. It was a nice-sized cut. From where I was, it looked deep too. Blood spread on her cheek.

I fought a smirk. Cashlynn was a ticking time bomb. It was surprising to even get notified she was here. I knew from the first time I brought her here it wasn't her scene. When I approached her, I noticed how she glared at Majesty. Now, seeing what she had done, had my dick hardening in my slacks. It should have pissed me off that she'd ruined one of my top money makers' faces, but seeing the lengths her clear jealousy led her to made me want to take her to my office and bend her over my desk.

"Nazai! Do you see this?" Majesty cried when I didn't respond. She winced and cuffed her wound again.

I pulled my phone out of my pocket so I could text Lucas. I knew he was working at his clinic tonight, but I needed him here.

"I hope she enjoys jail because I'm gonna—"

My mind flashed red and my eyes lifted, glowering at her. "You're not gonna do shit but keep pressure applied to your face and wait for my brother to arrive."

"What!" Her eyes bucked and she winced. "Do you see my face?"

"More than just your face will be ruined if you threaten my wife again." Fear filled her expression.

"You'll be compensated for the hours you missed tonight. Stay here, he'll be here shortly." I turned and left the dressing room. I adjusted my jacket and my phone vibrated. I saw it was River. I glanced at the message and smirked, then locked my phone and shoved it back into my suit pocket.

Walking through the club, I beelined to my section where Cashlynn sat next to my brother unbothered, as if she hadn't just sliced one of my employees faces. Stepping into the section, I walked up to Cashlynn who smirked when I got closer. I stopped in front of her and crossed my arms over my chest.

"You thought cutting my employee's face was funny?" I asked.

"You cut someone's face?" Ezra's eyes widened with amusement. "Damn, sis, I knew you had some bite in you."

Ignoring him, Cashlynn stayed staring at me. "She had it coming. I don't play nice or share. You should remember that." Her eyes cut into tight slits.

My dick twitched. One corner of my mouth rose.

"Fuck, you might fit in this family perfectly, Cashlynn. Bro, you better be careful, she's got that look in her eyes."

"Look?" I wondered with a raised brow.

"Like you should sleep with one eye open." He chuckled and stood. Ezra walked past me. I approached Cashlynn once we were alone.

"You know you just fucked me out of one of my top earners, right?"

She gave me a deadpan look. "Is that supposed to mean something to me?" Her head cocked to the side.

Chuckling lowly, I enclosed her by leaning over and placing my hands on the back of the couch.

"While I should punish you, I can't deny knowing the length you could go makes my dick hard. Is my brother right, Wildfire?" I asked before switching to Spanish. "Is there a little psycho running around in that head?"

Her cheeks flooded with heat. "Don't flatter yourself. I just don't like that she knew you were married and didn't care. It's disrespectful and I don't take that well."

My mouth ticked. "So you were jealous?"

Her eyes narrowed. "Jealous of what? This marriage isn't real but no one but us knows that. It's the principle of the matter." Again, I chuckled.

The fight in Cashlynn's eyes caused lust to balloon inside of me. My atoms were electrified. My eyes focused on her lips. I thought about how they looked wrapped around my dick and how beautiful she was with tears running down her face. She looked so wrecked with her eyes unfocused and dilated.

Fuck.

Now I wanted to do it again; to see her barely hanging on while she choked on my length.

My phone vibrated in my pocket. Keeping eye contact with her, I dug it out and peeked at the screen, seeing it was Lucas.

"I gotta handle this. But know this isn't over." I moved down just a whisper from her mouth. I waited to see if she would make the move, but she didn't, which caused me to grin. I pecked her lips then lifted. Cashlynn tried to fight her feelings for me but her actions today showed she felt something.

My phone vibrated again.

I sighed so I could go handle Majesty. "Oh, Bruce is gonna drive your car home and you'll ride back with me," I told her.

She cut her eyes at me.

I turned and left the section. There was only an hour left in the night; then the fun could begin.

"Where are we going?" Cashlynn asked when I led her down the steps.

The club was closed and the cleaners were here for afterhours cleaning. "You better not be on some funny shit."

"Don't worry. I'm not taking you to your death or anything." She narrowed her eyes at me then looked forward. We got to the end of the steps and approached the door a couple of feet away. Using my key, I unlocked it and pushed it open.

In the room was Lucas, River, and Ezra, and a gang of security. They all surrounded the man tied to the chair. Lucas had cleaned and stitched up Majesty's face before I sent her home. I made sure she would be paid for what happened to her. She was warned what would happen if she went to the police, but even if she did, I wasn't worried. The cops worked for us and wouldn't do anything. There was also an NDA in place for anything that happened and was seen at the club that protected me.

"Nazai!" Cashlynn perked up, looking around. Ted's eyes popped out and he looked around wildly.

"Mr. Tavarez! I'm sorry. I didn't know she was your wife!" he rushed out.

Pausing in front of him, I stared down at him with tight eyes. Sweat beaded on his forehead. He attempted to wiggle free.

Dragging my tongue across my top teeth, I looked over at Ezra. "You bring Wilma with you?"

He grinned and pulled his bookbag off his back, reaching inside and pulling Wilma out. He walked over to us and stopped next to me.

"Which hand did he grab you with?" I asked Cashlynn.

"I'm not sure." She stared at Ted smugly. Lifting my hand, I stroked my beard.

Ted's eyes were locked on the custom hammer in my brother's hands. "Tsk, too bad." I turned my head to Ezra, commanding him in Spanish. "Smash both of them."

Ezra's face lit up, showing all thirty two.

"As you wish," Ezra responded in the same language as he walked toward Ted. His eyes looked like they were about to pop out of his face. My face stayed blank when Ezra lifted Wilma and sent it down on Ted's hands. It was large enough that it slammed against a good part of the hand. The sound of bones crunching under the impact could be heard instantly.

Ted released a gut-wrenching scream. "No, please, please!" he cried when he saw Ezra moving to the other hand. The walls in this room were soundproof so I wasn't worried about anyone hearing him crying or screaming.

I turned to face the other men. They all worked under River and had been vetted. They were loyal and knew not to run their mouths.

"Unless you want to end up like Ted, I advise you to never put your hands on my wife." I made sure to make eye contact with each of them. "If you value your life, you'll take heed and not learn what will happen if you disobey me. Understood?"

"Yes, boss."

"You'll respect Mrs. Tavarez like you respect Mr. Tavarez," River cut in, eyeing each of his men.

"Now get the fuck out." I waved them off to leave.

They all turned and filed out. Once it was only me, my wife, my siblings, and River, I turned back to Ted. Blood dripped from his mouth and snot leaked from his nose, mixing with his tears. He dry heaved and his body jerked every so often.

"Can you hurry this along?" Lucas yawned.

"Ple-please. I'm sor-rr-ry," Ted stammered out. "I won't d-d-d-do it again."

I glanced down at Cashlynn. "Do you accept his apology?"

She was staring at him expressionless. She stepped forward and held her hand out next to Ezra. He looked at her confused.

"No one touches Wilma."

Cashlynn turned toward me with cold eyes. "Let her see the damn hammer," I commanded.

Ezra cut his eyes at me and grunted, then handed the hammer over. Cashlynn's eyes locked on Ted again who was crying and begging for mercy. She lifted the hammer and brought it down on the hand closest to her.

The scream he released was enough to bring a child nightmares. Pride exploded in my chest. I loved seeing how fearless Cashlynn was. She didn't even flinch when she sent the hammer down. It was clear she was perfect for me.

"You both are insane," River mumbled.

"Did you bring it?" I asked, turning to Lucas.

He nodded and reached behind him on the table and picked up the machete. He walked over to me and handed it over.

The fear that filled Ted's eyes heightened my senses. Blood pumped wildly inside me. My heart expanded and adrenaline rushed through my veins.

"And just in case you need an extra incentive not to put your hands on my wife." I looked at River. He walked over and used a key to undo one of his arms then held it in place. Grinning, I stepped closer, tapping the flat side of the machete against my palm.

"No, no! Help!" He strained to get out.

Lifting my hand, I sent the machete against his wrist, slicing his hand off. It plopped down on the plastic. Blood splattered from the wound.

"Damn, he just pissed himself." Ezra laughed.

I looked at Lucas. "Get him patched up, put the hand somewhere safe." It would be used to remind others not to touch what was mine.

He stared at me blankly but picked his doctor bag up and came close to me.

"Do you accept the apology now?"

Cashlynn turned with a half grin. "Now I do."

I'd never had the urge to punish someone for putting hands on a girl I was seeing. Cashlynn was different, however. Each day I spent with her, I found myself growing more fond of her. She was slowly making her way into my thoughts, even when I didn't want her to be. Crawling and embedding herself under my skin. I was the only person meant to touch and play with her. Anyone else who dared to try it would suffer the same fate as Ted.

"You gon' tell me what we're doing here?" River asked from the driver's seat of the car. It was one he used for off the grid jobs. There weren't too many houses on the dark, dead end street.

I flipped through the file Emmet gave me concerning Maddox then looked up at the house listed.

"It's simple, he did some shit he shouldn't have. Now it's time to make him pay." I dropped my eyes back to the file. Maddox was next in line to inherit the drug business. He was his dad's only kid. His mother passed away when he was young, the dad was rumored to have a hand in it. He still was working in rehab from Cashlynn stabbing him.

"And it just so happens that he's Cashlynn's ex-fiancé?"

"Even if he wasn't, he still needs to be handled. Him being the man my wife was engaged to is just a bonus."

Since Cashlynn told me what Maddox had done, I knew he couldn't go unpunished.

"I could be wrong but it almost seems like your marriage to her is real."

"You were at the wedding, weren't you?"

He smirked. "You know what I mean, you went from not wanting to marry to chopping hands off and now stalking her ex. You've got feelings for your wife, don't you?"

I stroked my beard and thought about it. While my relationship with Cashlynn might not be orthodox, the feelings I was developing for her were starting to consume me. The push and pull between us had become something I craved. While I used to be happy sleeping with different women all the time, knowing I was the only one who had been inside of Cashlynn and owned her pleasure brought me rising gratification.

"We have an understanding."

He chuckled. "That's an interesting take on things." He checked the time on the dashboard. "You know if you're late to your dad's retirement party your mom will have your balls, right?" Things had settled around us since the other night and the incident with Ted. My mom was celebrating my dad tonight and once Maddox was captured, that would gain my focus.

I glanced at the dash. He was right. My mom was making tonight a big deal. While my dad retired from being a judge years ago, the party to celebrate his retirement from his firm was tonight. My dad was well-connected from his twenty plus years as a judge, not to mention his years before as a high-powered lawyer. Since he was retiring completely now, it was up to Ezra to step up in the legal aspect and me with everything else. I'd turn thirty in two weeks and all that was left for me to fully take over was being announced as the family head.

"We'll make it." I made sure my personal shopper dropped off outfits for me and Cashlynn. All I needed to do was get home, shower, and dress.

My eyes narrowed when I saw a car pull into Maddox's driveway. "There he goes," I said, closing the folder.

River's demeanor changed and he straightened in his seat. Going into my pocket, I pulled out my black leather gloves then leaned down, unzipping the bag at my feet. I pulled out the rag and bottle.

"You keep watch while I grab him.," I told River, opening the bottle and pouring the liquid inside into the rag.

Maddox was smaller than me in height and size. I knew he'd give me no issues.

I checked the scene before climbing out of the car and heading toward the house. Maddox staggered out of the car, using his cane to walk. He was unsteady, even with the cane. By the way he swayed, I was sure he was drunk. I'd learned he spent a lot of time at bars and a lot of money on liquor by the financial statements Emmet included in his file. The more I read about him, the more I wondered how he'd ever ended up with Cashlynn.

Pulling my hood over my head, I crept across the street with my hands in my hoodie pocket. The rush from the hunt slammed into me.

Maddox fumbled with his keys at the door. He clumsily dropped them and cursed under his breath. Not giving him a chance to pick them up, I rushed him. He started to yell but was cut off when I wrapped my arm around his neck, squeezing tightly. He struggled to break free. My blood pumped excitedly through my veins as my heartrate picked up. I tightened my hold around his neck. He slapped my forearm. While it would have been easier to drug him the moment I noticed him, my blood boiled and I wanted to see him struggle and attempt to fight.

Eventually the struggle dwindled and his hits on my arm became fainter until he went completely lax against me.

Releasing him, I turned his body then leaned and picked him up, tossing him over my shoulder. I kneeled and snatched up his keys before heading back toward the car. I looked around, seeing we were still alone. River waited near the open trunk. Stepping to it, I tossed Maddox inside. River stepped forward, binding his legs and feet together then duct taping his mouth before shutting the trunk.

I rolled my neck between my shoulders. "Now we drop him off then get ready for the party."

"I thought it was just rumors but you really went out and married a Cavana. You're one crazy son of bitch for that." My body tensed when the hand slapped down on my shoulder. Turning, I made eye contact with Roger. He was a detective on Silver Stone's police force, but crooked as fuck.

The more he laughed, the more I felt my blood grow hot and my eyes tighten. I glared down at him and reached for his wrist, twisting it, causing him to wince.

"Wanna try that again?" I gritted.

"Hey man, I mean no harm," he groaned with his face twisting in pain.

My grip tightened. "Speak on my wife again and I'll slit your fucking throat, McKinley." I flashed him a crude grin before shoving him away from me. I turned back to the table, grabbed my drink, and walked off.

I had spent most of the night familiarizing myself with my dad's associate in the legal field. Most of them would be useful in the future. When Dad wasn't introducing me to people, he and Ezra were working the room.

I was headed back to the table where I left Cashlynn and Carson when I noticed Emmet and Lucas talking quietly amongst themselves. I squinted, noticing Emmet slide him a folder. Lucas looked around and nodded as Emmet explained something to him. Lucas nodded with an intense expression on his face.

Continuing to the table, I took a seat next to Cashlynn. She looked like she wanted to be anywhere but here.

"I'm confused. Your dad was a corrupt judge, right? So now that he's retired, how does your family expect to get away with the shit you do?" Cashlynn asked.

I gave her my attention. "And what exactly does my family do?" I smirked.

She rolled her eyes. "Don't act like you guys are as clean and righteous as the public thinks. Remember I know who your family truly is."

The corner of my mouth lifted. I brought my drink to my mouth, sipping it slowly and staring at her over the rim.

I lowered my glass and set it on the table. "Well, my darling wife…" I reached out and twirled the end of her hair around my finger. "Now that dear old dad is stepping down. It's my job to handle the business, meaning all jobs we take go through me. Ezra will continue being the family's lawyer and the connections my dad and my grandfather gained stay locked in the family."

"What I don't get is why it's not you going into law. You were forced to marry because you became the 'head of the family'." She made sure to put the last words in quotations. "But you own a club."

Leaning in my chair, I kicked my feet out under the table. "My main objective was to kill, running everything never appealed to me. The only reason Dad got into law and shit was to help the family business. I just so happened to be the oldest, so it fell on me. Ezra is into all that legal shit."

She squinted and searched the room until stopping where Ezra was. Lucas was talking with River. He was grinning and drinking from a glass.

"Ezra is so unserious though. I've literally seen him joke and laugh when slamming his hammer down on someone's hand."

I chuckled lowly. "What you don't understand is we've all been trained how to act in front of others. Ezra might joke and bullshit a lot, but my brother's a shark in the courtroom. We all have skills that work in our everyday lives. I might be a club owner, but I'm the cleanest shot you'll ever see."

"It's time for the family photos, come on you two," Mom said after she walked over. "The press wants to interview the family as well, then your dad will do his speech before we cut the cake."

"I'll just sit here," Cashlynn protested.

Mom narrowed her eyes. "When you got married to my son, you became a part of the family. So you're gonna be in the picture."

Cashlynn glared at my mom.

The stare off ended with Cashlynn rolling her eyes and cursing my mom under her breath. I chuckled as we walked over to where the rest of the family was.

"I don't get why I have to be involved in this. I don't even like the spotlight."

"Just smile and look pretty." I patted her head and she smacked my hand away.

The evening continued. Previous and current judges told stories about my dad, as well as DAs and a few members of the police force, including the chief and commissioner. The night ended with my dad giving some bullshit speech about how proud he was to have served the law for as long as he did.

"Wow, everything about your family is truly fake as hell. Your dad is the leader of secret criminals, yet he's giving a speech about respecting the law." Cashlynn mumbled.

"Illusions, Wildfire. Gotta love them." I winked at her.

"I'm proud to say my middle son Ezra will be continuing the law tradition. Many of you know he's a force to be reckoned with in the courtroom…" Dad said.

The end of the night came. Most of the people had left and only a couple lingered.

We were leaving the hall. Cameras flashing and shutter sounds surrounded us from the few reporters still on the scene who couldn't get in. It was dark out and my mind was set on finishing what I'd started with Maddox. He was currently being held captive at The Barn on the outskirts of town. I barely noticed the black car creeping down the street.

"Get down!" I heard one of River's guys who was working security yell before gunshots sounded.

Screams and panic replaced the celebration as bullets started flying. My family was quick to recover.

The car was outmatched by us along with River's men. I rushed forward to the sidewalk, constantly pulling the trigger. The back window was shot out and tires squealed as it skirted away.

"What the fuck was that!" someone yelled.

My blood boiled and my body pumped with anger thinking someone was brave enough to come after me and my family.

"Is anyone hurt?" Dad asked.

I looked around. Reporters were on the ground, all cowering along with some pedestrians innocently passing by. What surprised me though was Cashlynn right next to me with a gun in hand. With everything going on, I hadn't even seen her pull a gun out or start shooting with the rest of us. I didn't even notice she'd followed me onto the sidewalk.

"Who the fuck thought it was a good idea to shoot at the fucking Tavarezes. Do they know who the fuck we are?!" Ezra boasted, waving his gun in the air. He came over to where we were and narrowed his eyes on Cashlynn. "And sis, I ain't know you got down like that! You surprised the fuck out of me."

"Yes, that was unexpected," Dad commented as his jaw ticked and reddened. His eyes scanned the area then settled back on Cashlynn, sizing her up.

"I don't take getting shot at lightly. Regardless of how you feel about them, my parents made sure I knew how to handle a gun," she replied, her voice bland and her face calm but her eyes held a raging storm.

For a second I forgot my anger, staring at her in awe. There were so many things I didn't know about her it seemed, but now wasn't the time to try and figure it out.

My dad was checking my mom over. Chaos was on the streets as people were attempting to get off the ground. A couple of them crying out and groaning.

"Who the fuck would be brave enough to pull some shit off like that?" Lucas questioned.

I bit down on my back molars. "That's exactly what I plan on finding out." No one takes shots at the Tavarez family and lives to tell about it.

My body seethed with anger as I gripped the butt of my gun tightly, my eyes darting around the streets. Chaos broke out around us as everyone ran around in a frenzy. My heart pounded viciously as blood pumped wildly through my body. I rushed to Carson and helped him off the ground, quickly checking him over.

"Everyone head to the trucks now! Family meeting!" Dominic bellowed. His face was fire truck red and veins bulged from his neck.

I bit the inside of my cheek, not feeling this meeting he was calling. My mind was on one thing, finding out who'd shot at us and going after them.

"C'mon." I flinched when Nazai touched my arm.

"Don't." I shook him off, turning to glare at him. He matched my stare.

"Go to the truck," he gritted.

I wanted to fight him, but I knew now wasn't the time. I scanned the scene again. His brothers all looked on edge. Nora stood by her husband looking just as upset.

I didn't know what the plan was, but I was out for blood now. I had never been in a shootout before. Outside of when that bounty was placed on me I'd never had anyone try me before. When the gunshots rang out,

I didn't hesitate to snatch my gun and start shooting back. This was personal and whatever they had planned I wanted parts of it.

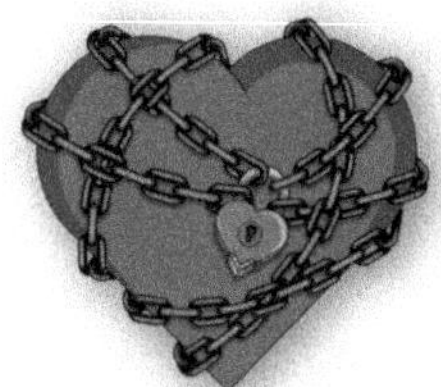

No one spoke as Dominic paced back and forth in front of the fireplace in his living room. Once we got to his home, we all piled into the family room and were now waiting for Dominic to speak

"Is no one gonna say anything?" I finally said, tired of the silence.

Dominic stopped pacing and focused on me. "Got something to get off your chest?"

"Yeah I do!" I shook Nazai off when he tried to grab me. "Some idiot tried to kill us and we're just sitting here looking at each other instead of going after them."

"We can't go after someone if we don't know who they are," River noted.

"Which brings me to, who the hell would be dumb enough to come after us?" Dominic's eyes traveled around the room.

"There's only one person who has known issues right now," Lucas stated. He turned to face me with a blank stare.

I cut my eyes at him. "This has nothing to do with me," I spat with my mouth turned up.

Nazai shut him down. "I handled that. The Rhodes know Cashlynn's off limits and called off the bounty."

"That's the only logical choice. None of us have beef going on right now."

"Even if it was the Rhodes they're not stupid enough to come after us while we're all together. It's not them."

"This is some bullshit!" Dominic rattled off in Spanish. Do you have any more enemies outside of your ex's family?" Dominic asked, focusing on me.

My tongue poked the inside of my cheek. "That's it. And Nazai is right, those idiots didn't do this. They don't have enough balls." I brought my apple juice I had in my purse to my mouth and took a sip. Not knowing who was after us had me unsettled. I wasn't used to being hunted. Just the month the bounty had been active made me jumpy and paranoid.

"Emmet, I want you to check out all of the surrounding traffic cams. See if you can get the plates of the car then run them. I spoke with the police at the scene and they're gonna be all on this. Someone coming after an ex judge is a big deal, they'll keep me in the loop, but this isn't on them. This is family business. If anyone comes up to any of you, don't say shit. Keep your eyes and ears open when you're out and watch your backs. River, I need your men in the streets, find out if anyone's talking about coming for the family. Nazai…" He paused and locked eyes with his oldest son. "This is the time you show you're not to be fucked with. I'm not passing the family down to you until I see you're built for this."

I could feel Nazai tense next to me. He adjusted his tie. "Cashlynn." My spine straightened and my lips pinched together, waiting for his next words. "You earned my respect today. I wasn't expecting you to pull out a gun and start shooting."

"I don't take threats against me lightly."

"You better be careful, bro, she might have a bullet with your name on it." Ezra laughed, but he wasn't too far off. There were a couple of times I was tempted to pull my gun on his brother.

"Shut up," Nazai gritted.

"Everyone's dismissed. I'ma make some calls to a few people who owe me favors and see if I can find anything out too." Dominic waved his hand in front of him.

I sat there trying to see if that was truly it. I turned to Nazai. "That's all he has to say."

Nazai's eyes landed on me. "Dad doesn't do anything without purpose. He's calculated. Once Emmet gets information on the car, we'll go from there."

I turned toward the youngest Tavarez. Since I'd been in this family, I'd hardly heard him speak. I knew he ran a PI firm and from how his family spoke on him, he was a whiz at computers. I saw him shooting at the car too, but his face was impassive, almost like he was bored right now. Like he felt my eyes, he turned and stared at me. It sent a chill up my spine at how expressionless he was.

Snatching my eyes away, I looked around the room. Dominic and his wife, who had been sitting in the chair close to him listening and observing, spoke quietly amongst themselves.

A faint beeping could be heard. "I got a patient," Lucas said, standing up to leave.

He turned to me and gave me a hard stare. Me and Lucas never had an issue since I'd been around, but I could tell he wasn't convinced tonight didn't have anything to do with me.

Regardless, that wasn't my concern. Maddox and his dad might talk a big game, but truthfully they were soft and not threats. Everything they did was for show. If anything, I was sure the Tavarezes had racked up enemies over time and this fell solely on them.

The street was dark and quiet outside of the sounds of crickets chirping. Two street lights stood on either side of the house, one flickering. As I watched the couple stagger inside the house, I waited, rubbing my gloved hands back and forth, across the steering wheel. The man was supposed to be the only person here, he was my target, but it looked like the girl was about to become a casualty too. His brother, who lived with him, had left when I pulled in, meaning the house was empty before they got here.

After the shooting the other day, I couldn't wait to take on another job, reaching out to my handler. Going to the gun range I learned Nazai had at his getaway house didn't help either. It took me two days to scope out my target before making my move.

I sighed, hating when the plan didn't come together correctly, but I didn't have time to wait around.

I gave it ten minutes before climbing out of the car. Making sure I had my black tool bag in my bookbag, I crossed the street and headed toward the house. I stayed on guard, walking up the driveway to the backyard. I hadn't had time to scope out the house like I normally did but I knew it had no security measures. I didn't know the details with this one, just that this guy had pissed off the wrong people. I didn't care either way, as long as I got paid at the end of it.

Adjusting the cap on my head, I kneeled at the backdoor and went into my bag, finding my break in kit. It took a couple minutes before I heard the small click. Putting everything away, I stood and crept in the house. It was dark inside. The closer I got to the steps, the louder the moans coming from the room grew. The girl was crying out loudly in an annoying manner.

Reaching behind me, I grabbed my gun, releasing the safety and going into my bag to grab my silencer then screwing it on. Slowly, I made my way upstairs. When I got to the door, it was partially open. I peeked inside and the girl's back was to me. She was on top of the guy, riding him with her head tossed back as her body bounced.

For a second, I froze, watching them. The guy grunted loudly, digging his hands into her ample sides.

I sank my teeth into my bottom lip. My hand on the gun tightened. The hair on the back of my neck rose and I was swarmed with heat. Before, something like this wouldn't have affected me. But now I couldn't help but think of how Nazai had taken me. It was only once, but it had been permanently instilled in my body. It was like he unlocked something inside of me that refused to go back in the shadows. I rubbed my throat, thinking of the soreness it once had from my encounter with Nazai. I kept seeing his heated gaze on me.

I shook my head. No, this wasn't the time for that. Right now this kill was my main focus.

Taking a deep breath, I closed my eyes and pushed the urges I was feeling away. Never had I been this distracted on a job before. The sound of skin clapping together caused me to open my eyes again. Now the guy was behind the girl, growling while she cried out as if he was killing her.

"I never knew voyeurism was your kink, Wildfire. I never would've guessed." Gasping, I quickly spun around with my gun pointed. My eyes widened seeing Nazai standing behind me with a crooked grin on his face. His eyes slid inside of the room then back to me.

"What are you doing here?" I hissed.

He stepped closer to me, the gun pressing into his chest. "You think I was gonna continue to allow my wife to sneak out of the house and not know where she's going?" My nostrils flared as I pushed out a heavy breath.

"You need to leave."

His smile fell and his tongue went across his top teeth. "Turn around."

My brows furrowed and my heart tripled in speed, bumping against my ribcage. "What?"

Instead of repeating himself, he grabbed my wrist and spun me around. His body pressed against mine and he lowered his mouth to my ear.

"Does it turn you on watching them?" he rasped.

A shiver shot up my spine as he wrapped his arm around my body, placing his hand on my stomach. Slowly he moved it down until he brushed the rim of my leggings.

"Does watching them make my wife wet?" I inhaled a deep breath and clenched my jaw as his hand slid inside my leggings.

My legs spread without a second thought and he brushed his fingers across my swollen bud, then moved to my opening.

"Mhm, you *are* wet." Nazai kissed the shell of my ear.

My eyes fluttered and I tried to focus. This wasn't how tonight was supposed to go. My chest rose and fell quicker. My knees buckled when he pushed a finger inside of me. I could feel his dick hardening and pressing against my ass.

"Now, let's see how good your focus is." He grabbed my hand with his other hand and wrapped it around the gun, lifting it.

"Nazai," I whispered shakily. My thoughts were scattered and my eyes were unfocused.

"Shhhh. I think they're about to finish," he whispered.

I fought to keep my eyes open as he pushed another finger inside of me. He moved them in and out of me swiftly and skillfully. I clenched my walls around his digits.

Nazai's finger fell on mine around the trigger. The gun leveled.

The girl let out a loud moan and the guy grunted as his body tensed.

Sweat covered his bare, wide back.

I tasted blood as I bit into my bottom lip, fighting to keep the moan in my mouth as my body trembled. Pleasure shot through my body. My pussy exploded like an overfilled water balloon.

"Now." He put pressure on my finger.

A faint sound left the gun and went through the back of the guy's head.

The girl released a loud yell when his body fell on hers. She scrambled quickly, attempting to push him off her.

I fell forward when his hand left my leggings and leaned my head on the door frame. My breathing was heavy.

"Mhm." Glancing over my shoulder I watched Nazai suck my juices off his fingers.

"You still got a job to do, Wildfire," he said, nodding with mirth on his face.

Slowly, I turned back to the door opening, keeping my eye on how the girl grew more frazzled on the bed.

I blinked quickly then pushed out a deep breath. My hand was slightly shaky, but I quickly pushed the door open. She was now sitting against the headboard with the cover clenched tightly to her chest. Her eyes fell on me and bucked.

"What, what!" she stammered. I lifted my gun and pulled the trigger before she could get the sentence out. Her eyes stayed wide as life left her body instantly. A rush of adrenaline filled my body.

"I knew there was something about you that was being hidden." Spinning around, I turned to face Nazai with a glower on my face. I ignored how my cum was running down my legs and the way my pussy throbbed.

"You shouldn't be here!" I growled, gripping the gun tightly. Lifting it, I brushed the silencer over my temple.

He raised a brow. His eyes moved around me to the dead couple on the bed. He stepped toward me and snatched the gun out my hand before I could blink.

"What are you—" My words halted when his lips slammed into mine.

"Nothing's hotter than watching you take lives. Fuck!" he muttered against my lips before savagely taking them again. His hand went to my side and he gripped it tightly. "Do you know how hard my dick is?" I moaned when he spun my body and slammed me against the wall.

"I shouldn't be surprised from how you shot your gun the other day with expertise." He bent down and nuzzled his face against the collar. "When I tracked you here, I thought I was gonna have to kill someone. Thought I'd catch you in here with another man. His blood was almost on your hands." The thought of Nazai killing someone over me shouldn't have made my pussy wetter but it did. It dripped down my leg like a leaky faucet.

"I gotta have you," he groaned. Stepping back, he reached in front of my leggings and tugged, ripping them. My mouth parted and my nostrils expanded. Heat flooded my stomach. He removed himself from his jeans and grabbed me by the thighs, lifting me.

"Ah," I cried when he lowered me onto his dick. It was painful at first. This was only the second time we'd had sex and he wasn't gentle. He pushed me against the wall again and pumped in and out of me. My legs went around his waist and my arms looped around his neck. I couldn't breathe as he fucked me mercilessly, his dick stabbing against my spot over and over.

"I swear I'll never get enough of this pussy. So fucking wet and tight," he gritted. "How do you feel knowing you're getting off while two dead bodies lay only inches away?" I shifted my eyes to the bed behind him. My heart thumped painfully, soaring and threatening to leap out my chest.

I attempted to speak, but my words got caught in my throat.

"Soon I'ma have this pussy molded for my dick only. I'ma fill it with my cum, over and over, until you become swollen with my seed." I moaned and closed my eyes. I was still taking my birth control pills so pregnancy wasn't happening yet, but for a second I could picture it.

He lifted the gun and rubbed the butt of it down my arm. I whimpered and clenched my walls. My stomach tensed.

"I could end you right now, Wildfire, and no one would be the wiser. No one would even miss you besides Carson." He pressed the gun to my neck.

The truth of his words caused something to twist inside of me.

"Ay, Jared. Man, where you at!" a voice called out.

My eyes snapped open and fell on Nazai. He didn't look bothered though.

"Yeah, I hope you're ready; we got another lick to hit," another voice said.

Fuck, fuck.

"Uh, oh, Wildfire. Looks like we got company." Nazai whispered in Spanish.

"Nazai!" I moaned.

"You better hurry up and cum unless you're an exhibitionist too." My eyes slid to the bed again. The thought of being caught didn't scare me, but knowing I was fucking this job up made my chest tighten.

Nazai pushed the gun closer into my neck and thrusted his hips up, fucking me roughly.

"Jared!" the voice called out again, closer now.

My walls clenched. Sweat beaded on the back of my neck. My body tensed for a second before trembling as I came. I clung to Nazai's neck.

"That's my girl!" he grunted in Spanish and exploded inside me.

The two of us were breathing heavily. For a minute I forgot we weren't alone. Nazai lifted me off him, causing me to wince. He brushed his hand over my collar just as the people appeared at the door.

"What the fuck!" My eyes whipped to the door.

The guy went to reach for his side. Before he could grab it, Nazai lifted my gun and pressed the trigger. His body dropped.

"The fuck!" the other voice called out.

When he became visible, Nazai shot him too. My brows shot to my hairline. I didn't expect him to be such a good and quick shot. I licked my lips. It was hot seeing him use my gun easily. He didn't bat an eye either.

He turned to me and leaned down, kissing me hungrily.

"Let's go," he said calmly, pulling back and bending to pull his pants up.

My brows furrowed. The way he just switched personalities and moods was eerie.

I grimaced, feeling his cum leak out of me.

My eyes bounced around the room. I noticed a tissue box on the dresser. Carefully, so nothing fell on the floor I walked over to it, wincing at the soreness. I picked a tissue out of the box and wiped myself.

"Yeah, gonna order a pepperoni pizza," he said behind me. I spun around and noticed he was on the phone. I wasn't sure why he thought this was the time to order pizza but I didn't have time to think about it. His eyes landed on me.

I licked my lips, trying to gather myself. Pushing out a deep breath, I went into my bag and grabbed my signature card. On shaky legs I moved to the bed, placing the card there. Going back into my bag, I pulled my secured phone out, taking a picture and sending it.

"The Queen of Hearts," Nazai said slowly, the realization hitting him as he eyed me.

Huffing, I didn't have time to explain.

I pushed past him and started out the door. This had gotten more complicated than it was supposed to be. I had never been this messy on a job before. I hadn't expected Nazai to show up either.

"Wait." He stopped me before I could walk through the front door. He pulled off the shirt he had on and shoved it over my head.

Scrunching my face I put my arms through the holes then stared at him.

"No one but me needs to see you dripping of me." Heat flooded my cheeks and I snatched the front door open.

We got outside and I saw River and a couple of other men outside. A cool breeze brushed over my lower lips through the shirt that went to my knees.

"What is this?" I spun around to face Nazai.

"They're gonna handle the cleanup," Nazai said, stepping next to me.

"How did they get here so fast?"

"You think I came here without backup? I didn't know what I was walking into." He smirked.

Rolling my eyes, I snatched my gun from him then stormed past them and headed for my car.

By the time I got to the car, Nazai had caught up to me. "Get in the passenger seat," he told me once I tossed my things in the trunk.

Glaring at him, I stalked to the passenger side and got in. My work phone vibrated and I saw it was a message from my handler confirming payment had been sent.

"Looks like there's more I need to learn about my wife," Nazai said, starting the car.

I cut my eyes at him but didn't say anything as I buckled my seat belt. I couldn't think straight. The last twenty minutes had my mind jumbled. Nazai now knew my secret; that I'd followed in my parents' footsteps. Now I wasn't sure what to expect going forward.

*S*ilver Stone, let's shine light on the shadows. We all know the key to anything around here is money. So it's no shocker that there's no one talking about the shooting at Dominic Tavarez's party the night before. There isn't even a police report. As you know, there have been rumors of his connections to multiple crime bosses, which isn't a shocker given how many get away with things in his courtroom. And his son represents them as well, isn't that a conflict of interest? Not to mention every single member of the family had a gun on hand. What respectable family is armed like that? It makes me wonder if the family pissed off the wrong crime lords they allegedly have allegiances to. For too long the wealthy have gone unpunished, and for too long they've been granted privileges just because they have money...

My jaw clenched as I continued to read the latest blog post by *The Shadows of Silver Stone*. Whoever they were had commented on the shooting that happened three days ago at my dad's retirement party. Whoever ran the page was obsessed with exposing how corrupt me and my family were. While many families, legal and illegal, were spoken on, lately whoever it was had been hyper-focused on my family in particular.

"Have you read this shit?" I gritted, lowering my phone and looking at my brother. "Have you been able to find out who's running this blog?" I asked Emmet while sitting across from him in his office. On top of being a professional hacker, he did freelance PI work, mainly for organized crime members who were looking for people who crossed them. On his desk sat four large monitors with a laptop in the middle. He had a large file cabinet on the wall. The room was decorated in black and red.

"No. I'm working on it, but whoever it is, is almost as good as me." His brows furrowed and creases formed in his forehead as he typed intently. "They think they're smarter than me but they're not. Each time I'm almost in, I hit a block, but I'm gonna figure it out."

One corner of my mouth lifted. One thing about Emmet was he took pride in his intelligence. I hadn't met anyone smarter.

"Fuck!" he growled and twisted to another computer. "They're trying to hack me back. Do they really think it'll be that easy?"

I had no idea what he was talking about. He started mumbling to himself and his face grew more intense. Emmet might be lethal, but he was a nerd at heart. Not much excited him, but things like this did.

"What about the shooting? Did you find anything?"

He paused and sat up straight. "I'm still working on it. I'm going through all the street cameras and any attached to the surrounding buildings. I'll have something soon."

I tapped my finger on my thigh. "One more question."

Emmet looked annoyed but gave me his attention. "At Dad's party I saw you give Lucas a folder. He still has you looking into Adrian?" One of my brows rose, referring to a ghost from the past.

Emmet hardly showed emotions. I loved my little brother, but he had one hell of a poker face and it always pissed me off. Out of all of us, Emmet stayed more to himself growing up. He did jobs with us and did his part in getting the information we needed. He had one hell of a kill shot too, especially with a rifle, but his secret keeping was vault tight.

"Why not ask him?"

I stroked my beard. "Because he gets touchy when it comes to her, so I'm asking you." I sighed. "Look, I'm just worried about him, E. He's been obsessed with finding her for the past fifteen years, you helping him only enables him."

"I'm not enabling him. Lucas isn't gonna let it go until he learns what happened to her. I would think you'd be happy if we could come to a solution and put it to rest."

I chuckled. "A'right. I can't argue with that. Just…if he seems like he's gonna crash out again, let me know. We don't know who's coming after us and everyone needs to be focused. If Lucas starts his shit again, that can put us all in jeopardy."

"You have nothing to worry about. If it gets bad, I'll tell you."

I nodded and checked my phone. "Good. Now thanks for this." I lifted the folder. It was why I'd come here originally and the blog just happened to be posted while I was here. I had Emmet look up everything he could about The Queen Of Hearts, not to mention Cashlynn's parents. Now, knowing who she was, I wanted a thorough analysis on everything before she broke into my house. Thankfully my brother was efficient and already ahead of the game. Both me and my dad had him investigate Cashlynn so it was no shocker he'd gone deeper and kept what he learned for when it was useful.

Emmet went back to his computers, basically dismissing me. It didn't bother me. I had more business to tend to once I left here.

"What is this? Why are we here? This better not be another sit down," Cashlynn ranted as we climbed out of the car.

"Just follow me. I'm sure you won't be upset once we get inside." The barn in front of us was in the middle of the woods in an abandoned area on the outskirts of town. It was in the back of the family meeting house. The barn had been completely gutted and remodeled. It was where we brought special cases that needed time to be handled.

Cashlynn looked around the area then rested her focus on me. She squinted at me but followed me anyway. Since I'd learned her secret she'd been staying out the way. Things have been hectic for me. With my birthday approaching, and me officially being named the head of the family, not to mention someone coming for us, my plate was full.

We walked up the dirt walkway. The sun was covered by clouds, which brought a nice breeze, offsetting the heat in the air. The sounds of the trees rustling around us along with birds chirping filled my ears.

I pulled the steel doors open and we walked inside. I led her to the room in the back where we set up for Lucas when he needed to do his doctor thing. In the all-white room were both Lucas and Ezra, and in the middle, tied to the hospital bed, was Maddox. Both of his eyes were black and swollen shut. He had knots covering his forehead and his lips were swollen with drips of blood surrounding them. He had bruises all over his chest. Since I'd taken him off his porch five days ago, I'd come here and worked him over. Lucas had him attached to an IV to make sure I could fuck with him and keep him alive. He made sure I didn't take it too far before the grand finale and used his doctor knowledge to help me torture him near death then bring him back.

"What are you doing here?" I asked Ezra.

"I'm offended! You have someone here, torturing them, and didn't include me and Wilma." He brought the hammer to his chest with an offended look on his face.

"This has nothing to do with you, that's why." Cashlynn stepped around me and slowly approached the table. The monitors attached to him beeped softly.

Maddox was unconscious but his chest rose and fell slowly. "Wake him up," she demanded with that same look in her eyes I had grown to recognize when she was serious.

She turned to me. "When did you do this?"

I crossed my arms and nodded at Lucas. "The night of my dad's retirement party."

She squinted. "That's why you were late?" The realization had her words coming out slower. My shoulders rose and my eyes shifted to Maddox.

Lucas walked over to the table and dug into his pocket. Cashlynn pulled the backpack she always wore off. She walked to the chair near the wall and tossed it aside. Her shoulders rolled back and she grabbed the ponytail holder off her wrist, pulling her hair up in a bun.

Maddox's eyes fluttered open and he groaned. I knew his body had to be sore from the multiple beatings I'd given him.

"Wake up!" Cashlynn walked to the head of the bed and sent her hand across his face.

He grunted as his head whipped to the side.

"Cashlynn," he coughed out and groaned.

"Shut up!" She hit him again. Her eyes were dark as coal. She leaned down and pulled something out of her sock. My eyes narrowed seeing it was her butterfly knife.

"What the fuck?" Ezra muttered. "You know your wife just walks around with knives hidden on her body?"

"Remind me what vital points I should avoid, to keep him alive, besides the heart," she said, turning to Lucas.

"There's a couple of other spots to avoid too." He stepped closer. He started pointing out areas. Lucas then walked to the table and picked up a pouch, then went to the IV stand and messed with it. "He's hooked up to an IV drip giving him fluids, so he'll last awhile."

"Wa-wai-waiitttt." Maddox's words were slurred. I was sure it was from whatever my brother gave him.

"What did you just give him? I don't want him numb to the pain."

"The medication will paralyze him but he can feel everything happening. "

A bone-chilling smile formed on her face. "Good." She looked around. "Can I get some gloves?"

Already one step ahead, I reached in my pocket and stepped forward with black leather gloves.

"I'm gonna enjoy this." She slid the gloves on.

"Ay bro, your wife is kind of scary." Ezra stepped closer to me. My smile widened. I had seen Cashlynn use her gun, but I was anticipating seeing how she was with a knife.

"You know, Maddox. I never really liked you." She pressed the knife against his neck and slid it down. "My parents were power hungry bastards who forced me to be with you because they wanted more power. Your daddy would have given them that." She lifted the knife and lodged it into the right muscle between his right pec and shoulder. His eyes widened with pain. "The only reason I came to your house after they died was because I needed a place to lay low and get things in order for me and my brother." She pulled the knife out and shoved it into another part of his body.

I stood back and watched with my brothers as Cashlynn went to work on Maddox. She was in her element and didn't slow down.

"Remind me not to get on sis's bad side," Ezra commented.

"Considering who her parents are, I'm not surprised she has this in her," Lucas commented.

While they conversed, I watched Cashlynn in awe. Seeing how she conducted herself without breaking a sweat made my dick grow.

"Do you guys have pliers or anything?" She turned and looked at us. Lifting her arm, she ran it across her forehead.

"Ezra, go grab some pliers," I said. We had a ton of tools in the other room for things like this.

"And shears!" she called out after him.

Ezra muttered something, but turned and did what I said.

Lucas stepped closer to the body and examined it. "He's stable, losing a good amount of blood. Heart rate elevated."

"As long as he doesn't bleed out before I finish, I don't care."

Ezra came back into the room with pliers and shears.

"Thanks." Cashlynn grabbed them then turned back to the body. She placed the shears over his chest, keeping the pliers in hand. Maddox had tears streaming down his face and blood running from the multiple wounds Cashlynn had inflicted. Hovering over one of the wounds she stabbed it with the pliers and spread the tool open. I grimaced but my chest swelled with pride as she repeated the motion a couple more times.

"You smacked my brother that day. I heard it." Dropping the pliers on the floor she grabbed the shears with a chilling expression on her face. She picked up one of his hands and placed a finger between the shears. "You should have kept your hands to yourself." She closed the shears, slicing his finger straight off. Maddox's eyes widened. He attempted to speak, but only indistinguishable sounds came out.

"Oh shit." Ezra laughed.

"Do you regret putting your hands on my brother?" She went to another finger and closed the shears around it.

Cashlynn was just as ruthless as I thought. I had to adjust myself as

I watched. My stomach fluttered along with my heart. Pride swelled in my chest. All I wanted to do right now was take her in the other room and fuck her roughly. She looked beautiful with a serious look on her face. She barely blinked this whole time, never asked for assistance. It was like she was working on autopilot.

"Now, I'm not a doctor, but I'm still sure my good ol' knife can do the final act." She grabbed his sweatpants. He had been wearing the same ones since I'd taken him. He had dried pee stains and a fresh wet mark on the front of them.

"What the hell?" Ezra grumbled and spun around.

I kept my eyes locked on Cashlynn's face.

"Your dad put a bounty on my head because I stabbed you, but you didn't die. Which, at the time, I would have said you were lucky because I *never* miss. But then again, if I would have killed you then, we wouldn't be having this moment now." She dragged her knife up his dick. "But did your daddy know you were a fucking pedophile. That you tried to force my ten year old brother to suck your little ass dick!"

Lucas's eyes widened while Ezra made a choked sound next to me.

I watched her grab his dick. For a second I clenched my jaw, not enjoying seeing her handle anyone's but mine. Seeing another man's dick in my wife's hand caused my body to go rigid.

"You should have never fucked with my brother or me. Maybe you would have had a chance in life, but now!" I winced when she replaced the knife with the shears, placing them at his dick and closing them.

Blood gushed from his wound.

"Did you just shit yourself?" Cashlynn laughed, grabbing his dick and moving to the top of his body. It took a struggle, but she pried his mouth open and shoved his dick inside, deep. He made a choking, gurgling sound.

"He's starting to stink. Can we finish this?" Ezra complained.

Maddox was barely hanging on. His heart rate was deadly low.

Finally Cashlynn grabbed her knife again and dragged it across Maddox's neck. Blood flooded out, covering the area.

She glared at him with tightly pressed lips. "Rest in hell, you sick fuck!"

Her eyes lifted, still with that lifeless expression.

"Big bro. I hope you never get on her bad side. You and your dick might be in danger." Ezra laughed.

Cashlynn's body was stiff. She seemed to dissociate.

I ignored him and stepped closer. Cashlynn watched me as I approached. I stopped in front of her and reached up, grabbing her by the hair and yanking her forward, slamming my mouth down on hers. Passion gushed up my spine. Seeing her work like that had me horny as hell.

"Fuck, that was sexy as hell. I knew you were lethal, but damn." I kissed her again, this time more heatedly. She moaned and I swallowed it up.

"Before you two decide to give us a show, we need to take care of his body and she needs to get cleaned up," Lucas commented.

I pulled back and stared into Cashlynn's now dilated eyes. Her breathing was heavy.

"You guys get started. I'ma show her the showers," I told them.

I grabbed Cashlynn's wrist and pulled her after me. We walked down the hall and upstairs to the shower room.

"We need to get you cleaned up." I released her then grabbed the bottom of her shirt, lifting it over her head.

I moved in and kissed right under her collar. My dick grew harder. Reaching behind her, I undid her bra and slid it down her arms.

"I've never been so turned on watching someone take a life, but right now I feel like my dick could burst," I rasped against her skin, grabbing her breast and messaging her nipple. "Did it feel good to finally make him pay?"

Pulling back, I stared into her eyes. They were burning with need but I could still see the darkness looming in them.

She swallowed hard and nodded. "Did it make your heart race when you were stabbing him?" I squeezed her nipple.

"Yes," she moaned.

Grinning, I moved around her to turn the shower on then grabbed my shirt and pulled it off.

"My brothers are gonna think you're a badass now."

"They should have been known that. I told you I wasn't the one to be fuck with."

Turning to face her, I saw she had stripped out of the rest of her clothes, causing me to follow suit. She stepped to me and sank her teeth into her bottom lip.

I reached up and grabbed her by the hair. "The Queen of Hearts *is* a force to be reckoned with. I had heard the rumors, even saw it the other night, but seeing it today was a completely different thing." I wrapped an arm around her waist and pulled her close to me. Her body slammed into mine.

"I wasn't The Queen of Hearts tonight."

I leaned down, kissing her shoulder. "Who were you?"

"A sister getting justice for her brother." I sank my teeth into her skin. My dick grew harder. I stepped back until we were under the water. It beat down on us as I moved my head lower to take one of her nipples into my mouth.

Spinning us around, I slammed her back against the shower wall and lifted her. The tip of my dick dripped of precum, aching for relief.

The beast inside me slammed against my chest cavity, begging to come to the surface and I was about to grant his request. I made sure to keep the look of blissfulness on her face as she worked in my memory to draw later. My sketchbook had become nothing but versions of Cashlynn without me realizing it.

I had been itching to take her since she'd first pulled her blade out, wanting to dominate and overpower her body, wreck her and leave my seeds dripping from her pussy while she cried out my name. I never knew a woman killing someone could turn me on like this, but Cashlynn seemed to be the exception.

My brothers weren't happy that they'd handled the majority of the cleanup but it got done. We ended up mailing the fingers Cashlynn chopped off to his dad then burning the body in the furnace in the back of the barn.

Now that we were home, Cashlynn went to her room while I went down the hall into my game room. Just like I expected, Carson was here. I noticed he spent most of his time in here or on his computer. We had yet to have a real conversation, but after learning what I had, I wanted to touch bases with him.

I stepped in the room and closed the door behind me. Carson was playing the latest 2K game. He was sitting in one of the beanbag chairs. When he noticed he wasn't alone, I noticed his body tensed. I went to the TV stand that held the controllers and picked one up.

"Let's run a game." Video games weren't my specialty but Cashlynn had bought Carson a bunch of games for my system when she went crazy spending to "punish me". The large, eighty-inch TV was set up on one side of the room, while the other had a foosball table, air hockey table, and a couple of arcade games.

He side eyed me with hesitancy on his face, but didn't protest. I turned the controller on and waited for him to get the game set up.

We selected our teams and the game started.

At first we didn't speak. I didn't know what I was doing, but Carson was a pro, easily scoring and taking the ball when my team had it.

I finally spoke. "Your sister told me why you guys were on the run." I noticed him flinch and blink hard a couple times, but he stayed quiet. He didn't talk much, unless it was to his sister. I paused the game for a second then turned to face him. "I want you to know you don't have to worry about Maddox anymore. He's been handled."

At first Carson didn't say anything. He twisted his body and stared at me. It was comical how much he looked like his sister when he had an emotionless expression on his face. He broke eye contact and looked down at the ground.

"You killed him?" he finally asked.

I smirked. Carson might be quiet and introverted but he wasn't dumb. He knew what went on around him. In a lot of ways, he reminded me of Emmet; he just lacked confidence.

"Nah, your sister did." He snapped his head up and his eyes lit up. How much he looked up to his sister was clear.

When he didn't speak again, I went to start the game but his voice stopped me. "Cashlynn is always protecting me. It's because of me so much bad stuff happens to us." He laid the controller on his lap. I didn't speak, not wanting him to stop talking. "I'm too weak to protect myself. My parents knew it and Maddox knew it. I hate it." He clenched his hands into fists. Carson lifted his head and looked me in the eye. "I don't want to be weak anymore," he voiced tightly.

"Then stop being weak," I commented. He looked at me confused. "Carson, in this world you have to demand respect to get respect. If people know they can fuck with you, then they will."

"My parents told me I was too weak to be in the family business and they wanted to—" He snapped his mouth shut and shifted his eyes away. My brows furrowed. Curiosity filled me at what he was about to say. "And Maddox told me I was a pussy so he was gonna treat me like one." His lips pressed into a straight line and hands clenched again.

"So what are you telling me this for, Carson? Tell me what you want."

"I want you to teach me to be tough. I want you to train me so no one ever picks on me again. I don't want to keep having my sister defend me. Cashlynn is so strong and she does everything for me, but I'm her brother. I should be the tough one standing up for her."

I didn't point out that he was years younger than Cashlynn, and that regardless, if I taught him anything, his sister would never stop defending him.

"A'right." I nodded. "You want to be toughened up. We can do that."

His eyes lit up. "Really?"

I shrugged. "Yeah, why not. We'll teach you some self-defense, get you out to the shooting range. It's not hard."

"Thanks."

A silent understanding passed between us. We turned to start the game again, but Carson paused it again.

"Nazai, I think my sister really likes you," he expressed. "She's never had anyone to look out for her and have her back before. I think it's different with you."

He didn't wait for me to comment back before he started the game again. I smirked and faced the TV. I too noticed the difference slowly happening in Cashlynn from when I first met her until now. She was still a hard ass and guarded, but each day I was around, it seemed that guard slowly lowered.

I sat on the couch, sipping my apple juice, scrolling through The Shadow of Silver Stone latest blog post when my name was called, gaining my attention.

Confusion hit me and my face balled up seeing my brother dressed and standing next to Nazai.

"What's going on here?" I asked, bouncing my eyes between the two. Both were dressed in dress pants and short-sleeved button ups.

"Carson's spending the day with me today," he said.

My frown deepened. "Uh no." I looked at my brother. "Carson, what's going on? Is he forcing you to go out with him?" I dropped my phone and sat up straighter.

Carson shifted slightly on his feet. "No, I want to go with him."

"You want to go with him? For what? You don't even know him."

"I am his new big brother. Don't you think we should spend time together?" Nazai grinned.

I reached over, setting my apple juice down, then stood up. "Actually, no I don't." My hands balled at my sides. "If this is some sick game, so help me…"

"Cash, it's not!" Carson interrupted. "I asked Nazai to hang out. We're gonna do guy stuff."

I cocked my head back. "Guy stuff? What exactly is guy stuff?"

"That's for us to know. Your brother's in good hands, Wildfire. You don't gotta worry. I'm not on any funny shit." My stance didn't soften. "I saw what happens to those who fuck with your brother. I got too much on my plate to add dodging knives in my own home too."

"Says the guy who tried to drown me and put a gun to my head."

He chuckled while my brother's eyes widened and fell on Nazai.

Nazai smirked. "Don't worry, kid, that's all in the past. Plus, your sister liked it. Ain't that right, Wildfire?"

My eyes narrowed. I turned them back to my brother, ignoring the way my stomach fluttered. "Carson, are you sure you want to go with him? If he's making you, then you can tell me."

"He's not."

My eyes bounced between them. Finally, I sighed and my shoulders relaxed slightly. "Okay, fine. But you better look out for my brother, Nazai. I don't know what you two are up to, but nothing better happen to him."

Truth was, I was starting to trust Nazai. After what he did with Maddox and let me have the kill, it showed maybe he wasn't that bad. Still, my brother had been through a lot. People preyed on him because he wasn't the toughest kid and I refused to let that happen to him again.

He smirked. "I got this. Let's go, Carson." He stepped into me and gripped the bottom of my chin, tilting my head upward. He licked his lips, making my heart lose its rhythm in my chest. "One day you're gonna realize I'm not your enemy and you can trust me." He dipped his head and kissed me. I sighed against his lips and closed my eyes, but it was over before I could fully enjoy it. That was another thing that scared me. I didn't flinch at Nazai's touch anymore. Kissing him wasn't awkward for me anymore. Sometimes I felt like a completely different person around him.

"A'right lets go." Nazai stepped away and turned to leave with Carson behind him. He unlocked the door and pulled it open. "Oh, my mom is on her way to get you. Make sure you're ready." He and Carson were leaving out front door before I could protest.

I stood there dumbfounded.

A second later, my phone vibrated on the couch. I glanced at it and squinted, seeing a text from Nazai's mom.

The in law: *Be there in 10. Be waiting in the lobby.*

"It's a shame you and my son have been married for almost a month and this is the first time we've gotten together since dress shopping." Nora took a seat next to me on her couch. "I got the pictures back from the photographer and they're stunning." She handed me the thick manila folder.

I glanced up at her then down at the folder. The last thing I expected was for her to bring me to her house. I didn't know much about my mother-in-law, except that she was part of the one percent of socialites in the city. She never left the house with a hair out of place or makeup not done. She was just who I'd picture when I thought of a high-powered, ex judge's wife with dark secrets.

Blinking slowly, I opened the folder and pulled out a pile of photos. My lips parted as I searched through them. I couldn't believe the girl in the photos was me. Although it was all fake, I looked like a real bride. Pausing on a picture of me and Nazai at the altar, I lifted it and studied his face. The way he looked at me made goosebumps form on my skin and my heart stutter. His eyes weren't the ones of someone marrying someone just because he had to. I could be mistaken but he actually looked like he adored me.

I swallowed hard, lowering the picture and continuing to skim through them. "The photographer did an amazing job, didn't she? I want to get this one framed." She grabbed the picture of Nazai putting the ring on my finger.

I sank my teeth into my bottom lip. My eyes dropped to my left hand where the large rock sat on my finger.

"Nice choice," I said, feeling a tingling through my veins. A weird sensation passed through me.

"You know my son's birthday is next week. Have you thought about what you're going to get him?"

"Wait, it is?"

Nora lifted her head and stared at me blankly. "You mean to tell me you married him and didn't even bother to find out basic information about him."

"Yeah, well it wasn't really on my agenda considering I hated your son when we first got together. Why would I?"

Nora continued staring at me with judging eyes. "You said hated. Does that mean your feelings for my son have changed now?"

I pressed my lips together tightly. I didn't know what I felt when it came to Nazai. I had never been in this situation before. Before him, boys and feelings were never even on my radar. I was raised to kill and keep my emotions bottled up. I'd never had a boyfriend before. It felt like I was being pulled in two different directions. Part of me thought I was catching feelings for Nazai. The other part still resented him for dragging me into this situation in the first place. My life was fine with just me and Carson.

Before I could answer, Dominic came into the living room. He loosened the tie on his neck and when his eyes landed on me, they widened in surprise.

"Cashlynn." He walked over to us and pressed a kiss on his wife's forehead then turned to me. "I'm glad you're here."

"Why?" Narrowing my eyes and furrowing my brows, I frowned.

"I need to discuss some things with you. If you'll come with me to my office."

I looked at Nora. "Go ahead. I never been the one for all that business talk." She waved me off and started collecting the pictures.

"Fine."

Dominic leaned down and whispered something in his wife's ear before kissing the side of her face and standing up straight.

"Follow me."

The Tavarez family house was huge, almost like a maze. As I followed Dominic, I realized just how big the house truly was.

We got to the office, and once inside, Dominic went behind his desk and took a seat, folding his hands on top.

Following suit, I sat on one of the chairs across from him.

"Who are you?" he asked.

I gave him a blank stare. "I'm sure you had Emmet do a search on me."

"You and I both know that's not what I mean. I mean the fact that you jumped into a shootout without blinking an eye then I hear about your torture of the Rhodes kid. So I'ma ask you again, who are you?"

"You act like you don't know who my parents were. It should be no shocker that I know how to defend myself. As for Maddox, he had it coming."

Licking my lips, I sat back in the chair and crossed my arms over my chest and crossed my ankles.

"Who do you think I am?"

He smirked. "I told my son marrying a Cavana was trouble, but after seeing you in action I see you could be an asset. My only question is can you be trusted?" His eyes narrowed and head cocked to the side. "My grandfather and father put a lot of blood, sweat, and tears into making our name what it is today. Not to mention all the things I've done to make sure the Tavarezes remain standing where they are. You might be married to my son and he may be due to take over, but I only see a threat to what I've worked so hard to build and maintain that will be eliminated." I didn't blink at his threat.

A normal person would be frightened by Dominic, knowing what he was capable of, but good thing I wasn't normal.

"If I wanted to harm your family, mainly your precious heir, I already would have. You keep forgetting one thing, Dominic. I didn't come after your son; he forced me to marry him. I was good before I met him."

Dominic smirked. "You mean when you were bouncing around low budget motel rooms to make sure no one cashed in on the bounty on your head." I bit the inside of my cheek and balled my hands into fists.

Dominic sat straight and loosened his tie more. "My son seems to think you're trustworthy and I trust my son's judgment or I wouldn't be about to hand The Bloodline to him. Do you understand what we do exactly, Cashlynn?"

My tongue dragged over my top teeth. "I know the rumors."

"And what are those rumors?" His voice was calm.

This time I leaned closer. "You guys are known as the cleaners. There's no proof it's you but apparently in the past your family was known to make other people's problems disappear and that hasn't stopped since you've taken over as head of the family, except that's not it, right?" I lifted a brow. "You also take the law into your own hands, right?"

"Do you know how we got started?" He didn't wait for me to answer. "When my grandfather came over here from the DR, he wanted to build a better life for him and my abuela. He had done some things back home to survive but wanted to leave that life there. My abuela was attacked and raped one night and you know what the law did? Nothing. All they saw were illegal immigrants who didn't matter. My grandfather did a lot of odd jobs when he came over here. He met some people who were able to help him track down who'd attacked my abuela and he made them pay himself. That's when he realized no matter how great they say this country is, there *are* flaws; one being how immigrants are treated. My grandfather took that knowledge and built the Tavarez name by handling trash the courts wouldn't. Eventually, he got noticed by gangs and other crime bosses, and they paid him to make problems go away."

"So knowing all that, why go into the same justice system you don't believe in?"

My question caused one corner of his mouth to lift. "Simple, to make sure my family is protected. When you have a man on the inside, you're less liable to get caught. Not to mention, the connections I've built have helped my family more times than I can count. Do you know why we've been able to stay hidden after all these years?"

"Because you were a corrupt lawyer and even more corrupt judge who makes sure of it."

He chuckled. "You're a smart ass," he remarked in Spanish. "My son has his hands full, that's for sure. We've managed to stay off the radar so long because we're good at what we do and we trust each other. Each person in this operation has a role. Do you think my kids are in their professions for the hell of it? Hell no, each of them is doing something that ultimately helps the business." My body went still. "Nazai, although I would have loved for him to go into law too, was groomed to take over the business. I know my son was destined to be a leader and born for greatness."

"So what, you just see your kids as assets?" I asked tightly, gripping the arms of the chair just as tightly. Déjà vu of being around my family hit me.

"All of my kids are smart and talented and they use those skills to keep this family running. Because we *are* a family. No, I don't just see my kids as assets, but they *are* assets. You can't build a tower without a foundation. Each of the skills my kids possess are building blocks. Those blocks are what makes the Tavarez family who we are."

I bit into my bottom lip. "I'm not a threat to your family," I said slowly.

"*Our* family, because whether or not either of us likes it, you *are* a part of this family now, Cashlynn. You might not want to tell me who you really are or what you do, but I didn't get to where I am by being dumb. I know in ways you are your parents' kid. And even though they were a disgrace as humans, they were good at their job. If they trained you to be nearly as good as them, then I'll be proud to have you on our team."

This time a sincere expression formed on his face.

I didn't confirm or deny anything. This conversation gave me a lot to think about. What Dominic didn't know was, the way my parents had trained me made them look like amateurs.

I jumped out of my sleep as my heart pounded in my chest, while clenching my covers tightly to my chest. The thunder went off again, louder this time. Rain poured and violently beat against the window near the bed. A few seconds later lightning flashed, illuminating the room.

Blood raced through my veins. I darted my eyes around the room before squeezing them shut as my muscles tensed at the thunder again. My breathing sped up and my chest became taut. I attempted to take a few small breaths to calm myself down, but the beating of the rain made it too hard.

Finally realizing sleep would not come easy, I snatched the cover off me and hurried out of the room down the hall. Stopping at the elevator, I hit the button a few times while bouncing my eyes around the dark hallway. Another wave of thunder came by, causing me to jump just as the elevator opened. Hurrying inside, I quickly hit the third floor button.

Pressing my back against the glass wall, I closed my eyes until the cart stopped and the doors opened again. Quickly, I rushed out of the elevator to Nazai's door, pushing it open and going inside.

He was still up in bed, an overhead light lit, aimlessly moving a black, charcoal pencil on a sketchpad. His movement paused and he glanced up at me.

"Well, this is a surprise." He smirked, eyeing me. My mouth clamped shut and I avoided his amused stare. "What can I do for you, wife?" Normally I wouldn't come into Nazai's room so easily. He hadn't pressured me to sleep next to him, although every so often he would come downstairs and carry me into his room.

"I—" Just as I was answering, thunder roared, causing me to jump and hurry across the room. I climbed into the bed, ignoring the embarrassment I felt, and pulled the covers over me. My eyes squeezed shut and I moved so my face was pressed against Nazai's body.

I felt him move around, heard a small click, then he was lowering himself so he lay flat. I didn't want to talk about why I was in here and thankfully I think he sensed that. Moving up, I planted my face in his neck, then breathed softly, finally feeling safe. He turned slightly and placed his hand on my hip. My body tensed every so often at the sound of the storm outside, but I tried to tune it out and find sleep again.

CHAPTER TWENTY ONE

"**S**tarting today you'll officially oversee the business, hijo. When you were growing up, me and you bumped heads a lot. We disagreed on a lot of things, mainly because you follow after me when it comes to being too strong minded for your own good, and you've got your mother's stubbornness." Dad paused and smirked. "But still I'm proud of the man you've become. With this business comes a lot of risk, but I know you'll continue to lead The Bloodline into success. You might not have followed in my footsteps with law, but you created your own path and now that you're married, it's time for you to not only continue our legacy but create your own. To Nazai! Happy birthday, son." Dad lifted his glass with my brothers, including River, following suit. We were currently at the family meeting house. It was the morning of my birthday and it was starting off just like I always knew it would, me being crowned head of the family.

"How does it feel, old man?" Ezra asked with a grin on his face.

"Like I can still whoop your ass in a fight."

He chuckled. "Good luck getting past Wilma."

I grinned at my little brother. "That's why God made bullets."

Dad laughed at the head of the rectangle table. It was the same table we had sat around plenty of times while he debriefed us on missions we were taking on. Emmet would provide the information while Dad would explain what needed to be done. I enjoyed what we did, killing with my brothers brought me joy. Killing period excited me but being in charge, knowing the shoes I had to fill, made my nerves a little rattled, but I was up for the task. I had been groomed to take over since I could remember.

"So since you're the head of the family now, what does it entail exactly?" Cashlynn asked next to me. She had been sitting silently since we'd arrived.

"It means now I distribute the jobs this family does."

"And how exactly do you do that? I mean, I know what you guys do, but I never understood how."

I smirked. "It's simple. My dear brother over there…" I pointed to Emmet. "…is a genius and created us a whole online portal where folks who know how submit requests, anonymously, and pay a shit load of money to have those requests fulfilled. Since neither parties identities are ever exposed, both remain protected."

She leaned up, tapping her finger on the table. "So you guys just don't take care of the shitty people, you take on kill requests too."

I grinned. "Bingo, wifey."

"And that particular information is sensitive and shouldn't be given so carelessly," Dad said.

"She's my wife and—"

"And I want in," Cashlynn cut in. She stared at me.

"We don't let women in the business," Dad said.

"Nah, Pops, you got it wrong. Cashlynn isn't a normal girl. Sis is as cutthroat as the rest of us," Ezra interrupted.

"He's not lying. I've seen it firsthand," Lucas agreed.

"And regardless of if you don't think women should be involved, you're not in charge anymore. I'm just as much of an asset as your other sons."

"Because you do the same thing as us." Emmet spoke up, gaining our attention. "I've been wondering what it was about you that bothered me. I've dug into your life from the moment you were born. I read everything about your parents and the people they were wrapped up with. Which, by the way, they were into a lot of sick shit. Finding out everything I did, I realized that you were keeping who you really are hidden."

"After what she did to Rhodes, I believe it," Lucas said.

Cashlynn snorted and leaned back in her seat, staring at Emmet. He might not talk much but when he did he knew how to make an impact.

"You ever heard of The Queen of Hearts?" she asked with a raised brow.

Dad's face pinched then his brows shot up to his hairline. "You're not about to tell us *you're* The Queen of Hearts," River chimed in for the first time before Dad could.

Cashlynn smirked. "You said it, not me."

"Well I be damned!" Ezra muttered. "I've heard about you, Wildfire. You're very sought out."

I cut my eyes toward my brother. "Cashlynn. Her name is Cashlynn."

Ezra tossed his hands up and grinned.

"That's because I'm great at what I do. I needed money and killing is what I was raised to do. The thing is, I know you guys make more than what I would make on my own, and I want in."

"My money is now your money, so you don't have to worry about that," I noted.

"Your money is *your* money. I've never been against making my own and I won't start now."

I chuckled at her stubbornness. My wife was prideful; that was clear. In time I planned to change that. Looking around the table I saw Dad still had a shocked expression on his face. I didn't think I'd ever seen him speechless before.

"The Queen of Hearts is one of the most well-known assassins around. You're telling me you're her?"

"Thank you," Cashlynn replied in Spanish instead of directly answering my dad's question.

Dad pointed a glare at me. "And you knew this?"

I nodded. "I did and I've seen what she can do. I'm bringing her in."

I could see it written all over his face. Dad wanted to protest, but instead he clenched his jaw and looked back at Cashlynn who had a satisfied expression on her face.

"Anyone got an objection?" I circled the table with my eyes.

No one spoke up. "I'll feel good with her covering my back," Ezra announced.

"Not on that, but I have news," Emmet said. "I was able to catch the car that shot up Dad's party on one of the street cameras." He typed on the keyboard in front of him. An image appeared on the screen on the wall. "The idiots were amateurs and used one of their cars. It was registered to a Victor Wallace." The driver's license popped on the screen.

"Who the fuck is that?" Ezra questioned.

I looked toward my dad but he nodded for me to take the lead.

I cleared my throat. "I don't know but we're gonna find out. River, I want you and Ezra to go snatch him up and bring him to the barn. Take Emmet too, find out whatever you can about this guy and why he was brave enough to come for us."

"I want to go too," Cashlynn interjected.

"You're not going anywhere."

"He tried to kill me!"

My nostrils flared and I straightened my spine. Her giving me backtalk, especially when I just was handed the reins and allowed her to join the team, wasn't what I needed.

"He tried to kill all of us. We have a system here and when you're needed I'll be sure to let you know." I cut my eyes at her. "I don't know how you handled shit before, but I'm the boss now and you *will* follow what I say."

Her lips pressed together, her cheeks puffed, and her eyes flashed with anger.

"Bro acting like we didn't see her cut a dude's dick off and feed it to him," Ezra mumbled.

"What the fuck?" River choked.

I stood up so everyone understood me. "I want him caught and brought in before my party tonight. Have him tied up and we'll handle him tomorrow." I made eye contact with everyone, leaving my stare on Cashlynn so she knew I was serious.

"And on that note, that's enough business talk. We need to celebrate my baby turning thirty." Mom walked in the room, holding a cake, with Carson behind her.

There was more I wanted to say but I saw the determination in Mom's eyes. "That's it for now. Handle Victor and we'll take care of the rest later," I let everyone know.

I sat back down and moved my chair closer to Cashlynn, leaning in so my mouth was at her ear.

"Try to undermine me again in front of everyone and me attempting to drown you won't be the only problem you have."

She snatched her head back and glared at me. Her hand twitched on the arm of the chair.

Winking at her, I gave my family my attention. Cashlynn had to learn I was the king of this castle and if she didn't fall in line, I had no problem showing her.

Getting off the elevator, I stepped onto my second floor and headed toward the room Cashlynn currently slept in. For a second I stared at the door. After we got home from the meeting, she didn't say much, mostly spoke to Carson before leaving. When I tracked her, I saw she went to the shooting range at my other house. Since learning I had one, she spent a good amount of time there. She must have not known we had one at the barn she could've used. I knew she wanted to make whoever shot at us pay, and so did I, but I also knew that wasn't a random shooting and it had to be more to the picture. I grabbed the doorknob and turned it, opening the door.

When I stepped in the room, she paused before spinning around and glaring at me. "I need to start locking the door." I grinned and gave her a onceover. The outfits my shopper picked out for the two of us complemented each other well. She wore a one shoulder mini dress with a structed drape detailing that stopped right at the top of her thighs. The blood red color looked good against her light brown skin. I wore a black Amiri polo and camel colored Hollywood trousers with white pockets.

"You look good in red." I licked my lips, taking her in one last time.

She huffed. "I don't know why that lady keeps buying me heels. I can't even walk in them." She rolled her eyes, sitting on her bed and taking the gold heels out of the box next to her, examining them.

Walking over to her, I kneeled, being careful not to crease my pants, and grabbed the shoes from her.

"About time you learn then, huh?" I grabbed one of her feet to put the heel on.

Again, she rolled her eyes. "Are you gonna take this off my neck? I think it's clear I'm not gonna run away."

My eyes flickered up to the collar on her neck. "Now why would I do that?" Finishing strapping the shoe, I ran my hand up her calf slowly, causing her to shiver. A smirk formed on my face.

"Maybe because I'm not a dog." Her voice came out strained and breathless.

"No but you got some bite to you though." I switched feet and reached for the other heel.

Cashlynn cleared her throat. "You know one reason I hate dresses is because there's less material to hide my weapons." My hand paused for a second. Again I flicked my eyes up. Cashlynn was used to being in fight mode. Even now she would briefly let her guard down before shooting it back up. I had a feeling it had to do with her parents. Even with Emmet's research, I still knew little about their relationship. Although from what I'd heard Cashlynn mention, I had an idea.

"Looks like you'll have to trust me to keep you safe if something goes wrong then."

She narrowed her eyes at me, but didn't respond. When I finished putting her shoe on, I stood and towered over her. My hand went out and brushed over the collar on her neck, grazing the cool heart lock.

"You ready to talk about the other night?" My finger slipped in the circle connecting the collar.

"What about it?"

"You climbed in my bed, which I'm not complaining about. It's about time we make adjustments with this sleeping arrangement anyways. I've been too lenient with you."

"Why have you? I mean you forced me into everything else. Why not your bed?"

"I've never had to force a woman in my bed before and I'm not starting now. Believe it or not, women would kill to be in your position.

Sometimes I wonder if I need to make that happen, find a concubine to occupy my bed at night since my wife continues to neglects me."

Her eyes cut into slits. She reached up and smacked my hand away from her. "The day that happens you better hope you had the best orgasm of your life because it'll be your last."

I chuckled at the deadliness in her voice, stepped back, and stuck my hands in my pockets.

One corner of my mouth ticked up. "Careful, Wildfire. I might think you actually care about me."

"I just won't tolerate being made a fool of or disrespected. I've killed for less." Her eyes turned cold.

I wasn't sure if she thought that was supposed to do something to me, but all it did was turn me on. Blood shot down to my dick.

"And as for the other night, it's no big deal. I don't like thunderstorms. A lot of people don't." She stood up and went to walk past me but I grabbed her.

"That's not good enough. That wasn't a normal fear." Her nostrils flared and she licked her lips. "It is my birthday; you really can't say no to me."

For a moment she stared at me without saying anything before pushing out a deep breath. "My parents used storms as a way to punish and keep me in line to make me stronger, they said. It started when I was six, it was storming out and they locked me in a shed overnight. Since then, I've hated them and I go back to that night." The way she spoke was as if she was revealing the weather forecast. Her voice was cool as a cucumber.

"The fuck." My eyes widened and my brows shot to my hairline. I didn't know what I expected her to say but that wasn't it.

She snatched away from me and turned, heading in the direction of the bathroom. Digging into my back pocket, I checked the time. My parents were throwing me a thirtieth birthday dinner. They'd rented out the private room at one of the high-end restaurants downtown. Afterwards, I would be celebrating at The District. Tonight was officially a new era in my life

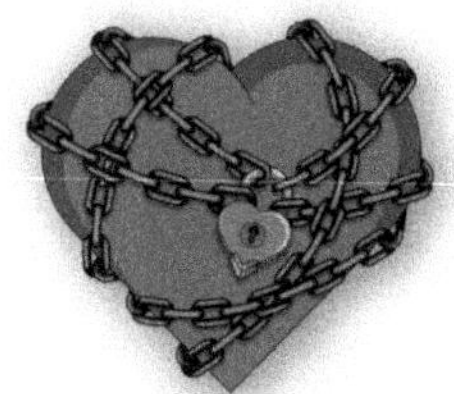

My party was in full swing. The District and Euphoria were maxed out to capacity. I had a full supply of drugs delivered before we opened to make sure we were fully stocked. We started down in The District, but once it started to fill up we went upstairs. I knew Cashlynn didn't care to be in large crowds and there was more space upstairs.

It felt good seeing the fruits of my labor. Starting this club put a strain between me and my dad at first. I built it from the ground up and even though the Tavarez family name helped it grow as quickly as it did, I put the footwork in to make sure it stayed running and successful.

"Are you sure you switched the pills?" I asked Lucas as we stood in the owner section of Euphoria. My eyes were on Cashlynn who was nursing a drink while sitting on the couch.

Lucas side eyed me with his face turned upside down. "Are you questioning my medical expertise?"

"I'm just saying it's been a month and nothing."

"It takes time. Learn to be patient."

My tongue dragged across my bottom lip as I brought my glass to my mouth and slowly sipped from it.

I walked across the section to where Cashlynn was sitting and sat down, placing my hand on her leg.

"Having a good time?" I asked.

"It's your birthday. I should be asking you that."

I leaned over and brushed my nose along her jawline. "True, but it's my job to make sure my wife is taken care of."

"I'm fine. You can go enjoy yourself if you want."

Kissing her, I made my way up to her ear. "Are you gonna let me have my way with you, you know, since it's my birthday?"

She breathed softly and brought her glass to her mouth.

"If I say no, are you gonna get a concubine?" Sarcasm dripped from her voice.

I pulled back and looked at her with a smirk. "Careful, wife, your jealousy is showing."

She rolled her eyes, making me chuckle.

"Don't worry Wildfire, you're the only concubine I want." I moved in and pecked her lips.

"You two are sickeningly cute," Ezra shouted dramatically over the music, gaining my attention. I turned my head to look at him, seeing River and Emmet with him.

"Did you guys get it handled?"

"He's delivered and waiting," River said.

"And I gathered all the information on him," Emmet said.

I grinned and nodded. "Good." Giving my wife one last kiss, I stood up. "Now it's a muthafuckin' celebration!" I shouted and lifted my drink.

"That's what I'm talking about!" Ezra was already heading for the drinks on the table.

A couple of bottle girls came over with happy birthday sparklers and bottles of Cristal. A few of the girls came in to dance for my brothers and River. Emmet, like I expected, declined and sat to himself, nursing a drink. Ezra and River enjoyed the girls naked and dancing for them. Lucas had disappeared somewhere.

"We can't have tonight go by without celebrating the boss man on his big day! Nazai, come to the stage," Ian, the club manager, called out on the main stage.

I glanced up and smirked before heading out of the section. "Make sure you keep an eye on my wife. She doesn't leave the section without one of you," I told Jackson who stood guard along with Luke.

"Yes, sir." He nodded.

I walked through the crowd, people were cheering and calling out my name. Happy birthdays were yelled all around me. I had to admit this was one hell of a way to start this next chapter of my life.

I sat down in my seat with my eyes locked on the main stage as my husband was placed in a chair in the middle of it. I worked on my second drink, never taking my eyes off the stage.

"You got that look in your eye," Ezra said, sitting next to me.

"What look is that?"

"Like you want to attack. Don't try no shit here, Cashlynn. Nazai won't be happy."

Lifting the corner of my mouth, I took another drink of the liquor. "The fact that you believe I care about your brother being unhappy is comical."

"I think you do." He leaned back, folding his hands and placing them behind his head. The guy on stage, who I learned was the manager of the club from his speech, was currently singing my husband's praises. "It's obvious you've been through some shit, Cashlynn. Your feelings run deeper for my brother than you show. You keep a good mask on, but I'm a lawyer, seeing behind masks is my specialty."

I ignored him as he stood up and walked over to River. Lucas and Emmet had disappeared somewhere but I wasn't sure where.

Standing up, I stumbled slightly. Since I was still fairly new to drinking, it hit me quickly. Needing to release my bladder, I headed out of the section.

"Boss doesn't want you wandering around," Jackson stated.

"Bathroom!" I shouted over my shoulder, heading toward Nazai's office. I continued to drink the contents of my glass. I wasn't sure what it was, but it helped ease my nerves from being in such an open space.

Once upstairs, Jackson waited outside at the bottom of the stairs with the other guard while I went up into the bathroom.

I sighed in relief as I emptied my bladder. Now I knew what they meant when they said liquor went right through you. After finishing and washing my hands, I went to leave the bathroom but paused when I heard the door to the office open. There was muffled talking and I pressed my ear to the door to hear clearer.

"The information you gave me was invalid, Emmet…again," Lucas complained.

"I told you it was a long shot, Lucas. I appreciate your faith in me, but at this point you've got to accept you're chasing a ghost," Emmet said.

"She's out there; I know she is. Your job, like literal job, is to find people, yet you can't locate one girl!" Lucas raised his voice.

"It's been fifteen years, Lucas. I'm good but I'm not a damn miracle worker."

There was some mumbling I couldn't make out. "I need you to look harder, Emmet. I'm not giving up until I have answers." I had so many questions about who and what they were talking about. Nazai's brothers were still pretty much a mystery to me, each like a puzzle that needed to be pieced together correctly.

I reached for the doorknob and pushed the door open. Both stopped talking and darted their eyes to me. Not bothering to say anything to them, I walked to the glass windows. The two didn't stick around long, giving me the office to myself, which was fine with me. My focus went to the stage where a large birthday cake was now being wheeled out. My teeth sank into my bottom lip, when a topless girl jumped out of the cake, shaking her breasts in my husband's face. My jaw clenched. My pocket knife was tucked in the strapless bra I wore under my dress. I itched to grab it and take it across the girl's neck.

The crowd loved it all, cheering and clapping. I didn't know this Ian guy but he had just made my list.

Frustration filled me as once again I was consumed with jealousy I didn't ask for. I spun around and looked around the office. My eyes dropped to his desk. I walked over and pulled on the drawers. They were all locked besides one. A medium-sized bottle of liquor was inside.

Pulling it out, I saw it was barely used. I uncapped it and walked back to the glass mirror. My eyes narrowed as I watched the girl climb out of the cake and strut to Nazai. She grabbed his knees and leaned over. Her breasts shook in his face. The green eyed monster grew inside of me. I took a drink of the bottle, my face balling up as the warm liquid hit my tongue and burned going down.

There was a knock on the door but my eyes stayed locked on the stage. I didn't know what pissed me off more, the girl in front of my husband or the fact that I was jealous about the girl.

"Everything okay, Mrs. Tavarez?" Jackson said just as Nazai leaned up and whispered something in the girl's ear. My grip on the bottle grew tighter. A shocked expression formed on the girl's face but she quickly replaced it with a smile and nodded, pulling up.

When the girl walked off stage, I took one last drink of the bottle then turned around, placing it on the desk, not bothering to close it.

"I'm good." My words were slurred. My body suddenly felt too hot and my head was fuzzy as I pushed past him and headed down the steps. Stopping halfway, I leaned on the wall and closed my eyes, taking a couple of breaths. Sweat pooled on the back of my neck.

"Mrs. Tavarez."

"I'm fine!" My eyes snapped open and I continued down the steps. Luke led the way through the crowd while Jackson trailed the rear. Just as we got to the section, I was pulled on. Before I could think, I went into my breast and grabbed my knife, flicking it out.

"Whoa there, Wildfire. It's just me." Nazai chuckled.

I blinked a couple of times, coming back into reality. My eyes narrowed and I didn't bother lowering my knife. The tip pressed against his neck. His grin grew.

"You think I won't do it?" I asked as my blood pumped wildly inside me.

His hand went to my wrist. I thought he was about to push it away but instead he pulled it closer with a drunken grin on his face. "Actually, I think the opposite." The knife punctured his skin.

"You two need to take this up to your office," River said, approaching us. We were right outside the section but I didn't care. I didn't care that there were loads of people around or half naked women dancing and serving drinks. Right now I had tunnel vision.

"Did you like that girl all over you?" I stepped closer, my voice menacing.

"If I did, I wouldn't have dismissed her." My knife dug deeper.

Blood trickled down his neck, coating the blade. The music around us seemed to suddenly disappear. My breathing sped up as adrenaline rushed through my veins.

Someone bumped into me from behind, causing me to stumble. My eyes bucked when the blade cut deeper into Nazai's neck than I intended. I always resharpened my knives after I used them so the steel blade easily sliced through his skin.

"What the hell did you do?" Lucas shouted. My hand was slapped down. My still wide eyes were now locked on the blood coming from Nazai's neck.

"Shit. Put pressure on it. Get me some napkins."

I was so focused on Nazai bleeding that I didn't notice someone approaching me from behind and a blade was now pressed against my neck.

"I don't care if you're his wife, you tried to kill my brother," Emmet growled lowly. The blade pushed against my skin.

My temples throbbed and I tightened my grip on my knife. Emmet didn't realize the mistake he just made.

Nazai narrowed his eyes at his brother, his hand cuffing the wound. "I love you, brother, but touch my wife again and you won't be performing surgeries for a long time." Then he faced me and Emmet. "Remove that blade from my wife's neck before it's a problem, Emmet." All playfulness had left his voice.

Lucas didn't look too bothered by his brother's threat. "Now isn't the time for threats." He hurried to add pressure to the wound.

"She tried to kill you," Emmet protested, knife still to my neck. "No one goes after my brothers."

"She wasn't gonna kill me, E. Everything's good. Take the knife from her neck. Now!" The last part came out in somewhat of a growl.

Emmet hesitated for a second and slowly removed the knife from my skin. I turned and glared at him, but he looked as unbothered as always.

"What the hell happened?" Ezra asked, coming out of nowhere.

"Our dear sister-in-law just tried to off our brother." He shot me a venomous look.

Nazai huffed out a laugh then winced. "She wasn't trying to kill me." Someone's tie was now being held to the wound.

Silently I shot my eyes to my knife. Blood still coated it. I still wasn't sure how to process how I felt right now. The ball of knots in my stomach refused to unravel. My heart hammered behind my breasts.

Too many things were swirling through my head, causing a murky storm of emotions to suddenly erupt.

"My bag's in my car, take him upstairs," Lucas demanded. Suddenly we were being rushed in the direction of the office I had just come out of. It seemed everyone was too lost in their own world to notice anything going on. My intentions weren't to cut Nazai, but after replaying him and the girl on stage over in my mind, I didn't feel bad about it either.

Turns out the knife went deeper than I expected. Lucas ended up adding eight stitches to Nazai's neck. Nazai had spare clothes in his office for whatever reason and decided to stay while I caught a ride home. I thought he would protest but instead he made Luke go with me and Devin drove us. He didn't say much in the office either, just stared at me as Lucas stitched him up. He dismissed everyone but the three of us and River. I could tell Emmet still wasn't happy about what had happened and even Ezra was side eyeing me. I was used to watching my back and being on guard, but I didn't like it in such an open setting.

When I got back to the penthouse, I dismissed the babysitter then checked on my brother. The effects of the liquor still had me somewhat fuzzy, but my mind was all over the place trying to understand what had happened earlier, so I grabbed a bottle of wine from the wine cellar and downed the majority of the bottle. Jealousy was a foreign feeling to me and I didn't know how to process or handle it. It scared me to know that in such a short time, I had developed enough feelings for my husband to want to physically harm someone else because of a lap dance at a strip club. It didn't make sense to me. I'd never cared about anyone else outside of my brother, not even our parents. I'd never felt the need to stake my claim or had the urge to literally slice someone's hands off for touching someone I deemed off limits.

Growing up, I wasn't impulsive; there were risks in what I did. Taking my time and not being sloppy was why I was great at what I did. Acting off emotions made you make mistakes and could get you caught. So tonight, when I snatched my knife out and brought it to Nazai's neck, it wasn't because I felt threatened or anything, it was solely because I wanted to harm him and the dancer who'd popped out that cake and that angered me.

I ended up finishing most of the bottle of wine and stumbled into the shower before retiring to bed. Since the night of the storm, I found myself in Nazai's bedroom. Usually I would start on the edge of the bed and at some point my body would gravitate toward him and I ended up tucked at his side. Cuddling and being able to sleep comfortably next to someone was new to me. My whole life was built around fight or flight, but those instincts seemed to be gone when Nazai came into the picture.

I passed out in a drunken slumber at some point. I wasn't sure when Nazai got in, but I faintly heard the doors open and close in his bedroom before drifting back off.

NAZAI TAVAREZ

CHAPTER TWENTY-THREE

When I got out of the shower Cashlynn was asleep, snoring lightly, laying on her back. Usually, she slept curled up in a ball as if she was trying to close herself off from the world, but tonight she was laid out with the covers only covering her lower half. I noted the bottle of nearly empty wine from the cellar I hardly ever used.

Smirking, I brushed my hand over the cut on my neck. I saw it in her eyes tonight, Cashlynn was acting off emotions, something I'd never seen from her before. Normally when I made her angry she snapped at me but never truly reacted in a way where I felt like she cared about what I did. Tonight though, she was acting like a pissed off woman. She normally closed her feelings off to anyone who wasn't her brother, but not tonight. No matter how good she had grown at masking her emotions, that all went out the window.

Wetting my lips, I skipped the briefs and headed to my side of the bed. Another thing, Cashlynn was growing more comfortable sleeping next to me. She tried to fight it, but since the night of the storm she always found her way close to me.

I went into my nightstand and grabbed the cuffs. They were long enough to give Cashlynn a little range, but still keep her secured.

Grinning, I crept on the bed and gently grabbed one of her hands, snapping the cuff around it and threading the other through the steel bars on my headboard before doing the same with her free hand.

I eyed her. The alcohol must have gotten to her because she wore nothing tonight, which was good news for me because I had plans for her. Since she'd put that knife to my neck, my dick had been hard, but I also knew I needed to punish her. What she did was reckless and shit could have gone left quickly. My brothers all wanted her head for cutting me, but I shut them down, especially Emmet. Many people let their guard down with him, but when pushed he was the deadliest of us all. Since he was silent most of the time, people never saw him coming.

Getting off the bed, I went to my walk-in closet and grabbed the bag I had tucked into the side. I thought it might take me a little more time to use this, but now it felt right.

Walking back to the bed, I went back into my nightstand and grabbed the blindfold, placing the bag on top of the stand and getting back on the bed. I eyed the front of her body. My hand brushed lightly over her breasts. She moaned softly and her body shifted when I thumbed her nipples. My mouth watered to taste the now hardened gum drops. Lowering my head, I flicked one with my tongue and sucked it in my mouth lightly.

Cashlynn shifted under me and I flicked my eyes up to see if she was awake, but her eyes were still closed. I moved to the other breast, quickly flicking my tongue back and forth over it. I grabbed the cover, pushing it down her body, happy to see she didn't have on any panties either.

"Were you waiting for me, Wildfire?" I muttered against her skin, prying her legs open and brushing my fingers over her mound down her wet slit.

A sigh-like moan fell from her lips and her back arched slightly, thrusting her body into mine.

My dick grew harder knowing her body was responding to me like this.

Pulling up from her breast, I licked my lips, thumbing her clit and sliding my finger through her forming wetness. Cashlynn shifted and moaned, mumbling something I couldn't make out. I grinned when her body twitched and a needy sound fell from her lips.

"I'ma take care of you, don't worry." I leaned up and kissed her lips.

Before I could punish her, I needed to be inside her. I couldn't explain it, but whenever I saw Cashlynn show that murderous, spitfire side of her, I couldn't think of anything else but taking her where we were.

Removing my hands from between her legs, I brought them to my mouth, sucking her essence off them. I was tempted to taste her more, but that would have to wait.

"You been a bad girl, Wildfire," I muttered, grabbing her by the hips and turning her on the side. I positioned myself behind her. Grabbing my dick, I positioned it at her entrance. I gave a few shallow thrust, my tip teasing her entrance.

"Wildfire," I whispered in her ear, kissing it. Wrapping an arm around her, I cuffed her breast and nipped her ear. A whimper fell from her mouth.

Her ass pushed back on my dick, taking more than what I was giving her. I kissed my way down her neck, kissing right under the collar. I pinched her nipples between my fingers and sucked on her skin.

"Nazai?" she moaned sleepily.

I pushed a little deeper inside her, loving how her snug walls hugged me. My teeth sank into her shoulder and she cried out when I fully sank into her. My strokes stayed slow as I moved in and out of her. Her pussy grew wetter.

"Wh-what you doing?" Her words dragged out with a moan.

I grinned against her skin. "Are you up now?" I kissed her shoulder. "You were a bad girl tonight, Wildfire. Cutting your husband, on his birthday, in the middle of his club." I sank my teeth into her skin again.

"Stop," she whined, pushing back against my thrusts. She went to move. "My hands."

Chuckling, I sped up my thrusts. "Oh I took care of them. You've done enough with them tonight."

"Release me!" She attempted to pull against the restraints.

"I don't think so. You're at my mercy tonight, wife." I twisted her nipples and tugged them.

"No, wait-oh!" Her head flopped to the side. Her pussy clenched around me and her body shook as she came.

"That's it. Give it to me, baby. Your pussy's been wet since I first touched it. Does being taken in your sleep when you're barely conscious turn you on?" She moaned and her body jerked again.

"I didn't know what you were doing."

"Didn't you, though? You were moaning and even pushed back on my dick when I was teasing you. Tell me, were you dreaming about me fucking you? Or do you just always want my dick in you now?" My strokes picked up, my pelvis slapped roughly against her ass.

"No, I-I don't know."

"You don't know? Admit it, you enjoy when I take advantage of you, don't you? If you didn't, you wouldn't be leaking for me." I nipped the nape of her neck above the collar. "Just tell me to stop, and mean it, and I'll pull out."

Cashlynn twisted her neck as best as she could and looked at me. Her eyes were dilated and burning with lust. She licked her lips before parting them. Her eyes rolled to the back of her head and her body shook as I reangled my hips and pushed deeply into her tunnel.

I moved in and pecked her lips. "You know what the perfect gift for me would be?" I made sure to keep my eyes locked on hers.

Abruptly, I stopped moving and pulled out of her. I released her body before flipping her on her back. I grabbed a couple of pillows, stacking them, then pulled her up slightly, giving her head a little height.

Hovering over her with one of my knees bent and my feet planted on the bed, I grabbed her by the hair, forcing her to snap her surprised eyes up at me. "Open that pretty mouth for me, Wildfire." My grip tightened on her hair.

Her eyes cut into slits and dropped to where my dick was now in front of her face. "C'mon, be a good girl."

Slowly her mouth opened and her eyes lifted again. Lifting the corners of my mouth, I slid inside. At first her lips wrapped around my dick and I felt her tongue on my tip. My nostrils flared.

Not bothering letting her do it herself, I yanked her head forward until her face met my pelvis. She gagged and choked, but that was like music to my ears. I didn't slow down, loving how wet her mouth grew as I fucked her throat. Her eyes watered and tears silently fell down her cheeks. I met the movement of her head, thrusting my hips forward.

Every so often I would hold her head in place until she choked and struggled to get free, restricting her oxygen. My blood hummed and sped through my veins. My heart thundered inside of me. Clenching my jaw, the tears coming down her face caused a dark desire to twist and intertwine inside me.

"I love seeing your tears while you choke on my dick. Something about you being helpless under me brings me joy." I grinned, causing her watering eyes to narrow. "I bet if I touched your pussy you'd be even more soaked than before, huh? You like to fight me, but you like when I use you too." Her mouth grew wetter.

This whole time I had been controlling the pace and movements of her head. When I was lax, her tongue would slide around my dick. When I pushed too far, she would attempt to fight it, causing her to choke more. It was *a beautiful sight.*

"Ready to catch my seeds, baby?" I asked just as I came.

"Shit." My head went back and I pushed deeper into her mouth. She bucked under my body and yanked on the chains, choking and sputtering around my dick.

I pushed out a heavy breath, lowered my eyes back to her, and slowly pulled out her mouth. Her cheeks were flushed and her lips a swollen mess. Holding my dick, I brushed it over her lips.

"Lick," I commanded. Her eyes beamed with anger, but she was also turned on. Her tongue poked out and she circled my tip with it.

Grinning, I nodded. "Good girl. Although I like your fight, I love you being compliant too."

Her nostrils flared.

Moving off her, I stared at the mess that formed. My cum dripped from her mouth and some ran down her chin.

Reaching up, I cuffed some and rubbed it in her skin. "I got one more thing that'll make me happy."

"No, release me," she rasped, pulling roughly.

I shook my head. "You're gonna hurt your wrists if you keep doing that."

"Nazai!"

Ignoring her, I moved to pull the blindfold over her eyes. "What the hell!" she shrieked. "Nazai, let me go now!" Her voice held a slight panic. It caused my blood to pump more.

I leaned over and grabbed the bag I had set down in the beginning. Knowing Cashlynn, she was gonna be pissed with what I had planned, but that was a bridge I'd cross when we got there.

"You know my brothers wanted to kill you tonight, right?" I slapped one of her breasts, causing her to wince.

"I'd like to see them try," she gritted.

I grinned. "Emmet would have if I didn't call him off." I eyed her breast that was now red with my handprint.

"I doubt he would have with all those witnesses. By the time they tried to move me, I would have taken him down."

Her cockiness made my dick stir again. If I didn't know my brothers, I would have believed her. Cashlynn was good at what she did; I could tell she was groomed for it and well-taught.

"You cut me in front of everyone."

"You know that wasn't on purpose."

Digging into the bag, I grabbed an alcohol wipe and used my teeth to rip it open.

"Do I? I saw it in your eyes, you wanted to hurt me." I wiped the nipple closer to me.

"What is that? What are you doing?" She panicked, yanking her hands.

"Don't worry about it. Focus on what I just asked. You wanted to hurt me, didn't you?"

"If I wanted to hurt you, I would have done worse than nip your neck."

I shook my head and huffed out a laugh. Grabbing the sterile needle, I fondled her nipple, causing it to grow harder. I got the jewelry and needle ready.

"Funny thing is I believe you, but still… something about tonight was different." I leaned forward, aiming carefully. "You were upset tonight and I want to know why."

"No I—what the hell!" she shrieked as the needle pierced her nipple. Her body jerked and my smile widened.

"Perfect." I admired her, pushing the bar through and twisting the end on.

"Nazai, let me go. Now!" Her voice trembled. She twisted her legs and her belly trembled.

"Careful, you don't want me to mess up." I moved to the other breast, repeating the same steps as before.

"I never told you, you could do this!" Her voice grew louder.

"You're my wife. That means your body is mine. Plus I'm sure you just came when I did the first one."

"Fuck!" she cried as I pushed the needle through the second nipple. It came out as a moan. Her hands clenched tightly.

When I was finished, I lifted and my dick was back hard now seeing my initials on each side of her nipples. Gently, I wiped the blood already forming. From the research and videos I watched, I knew it would be a little bit before I could play with them again, but I could live with it, for now.

Tossing everything back into the bag, I tossed it on the floor before getting back between her legs. I kept her blindfolded as I pushed inside her.

"Nazai," she hissed and tossed her head back.

"You've been the perfect present tonight, Wildfire. Just the way I pictured ending my birthday," I grunted, pumping in and out of her. Just as I thought, she was wetter. Her juices sloshing around as I moved caused me to go faster.

It was clear she didn't know how to react. I would imagine her body was floating on a bunch of emotions. I eyed her now pierced nipples and licked my lips.

Grabbing her by the thighs I lifted them and held them in place, watching my dick move. My next order of business was getting my wife pregnant. She claimed she wasn't ready for kids but the agreement we had said otherwise. Determination filled me.

"You ready to have my baby, Cashlynn?" I asked.

"What?" she sputtered.

Releasing one thigh, I reached up, snatching the blindfold off her eyes. They were unfocused and large. Tears clouded the lids.

"You ready to have my baby?" Quickly, she shook her head.

"No babies," she cried out, squeezing her eyes and balling her hands tightly.

One corner of my mouth ticked up. "That's what you say now. But what you gonna do once you're swollen with my seed?" Her breathing picked up.

"You're delusional."

Chuckling, I glanced down at her, open and receiving my dick. "I can show you better than I can tell you."

I pushed into her deeper. She continued moaning and clenching around me until I was releasing inside her and she was cumming around me.

Adrenaline still pumped inside me as I let her legs fall and slowly pulled out of her. She hissed. Her chest rose and fell quickly. Sweat covered both of our bodies.

Moving over, I reached in the nightstand to grab the key for the cuffs. Removing them, I rubbed the areas that were now red and slightly bruised.

"When I get back up, there'll be hell to pay," she panted with heavy eyes.

I chuckled and stood from the bed.

"Trust me, Wildfire. I was planning on it."

STOLEN MATRIMONY

CHAPTER TWENTY FOUR

I winced as my fingers grazed my nipples. They were swollen and finally free of the crusted blood caked on along the sides. The letters N and T were on each side, shining in what I assumed were real diamonds.

I pushed out a heavy breath and sank my teeth into my bottom lip. I should be furious that Nazai had taken it upon himself to pierce my nipples without my permission, but even I could admit how hot they looked. And when he did it, I came harder than I had since we started having sex. A shiver shot up my spine, speaking of sex. Between my legs was sore from the pounding and my lower lips were swollen as well. I was hazy in a drunken slumber when he snuck into bed and the last thing I expected was for him to fuck me awake. While I tried to be pissed off, I couldn't deny how good it felt too. A slight panic had flashed through me when I realized I was restrained and I felt his dick pushed at my entrance, but it didn't last long. A twisted sense of passion quickly replaced it. That panic quickly became exhilarating.

A bra was out of the question today, so I pulled my shirt down, examining the impression of the rings through the shirt I wore. Using the ponytail holder on my wrist, I pulled my hair into a bun at the top of my head and grabbed my black baseball cap, secured it on my head and hooked it around the bun. Satisfied, I turned to leave the bathroom.

My blood hummed in anticipation. The guy who had a hand in shooting at us had been captured and now we were headed to the barn to question him. I had been itching to get my hands on him since the shooting.

When I stepped out of the bathroom Nazai was standing at the end of the bed. His dark eyes found mine and his tongue went across his lips. My stomach flipped and filled with heat.

"You look like you're ready to kill." He smirked.

Rolling my eyes, I scoffed and went to the wall where my book bag was, picking it up and threading my arms through the straps. Turning around I faced Nazai and took him in. He too was dressed in all black.

"I'm ready to show why you don't fuck with Cashlynn Ca—Tavarez." I corrected myself at the last minute. It was the first time I had acknowledged my change in last name out loud. I could have kept my name after we married, but shedding that name felt like I was starting fresh and releasing a weight that had been bearing down on me. My brother was next for the change. Nazai's eyes flashed and his nostrils flared at my words. He stood straighter and rolled his shoulders back.

"Let's head out then." He held his hand out.

I stared at it for a second before making my way over to him and placing my hand in his.

"All you gotta do is tell us what we want to hear and this will be over faster," Nazai said, sitting in the chair in front of the guy they had secured in the middle of the room. All of the brothers, including River, were present when we got to the barn. The man's arms were chained above his head, while his feet were secured to the floor. His face was battered and bruised. Blood dripped from his nose and mouth. His exhaustion was clear.

"Fu-fu-fuck you," he spat, lowering his head.

Nazai smirked and nodded at River who hit the button. A buzzing sounded and Victor's body convulsed as electric currents went through his body from the attachments on his chest.

I brought my apple juice to my mouth, embracing the coolness invading my throat as my eyes settled on the guy. They had been working him over for the past twenty minutes but he was already roughed up before me and Nazai arrived.

"We can do this all day. Tell us who sent you after us," Nazai demanded. The man kept quiet. This time Nazai nodded at Ezra who grinned as he walked toward the guy with Wilma in hand. He pulled back before sending the hammer into the man's kneecaps. The sound of the impact filled my ears.

"Ah!" he bellowed. His body jerked and his legs attempted to buckle.

"Last chance."

Ezra went to repeat the motion.

"Wa-wait," he stammered. "Okay." Sluggishly, he lifted his head and made eye contact with me. "She was the t-t-target."

My blood ran cold and my eyes narrowed. I gripped the gun in my hand and lifted it, sending a shot, hitting him in the shoulder, causing him to yell out.

"What the fuck!" Ezra jumped back. "Your ass could've hit me!"

Ignoring him, I clenched my jaw and stalked toward him, ignoring the call of my husband, digging my glove-covered finger into the wound.

"Who sent you?" I gritted through clenched teeth.

The man screamed and attempted to move his body away. "Cashlynn!" Nazai called out, but again I ignored him. My ears were ringing and blood rushed through my body as my pulse raced. I dug my finger deeper.

"Rh-Rh-Rhodes!" he struggled out.

I snatched my finger from him just as my arm was yanked back.

"Don't touch me!" I snatched out of his hold, seeing red. My body shook with fury. The grip on my gun tightened.

"You need to calm down!"

"You guys weren't getting any damn were!"

"Why did they send you after Cashlynn?" This time it was Lucas talking.

I shifted my eyes over as he coughed. Blood poured from the wound

I'd just inflicted. His eyes were barely able to stay open and his head sagged.

"Hey, did you hear him?" I stepped next to Lucas.

"Bro, your wife is a menace," I heard Ezra utter.

Using the butt of my gun, I tapped it against his face.

"Revenge." He coughed blood. "Maddox stabbed." He coughed again. "He didn't forgive what you did."

My tongue dragged over my top teeth.

I turned and faced Nazai who had a hardened look on his face. He stalked past me and grabbed the guy, yanking his head up.

"Who was with you when you were shooting?"

The man attempted to shake his head. Taking a move out of my book, he pressed on the wound, causing the man to yell out.

"My cousins! Please," he cried.

"I got in his phone and have the names of the two guys he's referring to." Emmet spoke for the first time since I got here. I had been keeping my distance from him since I still wasn't feeling him holding the knife to my neck.

"Perfect." Before I could blink, Nazai went in the small of his back and put his gun to the guy's head. He attempted to plead his case but the bullet silenced him.

I spoke, causing Nazai's stoic glare to land on me. "I knew I should have killed both Neil and Maddox when I had the chance."

He stepped to me until he was towering over me. "Let's get one thing straight. I don't give a damn how badass you are. In here *I'm* the boss and you *will* follow my lead if you want to be a part of this."

My eyes narrowed. "I don't need you. I was handling things on my own before you."

Nazi lifted his clean hand and grabbed me by my bun, yanking my head, causing my knees to bend slightly. He stepped into me and my eyes widened feeling his semi bulge behind his slacks.

"You'll do what the fuck I tell you to do or I'll make you regret it. Don't fuck with me, Cashlynn, because it's a game you won't win." A low rumble sounded, causing my insides to scatter as if they had been electrocuted. He swiped his tongue across his lips. His eyes drooped. My breathing sped up as I swallowed hard.

"Bro, is this some kind of foreplay for you two?" Ezra questioned. "And sis, you could have warned me before you took that shot. What if you hit me?"

Blinking a couple times, I attempted to pull out of Nazai's reach, but his grip was too tight. "I never miss." I kept my eyes locked on Nazai. One corner of his mouth lifted and he lowered his face so his mouth was inches from mine. My hands balled into fists.

"Keep acting up and I'ma make you pay, Wildfire. My patience is running thin." He held my stare a little longer before releasing me, causing me to stumble back.

"River, I want eyes on Neil Rhodes. Any type of money he had coming in I want to shut down."

"What about Major?" River asked.

"I'll take care of Major."

"You know this all happened because you took on a debt that wasn't yours right," Lucas mentioned, causing me to cut my eyes at him.

"I never asked him to. I had the situation under control."

He gave me a deadpan look. "A quarter million dollar bounty on your head isn't under control."

"Enough!" Nazai shut us down, standing in between us. His eyes bounced from me to his brother. "I don't know what issue you have with my wife, but that shit ends now. I'ma make this clear to everyone in the room, disrespecting her is like disrespecting me."

"All this shit is because of her."

"Wrong. Maddox was a sick bitch who needed to be taken care of. He's been handled and now his daddy is next. Regardless of how you feel, they came for all of us when they shot up Dad's party. So know he's gotta pay."

He looked toward Ezra. "You and Emmet go handle the cousins. Make sure they know why they're losing their lives before you take them out. Me and Lucas will handle the cleanup."

"What about me? I—"

"You're gonna go sit over there and let us take care of this," he said, cutting me off.

I bit down on my back molars and inhaled a deep breath. I didn't like being dismissed. Part of me wanted to challenge him but instead I turned and stormed to where my bookbag was. Dropping my gun next to it, I snatched my gloves off and tossed them on the ground too. My muscles were tight and my body was wound tightly.

Pulling my ponytail out, I reached down, grabbed my things, and turned for the back of the barn to the steps that led to the shower room. No matter what, after a kill I always felt the need to shower. Today was no different. Nazai could throw his power around all he wanted, but at the end of the day, this was my fight to overcome.

The shower was nice, but it didn't relax my taut muscles. The fact that Neil had put another hit out on me caused rage to fill my body. The worst part was that he had put the hit out before even receiving parts of his son's body, meaning the threat Nazai gave fell on deaf ears.

When I got out of the shower, now dressed in a sweat suit, I noticed the barn was empty and Victor's body was gone. I looked around with my brows crinkled, wondering where everyone went that fast.

"Nazai!" I called out, getting met with silence. My lips pinched together and I started for the entrance when the lights went out, leaving me in a shadow of darkness. "Nazai!" I called out again, this time gripping the handle of my bag. "I swear to—" Before I could finish my words, the sound of thunder sounded through the barn, echoing off the walls, causing me to jump.

My heart slammed against my ribcage and my eyes bounced around the room. "Nazai." My voice was shaky. "This isn't funny." The sound of rain pouring sent an icy chill through my body just as the thunder rang out again. As far as I knew, it wasn't supposed to rain today, so I was confused about what was going on.

For a second, I froze. My body shook violently as my eyes bounced around the dark room. Hurriedly, I moved across the room until I got to the opening of the barn. My hand skated around it, attempting to find the door.

"C'mon. C'mon," I whined.

I couldn't breathe. My chest was too tight with anxiety. My lungs were barely able to function properly. My heartbeat elevated along with my pulse.

When the thunder went off again and something like a flash of lighting filled the barn, I yelled out and dropped to the ground. Squeezing my eyes shut, I balled my body up and curled my head into my lap. Memories of when I was younger and when my parents would trap me in the shed alone during storms burned in my mind. The way they would mock me and leave me without food and water caused my stomach to plummet. Tears pooled in the back of my eyes. Moving my balled fists to my ears, I squeezed them tightly. I tried to tell myself it would be okay as my breathing sped up and I rocked back and forth.

My stomach was a ball of knots, growing larger with each second. The rain seemed to pick up. It grew harder to breathe.

I wasn't sure how long I was stuck in that position, but when the door finally opened I was a mess. Tears ran down my face. My body was jerky.

The light from outside caused me to crack my eyes open and slowly lift them to find my husband standing in front of me. The clear sky hovered in the background.

"You look like you've seen a ghost, wife," he stated, crossing his arms over his chest.

Blinking rapidly I looked around, realizing the sounds had stopped as I slowly pulled my hands from my ears.

Heat flushed through my body. Slowly, on shaky legs, I lifted myself off the ground. My skin prickled and I grinded my teeth.

"Are you ready to respect me?"

With my breathing still heavy and my eyes cut into slits, I made my way to him. Squaring my shoulders, I pushed out a heavy breath and jolted my chin upward.

"Was that supposed to be your idea of a sick joke!" I bellowed, pushing him. "How could you? After I told you?" I babbled, unable to form a full sentence. My mind was a muddy mess and my body refused to stop shaking.

A hard unmoving expression was on Nazai's face. His eyes were void of emotion. He reached up and cuffed my chin, forcing my head to tilt upward. It pissed me off that even though I was upset and wanted to scream at him, Nazai's touch still caused my insides to melt and my body to relax. I welcomed his touch, no matter how I could get it. It was pathetic but I couldn't make my body reject it no matter how much I wanted.

"You need to learn who's in charge here. I'm the one with the dick in this marriage and I run things around here. If I have to break you until you figure that out, then so be it. You will learn to respect me one way or another."

The urge to fight flared in me. The fight and flight mode I had been trained in was determined to take over.

I went to pull away but Nazai was faster, releasing my chin and gripping the metal heart on my collar.

"Regardless of how hard your rebellion makes my dick, you, my wife, will learn to listen to me." He bent down and pressed his mouth against mine. My muscles quivered and my heart pounded. Opening my mouth, I took his bottom lip into my mouth and bit down roughly, causing Nazai to grunt. The taste of copper filled my mouth. His mouth curved into a smile.

When I released him, Nazai pulled back and flashed me a crooked grin after flickering his tongue over the blood on his lip.

"You making me bleed only makes my dick harder." He cocked his head to the side. "That fire inside you is hotter than ever, but you need to learn when to put it out."

For a second my eyes dropped to his center. My stomach did a somersault.

"Remember Cashlynn, I'm not your enemy unless you make me one." With that he turned to leave. I stood there frozen. I hadn't heard my real name fall from Nazai's lips in months, so I knew he was serious. My body was still rigid, and my breathing remained shaky as my tongue dragged over my now dry lips.

I closed my eyes and took a couple of deep breaths as I reminded myself that my parents were gone and storms couldn't hurt me, real or fake ones.

My eyes scanned the barn. It felt like the walls were closing in suddenly. I turned and hurried to grab my bag before rushing outside and inhaling the fresh air.

"You good, sis?" I jumped when Ezra grabbed my shoulder.

He lifted his hands in surrender. "You good?"

Instead of responding, I searched the yard, scanning the distance between the barn and house until I located Nazai who looked to be in a heated debate with Lucas while Emmet stood off to the side looking bored, fondling with his Rubik Cube.

When I approached them, both grew quiet and all faced me. "I'm ready to go home," I told him, ignoring the way both brothers were watching me. It was clear they weren't fans and the feeling was mutual.

"We'll finish this later," Nazai told Lucas and looked at Emmet. "I want whoever runs that page's information. Everything else takes second until we find out who it is." He narrowed his eyes. Lucas clenched his jaw.

I didn't know what that was all about and at the moment I didn't care. My head was in a bad place. Between learning the Rhodes were still after me and Nazai's twisted "punishment", I needed some time to regather myself before I snapped.

"**B**ro, I think you fucked up. Did you see how she was looking at you?" Ezra uttered as we watched Cashlynn make her way to my car. My eyes narrowed.

"Don't worry about my wife. I have everything under control." I waved him off.

I had speakers set up in the barn and connected my phone to put the thunderstorm sounds on. Since the barn lacked windows, the door being closed and turning the lights off caused it to go pitch black. Cashlynn needed to learn her actions had consequences. Regardless of how sexy I felt they might be, sometimes she needed to be knocked down a notch.

"You need to get a handle on her, Nazai. She's a loose cannon. Even bigger than Ezra," Lucas commented.

"What's that supposed to mean?" Our younger brother turned and stared at him with a bewildered expression.

"Sometimes you can be impulsive and ignore reasoning."

"Cashlynn isn't like that," I protested.

"She stabbed you last night." Lucas added.

A smirk formed on my face. "She didn't mean it. Cashlynn's bark is worse than her bite…most of the time."

"She could have shot Ezra today."

"Trust me, if my wife wanted to shoot him, she would have. I've seen her targets at the range and she's a great shot." Since she used the gun range at my house often, it wasn't hard to peek in on her and watch her. Cashlynn had a shot that almost came close to mine.

Lucas narrowed his eyes on me. "You're letting her get away with too much shit. If you don't get her under control, she'll fuck everything up. You think scaring her is gonna make her fall in line."

"I don't need you to tell me how to deal with my wife. My marriage is none of your concern."

Lucas stepped closer to me. "When your wife is irrational and it could affect the family, then it is my concern. Her recklessness might turn you on but not the rest of us. Now we're in a damn war because of her. Before you brought her in, the family didn't have these issues. She's gonna be our downfall."

I squared my shoulders and clenched my jaw. "If I remember correctly, I was put in charge of the family business so I'll handle things how I see fit. Anyone who poses a threat to my wife will be taken care of. Neil Rhodes made an enemy of us the moment he disobeyed my orders and came after us."

"I'm not gonna let that woman and her bullshit ruin everything we've built. Dad would have never let this happen."

"Dad isn't in charge anymore. I am."

"A'right y'all chill. This isn't even us." Ezra stepped up, bouncing his eyes between us.

"Lucas, enemies come with the territory. Even when Dad was in charge we had them because of who he was and people unhappy with some of his rulings. Shit happens. As long as we show them the Tavarezes aren't the ones to fuck with, we're good."

For once Ezra's point made sense. There was a reason he took after our dad with law, he was logical when need be.

"If you don't need me for anything else, I have a separate case I need to take care of," Emmet cut in. My youngest brother was always so quiet that at times I forgot he was there. He looked toward Ezra. "I'm gonna find out about the two cousins so we can take care of them."

Ezra nodded. "I gotta head to the office and meet with a new client anyway. Can you two get over your shit?" He looked between me and

Lucas.

The two of us stood in a stare off.

"I'm picking up a shift at the hospital tonight. Try not to get yourself killed by your wife in the meantime." Lucas waved Ezra off before turning to leave.

I gritted my teeth. While I understood Lucas's point, I didn't like being questioned.

"Let me know when you two take care of everything. Emmet, send me some cases that's been submitted." Since I was in charge now it was up to me to choose the jobs we took on. Business didn't stop because someone was dumb enough to come after us. My dad, his dad, and my great grandfather had built The Bloodline to what it was today and I didn't plan on ruining the legacy they'd created.

I turned and headed for my car. When I opened the door and climbed in, I looked over at Cashlynn seeing her head rested against the window while she snored lowly. I took a second to study her, the way her body curled into itself, yet her face was relaxed.

Today, as well as the other night, I'd seen true fear in Cashlynn's eyes. It was the only time she seemed human to me and allowed herself to be vulnerable enough to show her emotions. While I liked her fire, I realized I *loved* seeing that needy state within her more. She didn't need it, but it caused an urgency inside me to protect her because she was *mine*. Every time she showed a crack in that hard exterior, I found myself being more drawn to her. Her problems and fears became my own and that was what my brother failed to realize.

I studied the recent drawing I had done of Cashlynn while tapping my charcoal pencil against my sketchpad. A lot of the time when I pulled my sketchpad out, I let my imagination run wild, but Cashlynn had been my muse and my obsession. No matter how much I attempted to draw something new. I cocked my head and tucked my bottom lip between my teeth. The tears that were running down her face took me back to the other day at the barn. It had been three days since then and Cashlynn had been keeping her distance from me. She stayed locked in her room and didn't even come to my bed to sleep anymore. I let her wallow in her feelings for now while staying alert. My wife was spiteful. I knew that much, but she had yet to strike or counter what I did.

I checked the time and realized I had been lost in my sketch for the past hour. It wasn't finished. No, it seemed like every sketch I made of Cashlynn was missing something I couldn't pinpoint, but was determined to complete.

Closing my book, I set it and my pencil on my nightstand before kicking my feet over the bed and walking over to my closet to get dressed. Today I was taking Carson out for another training session. We were working on self-defense techniques. Eventually I wanted to take him to the range at my other house and get some shooting practice in. Carson might not be a killer like his sister, but his instincts were there, and he was smart too.

I looked around my walk-in closet, walking to the side that housed my lounging clothes. Grabbing the olive-green sweatsuit, I quickly changed and grabbed my black and green tennis shoes off the back wall before heading out.

Taking the elevator to the second floor, I first entered the room Cashlynn was staying in. I wasn't even sure if she noticed but I had been slowly moving her things upstairs into my room. After sleeping next to her there was no way I was gonna keep allowing her out of my bed. She had accumulated a nice amount of things at my expense since being here.

When I opened the door, I saw she was laying with her eyes closed on her bed and her wireless headphones over her ears. I knew she was meditating. It made me wonder if this is what she'd been locked in her room doing the past three days.

Deciding to leave her alone, I left and walked down to where I knew Carson would be, in the game room.

"You ready to go?" I called out, causing him to pause his game. He turned his head toward the door and faced me.

He blinked slowly. "Oh, yeah. I just gotta save this game." He faced the TV on the wall.

"Meet me downstairs." I turned to leave.

Pulling my phone out, I texted Devin to make sure he was waiting at the door for us then shot a text to Jackson to be on standby if my wife decided to leave. As much as I didn't want to agree with him, Lucas wasn't wrong, Cashlynn could be reckless, especially when her emotions were running high. My tracker could only do so much; I needed eyes on her at all times.

"What are we doing today?" Carson questioned when we got downstairs.

I glanced at him and smirked. "You'll see."

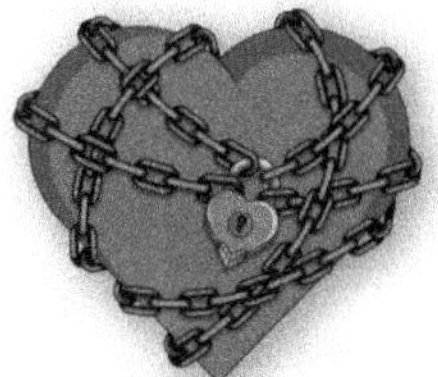

"Ow!" Carson cried out as I applied pressure to his wrist.

"C'mon, remember what I taught you. What do you do if someone grabs you like this? Focus!"

"You're grabbing me too tight," he gritted.

"You think someone coming after you is gonna give a fuck about grabbing you too tight? Their main objective is to hurt you. Now what do you do in this position?"

He glared at me and pinched his lips together. "Ah!" he yelled, rotating his wrist, then yanking his arm toward him. Pressure formed on my thumb causing me to release him. I lifted one corner of my mouth.

"Good, that was good. Now." I hurried around him and grabbed him in a chokehold. "What about now?"

I wanted Carson to learn how to protect himself without and with using a weapon. It was how my dad taught me and my brothers. In his words, you won't always have access to a weapon and if your hands didn't get the job done then you were finished.

Carson was tall for his age, I was six two and he was just below my chest. From what I remember from pictures I'd seen in the past, his dad was tall and it was clear he took after him. He was a lean kid though, one thing he needed to work on also was building muscle. He struggled under my hold at first, flailing his arms and attempting to wiggle his way out of my grip.

"All you're gonna do is tired yourself out," I grunted, tightening my hold.

Carson had the same fight and flight sense his sister did. I could tell he had some training, but instead of fighting like Cashlynn was accustomed to, he chose the flight method. He'd never had to learn to stand up on his own and face his own battles.

"You're a smart kid, Carson, but when put in a position to defend yourself, you shut down and panic. Keep your cool and eliminate the threat," I coached.

It took a couple minutes for Carson to calm down. His breathing grew heavier.

One of his hands came back, striking me in the face, before his leg shifted into mine, causing me to lose balance and fall back. I was proud of the move. What caught me off guard was when he pulled a knife out of his pocket and put it to my neck, close to where the stitches were.

I grinned.

"Looks like your sister isn't the only one who enjoys a knife as the weapon of choice."

"She told me to always be prepared and never leave home without it."

Nodding, I pushed myself up when he removed the knife. "Good advice, you never know how things will turn out. When it comes to a threat, take them out before they can get you, by any means necessary."

I ran my hand over my head and looked around my basement. The room I'd had his sister locked in was next door. This one I often used for training when I stayed here.

"A'right. Enough of that, let's put the gloves on," I stated and moved to the shelves on the wall. I wasn't sparing Carson. I was determined to toughen him.

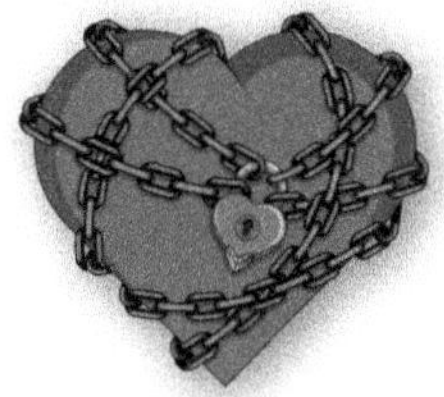

"Where are we?" Carson asked as we climbed out of the back of the truck.

"My brother Emmet's office," I announced as we walked toward the single door. We were done with training for the day. Over time Carson had got more comfortable and more fluid with his movements. He liked to think of himself as weak and when I first met him, I thought the same thing. But after working with him a few times before and then today, I learned he was far from weak. A little timid but it was clear he was trained the same as his sister. His movements were quick and persistent; he just lacked confidence.

An uncertain look flashed on his face. He looked around hesitantly. "Why are we here?"

Pausing, I looked down at my brother-in-law. "Many people underestimate Emmet because he's smart and quiet. He doesn't say much, instead he sits back and observes those around him. I haven't seen a security system or computer he can't hack." I glanced toward the building and tilted my head to the side, observing it. It was a single floor, metal, industrial-style building. The faint smell of salt water and fish from the shipyard not too far up the street filled my nose via the light breeze. The faint sound of a ship's horn sounded.

I looked back at Carson with a serious expression. "What people don't know is Emmet is probably the deadliest of us all." Carson's eyes widened. He knew what went on around him so there was no need to sugarcoat anything. "Many people thought it was Ezra because he was loud and loved to torture and play games with his victims, but in reality, Emmet is the one I wouldn't want to meet in an dark alley. Normally he stayed back, unless it was necessary. After me he had the best shot out of all of us. You remind me a lot of my brother, maybe not as intelligent, but when it comes to your instincts I can see the kill drive inside of you."

Not bothering to wait for Carson's reply, I continued toward the building. We walked down the small hall that led to the back where Emmet's office was. Pushing the door open, I stepped inside, and just as I expected Emmet, was hidden behind the multiple monitors on his desk.

"E!" I called out to gain his attention. Most of the time he got so lost in what he was doing that he tuned out everything else around him. "Emmet!" It took a few seconds but Emmet soon popped his head around the monitors.

"I need to talk to you." He stared at me with a blank face. He shifted his attention to Carson briefly before dismissing him and gazing back at me.

"What are you doing here?" he questioned.

"I need a favor." I walked to his desk. I waved for Carson to follow me.

"What?"

"Let Carson shadow you today."

Emmet's brows furrowed. "Why would I do that?"

"He's good with computers and I think he can be an asset, just needs the right training. You're tech savvy and—"

"I'm not a teacher."

One corner of my mouth lifted. "No, but I'm sure you can still teach him a few things. Even if it's with your PI stuff. Cashlynn mentioned he liked mystery stuff, right kid?" I glanced at Carson who seemed surprised I addressed him. He bobbed his head and examined the room.

"Yeah, it's my favorite."

"See. Let him work with you."

"I don't like working with people."

I huffed out a breath. Emmet had always been a loner. Usually when he did partner work it was with Ezra, besides that, if we weren't working as a group, he did things alone.

"Emmet, do me this solid a'right. The kid has skills, but he needs fine tuning. I don't know anyone smarter than you."

Emmet's blank stare went back to Carson. Carson averted his stare and shifted his body weight. He still wasn't as confident as I would like, but dealing with Emmet I didn't blame him. My baby brother's eyes were often calm, yet cold and unwelcoming. When he stared at someone like he was Carson right now, it was as if he was peering into their soul or looking through them.

"Fine. Whatever." He waved me off. His eyes narrowed. "I don't like fuck ups. You'll do what I say and don't get in my way.," Emmet uttered.

"Uh, yeah okay." Carson stammered and nodded.

I grinned. "You're in good hands with Emmet."

"Wait, you're leaving?" Carson's brows shot up to his hairline.

I pulled my phone out and clicked it a couple times, pulling up the tracking app I had in Cashlynn's collar.

"Yeah, I have other things to take care of." Seeing where Cashlynn was, I smirked and locked my phone back.

"This is for you too." Emmet grabbed a folder and a sheet fell on the floor in the process.

I went to pick it up and paused, noticing it was a digital photo.

"What's this?" I examined the picture with furrowed brows.

"Nothing, Here. It's the information on Neil." He went to grab the paper in exchange for the folder but I pulled the sheet back.

I squinted and my mouth parted. "Is this Adrian?" She looked older in the picture, but I could still see traces of the thirteen-year-old, mainly the distinguishable birthmark going through her right eye. "How did you get this?"

"It's a digitally modified photo of what she could potentially look like now." He snatched the paper from me.

My mood grew serious. "Emmet, I told you, you need to stop enabling him. Did you show this to Lucas?"

"He brought it to me." He thrusted the folder my way.

I sighed and grabbed the folder. "This shit's getting outta hand." I shook my head.

"If he wants to believe she's out there, then who are we to ruin it," he said. "Kid, grab a chair and sit down."

Carson jumped and quickly did as he said.

I wanted to say more, but Emmet wasn't the one I needed to talk with. This obsession Lucas had been locked into had gone on long enough.

"Take care of him," I said and turned to leave. "I'll be calling a meeting soon."

Emmet grunted in response.

I left his office and headed down the small hall that led to the entrance. Devin was waiting at the truck for me when I approached. My parents allowed Lucas to continue this search for a ghost because they didn't see it as harmful, but I was ready to nip it in the bud. It was time for my brother to move on with his life and I planned to make sure he did.

251

CHAPTER TWENTY SIX

I reloaded my gun and lifted my arms to aim at the target in front of me. Too much tension was building inside of me and I needed to release it. I thought about reaching out to my handler for a job, but instead I came to Nazai's other house and decided to use the shooting range he had built in the backyard.

For the past couple of days I'd been thinking about my childhood and growing up with my parents. Their parenting was unorthodox but it did help me become who I was today. I wouldn't be as strong as I was if they hadn't pushed me. I hated my parents and what they did to me growing up, but at the same time I appreciated them for helping me become who I was.

Movement from the corner of my eye caused my hand to freeze on the trigger for a second before pressing it and sending the bullet into the target. I lowered the handgun and removed one side of the headphones off my ear. I twisted my body to face Nazai who stood there watching me. His eyes shifted to the target, taking in where I hit, then back to me.

"You're a good shot," he noted.

My face stayed deadpan as I stared at him. "Why are you here?" I didn't have to ask how he knew where I was, either Jackson or this collar told him.

He smirked. "If I remember correctly, this is my house and my range. Am I not welcome here anytime I want?" His head tilted to the right with bewilderedness in his eyes.

I bit the inside of my cheek and rolled my eyes, turning to face the target again. "Whatever." I paused. "Wait, where's my brother?" My eyes narrowed.

"With Emmet." Nazai pulled a gun out of the small of his back.

My heart fell into my stomach and blood rushed through my head. "Emmet? Why the hell is he with that psycho? Are you out of your mind?" I went to rush past him but he caught my arm.

"He's good." His face grew serious.

"No he's not. Your brother hates me for one and if he does something to Carson I'll—"

"He's not gonna hurt the kid. Your brother is tougher than both you and him give him credit for."

"He's not like us!" I gritted. My muscles grew tighter. "He's not a killer nor is he meant to do what we do!"

"Carson might not be useful in the field, but he isn't useless. He has quick reflexes and he picks up on things quickly. Besides that, the kid is smart. All he needs is the proper training and he'll be a great asset."

I scoffed. "Asset. I hate that fucking word."

I turned toward the target and lifted my gun, aiming and pressing the trigger.

"It's clear your parents implemented skills in you that make you as talented as you are. The Queen of Hearts is well known for her flawless and clean kills. You don't learn that overnight. I don't know if your brother didn't learn it because he wasn't old enough but—"

"My parents were sadistic, sick, narcissistic assholes who didn't give a fuck about anyone but themselves. I could handle their fucked up ways but Carson was never built for it. They hated it and him for that fact." I faced the target and studied it. For the most part I had hit the center, only missing a handful of times.

"Your brother is obviously smart. They didn't care about that?"

I huffed out a laugh and rolled my shoulders back. "Carson learned how to code at eight years old from videos online. He's always been into gaming and his dream was to create his own video game one day.

My parents said it was a waste of time and became angry because he'd rather sit in front of a video game or computer instead of going out and putting a bullet through someone's skull." Lifting my arm, I pressed the trigger, not bothering to aim this time. "They saw my brother as weak, useless, and worthless, so they ignored him and wrote him off." Again, I shot my gun before turning back to face Nazai.

"I won't allow anyone else to make him feel like that. So whatever sick joke you and your brother have going on won't end well. Carson might not be built for the field but he's a good kid and doesn't deserve to be treated like less than because of that."

My grip tightened on the gun and I clenched my jaw. My stomach churned thinking about all the things I endured to take the pressure off my brother. It didn't bother me that I never got a hug or praise from them growing up, I learned at a young age to accept it. Carson wasn't easily able to write it off. He wanted what every young kid did, his parents' love, and tried hard to earn it. My parents thought it was funny and taunted him for it, claiming they were toughening him up, that was when I stepped in.

"That's not what this is. Carson came to me wanting to train and get stronger. As I said before, he's stronger than any of us thought and he picks up on things quickly. Emmet doesn't bat an eye when it comes to killing yes, but he only ever steps in when it's needed. We don't call him the silent assassin for no reason. He prefers to be behind a computer gathering intel for us. He's the perfect person for Carson to learn from."

Again, I chewed on the inside of my cheek. My muscles were twitchy. I didn't trust Emmet. He seemed to lack any human emotions and didn't say much. I had learned early on to trust my instincts and something about Emmet made me uneasy.

"My brother better be okay." I left it at that.

Husband and brother-in-law didn't mean a thing to me. If Carson was put in harm's way and hurt, I would slit both of their throats with a smile on my face.

I went to put my headphones back on but Nazai's chuckling caused me to halt.

"Wildfire, one day you're gonna learn to lower your guard and trust me."

"Maybe if you give me a reason to, I will," I spat, thinking back to the barn. I didn't open up easily, if ever, and Nazai using the time I had against me caused daggers to shoot into my chest. It made me angry, but even more, it hurt, sealing the locks that had been starting to crumble back into place.

Silently he watched me without blinking. His eyes scanned from my head down to my feet and back up again. He didn't respond, instead facing the wall and pressing the button next to him that brought the target closer to us.

"Your parents really fucked you up, huh?" I cut my eyes at him but didn't reply.

I didn't want to talk about my parents or what I went through with them. All I wanted was to continue shooting the target in peace like I had been. Nazai didn't grow up like I did. His parents spoiled and loved him. He might have been trained for the business but it didn't jade him or leave physical and mental scars on him. His family worked together to grow and become who they were. He would never understand the turmoil of having the ones who brought you into this world be your biggest bullies and tormentors.

"You're almost as good a shot as me."

I choked out a laugh and reached over to grab my apple juice. "My dad was the best shot I knew and I knocked him out of the water. When I say I don't miss, I mean it." I licked the remaining juice off my lips and set my bottle back down.

One corner of Nazai's mouth hiked up. "Is that right?" He studied my target sheet. "Care to wager?"

My eyes narrowed. "How?" This time his mouth lifted into a full smile. My stomach fluttered. Nazai had a beautiful smile, but I told myself not to trust it. He had different sides of himself. His smile might seem friendly, but there was a twisted side inside him that could flip on at any time.

"A full clip, fifteen rounds, and whoever hits the center the most wins."

I processed his words for a second. "Okay… I'll bite, if I win then what?"

"What do you want?" I studied Nazai. His dark eyes beamed with mischief and mirth.

"You have to pierce your dick."

Nazai's eyes bucked, and he sputtered. "What?"

This time my mouth lifted into a grin. "You heard me. Since you enjoy piercings so much then let's make it fair. If I win, you have to pierce your dick." I dropped my attention to his groin. The imprint could be seen behind the sweatpants he had on.

"Fuck." He laughed. "A'right, I'll bite. If I lose then I'll pierce my dick, but if I win you become my slave for twenty-four hours."

"Your slave?"

A playful grin formed on his face. "You heard me. For twenty-four hours you'll do what I want, when I want, without any complaint or fight from you."

I tapped my gun against my thigh. "You ever been told you're a control freak?"

He replaced the target sheets and hit the button to move them back. "Not confident enough in your skills?"

I snorted then turned forward. "Just don't chicken out when that needle comes into play." Grabbing my headphones, I placed them on my ears. If Nazai wanted to play, then I was game. Shopping was usually a hobby girls were into, but not me. I always enjoyed the way the sleek, heavy metal felt in my hand and feeling the kickback after I pulled the trigger. When I was younger, I spent a lot of time at the shooting range perfecting my shot. Nazai underestimated me, but he was about to learn his mistake for doubting me.

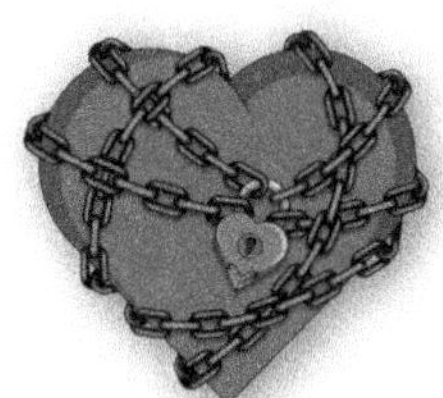

After leaving his other house and coming back to the penthouse, I showered and hid myself in my room while Nazai went and got my brother. I was still supposed to be upset with him after what he pulled at the barn, but today at his house I had fun with him. Nazai was competitive and a shit talker, but that wasn't what I enjoyed. Him enjoying shooting just as much as I did had me seeing him differently. The way he held his gun with confidence and how his arm flexed when he pulled the trigger was a turn on I didn't even realize I enjoyed seeing. He could handle a gun easily and it was clear that he had been trained properly. Nazai was an arrogant prick, but I respected that he knew his shit.

Nazai had dropped Carson off at the penthouse then left for the club. I didn't know if he was handling business or going there for pleasure, but I didn't bother to ask. My feelings for him were starting to confuse me. Normally the stunt he pulled would have had me putting a bullet through his eyes, but I didn't want to see him dead. Truthfully, the thought made my stomach turn. He proclaimed I needed to learn to trust him, but all I'd ever been able to count on was myself.

He did step up and help me get Maddox.

Squeezing my eyes closed, I pushed out a deep breath. My mind was twisted with uncertainty. He even had been spending time with my brother and Carson seemed to be comfortable around him. That didn't happen often. Carson had only ever been himself around me, but it seemed Nazai had found a way to break through that. Part of me felt like Nazai's actions were genuine, but at the same time I didn't know if his actions were all a ploy to make me bend to his will.

Stepping into the kitchen, I went to the fridge. I pulled it open, searching for something to drink, knowing I had to make a run to the store to get more apple juice. Lately I had been feeling thirstier than normal and had been consuming liquids, mainly apple juice, more than normal.

My nose scrunched seeing a full pack of apple juice right there on the center shelf. I picked up one of the bottles and examined it, seeing it was the same brand I always drank too. I knew I hadn't gone to the store to get any, so that left…

I shook my head. Nazai had an angle; I was sure of it. He did little things like this to draw me in and I didn't know why. We were married and he got his position in the family. I tried to stay out of his way. There was no reason for him to keep fucking with me unless it was a mental thing. From growing up, I knew mental manipulation well.

Carson had fallen asleep after coming home so I didn't get to speak with him about his day, but he seemed unharmed. For the first time in a while, I actually saw excitement and eagerness in his eyes.

"Fuck!" I opened the apple juice and brought the bottle to my mouth.

My head hurt from trying to figure out what was going on. Neil was out there and needed to be handled. That was where my focus needed to be, but it was hard when I didn't know if my husband was plotting on me.

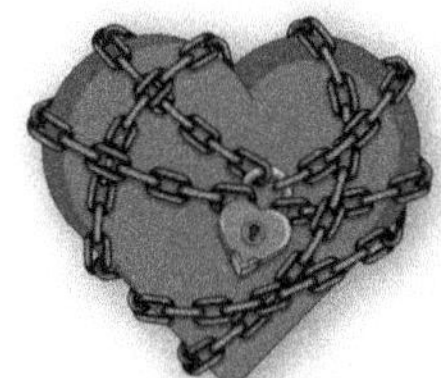

A groan left my mouth and my body shifted, feeling myself being lifted. I twisted and nuzzled into the hard body suddenly against me. My nose scrunched and my eyes fluttered before snapping open.

"What are you doing?" I mumbled.

Nazai stared down at me with dark eyes. "Enough of this sleeping away from our bed," he uttered.

"I don't want to sleep next to you," I lied.

Truthfully the past few nights sleeping away from him had been hell. Since the night of the storm I'd enjoyed being in his bed. My body always gravitated toward him. No matter how much I tried to deny it, I loved feeling his warm body against mine. For too long I'd had to look over my shoulder, but when I was next to Nazai, my body was at ease.

A lazy grin formed on his face. "You don't have to front, wifey. You like being in *our* bed. You're just pissed at me right now."

Instead of replying, I closed my eyes and leaned in, laying my head on his chest. I inhaled his fresh scent. He must have just gotten out of the shower. He was shirtless and his chest was still a little damp.

My body soon connected with the bed and I was on my back. Nazai's body hovered over me and I snapped my eyes open when he grabbed my hands and placed them above my head, holding them there.

"We need to set some things straight." His minty breath tickled my nose as he spoke just inches away from my face. "Stop trying to make me your enemy. The moment I put that ring on your finger, that shit went out the window." I bit down on my bottom lip when he pushed down, brushing his dick against my center. He was only in a pair of briefs, leaving very little between us. "I make a better partner, Wildfire. The more you fight me, the more I push back, and *I don't lose*. Me and you would be better as a unit if you allow it, you need to understand that."

My eyes fluttered when he pushed the T-shirt I had on up and pressed his growing dick against my clit. His eyes darkened with lust, glowing with a savage inner fire.

Nazai lowered his head and kissed up my jawline until he got to my ear. "What is it gonna take for you to trust me?" He took the lobe of my ear in between his teeth. His hips circled, causing friction against my clit. The sensation shot up my spine. My stomach fluttered with butterflies, my heart danced with excitement. It was strange how I went from not needing human contact to *craving* my husband's touch.

"Trusting will get you killed."

For a quick second disappointment flashed over his face. "That may be true normally, but at some point you have to learn to put your faith in others. You are *my wife* and that means you can put your life in my hands without worry. I thought you would have realized that by now, but if you need to be shown more, then I'm up for the challenge." He grinned against my ear as he ground harder against me. My hands shot up and gripped his shoulders, my eyes squeezed shut, and my body arched into him.

"Submitting to me doesn't make you weak, Wildfire. We can be partners in all this as long as you follow my lead when needed. I've seen what you can do and I won't *ever* try to change you. In fact, I love that shit. Keep that fire pumping. Keep that killer drive. Together me and you could make magic together, baby." A silent moan fell from my mouth as my head fell back and my body shook. His teeth sank into my lobe again before he pressed his lips against it to ease the sting.

My breathing sped up as I panted while my heart beat wildly in my chest cavity. Nazai hovered above me now, watching. My insides ran wild. Blood hummed through my veins.

Nazai leaned down and pecked my lips. My breathing halted seeing how his eyes bled with sincerity and seriousness. The hold they had on me suddenly made my throat tighten and my lungs constrict painfully. "Believe me when I say this is only the beginning between us. Buckle up, Wildfire, because I'm gonna show you just how magical we can be together."

CHAPTER TWENTY SEVEN

"**I** found out who runs the *Shadows of Silver Stone* blog," Emmet announced. Currently, we were at the farmhouse in front of The Barn for a family meeting.

"Who is it?" I leaned back in my chair and stared at the screen, waiting. Emmet tapped his laptop a couple of times before an image of a light skinned girl popped on the screen.

"Damn," Ezra mumbled, leaning forward, locking his eyes on the screen.

"Her name's Ziora Lambert. She's twenty-five years old. It took some time to get into her system because her firewall is almost as good as mine. She kept trying to out hack me, but I was smarter."

"The name doesn't ring a bell. What's her issue with us?"

Emmet tapped the keyboard a couple more times. "Apparently her thirteen year old sister was kidnapped nine years ago and turned up dead three months after. The cops never found out who it was, causing Ziora to take matters into her own hands."

"Did you say thirteen?" Lucas cut in, gaining interest.

I cut my eyes in his direction then spoke again. "Again, what does that have to do with us?"

"Nothing in particular. It seems the cops did a half ass investigation and Ziora proclaimed it was because her family was on the poorer side. Apparently the wealthy got more attention and help when they went missing while her sister barely got the coverage. The cops chalked it up to her being a troubled runaway. According to her site, it seems her mission is to uncover the corruption in the justice system and show how the wealthy population is full of snakes. One guy who was thought to be involved in her sister's disappearance showed up in dad's courtroom and the case got thrown out because of some technicality. And that's what put our family on her radar."

"Is it such a big deal that she's running her mouth?" Cashlynn spoke up on the side of me. "I mean she's just some low-level blogger who runs her mouth."

"You've never been in a family that's in the spotlight. The whole reason we've been able to stay off the radar is because our family is so respected in the public eye. He's retired now but our dad was one of the most respected judges on the east coast. Not to mention one of the youngest to take the bench. Him being disrespected is not tolerable," Ezra chimed in.

"Not to mention, Ziora has a large following. She keeps her identity hidden but I'm sure it was the girl disguised as a reporter at your engagement party and wedding. It's rumored she likes to take the law into her own hands and is determined to find out what exactly happened to her younger sister. I accessed her bank statements too and she gets donations from a lot of anonymous donors who help support her cause. We shouldn't just write her off," Emmet justified.

My hands folded over my lap and I stared at the girl on the wall. In the picture she had large brown curls that framed her round face, freckles across her nose, and high cheekbones. The photo more than likely was her license picture.

"We need to find out what she knows about us," I mentioned.

"I'll handle it," Ezra said, causing all eyes to fall on him. He was still locked onto the picture. "Send me her address and I'll pay her a visit."

"We don't need any more attention on us than necessary, Ez. I think Lucas sho—"

"I got it," he said, this time a little firmer. My eyes narrowed and I glanced at the screen.

"He can do it." Lucas waved us off. "I've got more pressing matters to handle. You said her sister was thirteen when she went missing."

"Lucas," I warned at the same time Emmet said, "Yeah."

"What does that have to do with anything?" Cashlynn asked.

"Where did it happen?" Lucas asked as he leaned forward, ignoring Cashlynn.

Emmet tapped the keys on his laptop a couple times and an old article popped on the screen. "On her way from school. She was on the volleyball team; on her way home from practice but never came home."

Lucas tapped his finger on the table. His jaw clenched.

"What else do you know about Ziora?" I asked, bringing the subject back to what was important.

"She's good at covering her tracks and practically making herself a ghost, but I did find some things…" Emmet went on telling us what he found about Ziora. While he spoke, I made sure to keep an eye on Lucas who had become twitchy, his face riddled with irritation. In the end I didn't think she could be a major threat, but I still didn't want to take any chances given her dedication to attacking my family's name.

River spoke up once Emmet finished his coverage of Ziora. "I found out where Neil's safe house is. Apparently, it's where he's hiding out."

"Where is it?" Cashlynn asked, sitting straighter. Reaching over, I placed my hand on her knee. She cut her eyes at me and I shook my head.

"What do we know about it?" I asked.

"He's got about nine or ten guys there with him. They don't look like major threats, just some low-level thugs he's paying to keep guard."

I nodded and glanced at Cashlynn. Steam damn near blew from her ears. Her face was red and her lips pinched together.

"Keep an eye on him."

"What? No we need to—"

I put my hands up to shut Cashlynn down then faced River. "Make sure your guys keep an eye on Neil so he doesn't disappear. Let him get comfortable then we'll take him out."

River nodded. "On it." He pulled his phone out.

"Also put the word out. There's a hundred and fifty thousand bounty on his head and I want him alive."

"Nazai," Lucas called out.

"That's it." I dismissed everyone, ignoring my brother's protest. "Until Neil is taken care of and we get a handle over the Ziora situation, we'll hold off on business."

Cashlynn sat next to me pouting, not happy about my decision, but I paid it no mind.

Before he could make an exit, I approached Lucas, pulling him to the side. "I know where your head is and leave it alone," I told him.

His expression was blank as he stared at me. "Lucas, you need to move on. Adrian's been gone for years and it's more than likely she's not even alive anymore. The more you obsess over her, the more you hold yourself back. Just because the girl that disappeared was the same age as her doesn't mean they're connected. Let it go."

His face stayed blank and he snatched away from me. "What I choose to worry about in my spare time is my business."

He went to walk away, but I grabbed him again. "This is me coming to you as your older brother. I'm worried about you."

"I'm fine. Adrian's body was never discovered which means there's no guarantee she was killed. Until I get shown otherwise, I'm not giving up."

This time when he went to leave I didn't stop him. I watched my brother stalk out of the large meeting room to the steps that led to the second floor of the house.

"What's his deal?" Cashlynn asked, approaching me.

I dragged my tongue across my top teeth. "His childhood best friend went missing when we were younger and since then he's been obsessed with finding out what happened to her. There were rumors of human traffickers who were going around snatching up kids and forcing them into work in some sex trade, but nothing concrete ever was found."

Cashlynn's face blanched. "Human traffickers?"

"I have some guys at the safe house keeping watch. Is there anything else you need from me?" River asked as he stepped to us.

"Nah, that's it. Thanks, man." He nodded.

"We should just take him out now. Why do we have to wait?" Cashlynn asked. Whatever crossed her face previously was gone now.

I flashed her a crooked smile. "Because patience is the key, Wildfire.

We'll get him, don't worry."

"You're still meeting me at The Grave tonight right?" River asked.

Digging in my pocket, I pulled my phone out and glanced at the time. "I need to go by the club first but yeah we'll be there."

"Who's we?" Cashlynn asked.

"Me and you, wifey." I winked at her.

Leaving them where they were, I walked over to where Emmet and Ezra were conversing. The picture of Ziora was still on the screen and she seemed to be the topic of discussion.

"We're leaving," I told them. "E, don't do anything that's gonna bring too much attention our way. I see the look in your eye."

He never took his eyes off the picture and waved me off. "I got this."

Shaking my head, I left them alone. Ezra was smart. I knew at times he could be erratic but he wouldn't do anything that would jeopardize the family or his reputation.

"The numbers are looking good. How's inventory?" I asked Ian. I had been relying on him a lot lately when it came to club business. The good thing was that Ian was reliable and trustworthy. Currently I was at The District, looking over the books. Both The District and Euphoria were exceeding expectations.

"I just sent in an order for more pills for Summer Bash. I think we're gonna pass last year's numbers."

I nodded. Every year we threw an event called Summer Bash. It was always the last weekend of August and we ran drink specials, girls free until a certain time, and deals on shots. Of course the secret menu was always a hit too.

"That's what I like to hear. Summer Bash is always a fan favorite. The girls in Euphoria make a killing too. Have you met with the Fire Marshall?" We always hit capacity with Summer Bash and in order for us to run the night with no interruptions, we had to rub a few elbows.

The Fire Marshall always got a hefty donation from us to leave us alone.

"Met with him yesterday morning."

I grinned. "I knew I made the right decision making you manager. I've been MIA but you've made sure things run smoothly around here. I'll make sure you have a nice bonus on your next check."

Ian nodded. "I 'preciate it, boss."

A knock on the door gained my attention. "Come in."

The door opened and to my surprise it was Majesty. I glanced at Ian. "Make sure the bar on both floors have their orders ready for me. I'll be down shortly."

"Will do."

Ian stood and headed for the door, closing it behind him as Majesty stepped in the room.

"You ready to come back?" I asked, leaning back in my chair.

Hesitancy filled her face and she nodded, slowly walking toward my desk. "I am."

I checked her face out. Lucas wasn't a plastic surgeon but the stitches he did on her cheek were clean, and now that they were out, I saw they'd left minimum scarring. Majesty must have seen I was staring at her face. She lifted her hand and brushed it over her cheek.

"We gon' have any issues with you?" I raised a brow.

She shook her head. "I just want to work." Majesty avoided my eyes.

The door to my office opened again and I was about to chastise whoever walked in without knocking until I noticed it was my wife.

"I thought you were waiting in the car."

She shrugged and walked toward me. "I got bored."

Carson was at my parents' house and instead of going home, Cashlynn wanted to come to the club with me, which caught me off guard but warmed my insides at the same time. The distance she used to keep between us seemed to get smaller each day and that was a win in my book.

"What are you doing here?" Cashlynn cut her eyes at Majesty, whose eyes widened with fear.

"I don't want any problems." She tossed her hands up. "I just came to tell Boss Man I'm ready to get back to work."

Cashlynn surprised me when she slid into my lap and leaned back on my chest. My hand went to her leg. Majesty shifted where she stood.

"Are we gonna have a problem going forward?"

Majesty quickly shook her head. "No," she answered in a shaky voice.

Cashlynn leaned down and pulled out her pocket knife, from where I wasn't sure, but the gesture caused my dick to stir. Majesty's eyes locked on the knife; her body trembled.

"And you understand my husband is off limits correct?" Cashlynn flicked the blade open and twirled it around. Her eyes narrowed on Majesty who swallowed hard and nodded.

"I just want to dance."

When Cashlynn got possessive over me, it always lit a flame of desire in me. The action was hot as hell and made blood rush to my dick.

"Then we shouldn't have any issues. You can go." Her voice and expression remained steady and monotone. She flicked her wrist dismissively.

Majesty didn't hesitate to turn and hurry out of the office.

Cashlynn twisted her body and peered into me. "Don't make me have to use this." Her blade flashed, causing one corner of my mouth to lift.

"What you gon' do, give me a matching cut?" Her eyes dropped to my neck.

"If I need to." She lifted her eyes to meet mine.

Her expression caused a fire to roar inside me. Reaching forward, I grabbed the heart attached to her collar and yanked her forward, crashing her mouth into mine. Long gone was the girl who used to shield away from my kisses. My heart swelled inside me. The blood in my veins electrified.

"Keep showing that possessive side and you won't be able to keep me off you, Wildfire." Her eyes became unfocused and her breathing picked up.

I licked her lips before bringing her bottom lip into my mouth, sucking on it. "Who do you belong to, Wildfire?" I growled against her lips.

"No one," she rasped, causing my smile to heighten.

"Still stubborn, but we'll fix that one day." I kissed her again while palming her breast, causing her to hiss. Her nipples were probably still sore from me piercing them. She hadn't taken them out, which shocked me, but I enjoyed looking at them as much as I could. Knowing she sported my initials on her body had me wanting to beat my chest like a caveman. I pinched where I knew her nipple was and she whimpered against my mouth.

"You are mine, Wildfire. Eventually you'll realize that," I murmured in Spanish.

The rowdy crowd around us grew louder as the two guys in the cage went hit for hit, neither of them letting up. The Grave was an underground cage fighting club. People went into the cage and didn't hold back as the crowd cheered them along. Bets were made against the fighters and the owner of the club made a killing on the fights.

"Tell me why we're here again," Cashlynn shouted, stretching her neck toward me. We were on the other side of the barriers that separated the cage area from the crowd. Behind us were a bunch of people standing and cheering and behind them were people seated, just as equally excited.

I leaned down and said, "River's gonna be fighting soon." I made sure to keep an arm around her waist and her body close to mine. Cashlynn wasn't a fan of crowds, and I knew that, so I made sure to keep her close. Usually I got one of the VIP suites up top, but tonight I wanted to be close to the action. The crowd here could get overwhelming if you weren't used to it. Adrenaline and emotions were always running high. A lot of money was typically at stake too, making people more irritable. Still, I always enjoyed coming here when I had time.

"He fights here? Why?" Her eyes stayed locked on the cage. I wasn't sure if she was aware of her actions but she pressed her body into me more the longer we stood here. I wasn't going to mention it either.

"After his parents were murdered, he had a lot of anger building and needed somewhere to release it. The Grave was a popular place known for its gruesome and no holds barred fights. What started off as a way to let off steam became a release for him and soon he was named the champ everyone wanted a shot to beat. Now he only comes when he needs a release."

"What about you? Do you ever get in there?"

I smirked. "I'm not the one for hand-to-hand combat for no reason. I'd rather shoot you and move on."

"And the winner…" the announcer started, lifting the hand of the bloody faced man.

"Damn, they don't play." Infatuation beamed in Cashlynn's eyes.

"No they don't. In there, they're like lions dying to take one out for the top spot. Till this day, River is still undefeated, so when he comes for a match it's always a big deal."

"Did you bet tonight?"

"Of course." I grinned. "When he wins I'll be a quarter-million dollars richer."

"You have that much faith in him."

My smile grew. "You haven't seen River in action."

The night continued and eventually it was time for the main event.

"We have a treat for you folks. It's been almost a year since we had him back here in the ring. Will he keep his undefeated streak? River the Destroyer!"

The crowd roared as River walked down the hall that led to the cage.

"The Destroyer huh?" Cashlynn asked with a lifted brow.

"That's right. Get ready to see why he got that name."

I eyed the stage. River's opponent was called to the ring and the crowd booed and cheered. Apparently this guy was a heavy hitter and had been on a winning streak.

River eyed the man like a hungry predator stalking its prey, waiting to pounce. No matter how many times he got in that ring, he always had that look in his eyes when it came time for his match.

The announcer spoke a little longer before stepping out of the ring and the bell rang. River didn't move at first, causing the guy to hit first. River didn't flinch. He always started the match the same, sacrificing a bit to gauge his opponent's power.

"Now it's time," I said, just as River went into attack mode, drawing another roaring cheer from the crowd. We could hear the crushing of bones from the first hit, causing the guy to stumble back. Spit and blood splattered from his mouth. River didn't stop there; he sent a series of hits the guy's way, two to the face and one to the body.

"Shit," Cashlynn gasped, gripping my wrist tightly with excitement pouring from her eyes. I smirked.

I knew she would be into this. Cashlynn wasn't like most girls. Things like this were a rush to her and I loved seeing her eyes come alive as she watched.

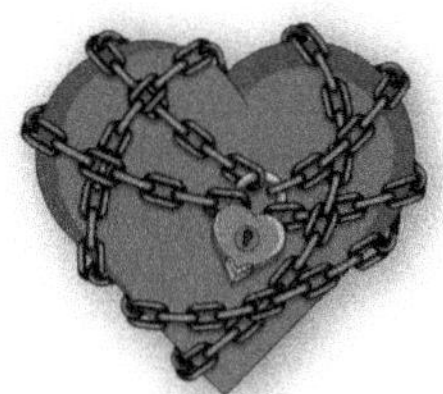

I grinned as I accepted the black bag of money from my winnings. River ended up taking the guy in under fifteen minutes. Part of me felt like he was playing with his food before he fully attacked.

"'Preciate it, gentlemen." I nodded and turned to leave the small room where the bets took place. Cashlynn was waiting outside the door for me. She pushed off the wall when I stepped back into the hall and her eyes dropped to the bag.

"We're finished here," I stated.

"That's what you earned tonight?"

My smile grew. "It is."

We started down the hall. "This was actually kind of cool. I'd heard about The Grave but had never been here before."

"Why am I not surprised you would be into something like this?"

She rolled her eyes and fought back a grin. Cashlynn was wound up when we first got here. Her mind was still locked on Neil and it didn't help that she'd run into Majesty at the club. It was a gamble bringing her here in order to distract her, but it seemed to do the job.

"Nazai!" My name being called caused me to pause. I looked up and saw Easton, the guy who ran The Grave, approaching. His eyes flickered to the bag in my hand and his mouth ticked. "Long time no see. I see River is still winning you money. I was glad when I received a call from him to put him on the roster."

I snorted. "That's because he makes you a shit ton of money too."

Easton grinned. "That he does. I wish he would consider coming more often, he knows how to bring out the crowd." His eyes shifted. "And who's this beauty?"

"Yeah she is a beauty, isn't she? This is *my wife*, Cashlynn."

"I remember hearing about you getting married. Shame I couldn't attend the wedding." His head tilted to the side and he sized her up as he licked his lips. My stomach churned and my eyes narrowed. I slowly dragged my tongue across my top teeth and stood straight.

"Careful, Easton, don't let your eyes get you in trouble. She is *mine* after all."

Easton didn't look fazed. "I mean no disrespect of course, Nazai. Just paying the lovely lady a compliment."

"Thank you." Cashlynn spoke up. "Nothing wrong with compliments." She cut her eyes toward me.

I twisted my body and gazed down at her heatedly. "You're right. They can look, but only I can touch right, Wildfire?"

Her cheeks flushed. "Not answering that." She averted my gaze and shifted on her feet.

I flashed a crooked grin then faced Easton again. His eyes bounced between us. "Mhm, I won't keep you two longer. I need to go find out my earnings after all. Cashlynn, it was nice to meet you. Nazai, please come back soon, you and River." He stepped around us and continued down the hall.

"Charming," Cashlynn muttered.

We continued down the hall and met with River who was walking toward us with his duffle bag thrown over his shoulder.

"Give me a second," I told Cashlynn, stepping away from her and meeting River halfway. I studied my friend for a second. There was still a storm in his eyes, his muscles were tense.

"There's the champ." I smirked, causing him to chuckle.

"I see you did good tonight." He nodded toward the bag.

"Always, brother. My wallet always appreciates your talent."

He chuckled again. "Yeah, like you need more money."

I shrugged. "Never can have too much." I studied him again. "How you feeling?"

"That was light work. I don't know how that guy won so many fights in the first place, I barely broke a sweat."

"I'm not talking about that. I mean, do you feel better?"

River's eyes shifted behind me, becoming distant. "As good as I'll be. Me beating the shit out of someone isn't gonna bring my parents back but it helps me release the anger that them being gone caused."

I nodded. This time of the year was always rough for River because of the anniversary of his parents dying. He was only fifteen when they were murdered but he never got over it. When he moved in with us, he got into a lot of fights because he didn't know how to properly grieve them. My parents never held it against him though. When we were seventeen, he fought his first fight at The Grave.

"You know I got you, man. If you want to talk or whatever. You're my brother." River had come a long way. He might work for me as security, but I never saw him as an employee or less than because he wasn't blood. I saw him just as I saw my actual brothers. The two of us had been through a lot of shit together.

This time River looked at me with one corner of his mouth tilted. "Don't go getting sappy on me."

I chortled. "Fuck you."

He joined in then looked behind me again and paused. His eyes narrowed. "Nazai," he said suddenly.

"What?"

He nodded, causing me to turn. My nostrils flared seeing a man in Cashlynn's face. Heat flared through my veins, causing my stomach to boil.

"Hold this." I lifted the bag and pushed it into River's chest, causing him to grunt. Spinning around, I made my way back over to Cashlynn.

"A beautiful lady like yourself shouldn't be standing here all alone," the guy slurred to Cashlynn. His body swayed. Mirth mixed with annoyance passed over Cashlynn's face.

"I'm not alone and you need to back up."

The guy grinned. "Well whoever left you alone is a fool." He grabbed her hand. My blood grew hotter as my heart pumped in my chest cavity. No one other than me had the right to touch Cashlynn.

"I'm in a good mood so I'm gonna give you till the count of three to—" Before Cashlynn could finish her sentence, I grabbed the guy by the head and shoved him against the wall. I grabbed one of his arms, pulling it behind him, causing him to groan.

"You really shouldn't touch what doesn't belong to you," I snarled, slamming his face into the stone wall.

"Fuck. My nose!" he cried.

I pulled his arm up higher, sure his shoulder was close to dislocating. He cried out again and withered under me.

"Let this be a lesson not to put your hands on someone's wife. Next time you might end up losing them." Again, I slammed his face against the wall. Blood coated the wall. I turned and shoved him away from me. He stumbled and clutched his face.

"I didn't need you to come to my rescue," Cashlynn noted.

Spinning to face her, I gazed down at her. Her mouth said one thing, but I saw the passion in her eyes. My actions turned her on. Her eyes darkened and her cheeks were flushed. I stepped into her and she inhaled a sharp breath.

"Oh I'm fully aware." I lifted one of my hands and cuffed her cheek. "But what kind of husband would I be if I didn't step in? Never question me when it comes to coming to your aid." I ran my hand over the collar on her neck. Her nostrils flared and she tucked her bottom lip into her mouth. The air felt electrified around us. Suddenly, all I could think about was pressing her against the wall and claiming her in front of everyone, so no one tried to approach her again and knew who she belonged to.

"A'right, before you two start fucking, let's get out of here," River grunted. I had forgotten he was even close by.

Cashlynn swallowed hard and cut her eyes at him. "No one's fucking."

He smirked. "Yeah, by the way the both of you are looking at each other, I doubt that." He pushed the bag of money into my hands.

The three of us started down the hall toward the entrance. I pulled my phone out to let Dante know we were headed out so he'd be waiting. I glanced down, feeling an arm brush against me. Cashlynn had moved closer to me but I wasn't even sure if she realized it. This was becoming a habit of hers. Whether she meant to or not, her body gravitated to mine. I wouldn't call her out on it because I craved her touch just as much.

CHAPTER TWENTY EIGHT

"Hey, bud. What you doing?" I asked, sitting next to Carson at the kitchen table. Lately he'd been coming out of his room and the game room. He actually seemed like a completely different kid.

"Coding," he mentioned, tapping the laptop screen. I glanced at the screen and squinted, trying to follow whatever he was doing.

"Coding what?"

"Can't tell you."

My brows lifted. "Why not?"

"Because. Emmet said it's a secret."

My jaw clenched. The past week he had been working with Emmet a lot at his office. Whenever I tried to find out what exactly he was being taught, he always told me he couldn't tell me.

"Is Emmet nice to you? He doesn't give you any issues right?"

Carson paused and shook his head. "No. He's really smart and he's teaching me a lot of things." The eagerness couldn't be hidden from his eyes.

Reaching out, I grabbed my apple juice, bringing it to my mouth. "That's good. You seem to like what he's teaching you too."

He nodded then looked around before leaning closer. "He showed me how to hack into a security system yesterday. He knows a lot of cool stuff about computers and he's really smart. A little scary, but it's okay; I can handle it."

It was comical to me that he said it like it was a big secret. I worried about my brother, but it was clear he was enjoying whatever he was learning from both Emmet and Nazai.

"That's cool." My finger tapped on the table. "I was thinking though. School will be starting soon and—"

"I don't want to go."

"Carson."

"I want to be homeschooled like you were."

I chewed the inside of my cheek. I was only homeschooled because my parents felt me going to real school would hinder my training. It also was a way to control me by having minimum contact with the outside world. I didn't want that for my brother. He was coming out of his shell and I thought being around kids his age would help that even more.

"Don't you want to be around kids your age?"

He shook his head then focused back on the screen. Carson was only ten but had been through so much. Like me, he probably didn't even know how to function properly in the general public.

"Okay, I'll consider homeschooling, okay?"

He nodded, but kept his eyes on the computer.

Seeing he didn't want to talk anymore, I grabbed my apple juice, then ran my hand over his head before heading for the elevator. Thinking about Carson and school reminded me that in all of this time I'd never handled making sure he couldn't get taken from me, not that I would let that happen. But for him to be enrolled in school, I would need to show I had a legal standing with him.

I took the elevator to the third floor. I realized I no longer walked on eggshells around the house. I had been sleeping in Nazai's room and he thought I didn't notice that he had been moving my things from the original room I had deemed mine up to his.

When I stepped in the room, I heard the shower running from the open bathroom door. I glanced toward it, feeling heat swell in my stomach as my pussy pulsated. *Sexual desire* was so foreign to me that when it hit, it caught me off guard. Nazai was so dominant in the bedroom and I thought that would turn me off, but it did the complete opposite. I normally didn't take well to someone trying to control and overpower me, but with sex, it was like all that went out the window. I didn't know what Nazai had done to me, but my mind thought about him inside me too often and my body craved his warm flesh against it.

Blinking rapidly, I debated if I should go into the bathroom. I'd never initiated sex between us before but I found myself wanting it more and more.

No.

I pushed out a heavy breath. I needed to maintain some kind of dignity. If I gave in, I knew Nazai would never let me hear the end of it.

Moving to the bed instead, I decided to wait for him when something on his pillow caught my eye. I stepped closer to the head of the bed and peeked at the bathroom door, still hearing the shower run. I bit on the corner of my bottom lip and wet my lips. Often I had seen Nazai scribbling in this sketchpad but never bothered to ask what he was doing, but now that it was out in the open, my curiosity got the best of me.

Reaching for it, I checked the bathroom door again before opening the sketchpad. I inhaled a sharp breath as my heart stuttered and my stomach did a cartwheel. My lips parted and my eyes widened taking in the drawing of me. It was spot on when it came to details. A scowl was on my face, my hair tied into a ponytail, my eyes narrowed. It was as if I was looking at a photo.

My heart felt like it had been shocked back to life when I flipped the page and saw another sketch of me. This time, I was sleep and tangled in the sheets. It seemed as if my lungs forgot how to function properly as I continued looking through the book. Every page was a different sketch of me, down to the first day we met when I broke into his house and he chained me in the basement. I closed my eyes and took a few breaths to try easing my racing heart. It seemed like forever since that day, the day my life changed forever. I was a wife now, married to a leader of a murderous crime family. Nazai didn't try to change who I was either, he embraced it, even instigated it at times. A lump formed in my throat as a gnawing feeling clawed at my chest.

"They say curiosity killed the cat." I jumped and the book fell on the bed. Snapping my eyes forward, I looked at Nazai dressed in only a towel wrapped around his waist while he used another to dry himself off. My mouth grew dry and my pussy throbbed.

"I…" My eyes went back to the book. "These are all of me!" What the hell was happening to me? I didn't get flustered easily.

"They are," he agreed. His mouth ticked upwards.

"Why?"

My mouth opened when he pulled the towel from his waist, exposing his semi-hard dick. A rush of air pushed through my nose. He strolled closer to the bed and his dick bounced against his thigh. I swallowed hard.

Once he was in front of me, he reached down and studied the sketch I stopped on. It was one of me lying in bed with my headphones on. My eyes were closed and my face appeared relaxed.

"It seems you fascinate me, Wildfire. You've become an obsession I can't help but recreate over and over."

Nazai's eyes lifted with sincerity. It caressed my insides and caused them to explode with a yearning desire. Again, my heart stuttered.

I ran my eyes down his body, tracing his wide chest and the outline of his ripped abs until I got to the groomed hair on his pelvis and the bulge that rested beneath it.

"You can't say things like that to me.," I told him tightly, feeling my chest grow taut with anxiety. I didn't understand what was happening. His words didn't make sense to me.

Nazai licked his lips. His smoldering stare became overwhelming, making every atom inside me become alive. "Why not?"

"Because and stop looking at me like that."

His mouth ticked. "Like what? Does it make you uncomfortable?"

"Like that. Like you care about me. And put some clothes on!" My hands clenched at my sides. I couldn't think properly with him standing in front of me naked and smelling like fresh sin. His words had me feeling unbalanced and I didn't like that.

When he reached up and fiddled with my collar, I didn't blink. My body stiffened.

"You're not used to someone giving a fuck about you, so you doubt my intentions, but I keep telling you they're genuine. I don't want to be your enemy, but at the same time I want you to fight me. From the moment I caught you in my shower, my infatuation with you started and it's only grown. These drawings don't even compare to how much you consume my thoughts."

My teeth sank into my bottom lip when he released me and turned away with his book in hand.

"Tonight's Summer Bash at the club. Try not to use your knife on anyone." He tossed a smirk over his shoulder and headed for the closet. My skin felt too tight and itchy, as if fire ants were running wild under it. Nothing made sense. Since I was born, no one had given a fuck about me until Carson was born. He was the only person who ever loved me and that was only because we were literally all we had. Nazai's confession of having feelings for me, *real feelings,* didn't make sense. He had only known me a few months and most of that time was spent with us at each other's throats. So how could he have feelings for me?

"I didn't say I was going to the club tonight," I called out shakily.

Nazai poked his head out the closet. "You don't have a choice."

I scraped my teeth over my bottom lip. "If I agree to go, I need a favor from you."

Nazai stepped out the closet now in a pair of boxers and a couple hangers with clothes on them in hand.

"What's that?"

"I need to talk to your dad."

Pausing, Nazai raised a brow and eyed me. "Why?"

"I know he has to have some connections that can help me get legal custody of my brother. Eventually I want him to go to school and live like a normal kid."

"You do realize his life isn't normal, right? He's surrounded by killers and corruption daily."

"Doesn't mean I can't try to give him a life outside of this. My parents kept me isolated from society, basically trapped in a prison, because they didn't want me exposed to the outside world. They wanted to mold me and control me and that was easiest if they made sure I didn't know any better. All they cared about was my training and making money. I don't want that life for my brother. He deserves better than that." My muscles grew more taut with each word I spoke.

Nazai stared at me for a long while, not speaking right away. "I'll talk to him. I'm sure he knows someone."

Stiffly, I nodded. "Thank you."

A crooked grin formed on his face. "No problem, wifey." He winked. Heat submerged through my body.

"Are you going to stop drawing me?"

He licked his lips and ate me up with his orbs. "Now why in the world would I do something crazy like that?"

My leg bounced wildly, my eyes darted around the club with my bottom lip tucked into my mouth as I tried to calm my nerves. I had been unsettled since I laid eyes on Nazai's sketchpad. Between my legs continued to throb and leak each time he walked into the section. Apparently tonight was one of the biggest events The District threw, so he was in high demand up- and downstairs. I wasn't even sure why he was so persistent that I came because I'd barely been able to lay eyes on him longer than two seconds before he was whisked away. Ezra was here, but downstairs for once, so it was just me in the section.

Slowly I sipped on the lemon drop and observed the scene. On the floor, a bunch of girls were giving lap dances and men made it rain. The last girl on stage had just made her way to the back and I knew it would be a small gap until the next girl's set. The music was loud, causing the bass to thump in my chest.

"Fuck, we're gonna make a killing tonight." I flickered my eyes up as Nazai made his way closer to me. Dressed in a wine red, short-sleeved button up that hugged his arms and black slacks. He made his way to the couch and sat down, tossing his head back and closing his eyes. I studied his face for a second before shifting my eyes down his body, admiring how the button up looked against his gingerbread skin. His chest looked broader behind the material. Continuing down, I paused at his dick. I could see the bulge under his slacks. Heat flooded my stomach. My veins buzzed as if bees were running wild through them.

I licked my lips and shot my eyes up when a deep, low chuckle left Nazai's mouth. He was eyeing me through low eyes with a crooked grin on his face.

"See something you like."

My cheeks heated. Since he had stripped out his towel I'd wanted him to take me, but I'd never been the initiator when it came to sex. I always acted as if I didn't want it, but in reality I loved feeling Nazai inside me and the way he roughly took advantage of my body. Although I was growing more comfortable when it came to the act of sex, I still felt awkward when it came to the thought itself. Nazai was more experienced than me and he never seemed to complain at my performance in the bedroom, but if I initiated things then would he expect me to take the lead? Would I even want that? In my life I was so used to being the leader and problem solver. I was never meant to be a follower, but with Nazai, in the bedroom, that all changed. My body seemed to submit willingly, no matter how much my mind protested.

It was one reason I'd been so unsettled. My body craved my husband and I felt foolish because I wasn't sure or comfortable enough to vocalize that without fearing I sounded pathetic or looking like a fool.

My stomach stirred and I attempted to swallow around the lump forming in my throat.

"I need you to do something for me," I stated. My eyes darted around before focusing back on him.

Nazai raised a brow. His darkened eyes ran over my body, causing my breath to hitch. My skin tickled with desire. My heart thudded inside me wildly.

"I want whatever you gave me the first night you brought me here." Swallowing hard again, I quickly downed the rest of my lemon drop. I remembered how open and carefree I'd felt when Nazai fed me the drug. My mind didn't care about anything but feeling good. There was no reason to overthink things outside of gaining pleasure.

For a second he seemed confused by my request before one corner of his mouth ticked and his eyes brightened with interest. My cheeks grew hotter.

"Don't make it a big deal," I gritted.

Leaning forward, his large hand went to my thigh and he gripped it tightly.

"You want me to drug you? Is that what you're telling me, Wildfire?" His voice came out in a low, gritty, rumble.

"Wouldn't be the first time." My tongue swiped over my lips. My nerves were running wild and my body felt jittery but I refused to break eye contact.

Nazai's eyes' bounced around my face for a second before he nodded and dug into his pocket for his phone. After unlocking it, he tapped the screen a couple of times. I inhaled a deep breath, ignoring how my heart slammed violently against my ribcage.

It didn't take long for a girl to come to the section with a drink on her tray, next to it was a small baggie. Nazai took both before waving her off. I eyed the baggie with the small white pill inside. My stomach clenched.

Nazai went to hand it to me but I shook my head. "Make me take it, like you did the first time." Lowly, he chuckled and leaned forward, setting the cup on the table along with my martini glass.

I watched him sit back and open the baggie then take the pill out. He placed the pill on his tongue then cuffed the back of my neck, pulling my face forward and crashing his mouth into mine. I moaned and opened my mouth instantly, loving how his tongue felt against mine. The pill slipped inside my mouth and I swallowed it hungrily. Nazai's tongue swiped across my bottom lip before he pulled back and studied my face again.

His phone vibrated on his lap, but his eyes never left mine. I blinked slowly while panting.

When he finally checked his phone, he cursed lowly and closed his eyes, pushing a deep breath out.

"I need to run downstairs and take care of something." His eyes penetrated me. Reaching up, he grabbed me by the jaw and gripped it tightly. "Do not leave this damn section. Do you understand me?"

The authority in his voice caused between my legs to leak more and pulsate with need.

"I'm not."

His jaw was set and his eyes were hard. I didn't know if it was because of the text he got or the thought of me leaving.

Finally, he lowered his hand to the collar and forced me forward, taking my mouth aggressively.

"I'm gonna have a time with you," he muttered before releasing me.

I watched as he stood and walked toward the entrance of the section. He leaned in and whispered to Jackson before glancing back at me. The possession that now bled from his stare made my insides quake and goosebumps cover my arms.

Snatching my eyes away from his, I glanced at the untouched drink, quickly snatching it up and downing the contents. My nose scrunched and my chest burned as the liquid went down.

I wasn't sure how long Nazai was gone, but eventually that light and floating feeling filled my body. My skin felt sensitive as blood raced through my veins, humming and scorching with fire. Between my legs pulsated, causing me to shift to ease the overwhelming feeling building.

Eventually, Nazai made his way back and by then all I wanted was for him to take me and own my body.

At first, he ran his eyes over me. "How you feeling?" he asked with a smirk on his face. Moving to the edge of the couch, I reached forward and grabbed his dick, causing his brows to shoot up.

"I need you," I replied shamelessly. Pride had left the building.

"What do you need, Wildfire?"

I squeezed his bulge, causing his nostrils to flare and his eyes to flash. "You."

Moving closer, Nazai reached forward and gripped my chin, tilting my head.

"You want me to fuck you?"

Licking my lips, I nodded. "Yeah? You want me to bury my dick inside that pussy and pound it until you're begging for relief."

My eyes fluttered and a moan escaped my mouth. "Yes!" His smirk grew.

By now I was rubbing on his dick, feeling it grow under my touch was hot as fuck. "I can fuck you, right here. Bend you over and push inside you for everyone to see."

The thought had my breathing speed up and stomach flipped. "No." For a second my lust was replaced with anger. "No one sees your dick."

"No? Why not?" Teasing played on his face and in his tone.

"Because, it's only for me." I gripped him tighter, causing him to grunt.

Nazai leaned over, allowing his mouth to hover inches above mine. "Mhm, look at you being all possessive. That's hot as fuck." Pausing, he licked his lips before his teeth sank into his bottom lip. "Tell me exactly what you want, baby. Tell me what you and that pussy want."

A volcano exploded inside me, causing lava to flood my body. My body ached with need for the man standing in front of me. Blood rushed through my head, making it spin.

Nazai leaned closer and inhaled a deep breath in the crease of my neck before licking a line from my collar up to my ear. Pleasure gushed up my spine. His hand cuffed my breast and gripped it securely.

"Take me to your office. Now." My chest rose and fell quickly. My palms became sweaty. The fullness between his legs filled my hands.

"As you wish, wife," he growled, leaning down and licking my lips before sucking on my bottom one. Reaching up and grabbing his face, I kissed him more feverishly. I shifted in my seat as my clit filled with blood.

"Fuck. Let's go." He tore away from me and peered into me with hunger-filled eyes. I loved when he had that look in his eyes. I'd never felt desired before but anytime Nazai looked at me like he was now, I knew he wanted me. It made me feel powerful and as much as I didn't want to admit it, I craved the attention.

He pulled up and held his hand out. The moment I placed mine inside his, he was yanking me up and stalking out the section. I stumbled some, but moved closer to him once we were in the crowd. They still made me uneasy no matter how many times I had been to the club.

Nazai didn't slow down, easily maneuvering through the large body of people. My body tensed with expectation.

We got to his office and he slammed the door shut, locking it behind us before releasing me.

"Strip," he demanded, staring at me lustfully. My knees buckled while electricity surged through me. I was wearing black shorts and a silk button top that had the first two undone, but my body felt as if I was bundled up in a hundred degree weather.

Nibbling on my bottom lip, I shakily fumbled with the top of my buttons. Once undone, I slid it off before moving on to my shorts.

Nazai stalked toward me just as I pushed the shorts down and grabbed my hair roughly. Leaning down, his breath brushed across my face as he spoke. "I can't wait to feel your pussy wrapped around my dick. Tell me who owns this pussy, Wildfire." He cuffed my pussy through my panties. I moaned and squeezed my eyes shut. Flashes of colors exploded behind my lids as he pressed against my clit.

"Who does this pussy belong to? Who's the only one who can give you what you need?"

"You," I whimpered. The drug made everything more needy. I was painfully turned on and needing relief.

"That's right," he hissed with a growl. "Only me."

Before I could speak, he moved us toward his desk before spinning me so my back was facing him.

"Hands on the desk." My heart lurched and my stomach fluttered. Doing as he said, I placed my hands on the smooth, wooden surface. A few seconds later his gun landed on the desk next to my right hand with a small thud.

Nazai yanked my panties down, causing me to hiss from the slight burn of the material rushing down my skin, then he kicked my legs open. He pressed into the small of my back, causing me to lean forward.

"Your pussy's soaked. I can see your juices seeping down your leg." His finger brushed my inner thighs, making my legs tremble and prickle with goosebumps.

Anticipation built inside me. My chest tightened with yearning.

I jumped, releasing a loud cry when I felt Nazai's tongue drag over my lower lips. He flicked his tongue back and forth, causing me to squirm. I pushed backwards, craving more. He devoured my pussy, sucking my lips into his mouth and swirling his tongue.

I couldn't breathe. My senses were overloaded with pleasure. Moaning, I went to reach behind me but he pulled back, causing me to whine.

"Hands on the fucking desk," he growled. Wanting to feel his mouth again, I quickly did as he said, balling my hands into fists. His fingers spread my pussy and he forced his tongue inside, darting it in and out. His beard tickled the inside of my thighs, causing me to shudder.

"Do you like me fucking this pussy with my tongue, baby?"

Baby.

The endearment almost caused as much excitement in me as wife and Wildfire. I'd never had a pet name before and it was so general, but with Nazai I knew it was more personal and that thought alone made me feel special.

A loud whimper escaped my lips when he sucked my pussy inside his mouth. My stomach tightened and my body jerked as I came. My nails dug into my palms as my fists clenched tighter. His lips and the way he ate me was so skillful and for a second jealousy pooled in my gut thinking about how he'd learned these skills and how many women might have experienced this same sensation. Just before the anger could ruin things, I jumped when his tongue dragged back and my ass cheeks widened. He swiped my back hole before sucking and swirling his tongue around it, while shoving a finger inside my pussy.

"Oh, ah," I cried. No one had ever touched there before. That floating feeling in my head intensified.

My walls clamped around his fingers as my body trembled again.

I panted heavily, causing the papers on his desk to ripple.

I heard ruffling around me and just when I was about to see what was going out, I felt the blunt tip of his dick at my entrance. My blood surged.

One of his hands went to my hair, which I knew was completely sweated out and unruly at this point, and the other to the small of my back. He didn't give any warning as he thrust inside of me, causing me to cry out.

Not bothering to give me time to adjust, he moved in and out of me with urgency. His hand curled in my hair and he yanked my head back, stretching my neck backward. The way he was fucking me almost felt like he was punishing my pussy. Since I didn't have a bra on, my breasts rubbed against the smooth, cool oak, only intensifying the pleasurable sensations soaring through me.

"Put one of your legs on the desk," he demanded in a low throaty tone. I had to blink a few times to make sure I heard him correctly. Nazai paused his assault. The hand on my lower back, reached for one of my legs and lifted it. I was caught off guard in the new position, but when

Nazai started to move again, I understood. I hissed at the long deep strokes he gave me, feeling it more than before.

"I could fuck you all fucking day and it not be enough," he growled as I whimpered. He leaned in, only making him push further inside me. I wasn't sure how but I swore he was touching the bottom of my stomach. His teeth nipped the top of my ear and his warm breath caused the hairs on the back of my neck to rise. "I saw the way you watched me tonight. The lust that radiated from your eyes. Tell me, wife, have you been thinking about me fucking you all night?"

My words became trapped in my throat as I attempted to answer. My eyes slammed shut and scalding lava piled in the bottom of my stomach. My body felt alive for the first time, every stroke and touch only made it more satisfying.

"That's why you wanted that pill, huh? So I would fuck you." He scraped his teeth along my jawline. "But you know I would have fucked you regardless, baby. The way this pussy molds to only *my* dick makes it hard to stay out of."

"Nazai. I can't," I stammered as my eyes rolled to the back of my head and ecstasy shot through me.

Suddenly, Nazai snatched out of me in the middle of my orgasm. I was about to complain until he spun me around and lifted me, placing me on his dick. Then he was back inside of me. His mouth lowered and he took my breast into it. I cried out as he hungrily tongued my swollen nipple. Since they'd been pierced they'd been ten times more sensitive. They were still slightly sore, but I didn't care; it only made the sensation better.

My arms went around his neck and I tossed my head back as he bounced between my breasts, teasing and sucking my nipples. He pulled on one with his teeth and my walls clenched around him. Heat sizzled through me and my head spun.

"Your pussy is like heaven, baby. Taking everything I give and only growing wetter. You never have to be afraid to ask for this dick because I'll willingly give it to you every time." He lifted his head and gazed into my eyes. My lips parted as I breathed heavily. I watched as sweat beaded on his forehead and ran down his face. His plush lips glistened when he swiped them with his tongue. He grabbed my hair again and pressed his forehead against mine.

The way his orbs burned into me had me feeling too open and exposed. I didn't want him to know why I needed the drug tonight, but my husband was smart. It didn't shock me that he'd put two and two together.

"Look how my dick is stretching out your pretty little pussy, baby," he murmured in Spanish. "Fuck! I love seeing you wrapped around me, knowing no one else has touched you."

I moaned and flicked my eyes down, watching his length move and out of me. It glistened with my juices.

"If you ever tried to give it to someone else, I'd cut their throat then fuck you in their blood until you forgot ever having the thought." His voice was a low, threatening rasp. I moaned and fluttered my lids, tickling my cheekbones. When I looked back into Nazai's gaze, his eyes were burning with fire.

"Do you like that? The idea of me killing a man because he dared to touch what's mine?" he continued in his father's native tongue.

"Yes," I whimpered without shame. His possessive words flooded my chest and caused my heart to tremble erratically. The thought of Nazai losing his control because of me turned me on like no other.

He growled and sped his thrusts up, causing my body to jerk roughly. He had a bruising hold on my side. His eyes were the color of the midnight sky in the country.

"Tell me, Wildfire. Tell me this pussy is mine."

"It's yours," I breathed, biting down on my bottom lip. I didn't care about anything else right now but the pleasure he was bringing me. It didn't matter that we were in the middle of his office during one of the busiest nights at his club. All that mattered was how amazing my body felt and that Nazai was the cause.

"No one else can *ever* have it."

"No one."

"Only me."

"Only you."

As if those were the magic words, he pushed inside me deeply, making me cry out and tighten my hold on his neck. This time it was me slamming my mouth into his, but he barely let me maintain control as his tongue forced its way inside my mouth, owning it. The feeling of his warm release shooting inside of me had me moaning and cumming again. I shook violently against him, pulling away from his mouth and shoving my head into the crease of his neck.

"Fuck, you drained me so fucking good," he grunted, still slowly pushing in and out of me. His dick twitched and I whimpered against his skin.

This was what I needed, what I'd craved since seeing him come out of that bathroom in only a towel. I might not have been able to flat out tell Nazai what I wanted, but I was grateful he caught the hint and followed through regardless.

CHAPTER TWENTY NINE

Cashlynn lifted her head from the crease of my neck. Her cheeks were flushed and her eyes were glazed over and unfocused. Sweat beaded on her skin. Her breathing was heavy and minor tremors passed through her body. I ran my eyes down her frame, pausing at her breasts. My initials glistened brightly.

"I'm not done with you," I announced, running my hand between the valley of her breasts and licking my lips, savoring the lasting taste of her essence. She moaned and her stare wavered. Moving my touch to her breast, I brushed over her hardened nipple. "When we get home, I want you all night." Leaning in, I swiped her bud with my tongue and circled it before pulling, causing Cashlynn to hiss and clutch my arms. I knew the drug in her system had her body more sensitive to touch and heightened her senses.

I grinned and lifted my gaze into her eyes. All night I'd noticed how Cashlynn watched me with lust in her eyes. She looked like she wanted to jump on me all night but held back. Even back in my bedroom I saw the desire beaming from her but she never acted, instead she looked uncomfortable and uncertain. Cashlynn had an issue with displaying her emotions, especially ones that were new to her. If she needed a push to

"I need to clean up," she uttered breathlessly.

Glancing down, I watched the way my juices and hers coated the inside of her thighs. Possession grabbed at me.

"I don't know… I like seeing me seep out of you." I reached down and touched her pussy, pushing the mixture back into her. Her leg twitched and she bit into her bottom lip. I had just pulled out of her and already missed her snug walls wrapped around me.

Removing my hands from between her legs, I helped her off the desk. She stumbled, causing me to steady her.

Cashlynn looked up at me with confusion flashing over her face while she blinked slowly. "My head is spinning," she groaned, leaning into me.

"We'll get you some water," I said, positioning her against the desk. I lifted my slacks and briefs from around my ankles, rebuttoned them, and headed over to the mini fridge on the wall. Grabbing a water, I went back to Cashlynn, opening it and handing it to her.

"Drink."

She took the water and took a large gulp. "It's so hot."

I smirked and looked around. "Let's get you dressed."

Moving around my office, I collected her clothes then walked back to her. The water was gone, but her body was still flushed. Kneeling, I helped her into her shorts, not bothering with her panties, then stood to put her shirt back on.

"You need another water?"

Cashlynn shook her head as her body sagged into me. "Sleepy."

I chuckled.

Making sure I grabbed my gun and tucked it into the small of my back, I led us out of my office, keeping a hold on her so she wouldn't fall down the steps.

"Sir, there's someone waiting near the bar who requested to speak to you," Jackson said.

"Who is it?" I asked, tucking Cashlynn into my side. I enjoyed high Cashlynn; she didn't give me any lip and complied easier.

"Not sure. I can ask."

I shook my head. "Nah, it's probably a guest. Where's Ian?"

"He didn't want Ian. He wanted the boss."

I sighed and nodded. "A'right." The last thing I wanted to do was deal with a complaint after having a mind-blowing orgasm.

We moved through the club. The crowd was thicker than before we went upstairs which wasn't shocking. It was going on one in the morning and there were no signs of slowing down.

"Where is he?" I asked Jackson when we got to the bar. "Stay here," I told Cashlynn, placing her on the stool.

"You're not the boss of me," she complained, giving me a pout.

Grinning, I moved in and pecked her lips. "I am. We both know that." Her bottom lip poked out more and her eyes lowered.

"Sabrina!" I called out to the bartender, lifting my hand to gain her attention.

"Wassup, boss man?" she shouted over the loudness.

I leaned in. "Get my wife a water."

She nodded.

After making sure Cashlynn was good, I turned to Jackson. "Where is he?" I looked around, not noticing anyone.

He frowned and did the same. He spoke into his earpiece. "Where's the guy who wanted Mr. Tavarez?"

Impatience filled me. "It seems he left to go downstairs." Jackson's eyes scanned the area again.

"I'm not going down there right now. If he needs me, he'll make his way back up here." The District was always so much more congested than upstairs. I didn't have it in me to deal with the unruliness.

I checked in with the bartenders, making sure everything was running smoothly and they didn't need anything before giving my attention to my wife.

"Let's go back to the section," I announced to Cashlynn, helping her off the bar stool.

She clutched her water and stumbled into me. "I always forget how much of a lightweight you are." I laughed, leading us to the section.

I noticed Ezra was now in my section receiving a lap dance. Out of all my brothers, he spent the most time here, so it didn't surprise me.

"Cashlynn Cavana!" someone shouted over the music when we were inches from my section.

I frowned and spun around. "Her last name is Tava—"

Everything happened quickly. The man standing behind us pulled a gun from the inside of his brown leather jacket. The sound of the music drowned out the sound of the shot.

"Neil said an eye for an eye," he aimed at my wife and pulled the trigger.

Instantly reacting, I pushed Cashlynn out of the way as the gun sounded off. A burning sensation slammed through the upper part of my body. I stumbled slightly, feeling the bullet rip through my flesh. He released two more, causing the people close by to make note of the gun shots. Chaos erupted around us and everyone was yelling and screaming. Everything burned, but I pushed through it.

"Code red!" I heard Jackson shout.

I gritted my teeth and quickly reacted, pulling my gun out, firing a shot. It hit the guy and Jackson quickly tackled him.

"What the fuck!" Ezra rushed over, gun in hand.

"Fuck, take his ass downstairs!" I shouted at Luke who rushed over too. I held my arm as blood seeped out of my wound, covering my hand. My right arm felt heavier than normal. An aching throb pulsated through me with each heartbeat.

"Nazai!" Cashlynn yelled, scrambling toward me from where she had landed on the floor.

"We need to get him to Lucas!" Ezra shouted.

"Call River and tell him to get here!" I demanded.

Too many things were going on around me. People in the club were all rushing to get to the stairs to leave. Adrenaline pumped through me as the lights from the club began to blur. My breathing became ragged, making it hard to fill my lungs properly.

My knees buckled, causing me to stumble. Before I could hit the ground my body was caught. "I got you, bro. Get the fuck out the way!" Ezra shouted.

My ears rang and everything spun before blackness overtook me.

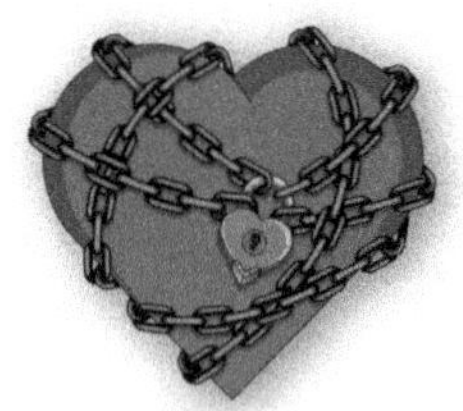

My head throbbed as I slowly attempted to open my eyes. Confusion filled me at the bright lights hovering over me and the faint beeping sound around me. My head felt fuzzy and my sight was blurry. It felt like my body was being weighed down by pounds of heavy weights.

Pain seared through me when I attempted to lift. "Don't move."

The voice caused my eyes to shift over and Lucas stood next to me with a blank expression on his face. He shifted his eyes to the machine next to where I lay.

"Lucas?" My throat felt scratchy and dry as if I had swallowed sand. "Where?"

"You're at the clinic. How you feeling? Do you remember what happened?"

Closing my eyes, I pushed out a deep breath as scenes flashed in my head.

"I was shot," I gritted.

He nodded. "Once in your right arm, that went through and through, and then another on your left lower side. That one I had to remove the bullet. Nothing major was hit. You'll be sore for a while but you'll recover fine."

The door opened, and Ezra and Cashlynn came storming in.

"About time you woke up. How you feeling, bro?" Ezra asked.

"Like I got shot. What happened to the guy?"

"River showed up after we left and had him taken to the barn after Ian dealt with the police."

"How the fuck did he even get inside with a gun?" Lucas questioned. My jaw clenched. That was a good question. There was no way he should have even been allowed inside with a weapon. Only me, my family, and River's people were allowed inside with one.

"I don't know, but I'ma find out. The guy mentioned something about Neil," I announced. Things were still fuzzy but I remembered that fact.

"We're already on it. He's in the wind," Ezra noted.

Again, I gritted my teeth. "Raise his bounty to five hundred thousand. I want his fucking head!" I was furious. My blood boiled as my heart pounded in my chest.

Shifting my attention, I eyed Cashlynn who had been quiet, which wasn't like her. I studied her. Her body was stiff, arms crossed over her chest with a blank face.

"Give me a second with my wife," I demanded, never taking my eyes off her.

"Don't do shit that'll bust your stitches," Lucas expressed. His eyes leveled on me then bounced to Cashlynn. "No fighting or fucking."

He and Ezra left the room we were in. Cashlynn didn't move. Her eyes remained unblinking.

"What the hell you doing all the way over there? C'mere." I nodded and shifted in the bed, causing me to grunt. I knew my brother had me on pain meds, but the dull aching couldn't be ignored.

Cashlynn's eyes dragged down my body. It could have been the pain medicine but I swore I saw sadness pass through her face as she eyed me before her eyes hardened and she clenched her jaw and her arms fell from her chest. She balled her hands at her sides and stalked toward the bed.

"You took a bullet for me," she stated. "I was caught off guard and you had to save me." Her voice was strained as she spoke.

My eyes narrowed. "Wildfire—"

"Why?" She cut me off. "Why would you do that?"

I studied her face. She looked to be having an internal battle.

"Cashlynn. You are my wife! I don't know what else I have to do to prove I have your back. I wasn't about to sit back and watch you get shot."

"If I was paying more attention and watching my surroundings I would have noticed. And then you wouldn't have been shot."

My brows furrowed. "No. That guy slipped in somehow; he caught us all off guard. You need to realize you're not alone anymore. You have people that have your back."

I was caught off guard when she leaned down and quickly kissed me. "Thank you." Her cheeks tinted red and she hurriedly stood.

She licked her lips. Confusion raced through her eyes and her weight shifted. "Neil isn't gonna stop until we kill him. This is the second time he's come for me." Her eyes flashed. "I should have taken him out when I had the chance."

My eyes narrowed. "Don't go do something stupid."

"Stupid is letting him still breathe after we found out he shot at us the first time! I should have taken care of him right after I killed his damn son!" Her hands shook at her sides and her eyes burned with intensity.

The doors opened and Ezra came back into the room. "River's on the phone." He put it on speaker.

"Nazai."

"How the hell did your men lose Neil?"

"Turns out he had a tunnel built in the house. By the time we were inside we realized he was long gone. We cleared the house of the couple of men who lagged behind."

"Fuck! And the guy who shot me?"

"Tied up in the barn. You hit him when you shot, but we manage to stabilize the wound."

"Get whatever information you can out of him but don't kill him."

"Wait for me." Cashlynn spoke up, causing me to cut my eyes over to her.

"No."

"You don't get to tell me no. He tried to shoot me!" She stood stiffly.

"And River can handle him. You're not going anywhere."

Her cheeks puffed and her nostrils flared. "River, find out how the hell he got inside the club with a weapon and what he knows about Neil."

"I'm on it." He hung up.

Tension was thick in the room until Ezra spoke. "I'll head to the barn and help River. Wilma's been wanting some action anyway."

"I'll go with you."

"You aren't going any fucking where!" I shouted, causing pain to ripple through me. The machine started going crazy next to me. "Until Neil is handled, you'll lay low."

"I can take care of myself! I have been my whole life."

"You're not invincible! Go sit your ass in that chair and—"

"What the hell is going on?" Lucas stormed inside the room and made his way to the machine. He tapped it a couple times and then gave me a onceover. His eyes bounced between me and Cashlynn. "Didn't I tell y'all no fighting?"

"Sis, just chill here. I don't need you throwing up again anyway."

"Throwing up?" I questioned, ignoring Lucas.

"It's nothing."

"She threw up?" I whipped my head to Ezra.

His nose scrunched. "Yeah, when we first got here."

"It was the alcohol and pill I took mixed with the anxiety of everything. It's no big deal." She waved Ezra off.

I narrowed my eyes on her.

"I flushed her system; she should be fine now," Lucas stated.

"I'm out. I'll keep you updated with what we find out." Ezra turned to leave.

Cashlynn looked annoyed. "I don't like being treated like a damsel in distress."

"Your husband was shot. Sit your ass down and comfort him," I said, causing her cheeks to flush. She darted her eyes to the side.

"Soon as the IV finishes, you're good to go home. I'm sending you home with pain meds and some antibiotics too. I know your ass ain't gon' listen, but you need to take it easy the next couple of days, Nazai."

"I hear you, bro."

He muttered something then lifted the sleeve of the gown to check the wound and moved to my side.

Staring back at Cashlynn, my mouth lifted in a lazy grin. "Come sit." I nodded at the chair close to the bed. Exhaustion hit me out of nowhere. A yawn left my mouth.

Cashlynn glanced at Lucas before slowly moving and taking a seat.

"Are you still feeling sick?" Lucas asked Cashlynn.

"I'm fine."

He eyed her intensely then nodded. "A'right."

My brother turned and left the room, leaving me and Cashlynn.

Silence passed through us as my eyes grew heavier. I wasn't sure if she said it or I imagined it but as I faded into darkness, I could have sworn Cashlynn whispered, "I'm glad you're okay."

"**D**o we know how he got in with a gun?" I stood outside of the bedroom listening to Nazai talk on the phone. We had just gotten home from Lucas's clinic and I went to check on Carson who was up gaming.

"Ted. Apparently he wasn't over you cutting off his hand." River laughed.

"And where is the fucker?"

"Both are at the barn locked up. Though the guy that shot you was in bad shape. I don't know how much longer he'll last."

"I'll be by in the morning to take care of them."

"You know you're gonna hear Lucas's mouth." Again, River tittered.

"He'll be a'right. If I bust my stitches, he'll just have to restitch me up. Those fuckers think it's okay to come for me and my wife." The low boiling rage in his voice made the hairs on the back of my neck rise and my stomach stir. My hand went to the center of my chest and I attempted to rub out the tightness that formed from his protectiveness. I was still in shock that Nazai had taken a bullet for me. I was so out of it from the E pill I took, mixed with the alcohol and orgasm, that my reaction time was slowed and my mind wasn't as present as it normally would be. By the time I realized what was happening, I was on the ground and Nazai was shooting back.

I pressed my back against the wall and sank my teeth into my bottom lip. I'd never gotten caught slipping as bad as I had tonight. Nazai was proving to be a distraction I didn't need, but the bad thing was I couldn't find it in me to fight the feelings he gave me. The more I tried to fight it, the more I craved being near him.

My teeth scraped over my bottom lip as Nazai finished up his conversation. Knowing the two men that played part in the shooting were waiting for their fate lit a fire in my veins and caused my heart to pump wildly. My pulse pounded in my ears and my skin prickled.

He said he wanted me to stand down tonight, but that was one command I couldn't follow.

I pulled down the dark gravel pathway surrounded by trees and only lit by my headlights. Thankfully the medicine Nazai was prescribed made him drowsy and by the time I got out of the shower, he was knocked out cold in bed.

I rode past the big white house the family met in when we came to the property back to the barn. A good thing about the area was that it was abandoned, in the middle of nowhere, and the Tavarez family owned a good amount of acres surrounding it.

Cutting my car off, I pulled my hair into a ponytail and grabbed my baseball cap, placing it on my head. I turned my phone off and placed it in the glove compartment before reaching into the back seat for my bookbag. I dug into my bookbag, grabbed my black leather gloves, and slipped them on my hands then climbed out the car.

The air was eerie and stiff. The wind caused the trees to ruffle. Crickets sounded around me. There were no lights near the barn.

Leaving my car, I headed for the barn. Because I paid attention, I was able to insert the code to unlock the door. After hearing the click, I pushed the double doors open. On the wall I hit the button for the lights.

I thought I was gonna have to head to the back where they had the holding cells—each with steel doors and slidable, rectangle peep holes that could be opened to talk to and see whoever was on the other side—but instead I saw two people in the middle of the barn tied to chairs. Their heads leaned forward and their bodies sagged.

Bringing my bookbag forward, I reached in and grabbed my gun, making sure the safety was off. I tossed my bookbag on the ground near the doors and stepped forward.

Electric currents ran through me and amplified my heartbeat. I always felt high when I was preparing for a kill.

Ted's head popped up, hearing me approach. The other guy barely looked like he was breathing.

"Wake up, bitches," I announced, bouncing my eyes between them. They were facing each other. I dropped my eyes to Ted's missing hand and smirked.

"You just couldn't let it go, huh?" I taunted, shaking my head. Both had their mouths taped shut.

His eyes cut into slits. I swiveled my attention to the other guy. Stalking toward him, I tapped my gun against his head.

"Wake up." I grabbed the curls on top of his head and yanked. His eyes fluttered and he groaned. His arm was wrapped and that must have been where Nazai hit him.

"You thought it was smart to come for me?"

He grunted.

I lifted my gun, slammed it against his head, and released him. Stepping in front of him, I eyed him and dragged my tongue across my top teeth.

"You shot my husband twice." I pointed my gun and sent a shot through each knee cap. He cried out behind the tape. He wiggled and attempted to free himself. My vision turned red as I stared at him. Knowing he'd gotten that close to possibly taking me out caused my ears to pound. My breathing increased. The back of my neck grew hot. My heart was like a raging bull in my chest, wildly pounding into my ribcage.

Stalking toward him, I lifted my leg and sent my shoe into his chest, causing him to fly back. I stood above him and glared down. His eyes widened in fight. Fireworks of excitement exploded inside me. It brought me joy knowing I was the cause of that fear. "And then you truly fucked up by making me your original target. I hope your life was worth being Neil's bitch." He mumbled behind the tape, quickly shaking his head side to side. "Have fun in hell." Pointing the gun at his head, I pressed the trigger. The shot was clean, a bullet between the eyes.

Inhaling a deep breath, I closed my eyes and rolled my shoulders back. Turning, I faced Ted. Sweat beaded on his forehead. His eyes locked on the man's dead body now on the side of me.

"You're the reason he got inside the club." I went into my pocket and pulled my butterfly knife out, flicking it open.

I tucked my gun into the small of my back and slowly walked to Ted. His eyes ballooned in fear. His body shook and he shouted behind the tape.

"You should have just let it go after you lost your hand, but no." I grinned, placing the blade against his face and dragging it down, slicing his cheek. It slit open as if I was cutting into butter, blood leaked and dripped down his face. He screamed and attempted to move out of my reach.

"I planned on coming and finishing this quickly, but I don't like snakes." I lifted the knife and studied it. The once silver blade now was stained with his blood. My grin broadened. A warm glow flowed through me. "Did you know the best way to kill a snake is to cut its head off?" I narrowed my eyes on him.

Quickly, Ted shook his head. "How long do you think it'll take me to remove your head with my knife?" I placed the metal to his neck. I slid the blade slowly, making sure to drag it out.

"Stop!" a deep voice bellowed from behind me, causing me to freeze. I dropped my eyes to where the blood was seeping from Ted's cheek and now his neck.

Inhaling a deep breath and pushing it out, I pulled up and spun around.

I bit the inside of my cheek seeing Nazai standing at the entrance of the barn. His eyes were an icy storm and his lips were tightly pinched together. He slid his attention to the dead man on the floor and his jaw ticked. When he turned to face me, I fought not to shuffle under his glare.

"I thought you were sleep," I said.

Nazai didn't respond. He slowly made his way toward me. Each step he took caused my heart to tick loudly.

Stopping in front of me, he gazed down at me. I was about to speak when his hand went to my neck. My eyes bucked as his grip tightened.

"What the fuck are you doing?" he growled.

"Let me go!" I used my free hand and reached for his wrist. I struggled against his hold.

"Didn't I tell you to stand down?" He yanked me forward.

"He tried to kill me. He shot you!" I strained to get out. My throat burned. Air became hard to retain. My vision grew fuzzy.

Nazai's nostrils flared. "And we were going to handle him but not like this. What did I tell you about following my lead?"

He loosened his hold slightly but didn't release me. I blinked slowly as my breathing sped up. "You took a bullet for me. So I owed you."

"You owed me?"

I jerked a nod. "He shot you and if you thought I was going to let him get away with that, you were mistaken." Seeing Nazai in that hospital bed, knowing it was because he was protecting me, set something ablaze in me. It felt like my chest cracked open and released something that had been hidden away. For the first time I felt like someone other than my brother cared if I lived or died. It made my heart do a silly dance. It was hard to explain the wave of emotions that passed through me because I was used to being disposable, but with Nazai I was learning that wasn't the case.

Nazai's eyes flashed and darkened. "You did this for me?"

Slowly, I nodded. His eyes shifted to the side where Ted sat bleeding, then came back to me. Flaring his nostrils again, he leaned forward and captured my mouth with his. He kissed me roughly before sinking his teeth into my bottom lip. I grunted and moaned against his lips. A metallic taste filled my mouth when he pulled away.

"You need to fucking listen."

"They had it coming." I swiped my lips; blood coated my tongue. My eyes narrowed on him. "Should you be out of the house?"

Nazai ignored my question and finally released me, turning to Ted whose eyes bounced between us. "Carry on," Nazai told me, stepping back. I was surprised by his words.

I knew this wasn't over, Nazai didn't like it when I went against his commands, but that was a problem I would worry about later.

Someone pounded on the door in a hurry as I stepped out of the kitchen with my apple juice in hand. Nazai unlocked and pulled the door open.

"Mom, Dad, I wasn't expecting you two." It was a good thing he had such high security in this place and could see who was always at the door since he never bothered to ask who was on the other side.

"Nazai!" Nora rushed her son with wide, wild eyes filled with concern. "Why are you out of bed?" She whipped around to face me. "He was shot, aren't you taking care of him?"

My eyes narrowed. "I didn't tell him to get out of bed."

"Mom, I'm good. Lucas said I can move around, just have to take it easy."

"No, you should be in bed."

Dominic spoke up, stepping forward.

"Nora, leave the boy alone. You don't need to baby him."

"Pops is right, I'm good. I took my pain medicine and I only came down because I saw you two were coming up." Nazai was stubborn, I learned that quickly, so if he was in any pain he wasn't gonna admit it.

"We need to talk," Dominic told Nazai, leveling a stare at him.

"We can talk in my office." Nazai nodded. His eyes found me and he scanned me. He hadn't mentioned last night since we got up so I'd been on edge waiting. After killing Ted, he called for cleanup then we headed home. He barely said a word to me which was worse than him "punishing me".

Dominic and Nazai left the living room, heading for his office, leaving me alone with Nora. She stared at me for a second, observing the room. Her eyes paused on the newly replaced fish tank and she walked over to it.

"Were you there when my son was shot?" she asked after a while. Her back was still to me as she studied the exotic fish.

"I was."

"Mhm." Nora turned to face me with a look of disdain on her face. "And what did you do when he was shot?"

One of my brows rose. "If you have something to say, then say it." I crossed my arms over my chest and rested my weight on one leg.

"My family hasn't been shot at; then my son brings you in the picture and there's been two shootings, one where my son was hit."

I poked the inside of my cheek with my tongue. I had let the first threat Nora tossed my way slide, but she wouldn't get a second. The warning in her eyes and tone was obvious. "Your son was shot because he took a bullet for me. Every action your son does is because he wants to. If you want to blame someone, then go dig up the man that shot him and yell at him." Not bothering to stick around to continue the back and forth, I turned and headed for the elevator to go upstairs. My stomach still felt funny and a headache was forming. The last thing I was about to do was argue with my husband's mother.

CHAPTER THIRTY ONE

"So which one told you?" I asked Dad once I was behind my desk, sitting down. My wounds ached faintly but I ignored it. I wasn't about to let flesh wounds keep me down.

"Now, son," he started in Spanish. "Do you think there could be a shooting at your club and I wouldn't hear word of it? I'm retired. Not dead."

I smirked. Of course he would hear about it. Right before they arrived I had been reading the latest blog post from *The Shadows of Silver Stone*. According to them, my family's corruption and shady dealings were finally catching up with us. It amazed me how she could be right and wrong at the same time.

"Now explain what's going on. You haven't even been over the family for three months and you're already getting shot and bringing unneeded attention to yourself."

Stroking my beard, I leaned down and gave Dad a summary of what'd been going on. He didn't interrupt, his face stayed blank.

"So you mean to tell me the moment you take over things, instead of continuing business like it's been running, you decide to kill your wife's ex-fiancé and start a war with his family, leading you to getting shot?"

My shoulders lifted. "My wife's enemy became my enemy. She had an issue and I did what I needed to do as her husband. You would have done the same thing for Mom. Hell, the whole reason we're in this line of business is because your granddad was getting justice for his wife who was attacked and never got any."

One corner of Dad's mouth lifted. "No need to justify anything, hijo. I never said your actions were wrong. However, you must know that by bringing a war to the family you put targets on everyone's backs. As the head of the family, it's up to you to keep the peace and make sure shit runs smoothly."

"I don't need to be reminded of what my duties are. When there's a job worth taking, I will make sure we handle it. This is a minor situation that will be taken care of. Neil isn't a threat or anything I'm worried about."

Dad's jaw clenched. "And the man that shot you?"

My smirk heightened. "My wife took care of him."

In true Cashlynn's fashion, she went against what I said and did what she wanted. Since I had grown accustomed to sleeping next to her, I realized she was no longer in bed with me and I knew where she was headed before I even checked the tracker. I was pissed that she'd acted on her own and went against what I said, but her reasoning made sense. Not only was she upset that she was the target, but she wanted revenge for *me*. The Cashlynn I first married would have never made that the reason, so it was hard to be too upset with her.

He shook his head. "That wife of yours is a problem, but she also seems like someone that's good to have on the team."

I couldn't agree more. Cashlynn fought me ninety percent of the time, but she was loyal. Gaining her trust wasn't easy, but slowly I was starting to see it happen.

"I can't believe I agreed to this shit," I mumbled, shifting in my seat.

Cashlynn snickered and crossed her leg at the knee while leaning back in her chair. "Don't make bets you can't win." Her head cocked to the side.

My mouth turned upside down at what was about to happen. The day we made the bet at the range I hadn't expected to lose. I was confident in my aim and knew I always hit my target, but it seemed my wife was better. The shooting prolonged her winning but she made sure to cash in when things were taken care of.

"I'm still wounded and here I am about to put another hole in my body. My dick at that." I grimaced.

There was a knock on the door and a girl peeked her head inside. "All ready?" She smiled, stepping inside of the room and closing the door behind her.

"If that's what you want to call it." I glanced down. All I had on was my briefs.

"There's no boy piercers?" Cashlynn asked, giving the girl a deadpan glare.

Me and the girl spoke at the same time.

"No guys touching my dick."

"I'm the only piercer here today."

Cashlynn's eyes narrowed as she watched the girl walk to the sink and wash her hands. She slid her eyes to me, causing me to smirk. Her jealousy was always cute to me. She reminded me of a little lap dog, cute to look at but vicious when poked.

"Okay, we're piercing the penis, correct?" The girl sat on the stool and faced me.

I cut my eyes in Cashlynn's direction before giving a stiff nod.

"Perfect. Do you know where? Go ahead and pull down your boxers."

Cashlynn cleared her throat. "Before we do that, I want to make something perfectly clear. We're here for you to pierce and that's it. No fondling or funny shit." She pulled her knife out and placed it on her lap. "Let me see anything unprofessional and you won't like the outcome."

Cashlynn's words sent a chill down my spine but also caused blood to rush to my dick. She stared at the girl with a look that could freeze the sun. Fright filled the piercer's eyes as they widened. She looked from me and Cashlynn. I shrugged and pulled my dick out.

The girl swallowed hard and wet her lips. "I-I p-p-promise no funny stuff." She lowered her eyes to the blade.

I shook my head and reached over, tapping Cashlynn's hand. "Now, now wife. No need to be jealous. Remember, *you* made this bet." I faced the piercer again. "I want to get the frenum."

Cashlynn glared at me. "Just make sure you two keep it cute."

Smirking, I sighed and shook my head. Getting my dick pierced wasn't exactly something I saw for myself, but I was a man of my word. I lost so I was gonna take the punishment like a man. Plus, I had done some research on the different types you could get and the one I chose would be beneficial to the both of us.

I was scrolling through my phone when something was tossed on the bed, gaining my attention. My brow raised seeing Cashlynn kneeling in front of me.

"I'm not supposed to have sex or anything until my dick heals more, but if you're down I'm not gonna turn you down."

She poked her lips out and rolled her eyes. "That isn't what I'm doing." She pushed up the sleeve of my short sleeve shirt.

I watched as she removed the dressing on it then reached for the bag on the bed. "This is a surprise."

"You took a bullet for me so I figured I can make sure your wounds don't get infected." I grinned as I watched her care for the wound. It had only been a couple of days since my shooting and I didn't plan on her being my personal nurse. She moved like a pro, which, knowing her background, I wasn't shocked.

"You parents showed you how to do this?" I asked.

She didn't miss a beat as she redressed the wound. "Yeah. When I was thirteen, I got shot in my leg. My parents put me through some stupid ass training drills and I got too cocky thinking I couldn't be touched. It was just a flesh wound but my mom showed me how to clean and dress it if I ever found myself in trouble."

I stared at her in disbelief. "What the fuck! Your parents raised you like you were going to war."

She snorted. "War probably would have been easier than growing up with them. I wasn't allowed to be weak in my parents' house. With the job we did, I never knew when things could go south so I always had to be prepared."

Her words sounded routine, almost as if they were drilled into her. "That's fucked up."

She shrugged and moved to grab the bottom of my shirt. Instead I beat her to it and lifted it. "Help me take it off."

Her eyes flicked up to me before nodding. I winced at the slight pain that shot through my arm.

"When did you become the Queen of Hearts?"

"I was seventeen when I took my first solo job. I wanted my work to be known, but my identity to stay hidden."

"So where did the name come from? The whole card thing?"

She paused after removing the dressing from my side. "Believe it or not I loved *Alice in Wonderland*. I thought the Queen of Hearts was a bad bitch with how she took over Wonderland and had everyone scared of her, so I used that name and the cards. Just became my signature." She shrugged.

I was astonished, not only at her answer but that she'd chosen to share that information with me as well.

"I would have never guessed that."

"I didn't have much of a childhood, but the small moments I was able to experience I cherished." This time her voice was small.

I stared down at my wife, watching as she expertly cleaned and redressed my wound. It felt like another layer was peeled off the onion sitting here talking to her. It was clear she wasn't used to opening up and showing any vulnerability because she made sure to keep her eyes on the wound and avoid my gaze.

When she was finished, she went to stand. "There, you're good now."

"Hold up." I stopped her, reaching out to grab her collar. I pulled her forward. "Thank you for that."

She shrugged. "Don't mention it."

I studied her eyes. They seemed a bit lighter than I was used to. The guard around them wasn't as strong either.

Cashlynn cleared her throat. "I'm about to get in the shower." Her eyes left mine. She was fine with eye contact when it was a face off, but she struggled to keep it in an intimate situation. I hoped over time she could get past that.

"Tell me something good, Ezra." I stepped into his office at his law firm. He was the family lawyer, so he handled the police when things happened, like the shooting at the club.

"The investigation was closed. There're no witnesses, no evidence, no shooter, and no proof anything went on." I nodded, taking a seat.

"So we're clear to open back up?"

"Yeah whenever you're ready."

I nodded. "That's what I like to hear. And what about the other problem?" I leaned forward. "I saw the post Ziora made after the shooting."

A wide grin formed on Ezra's face. "Oh, I've been keeping an eye on her. She's harmless." He licked his lips.

I saw the predatory look in his eyes. "Ezra. Remember. don't be on any funny shit with her. You're supposed to get her to stop tarnishing our family name and that's it."

"I'm handling it." He waved his hand.

My eyes narrowed while his smile grew. "We need to get her off our back. Her blog needs to stay focused on exposing any other family but ours. That's what you're supposed to be handling."

"That's what I'm doing. You can't plan an attack without knowing your target, right?" He grinned.

I stroked my beard and sighed. "Regardless, we need to shut her shit down. Emmet's been working on shutting her page down, but according to him her shit's as lethal as something he'll do."

"Yeah he told me." He scratched his chin. "I believe she's harmless though. She does kick boxing twice a week, but I don't see her as a threat."

My eyes narrowed and I shook my head.

"Anyway, let's talk about how your wife is just running around offing muthafuckers. She really snuck out and killed the shooter and Ted."

I smirked. "She did."

He shook his head and whistled. "I knew sis was one you had to watch. I saw it in her eyes that night, she wasn't gonna let it go."

I didn't try to stop the grin from forming on my face. "Yeah that's my Wildfire."

"Damn, I never thought I would see the day. At least not anytime soon." Ezra chuckled.

I stared at him confused. "See what?"

"The day you actually fell for your wife. When you first got with her I thought it was more to rebel against Dad since he didn't care for her family and was forcing you to marry, but you're falling for her."

My tongue went across my top teeth. I thought about his words. Over the past few months I did find myself more intrigued with my wife. She kept our marriage interesting with her lively spirit too. She was unpredictable and kept me on my toes, but it was exactly what I was missing with all the other girls I had been with previously.

"Maybe," I stated, stroking my beard again.

Ezra's eyes shifted to something on his desk before widening. "Shit," he exclaimed suddenly. He stood up. "I gotta head down to the courthouse."

Standing with him, I watched him move around his office. My brother was the most playful out of all of us but he wasn't the one to sleep on in the courtroom. When it was time for him to get down to business, he never cut corners, and that was why he was so highly sought out.

CHAPTER THIRTY TWO

My hands rubbed against the steering wheel as I sat in my car, across the street from the tattoo shop, waiting for my target to walk out. It was closing time and I was waiting for the piercer to walk out. I played it cool while in the room, but knowing she'd touched my husband's dick didn't sit right with me, even if I was the one who implemented it. Her smile was too big when she spoke to him too. She acted as if I wasn't there, only making conversation with Nazai who seemed to take joy in my annoyance. I waited a couple of days to scope her out before I decided to make my move.

I tapped my finger on the steering wheel and twisted my lips to the side, feeling myself grow impatient. I checked the time; the shop had closed fifteen minutes ago.

Just when I felt my patience running out, the doors to the front of the shop opened. I sat up straighter. The piercer and a guy walked out. They spoke for a few seconds before she smiled and waved, heading down the street. I watched her get to her car and climb inside. After a few seconds, she pulled off with me behind her.

My phone vibrated and I peeked at the screen, seeing it was Nazai. I quickly grabbed it and silenced it before turning it off. He could track my movements; there was no need for us to talk right now.

The girl drove about twenty minutes before pulling up to a small, single level house. She parked in the driveway and turned the car off. The lights were off in the house and there wasn't a garage to hide any other car. I parked across the street and turned my car off. The girl was oblivious to her surroundings. She stepped out of the car, smoking and looking down at her phone, tapping away on it.

Reaching over I grabbed my black hat and placed it on my head, sliding it down over my eyes. I grabbed my gun out of my bookbag that rested on the passenger seat and climbed out of the car.

Checking my left and right, I hurried across the street just as she reached her door. She took one last hit of the cigarette before tossing it in the flower bed next to her small stoop.

As soon as she opened the door and went to step inside, I ambushed her, shoving her, causing her to stumble forward and drop her phone.

"What the fuck!" she shouted.

"Shut up!" I shut the door behind me and looked around.

The house was quiet and smelled of lavender. My nose twitched.

The girl spun around and her eyes widened seeing me with my gun pointed at her.

"I don't have any money!" She tossed her hands up.

I snickered. "I don't want your damn money."

She swallowed hard. "Then what do you want? I don't have much." Her voice was shaky as her eyes locked on the gun.

A crude grin formed on my face. "The other day, you touched something you shouldn't have." I lifted my hat slightly. She squinted for a second before widening her eyes.

"It's you. Look, I was professional when I did the piercing!" she stammered. Her body shook and she stepped back.

"Doesn't matter, you still touched something that was mine." Her eyes bounced from me to the gun before turning and attempting to rush off.

I was quicker. Launching forward, I grabbed her by the hair and shoved her to the ground, causing her to cry out.

"Please, please. I was just doing my job!"

"Shut up!" I shoved her forward.

She quickly turned to face me, holding herself up on her forearms.

Tears rushed down her face.

"Don't do this. I promise I won't go to the cops."

"I know you won't." Again, I lifted my gun. "I hope you enjoyed touching my husband's dick, because it's the last one you'll ever hold." I pressed the trigger, sending a bullet through the center of her forehead. Her body crumpled with a small thump. A calm feeling filed through my veins. I pulled out my phone that I normally used for kills, since it was encrypted and couldn't be tracked, and took a picture of the girl before turning to leave. I didn't feel bad for taking the girl's life. My feelings were invested in this marriage now and that was something I didn't take lightly.

The doorman nodded at me with a smile once I got to the penthouse lobby as I walked past him and headed for the elevator. Nazai didn't know what I was up to while I was out but I was sure he wouldn't be happy about me ignoring him.

Now I was stepping inside his room, wondering what I was walking into. Nazai was lying in bed. his eyes locked on the door.

"Oh look, it's my missing wife," he said, setting his phone to the side. "Why were you downtown?" I ran my eyes over him, taking in his ripped body. Even with the dressings from his shooting, I could never deny how handsome my husband was and just thinking about him with anyone else, or someone else touching him, made my stomach turn and my blood run hot.

Instead of answering him, I walked to the bed silently. I dug into my back pocket, pulling the phone out and clicking on it, then tossing it on his chest.

He stared at me confused then reached for the phone as I moved toward the bathroom, needing to shower my kill off me.

"This the piercer?" he asked.

Not facing him, I paused. "It is."

"You killed her?"

"Doesn't it look like it?"

Nazai chuckled. "Is there a reason why?"

This time I turned back and looked at him. Mirth filled his eyes with a crooked grin plastered on his face.

"Because she touched something that didn't belong to her."

He glanced at the phone again. "You know we went to her, right?"

"And she fulfilled her duties. Too bad it cost her life." I glanced at the phone. "Let this be a lesson. Last time your neck was cut, this time a girl lost her life, next time I might have a bullet with someone else's name on it." My voice stayed calm and I locked my eyes on him, but my stomach roared with jealousy.

Nazai chuckled again. "No matter how threatening you try to be, your jealousy will always be sexy as fuck to me. Knowing you'd kill over me shouldn't turn me on like it does. If I could right now, I'd have you climb on top and take me on a ride." He licked his lips, eyeing me hungrily. My stomach exploded in excitement, goosebumps covered my arms, and between my legs throbbed with want. "Lesson heard loud and clear, wifey."

"Good." I cleared my throat, then spun around, rushing into the bathroom and shutting the door behind me. My heart raced, slamming against my ribcage. A tightness filled my chest when the reality of what was happening hit me. I inhaled a deep breath and swallowed hard.

I was falling for my husband.

"Don't go in here reckless," Nazai said, his eyes leveling on me then cutting them into slits.

"I don't need you to tell me that," I responded, matching his stare.

"Do you know how many people are inside the church?" Lucas asked from across the table.

We were at the family meeting house and it was time for us to infiltrate one of Neil's safe spaces. Rumor had it he had been seen coming in and out of an abandoned church. It had been a week since Nazai had been shot and he finally made the call to go after Neil. I was becoming anxious, sitting around and waiting had never been my strong suit.

"Mommy would have our balls if she knew we were about to go shoot up a church," Ezra noted with a chuckle.

"He uses it as a front anyway. It hasn't been active in years," Nazai said, then turned to face his youngest brother. "Emmet, pull up the floor plans." It was unconventional, having to go shoot up a church, even if it wasn't in use anymore.

We turned toward the screen as Emmet pulled up the floor plans. "My men have been keeping an eye on things. It looks like he keeps four guards there around the clock," River chimed in. "Two in the front of the church. Two in the back. We estimated about four or five inside as well."

Nazai began speaking again, but I tuned him out, studying the floor plans. The church wasn't extra big and going in blind wasn't exactly the best move, but we didn't have a lot of options.

"Emmet, the parking garage across the street gives you full view to let shots off, right?" Nazai asked his brother.

"Yeah, I'll have a clear view and will be able to keep an eye out."

"Good. You take out the two front guards, then River, you go along the back and take the back ones out. Once that's handled, we'll go inside."

"You're still not a hundred percent. I'd much rather you sit this one out, but I know you won't," Lucas interrupted with a frown.

"You know me well, brother, and if anything happens, you'll be right there to help." Nazai grinned.

I spoke up. "I want the kill shot when we find Neil." My nerves were running wild as if they had been electrocuted. My heart raced with anticipation. Once Neil was taken out, the Rhodes would officially be off the market and no longer an issue we had to worry about. Their operation had been shut down by Major so their funds weren't coming in like they used to. Neil would have been smart to just leave town instead of sticking around for revenge.

Nazai turned and stared at me. I couldn't read the look on his face, but he didn't argue with me.

"In and out. We'll only have a limited time before the cops come and that's even with our contacts. Don't bullshit around and make sure you stay on guard."

Nazai eyed the table. Everyone looked like they were ready for business. This was the first official mission I would go on with everyone. I was used to working alone and handling things on my own so this would be new. As long as no one got in my way, I would play along.

Checking my gun, I made sure it was loaded and the safety was off as we waited for the signal to let us know it was good for us to go inside.

"Cashlynn," Nazai called out. My eyes left the gun and went to him. I knew whatever he was about to say had to be serious because he never used my real name when addressing me.

"Be smart when we go in there."

"You don't have to tell me that. This isn't my first kill."

"But it's your first time working with us. We don't go into situations being reckless and we make sure to have each other's backs. Don't go in here with a solo mindset and keep your eyes open. River did his best scoping out the area but we don't know exactly how many men could be inside of here."

I could tell by the look in his eyes he was serious. He wasn't saying this to piss me off, but more so to warn me or maybe because he cared. I tucked my lips in my mouth and gave him a stiff nod.

"Ezra, you too. Don't be on any reckless shit," he said.

"I got this, big bro." Ezra waved him off. I stared at the back of his head from the back seat of the truck. He was calm and collected. It was hard to believe he was a high-powered lawyer in the daytime. Lucas was in the driver's seat quietly staring at the church across from us diagonally. The sun was setting, the sky was a dark tint of orange, purple, and red. This street was on the lower end of the city. Most of the buildings were abandoned and had been taken over by gangs. Crime was high in this area and it was why the Rhodes operated successfully here.

I watched as one of the guys in front of the church fell in amazement. I remembered Nazai mentioning Emmet was a sniper but seeing it firsthand was different. Before the second guy could react, he was taken down too. I made sure my hat was on my head.

"Front cleared," Emmet said into our earpieces. It wasn't long before River's voice sounded too. "Back cleared."

"Let's go."

We filed out of the car and headed for the church. The street was clear of any unwanted eyes or attention.

"Ready?" Ezra said once we got to the door. We nodded and he grinned before sending his foot into the door, making it fly open.

"The fuck!" someone shouted, followed by a shot. The guy in one of the pews went down easily. We moved down the aisle. Quickly, I lifted my gun and aimed, pulling the trigger seeing movement coming from the side.

Shouting and movement could be heard from the left hallway.

Shots came from out of nowhere, bullets whizzed past us.

"Fuck, get down!" Lucas shouted.

Hurriedly, we continued, dropping down. Nazai lifted and sent a shot forward. A grunt sounded. The sounds of the guns going off echoed off the empty walls.

Ezra, not bothering to wait, rushed forward. "Ez!" Nazai called out but he ignored his brother. Not wanting to miss the fun, I followed him. Ezra shot the guy Nazai had already taken out one last time before moving down the hallway.

A shot rang out toward the end of the hall. "It's me!" River said into the earpiece and soon rounded the corner coming into view. "It's clear back there."

"No sign of Neil?" Nazai asked, kicking open a door and pointing his gun.

"No."

"I don't think he's here.," Ezra said once we checked all the rooms. In the distance a few shots could be heard.

"Emmet, what's it looking like out there?" Nazai asked into his earpiece.

"Still clear. No sign of Neil," Emmet answered.

I gritted my teeth. The hide and seek was growing old. If he truly wanted to get revenge for his son, he should show face and handle things accordingly.

"We're gonna check the basement." Nazai nodded at River.

"I'm coming with you," Ezra said.

"You two check the last three rooms down there. If I remember correctly, it's an office, kitchen, and bathroom," Nazai told me and Lucas. We looked at each other. I knew he wasn't my biggest fan.

"Yeah a'right."

We separated and they turned toward the basement door.

"I'm going to check the office," Lucas said, moving right.

Nodding, I went to the half-open door and stood on the side of it. Holding my hand securely, I counted to three before pushing it open. It was a single bathroom, with only a sink and toilet.

"Damnit," I groaned.

I wasn't sure when the last time Neil was here, but it was clear it hadn't been anytime lately.

"Office's clear," Lucas said.

"So that leaves the kitchen."

Pushing out a deep breath, I readjusted my hat and followed Lucas. It looked like we had taken out everyone up here. There weren't too many of Neil's men, just like River had mentioned at the meeting.

I opened the door close to the opening of the kitchen, seeing it was an empty storage closet. The kitchen led into the dining room and it looked like neither had been touched in a while.

I turned to let Lucas know everything was clear in the kitchen when I noticed a guy creeping toward Lucas.

"Lucas, duck!" I shouted, lifting my gun.

His eyes widened and he did as I said. The guy looked surprised and tried to hurry to point his gun at me but I was too quick. My finger pressed the trigger and the bullet pierced his chest.

He went down instantly.

Lucas rushed the guy, sending two more shots into him.

"Fuck, where did he come from?"

I looked around. "Over there."

We headed in that direction. "Thank you," Lucas mentioned when we got to the open door.

I faced him and bobbed my head. "You're welcome."

No one else was inside the small room. It looked to be another storage room but was now empty.

"The cops finally got wind of the shootings. They're on the way," Emmet said. He had a scanner with him that was tracking police movement.

"That's fine. The basement's clear. Neil's not here," Nazai said into the headset. "We can head out."

Annoyance filled me. "Damnit!" I stomped my foot. I didn't know where his ass was hiding but I was over it.

"C'mon," Lucas said, heading for the main doors that led back to the kitchen.

We left, making sure to still be on guard.

By the time we got to the main doors of the church, Nazai and them were getting there too. The distant sounds of sirens grew in the wind. We hurried across the street to where the two trucks were.

"Hurry up," Emmet said, already back in the truck.

We filed inside and I snatched my hat off, tossing it to the ground. "This is bullshit!" I shouted.

"Now what?" Ezra asked when Lucas started the car.

"Now we wait. We've taken out his men here. He knows the place he once thought was safe is out. There's a bounty on his head. He's like a roach scrambling now. All we have to do is wait for him to show his face, then we take him out," Nazai replied. "The other places he was known to operate out of were abandoned according to River."

I didn't like the plan but I knew there wasn't much else we could do. This was the second time Neil's men had been taken out and he'd avoided death. It was clear time was not on his side. Nazai was right; it was only a matter of time before he came into the light.

NAZAI TAVAREZ

CHAPTER THIRTY THREE

I lay in bed smiling as I listened to Cashlynn throw up for the third time this week. She thought I didn't notice when she got up and went into the bathroom, but it was happening more frequently. Too frequent to ignore.

It had been a few days since we'd raided the church we thought Neil was hiding out at and he hadn't shown himself yet, but I made sure River had his guys around at all times. Neil was gonna get desperate and I wanted everyone protected.

My arm that was shot was a bit stiff as I climbed out the bed and headed for the bathroom, where the door was closed. Grabbing the handle, I pushed it open and leaned on the archway. Cashlynn was on her knees, gripping the toilet, releasing her stomach. I waited for her to realize I was there. After wiping her mouth and flushing the toilet, she lifted her head and her eyes widened upon seeing me. Her skin was pale, her cheeks were flushed, and her eyes watered.

"You feeling sick?" I asked as she walked over to the double sink to wash her hands and rinse her mouth out.

"No. I'm fine."

I smirked. "Just in case, I think you need to look under the sink and grab what's under there."

She looked over her shoulder at me confused. "What's under there?"

"Look."

After drying her hands, she leaned down and opened the cabinet.

"What the hell is this?" She shot up with the pregnancy test box in hand.

"What does it look like?" I cocked my head to the side and raised a brow.

Her mouth turned upside down. "Why would I need this? I'm on birth control; there's no way I can be pregnant."

My smile broadened. "Funny thing about that."

Her eyes narrowed and her mouth pinched. "What's that mean?"

"I told you in the beginning, I needed an heir by the end of the year. You were dead set on not getting pregnant anytime soon, so I had to take matters into my own hands."

Cashlynn's body tensed. Her grip on the box tightened. "What the hell does that mean?" she asked tightly.

I crossed my arms over my chest and ran my eyes over her body, pausing at her midsection. I had suspected for a few weeks that she might be pregnant. It was why I had the pregnancy test waiting for her.

"I had my brother get me some sugar pills and switched them with your birth control pills."

Her mouth widened and her brows shot to her hairline. For the first time I had left her speechless. Her right eyes twitched and her nostrils flared.

"You did what?"

I shrugged and stood straight. "Since you refused to do what I needed, I decided to take matters into my own hands. When you agreed to be my wife, you agreed to give me a baby too."

"I didn't agree to this shit!" she shrieked, waving the box. Her body trembled. "You blackmailed me into marrying you and I told you I didn't want a baby right now!"

"That didn't work for me," I told her calmly. It was clear she was a second away from exploding and I was preparing myself. When she found out what I did, I expected for her to react badly. Cashlynn didn't like being forced against a wall or into something she didn't want to do.

Cashlynn blinked rapidly, her eyes bouncing between me and the pregnancy test in her hands.

"Just take the test and—"

I moved quickly when she launched it at me. "I'm not taking the fucking test!" Her honey-colored orbs were like sharp lasers blazing into me. Her face glowered in a mask of rage.

"I can't believe you would do this!" My brows drew together. It could be a mistake but I thought I might have heard a bit of hurt in her angry tone.

Cashlynn stormed toward me and I expected her to attack me, but instead she shoved past me. I turned around, watching her move around the bedroom like a tornado, eventually stalking out and slamming the door behind her.

"Well that went better than I expected," I mumbled.

Dropping my eyes to the floor, they landed on the pregnancy test and I couldn't help but grin. If Cashlynn was carrying my baby, then this marriage was about to get a lot more interesting.

"You're right; the kid has good instincts," Lucas mentioned, watching Ezra and Carson spar with one another. We were currently at the farmhouse, in the basement. Although impulsive at times, Ezra was the best hand-to-hand fighter out of the four of us. The two had on boxing gloves and headgear. Carson wasn't doing bad holding his own either. I was gonna have River train him but he had a job under his security firm today.

"Told you. I've been training him for a little over a month and already see improvement in him. He's been working with Emmet too; he's into technology and shit."

Lucas rubbed his chin. "You plan on bringing him in the business?"

"Right now? No. I doubt his sister will let me anyway." I chuckled. "But in the future if he wants to?" I shrugged. "Even still, he needs to learn basic skills and stop being so scared of everything."

Lucas nodded in agreement. His eyes fell back on my brother and Carson. "So what did you call me here for? I assume it wasn't because you want me to teach him how to do medical shit. Did you bust your stitches?" His eyes swiveled to me and he narrowed them.

"Nah, I actually got some good news I wanted to share in person." My mouth lifted into a wide grin. "Cashlynn's pregnant." Pride swelled in my chest. She might not have taken the test, but the signs were obvious.

"Damn, for real? It's about time! I bet she was surprised." He chuckled.

"Hell yeah, I thought I was about to prepare for war."

He shook his head. "If I thought I was preventing pregnancy only to learn my prevention was tampered with I'd be ready to go to war too."

I shrugged. "She'll get over it. The end of the year was growing closer and we were running out of time." An heir was needed within the first year of marriage. Her being pregnant now would make that happen and be one less thing to worry about later. Plus, I was excited to have someone to pass my legacy to when the time came.

Lucas lifted his hand and patted my back. "After we raided that church, I grew respect for your wife. She saved my life, but I also learned she's someone that you shouldn't fuck with. I would sleep with one eye open."

He turned and walked to where the sparing was. I pulled my phone out and went to my tracking app, checking to see where Cashlynn was. She was at my other house, using the shooting range I assumed. It seemed to be her favorite place when she was upset.

My attention was caught when Carson flew back on his ass, bouncing off the mat.

"Damn," Lucas muttered.

"Shit, Ezra, You had to hit him that hard?" I slid my phone back into my back pocket and walked closer to where they were.

"He was distracted. Distractions will get you killed," Ezra explained.

I walked to Carson and held my hand out, helping him up. "You good?"

He nodded. "I'm fine." He cut his eyes at Ezra who was smiling at him.

"See he's good. I ain't even hit him that hard."

"It's been a minute since we put the gloves on. You tryna run a round, doc?" I asked Lucas.

"These are million dollar hands. Do you think I'm gonna risk them?"

I waved him off. "If you're scared you can admit it, little bro. I'll go with Ezra."

His eyes narrowed. "One round, but we need to take it easy; you're still healing."

I waved his concerns off. "That's what I like to hear."

It had been a minute since I'd sparred with any of my brothers. We used to do it a lot when we were growing up. My dad made sure even though I was the only one to go the assassin route that all of us were trained and prepared for anything.

I was mid cut into my steak at my dinner table when Cashlynn came into view. Sticking my fork into the cut piece, I lifted it to my mouth while watching her. She stood where the living room and kitchen connected, watching me with a blank expression on her face.

"You gotta be hungry. Come over here," I said. She had been at my other house all day. From what Luke and Bruce said, she hadn't eaten anything and spent most of her time at the range.

Her eyes bounced around the dining room, her lips twisted and hands balled as she slowly strode toward the table. She went to sit across from me but I stopped her.

"Uh, uh. Over here." I reached for the chair at my side, pulling it out.

Her brows drew downward in a frown but she did as I said. A crooked grin split my face. Cashlynn plopped down in the seat and I cut into the medium well NY Strip and picked a piece up with my fork, holding it out for her.

Her eyes cut into slits and dropped to the held-out fork. "I know you're hungry and you need to feed my baby." As she snapped her eyes up, they burned with defiance. Her mouth tightened. I shoved the fork closer. Slowly Cashlynn moved in with her mouth open and snagged the meat.

"Good girl. Another." I grabbed another piece of steak. Between the bites of steak, I made sure to give her some of the garlic mashed potatoes too. Her tongue slid across her bottom lip, collecting some food caught on it.

Time passed and soon the plate was empty and I was satisfied.

"Now don't you feel better?"

Cashlynn stared at me with an emotionless expression. "You take joy in what you did, don't you?" she finally asked.

"I'm not upset at it." I picked up the glass of brown liquor and swirled the ice around.

"You shouldn't have messed with my birth control. I'm so tired of my choices being made for me." Her hands balled into fists and slammed on the table. Her voice was shaky as she continued, "Since I was a kid my life has never been mine. My parents forced me into the life they wanted for me. I was forced to be a parent to a child I didn't birth. You blackmailed me to marry you. And now you're forcing me to be a mother. I told you that's not what I wanted!" With each word she spoke, her voice grew louder, with a growing edge. Raw hurt glittered in her honey eyes.

Setting the glass down, I twisted so I was facing her fully. "If you're scared you won't be a good mother then—"

"That's not the issue here!" Cashlynn shot out of her chair and stormed across the room until she got to the large windows. I had the automatic curtains open, giving a full view of the city lights below and darkened sky above.

Her stance remained stiff with her shoulders full of tension. Standing up, I followed her and walked over to her, pressing my body against her and moving her hair off her neck. Leaning down, I inhaled her scent and closed my eyes.

"Then explain it to me."

All day I'd been battling my feelings, trying to deny the obvious truth of what was going on in my body. For weeks I'd been feeling off. My breasts had grown achy. I'd been sick and throwing up more and having more random headaches. I kept trying to tell myself it was a bug that would soon pass. When Nazai admitted to tampering with my birth control, I was livid. The terrifying realization of what was to come hit me like a raging truck.

I spent today taking my frustration out at the gun range at Nazai's other house. Each time I pulled the trigger I tried to picture Nazai's face. He had gone against my wishes for his own gain.

Growing up, I'd never felt like my life was mine. My parents had decided when I was born what I would grow up to be. I didn't mind killing, actually enjoyed it, so I didn't fight it once I was brought into the life, but that didn't take away the fact that the choice had never been mine.

Nazai kissed the nape of my neck, just above the collar. His warm breath tickled my skin. I wanted to push him away, but part of me couldn't deny wanting his touch.

"My parents only had me because they needed someone to join the family business," I started, staring out into the night sky. "They were never nurturing parents. They didn't hug me or tell me they loved me. All they did was train me to be a heartless killer. Growing up I saw them easily dispose of those who were deemed useless to them. Because I never wanted to be in that boat, I made sure to comply with everything they threw at me.

"I was homeschooled until I was thirteen because they never wanted me influenced by anyone who could make me want to go against what they wanted. When Carson was born, my parents couldn't be entertained with an infant, so they pushed him on me. I didn't know shit about raising a baby; I didn't even know how to show affection, but I tried. Early on it was clear to see Carson wasn't built for the assassin life. He was soft hearted, always smiling and wanting to play, you know, be a normal kid and my parents hated it, so they ignored him most of the time."

Pausing, I melted into Nazai when his hand wrapped around my midsection. I tried not to flinch when his hand rested on my stomach. I chewed the inside of my cheek. Talking about my childhood brought back a lot of different emotions. My heart felt like a weight in my chest.

"I was sixteen the first time I took a life, seventeen the first time I took a solo job. I trained and trained so my parents would leave Carson alone and allow him to keep being a kid. He was the first person to ever smile at me and genuinely be happy I was around. It was also the first time I loved someone and I knew I needed to protect him at all cost." A heavy sigh left my mouth. "The older I got, the more I saw my parents fucked up ways. They were into a lot of shit, more than just killing." My jaw clenched painfully hard.

"I never was taught what a good parent was. I didn't see it growing up. I was raised to be a killing machine. I don't know how to love or receive it. My parents raised me to be fucked up. Why the hell would I want to do the same when it comes to my own child? Why would you even want that with me?"

Nazai's thumb stroked my stomach lightly. His teeth brushed over my jawline before he pressed a kiss into it.

"You're saying all that, but you forgot that you already raised a kid, Cashlynn. You just said that you've been taking care of Carson since he was born. Regardless of if it was voluntarily or involuntarily, you need to give yourself more credit. Your parents are gone now. If you keep holding on to what they taught you, you'll be chained to them for the rest of your life."

My eyes closed. A tumble of confused thoughts and feelings assailed me. A warning voice whispered in my head. Since Carson had been born, my focus had been to protect him and keep him out of my parents' clutches. It wasn't too hard since my parents ignored Carson once they realized he wasn't built like us. Up until their last moments played in my head, the anger I felt toward them trampled in my chest.

Slowly blinking my eyes open, I bit into my bottom lip until I tasted blood.

"I killed them," I admitted out loud for the first time.

"Killed who?" Nazai kissed up my jawline.

"My parents. Everyone thought it was a robbery, but it was me. They weren't happy with how Carson turned out and I overheard them talking about selling him."

"Selling him?"

I became numb with increasing rage. My body ran hot and trembled with fury.

"Turns out my parents were into human trafficking. I don't know how they got involved in it or who they worked with but they planned on selling my brother off to whoever they were working for. Apparently a young, prepubescent, virgin boy would make them a lot of money and they decided it was the only way he would be useful. They saw my brother as some cash cow and didn't give a damn about giving their child up. I couldn't let that happen and I couldn't stand around and keep letting them do fucked up shit for their own selfish gain. So I killed them."

I remembered the rush I felt as the bullet went through my parents' heads. I made sure to wake them up so I would be the last face they saw before they met their end. Till this day I hadn't felt an ounce of remorse and would do it again.

It caught me off guard when Nazai spun me around and pressed my back against the glass. His body pressed into mine and he nuzzled his face into my neck.

"So you killed them in cold blood to protect you brother, huh?" he breathed in a husky tone. A tingling formed in the pit of my stomach. "I could picture it, you standing over them with your gun pointed, expressionless, dressed in all black. I know you looked sexy as hell." My heart jolted and my pulse pounded when his tongue grazed my skin. His breathing grew heavier, causing goosebumps to scatter across my skin.

"You say you don't know how to love or nurture but you did what you needed to do to protect your brother. Since the moment I met you, you've been doing it. I have no doubt you would do the same with our child."

His hand brushed across my stomach. "When I decided to make you my wife, it was because I saw something in you I knew I needed. I still see that. This whole marriage you've challenged and pushed me. You've cut me, you cursed me out, you've threatened me and that fire has been the driving force behind my feelings for you. It's the main thing that attracted me to you. So don't worry about what you think you lack because I don't see that shit as a flaw."

Nazai moved his hand down and pushed it under my shirt. His bare hand felt warm against my stomach. He didn't stop moving his hand up until he got to my breast, cuffing it through my bra.

"You're gonna have my baby and be the best fucking mom too," he growled. I moaned when he slipped his hand inside my bra and fondled my nipples.

"Tell me, Wildfire. Tell me you want to have my baby." His teeth nipped my skin. My breathing sped up in an uneven rhythm. Nazai grabbed the bottom of my shirt and lifted it over my head, tossing it to the side.

"Your breasts already seem heavier than normal. Are they more sensitive?" His head dipped and he bit the top of my cleavage, making me cry out. My hands went to his shoulders. He explored my skin with his mouth, sending a shiver up my spine. Closing my eyes and tossing my head back, I clenched my legs as my wetness grew.

"Are you gonna have my baby?" He licked the bite and sucked it roughly. "Tell me you're gonna have my baby."

It became hard to breathe as my heart beat wildly while a million butterflies fluttered inside my stomach. He moved his hand to my jeans and undid the button while kissing his way between the valley of my breasts. My chest rose, wanting to feel him more.

"She's wet for me, huh?" His hand slid into my now opened jeans and brushed over my pussy.

A whimper fell from my mouth. Blood rushed to my clit, it pulsated with need.

"Yes," I whined, rolling my hips.

"These are too fucking tight." He pulled away and kneeled. I watched him in a lustful haze as he pulled my jeans along with my panties down my legs, helping him remove them.

My knees buckled when he kissed the inside of my thighs, making his way up to my pussy. He inhaled a sharp breath.

"You always smell so fucking good." I cried out again when his rough tongue ran up my pussy and he pulled my clit into his mouth.

"Are you gonna have my baby?" His tongue skillfully flicked against my lower lips. My hands went to his shoulders, gripping them tightly.

His teeth suddenly sank into my clit, sending a jolt of lightning up my body. "Oh fuck!"

"Tell me." Again, he sucked and rolled his tongue.

"Yes, fuck yes!" I whined when he pulled back and kissed my pussy teasingly.

"That's what I like to hear." He lifted to his feet and gazed down at me. His lips shone with my juices along with his beard.

"Taste how good you are." He stuck his tongue out. My heart stuttered as I leaned up and sucked his tongue into my mouth. He gripped my sides tightly, pulling my body closer to his. I became drunk off my essence.

"Can't wait to see how full these get," he rasped, cuffing my breasts. When he flickered his eyes to meet mine, my breath became caught in my throat at the intense emotions coming from them. "You and my baby won't ever have to worry about anything. I didn't think it would happen so soon but I fell in lo—"

"Don't!" I begged, lifting my hand and covering his mouth. My heart fell into my stomach. The words that he was about to say, I wasn't ready to hear. "Not yet. I just can't," I whispered.

He stared into my eyes deeply and cuffed my cheek. "Okay." He pecked my lips. "Okay."

Nazai fumbled with his sweats, then leaned down, picking me up with my back still against the glass before lowering me onto his dick. A low moan fell from my lips as he stretched me good. My walls grew wetter the more he sunk into me.

I wrapped my arms around his neck and my head fell back as he began moving in and out of me.

"What about your piercing?" I asked the moment I felt it inside of me. It rubbed against my insides, intensifying the pleasure he brought me. He was supposed to use condoms for the next few months while he healed.

"Fuck this piercing. I'll never use a barrier between us. I only ever want your juices to touch my tongue or dick." I moaned at his crude words. The cool glass felt good against my warm body. I was glad we were on the highest floor, otherwise people would get an eyeful.

"Your stitches."

"Fuck these stitches," he said tightly.

Nazai lowered his forehead onto mine as he pushed into me, his piercing tapping against the spot that caused my body to tremble. Pleasure shot through my body and my walls clamped around his dick. I bit into my bottom lip, attempting to push down the whimper desperate to escape.

"I feel your walls tightening around me, you ready to cum, baby?" he rasped as he pushed up while pulling my body down. Heat spread through me as if I was in a sauna.

"I wanna feel you wet my dick up more. Go 'head, be a good girl and let me have it." He pecked my lips, sucking my bottom lip into his mouth.

My eyes rolled to the back of my head as an orgasm exploded through me. "Fuck, we always make magic together, don't we? You love the way I abuse this pussy, don't you?"

I nodded, my brain currently a pile of mush. Ecstasy replaced every thought, ridding my mind of anything but the pleasure Nazai brought my body.

"I know. Since I popped that cherry and you bled on my dick, I've been obsessed with your ass too. You knew that though, didn't you?"

Again unable to form words, I bobbed my head. His forehead pressed against mine again. His heavy breaths brushed over my face. My lips parted and a small gasp escaped.

He moved his hand to the collar on my neck and tugged on it. "You became mine the moment I chained you up in my bedroom." The raw possession in his voice wrapped around my heart and hugged it securely.

"Yours," I breathed, clenching my pussy around him. His strokes were slower, but still just as deep. I felt him everywhere. My pussy gushed like a raging lake on his length. My stomach grew tight with desire. My heart pounded like a drum.

"Mine." He captured my mouth again. Bolts of electric shot through my veins as I came again. He swallowed my cries, pumping into me a little quicker before releasing inside me.

"Does it feel good when I cum inside you? Knowing that I own you?"

"Yes," I sighed.

"I love knowing you got me inside you too baby." He pecked my lips. "I love knowing that every inch of you is *mine.* I love…" He kissed me again, this time moving along my jawline. The ghost of the words left unsaid lingered between us.

I was still against the whole pregnancy thing, but I'd make that a conversation for tomorrow.

"You're lucky the stitches were ready to come out," Lucas complained as he checked over Nazai's wounds. Nazai called him over when we got up to check him out, after realizing he might have overdone it last night.

"Even if they weren't, you could have just stitched me back up, right?" Nazai grinned at his brother who glared at him.

"I told you to take it easy until you healed, but you act just like Ezra, never fucking listen." He wiped the wound.

"They were flesh wounds. You act like they were life-threatening."

"That's not the point. Does this hurt.?" He pressed the wound on his side.

"Just tender."

"That's to be expected. They both look good, but I would still take it easy because they're still healing. Continue to clean them with antibacterial soap and use this ointment on it." Lucas went into his bag and pulled out a small, rectangle box and tossed it on the bed.

"I need you to do another favor for me," Nazai said as Lucas started cleaning up. His eyes fell on me. Cutting my eyes into slits, I shook my head.

"We need to find out how far Cashlynn is." This morning I sucked it up and took a test. I barely was able to pee on the stick before it popped up positive.

"I'm a surgeon; not an obstetrician."

"Then I need a name to one. A good one."

Lucas turned and focused on me, one corner of his mouth rising. "I guess congrats are in order, huh?" I rolled my eyes and crossed my arms over my chest. A low laugh left his mouth. "I'll make some calls for you. In the meantime, no wild shit. I know that isn't good for the baby."

"Yeah, yeah," I mumbled.

Again, he chortled and stood. "A'right brother, if there's nothing else I'll see myself out."

Once we were alone, Nazai lifted his head and stared at me. "You know Lucas had a point right?"

My brows scrunched. "About what?"

"You not doing any wild shit. With Neil still out there, you need to be more lowkey and no more killing while you're pregnant with my baby."

"I'm not changing my life and living in a bubble just because you trapped me."

He grinned. "Of course you are, wifey." He stood and crept toward me. Towering over me, he cuffed my chin, forcing my head up. "If anything happens to my baby because you're being reckless, I promise I'll make you suffer a fate worse than death." His eyes darkened along with his tone. The smile that formed on his mouth sent chills down my spine. "Understand?"

I snatched out of his grip. "Don't threaten me."

He brushed his hand down my arm and tilted his head slightly. "Oh it's not a threat, Wildfire, it's a promise." He bent down and pecked my lips. "Now I got some errands to run. Don't leave this house without a guard with you and let me know when you leave too."

"Why? You have my location."

"Doesn't matter." He tapped my nose. "Now smile and tell me you'll miss me when I'm gone."

My mouth turned upside down and he laughed. "It's okay, I know you will. I'll miss you too." He kissed me again, this time longer and harder. I sank into the gesture easily, enjoying the feel of his lips against mine.

"Take it easy today. I'll be back later," he muttered against my lips then pulled back.

It felt odd having someone worry about my wellbeing, even if part of it was because I was now carrying a life inside of me. It felt good in a way. It made me feel like for the first time in my life, someone outside of my brother truly cared about me.

"**W**hat brings you by?" my dad asked as my mom settled in on his lap. My nose scrunched watching her leaning back into him and his arm going around her waist. I could tell my dad had been taking his retirement seriously. He looked less stressed and he was even dressed down, something he hardly did.

"I have some news you'll be interested in," I replied.

His eyes found mine and his brow rose with interest. "You handled your problem I hope."

"That's being taken care of, but this news is even better."

Both of my parents focused on me. "Don't keep us waiting. Tell us what it is," Mom encouraged.

"The final part of the takeover has been taken care of."

At first, both looked confused by my words. Before long, realization filled my dad's face. "You mean?"

I nodded. "Cashlynn is pregnant."

Mom's eyes shot open and filled with excitement. "Oh Nazai. I'm going to be a grandma?" Mom asked in Spanish, hopping out of dad's lap and rushing toward me. "That makes me so happy!"

I laughed as she leaned down to hug me.

"How far is she? When did you find out? Is she taking care of herself?"

Mom pulled back and looked at me.

"We don't know yet. I'm waiting for Lucas to give me a doctor's name. We just found out. And she's fine."

Mom grabbed my face and bounced her eyes around it. "You're about to be a father. That makes me so happy. You're turning into such a fine young man. I'm so proud of you!" she gushed, still speaking my father's native language.

The corners of my mouth lifted. "Thanks, Mama." I swiveled my eyes to my dad, who hadn't said anything.

"Are you happy now? You wanted a marriage and a baby and that's what I did."

That look I normally saw him wear when he was deep in thought over a case covered his face.

"Of course he's happy! It's our first grandchild. Cashlynn needs a doctor ASAP. She already needs to start prenatal. That girl is a wild card, I'm going to have to talk to her about that." Mom got lost in her own world, turning and leaving the room while still making a list of things out loud.

"You don't seem very excited." I leaned back in the chair I was sitting in and crossed my arms over my chest.

"Did I ever tell you why I was so against you marrying a Cavana?" he asked.

"No, but after learning more about them recently I can only imagine."

He leaned forward, resting his elbows on his knees. "The Cavanas had their hands in a lot of shady shit. They had no integrity or morals. I know that might sound hypocritical considering what we do in the background, but we also have boundaries and things we'll never be mixed up in. I don't work with anyone I can't trust and they were contracted with a group of people who hired me to work in their defense when I was still a lawyer. I know when you're dealing with criminals you have to always watch your back and keep your eyes open, but even then I prided myself on always standing on my morals. The Cavanas didn't hold that same standard, they didn't care who they had to run over and sell out to get what they wanted. In the end they turned on the same people they were working for because the price was higher on the other side.

"When greed leads, eventually you will crumble. At some point you have to have a code and they have none. I don't like having to look over my shoulders when I'm doing business. There's already enough risk with the kind of people we work for and with. When my grandfather started The Bloodline, he made sure to build it on loyalty. That's how we've been so undetected and successful. When I took over I wanted to take this business further than just killing, I wanted to create a legacy each of my kids could build their own branch from and that's what I did. You each have unique skills and jobs but come together to form a well-oiled ship. Once you add in people who only are driven by money, that ship will eventually crumble."

"Cashlynn's not like that," I protested, cutting him off.

"I'm seeing that, but you have to understand where I'm coming from as well. A lot of people refused to work with the Cavanas because of how shady they were. Cashlynn doesn't seem to have their mindset, but are you sure she's fit to be a mother?"

I bit down on my back molars as my body went stiff, playing his words over in my head. "Out of all the women I've been with, I don't think there's one more qualified," I confessed truthfully. All the women I'd dealt with before Cashlynn were superficial. They didn't hold substance nor did they have traits that showed they would be able to nurture a child. Most of the time I wanted a body for the night and nothing past that. With Cashlynn, things were different, everything about her was new and exciting. Dealing with her showed just how much I'd been missing out on.

"You fought hard against getting married and having a child, yet you seem to be falling into the role so easily." Dad smirked.

"Yeah… well, when you find a woman like my wife, you can't help but want to explore the relationship more." I shrugged.

Dad stared at me intently. "You seem to have it all figured out then. You're a smart man. Me and your mama raised you right. I had no hesitation with handing The Bloodline over to you and I trust you know what's best for you and the family you're creating," he said, then switched to his native tongue as he continued. "Congratulations, son. I'm proud of you."

"Thanks, Pops."

I stuck around my parents' house a little longer, and on my way out, my mom called out to me.

"Can you try and get ahold of your brother? I've been calling him all day and he hasn't answered."

"Which one?" I had a feeling who she was talking about before she even responded.

"Which one stays stressing me out? That damn Ezra."

I nodded. "I'll stop by his house on the way to the club."

"And tell him to call me. I tried to call Cashlynn too, but she didn't answer either." Her eyes narrowed, making me chuckle.

"I'll have her call you, Mama." I leaned over and kissed her cheek.

Stepping outside their house, I eyed the large open yard in front. The bright green grass was freshly cut. The smell of flowers blew in the wind. My mom made sure it looked like something right out of *Better Homes & Gardens* magazine.

I headed for my car, parked in the large driveway.

After my own failed attempt at getting ahold of Ezra, I stopped by his house since it was on the way to The District.

Pulling up to his house, I cut the engine and stepped out of the car, making my way to the house. Ezra's car was parked in front of his garage so I knew he was home. Ezra lived in a high-priced area. Most of his neighbors were doctors, other lawyers, or held other jobs like them. Walking to the door, I tried to pull the screen door open, but seeing it was locked, I opted for the doorbell.

Just as I was about to hit it again, I heard the locks move then the front door opened. Ezra was dressed in a suit which meant he more than likely had just gotten home from the office. He unlocked the screen door and held it open.

"Big bro, wassup?" He grinned.

"Your mama been trying to get ahold of you." I stepped in the house.

My eyes circled the small entryway.

"I just got home. I've been in court all morning." He loosened his tie and started toward his living room.

"Make sure you call her."

"I will… later."

"You look stressed. Everything good?"

"Court kicked my ass today." He yawned, plopping down on his couch.

"You started your trial with Felix Benson?" I asked, referring to Wise's little brother. He was caught up on racketeering charges.

"Yeah. The little cocky bastard pisses me off. If I wasn't being paid so good, I'd hand him off."

My brows furrowed hearing thumping from overhead. "Someone else here?"

A sly grin formed on Ezra's face. He leaned back and kicked his feet out, crossing them at the ankle.

"Let's just say that blogger chick won't be an issue anymore." Mischief played in his eyes.

I studied my brother and flicked my eyes upward. "What the hell did you do?"

"She caught me breaking into her house so I had to do something to calm her down."

"I told you to scare her, not kidnap her."

"You chained your wife in your basement because you found her in your house. Are you really the one to talk?"

Laughing, I bobbed my head. "Touché, but what's your plan? You can't just keep her here." Our family had too many connections to be worried about him getting in trouble, but he still couldn't be too reckless. My brother normally wouldn't do something this outrageous and risky without a plan.

He shrugged. "I haven't decided yet, but me and Miss Ziora are gonna come to an understanding before I let her go." The twinkle in my brother's eyes showed me it was more to the story.

"As long as you know what you're doing. Don't fuck this up, Ez."

"I won't. Don't worry."

"Good. Keep me in the loop and let me know if you need me." I stood to leave.

"What's the status on Neil?"

"I got Emmet checking a new angle to find him." Neil was hiding well. I had spoken to Major and he had no insight on where Neil could be. Once he realized Neil was into shady side dealings and trying to undermine him, he washed his hands with him and left him to fend on his own.

"Call your mama!" I walked to the entryway. The banging sounded upstairs again. I glanced toward the steps and shook my head, opening the door. I didn't know what the hell Ezra was up to, but if I knew my little brother, it would turn out to be entertaining in the end.

My phone rang, interrupting my concentration as I went over things for the club. The shooting didn't slow business down, if anything it only made it increase. I was debating if I wanted to increase the number of pills I brought into the club again. With business increasing, the demand for them was too.

I checked the screen and saw it was Emmet calling me. I had been waiting for his call all day.

Quickly, I grabbed my phone and hit the green button to answer.

"E, tell me something good." I tapped my pen against the desk.

"I found him," he said, piquing my interest.

Sitting straighter, I gripped the pen tightly. "How? Where?"

"He's driving his son's car. Once I hit a dead end with his car, I thought about it and realized there could be more cars he has access to. I hacked the BMV and saw he was a cosigner on his son's car. Using the VIN, I was able to hack the GPS and locate him.

A smile split my lips and I stroked my beard. "Where did you find him? How do we know he's there?"

He grunted. "I wouldn't bring you any information without checking my facts." That was true. There was a reason my brother had taken his skills and opened an PI business. "He's hiding out in The Sticks."

"The Sticks, huh?" I dragged my tongue over my teeth. While Silver Stone was a wealthy city, there was a small part considered to be lower class. The Sticks was gang driven and known for killings, prostitution, and drugs.

"I looked up the address and it looks like the house belonged to his aunt. She's in a nursing home, but he still maintains the house for her."

"Send me the address." I reached for my computer to shut it down. My blood pumped with anticipation. Neil had been given too many chances and now it was time for him to answer for it all.

"Already ahead of you."

I pulled the phone back and checked my texts. "Got it."

"Good. Let me know if you need anything else." Before I could reply, he had hung up. That was fine though. Emmet had done his part and this wasn't his or any of my brothers' fight. It was time to end this fight and finally move on.

"**W**here are you taking me? What the hell is going on?" I asked, looking around, attempting to gauge exactly where we were.

Dante, Jackson, and Luke stayed silent. My legs bounced as my irritation grew. I wasn't sure what was going on, except Nazai had called and told me Dante was waiting for me downstairs. No one told me anything further than that. My stomach had been funny all day and the last thing I wanted to do was play games.

The area we were in wasn't too far from the church we had attacked just last week.

The street we turned onto was full of rundown houses. Some looked better than others but they all could use some upkeep if you asked me. When the car stopped, I went into my hoodie pocket and gripped my gun. The moment we started toward The Sticks, I went into my bookbag and grabbed it. While I didn't think Nazai would do anything to put me in harm's way, I wasn't going to be caught off guard again.

The back door opened and Jackson was standing outside of it. My brows furrowed. Dante said nothing. Luke was now out of the car.

Tossing my hood over my head, I slowly slid out of the car. My hand gripped my gun tightly and my finger rested on the trigger.

"This way," Jackson said, preceding me across the street. It was late at night so the street was dead besides the few houses with lights on and a couple cars that passed from the main street we'd turned off of.

Jackson opened the door to a red house. From the streetlights, I could see the paint was chipped and one of the front windows had a broken shutter.

My frown deepened. "What the hell is this?" I stopped, not wanting to go further. Staying alert, I bounced my eyes around the entry of the house and the porch we were on. My heart pounded rapidly.

"Everything's fine, Wildfire. You can release the gun." Nazai came out of the darkness into view with a crooked grin on his handsome face. He dropped his eyes to my mid-section before lifting them back to my face.

"Nazai? What the hell is this?" I stomped past Jackson to my husband.

He reached out and pushed my hair back. "You just wouldn't be you if you weren't difficult, huh?"

I bit the inside of my cheek, attempting to keep my irritation down. "I don't like being thrown into situations without knowing what's going on."

His smile grew. "Fair. Follow me." We walked to the back of the living room into the kitchen. I was confused until I laid eyes on Neil who was beaten and hanging from the fan of the low ceiling.

"Now, aren't you glad I brought you?"

Smiling, I walked further in the kitchen and circled Neil.

"How did you find him?"

"Emmet's the best in the business."

"Mhm." I noticed the bruising on his face. His head lifted slowly and his eyes fluttered open.

"It's…you," Neil strained out. His lip curled into a snarl.

"Hello, Neil. I heard you were looking for me." I grinned.

His nostrils flared and his eyes burned with hatred. I was caught off guard when he attempted to lunge at me. Nazai grabbed me, pulling me back.

"You bitch. You killed my son!" he bellowed.

Nazai released me and stalked toward Neil, cocking his arm back and sending his fist forward. "Watch your fucking mouth when addressing my wife."

"Fuck you and your wife" He spat, but Nazai avoided it.

He threw two more punches at Neil, the impact of his fist connecting sounded throughout the room.

Blood gushed from Neil's nose. It made my stomach churn and I held my midsection. It was clear the baby did not agree with the sight in front of us.

Nazai stepped back and flicked his glove-covered hand, flinging specks of blood.

"Now I planned on making this easy because I just wanted you gone, but since you want to continue being disrespectful, all that's out the window." I watched in curiosity as Nazai walked over and grabbed a chair from the table. He sat it down and looked at me.

"Take a seat, baby. Enjoy the show." I wondered what he had planned but I didn't question it.

"You know when you sent someone to shoot me, I was hit twice, right?" Nazai spun around, facing Neil who was now breathing heavier.

"I hate that I hired such an idiot and he missed. You should have died." Neil leveled his eyes on me.

I smirked. "Too bad only your son suffered that fate." I crossed my leg over my knee.

"Bitch!" he spat.

"Uh, uhn!" Nazai pulled his gun out and aimed it. He pulled the trigger, sending a bullet into Neil's right arm.

"Fuck!" he cried out.

Nazai pulled it again, this time hitting Neil in the side again, causing him to cry out. His body jerked. "Doesn't feel good, does it?"

Nazai looked around. "Now I wondered what would make this experience more enjoyable for my wife? She already took out your pedophile ass son."

"Pedophile? My son wasn't a fucking pedophile?" he gritted.

I laughed. "He was and that's why he had to die! I wish I could kill him all over again too," I called out.

Nazai looked down at me and smiled. His eyes were filled with adoration and warmness. "Now, now, wife. Just sit there and look pretty. I got this."

I cut my eyes at him. Nazai tucked his gun away and walked to a gas can near the wall. Picking it up, he walked back over to Neil.

Neil's panting was heavier now. His eyes widened as he watched Nazai. Amazement filled me as I watched him spray Neil with the fluid.

"No, what are you doing?" Neil coughed out, blood now dribbling from his mouth. His wounds leaked. He attempted to break free, but Nazai had him secured well.

"I told you I'm tired of playing with you. You've had me chasing after you for too long. So now I'm going to show you what I do to people who waste my time."

Nazai dug into his pocket and pulled out a book of matches. Neil quickly started shaking his head from side to side.

"Please, no, no!" he begged. His body twisted and turned.

"Too late. Give your son a fuck you in hell." Nazai struck a match and tossed it. Flames instantly engulfed Neil's body, rushing up from his legs to his head. His screams were gut wrenching and struck my eardrums.

"Nazai," I mumbled, holding my mouth over my hands. My stomach grew queasy as the smell of burning flesh flooded my nostrils. His skin began to char as he screamed and struggled to break free. The flames crackled and popped as the oxygen around us enhanced them.

"Nazai," I called out again. Bile built in the back of my throat.

The rope holding Neil gave way and his burning body went crashing onto the ground. He was barely able to move. His body twitched as it continued to burn. His screams had died out. The smell of his flesh melting away intensified.

I hunched over, holding my stomach, attempting to swallow the bile threatening to come out. My eyes watered and my skin ran hot.

Nazai pulled his gun out and aimed it, pulling the trigger and finishing Neil off.

"Now it's over." Nazai turned and looked at me. His eyes bucked realizing the state I was in. "Shit!" He rushed toward me and grabbed me. "I guess my baby doesn't agree with burnt flesh."

He assisted me out of the kitchen toward the door. The fresh, cool air felt like heaven against my hot skin.

"Get this handled," he told Jackson as we passed him.

"Will do, boss."

Nazai led me to the truck where Dante was waiting on the outside. I took a few deep breaths of the clean air.

"How you feel now?" he asked once we were in the truck.

I held my chest and closed my eyes. "Better. Especially now that he's gone."

Nazai's hand landed on my thigh. I peeked open an eye and looked over at Nazai. "I told you to leave it all to me. No one threatens my family and lives to tell about it."

A week had passed since Nazai killed Neil and things were starting to settle. I had seen a doctor and learned I was eight weeks along. I had gotten pregnant the night of my wedding when Nazai took my virginity and hadn't known it. It worried me since I had been drinking and had taken drugs, but the doctor said everything looked fine.

Now we were at the meeting house while Nazai led a meeting. I was starting to learn how things ran here. Each brother ran their own businesses, but there were times they needed to come together and work a job. Each brother was like a piece of the puzzle. Emmet was the brains who got the jobs in motion. Ezra was the legal help who stayed on standby if the family needed representation, but he also didn't hesitate to take a job. Lucas was the doctor who patched everyone up when needed, but he and Emmet rarely went on jobs unless more hands were needed. Even River, as the muscle and protection, played a part in the puzzle. Then there was Nazai, now the leader, but once happily took the kill jobs. It was amazing watching all them co-exist and work together because I had never seen this before. Even when my parents were alive, it was always every man for themselves.

A lot of the freelance cases they handled dealt with attacks and assaults against women and children. When they used the portal Emmet had set up, the jobs could vary.

"Tell me what's going on with the blogger, Emmet? Were you able to get inside her files when Ezra brought you her laptop?"

"The laptop was wiped clean."

"What? How the fuck did that happen?"

"She had magnets set up that crashed her system if the laptop ever passed through her door. I'm sure whatever was wiped is backed up somewhere, but it's gonna take some time to get it. Her security is tight and she's not an amateur. It's clear she's been heavily looking into the trafficking and missing kids in the area. It's obvious she hasn't let what happened to her sister go. I'm not sure what she has on our family, if anything, but I plan to find out."

Nazai pushed a heavy breath through his nose and rolled his neck between his shoulders. "And Ezra?"

"I'm handling it," Ezra replied. By the tick in Nazai's jaw, I could see his patience was growing thin with his brother.

"Make it sooner than later. We have much more important shit to worry about."

I zoned out as Nazai continued talking. As much as it annoyed me that I couldn't go out in the field like I wanted, I couldn't lie and say it didn't feel good to finally be able to sit back and not have to worry about anything for a change.

When the meeting was over and everyone prepared to leave, I watched as Carson followed Emmet. He was still mentoring my brother and Carson was enjoying himself. My brother was no longer that timid kid he once was and that made me happy. All I wanted was for him to be accepted and have confidence in himself.

"I spoke with my dad this morning. His lawyer friend is working on the paperwork to make us Carson's legal guardians. He's gonna make some calls and get it moved up and processed too."

"Us?" I asked with my brows scrunched together.

Nazai enclosed me in the chair, placing his hands on each of the arms and leaning down. "Well of course, Wildfire. You are my wife after all? Wouldn't that make the most sense?"

He grinned, causing my cheeks to heat. "I just wasn't aware that's what you wanted. You don't have to do that." My eyes shifted to the side.

"I know I don't *have* to do it, but I'm *choosing* too."

Slowly I moved my eyes back to meet Nazai's. It was hard to believe we had only been married two months but had come this far. I still struggled with not being so defensive and allowing him to lead, but I was trying. Nazai had brought a lot of changes in my life, most importantly he showed me what love looked and felt like. We might not have expressed the words, I didn't even know when I'd be ready to hear or say them, but I knew this wasn't the same cruel man I'd first met when I broke into his house.

I was brought back to reality when Nazai leaned in and pecked my lips. "What's got you thinking so hard?"

I scraped my teeth over my bottom lip. "Just thinking about how I made your life better by breaking into your house."

He laughed. "I think you got it backwards, baby. Your life was shit until you met me."

I rolled my eyes, making him laugh harder. I would never admit he had a point. If I hadn't broken into his house, that day me and my brother might still be on the run and we would have never found out what it felt like to have a real family surrounding us.

Curiosity filled me as I followed Jackson through the steakhouse doors. We were in downtown Silver Stone and it was a little past eight in the evening. I looked around, noticing the dining room empty outside of a couple of staff.

Two weeks had passed since Neil was killed. Nazai had been taking his role seriously, making sure each brother ran their part of the business fluidly. He had taken one killing job since and the two of us argued when I wanted to accompany him. I ended up staying at home after he reminded me of how my stomach became upset when he killed Neil. It pissed me off but made sense. Morning sickness was still kicking my ass every morning. My doctor had called in some medication to help me so I hoped it would take effect soon.

I paused when I noted Nazai in the center of the empty room sitting at a table. A pink, off the shoulder dress and clear heels were sitting on my bed when I got out of the shower with a note telling me to get dressed and Dante would be waiting for me within the hour. As far as I knew, we didn't have anything planned when it came to engagements, so I was confused.

My eyes scanned the dining room again before falling back on my husband who was now standing with a smirk on his face. Swallowing hard, I slowly walked toward the table.

"Good to see you following directions, wife," he said, approaching me. My eyes narrowed. He wrapped an arm around my waist and pulled me closer.

"Nazai, what is going on? Why is this place empty?" My nose scrunched while my stomach growled at the sweet aroma coming from the kitchen a couple of feet away.

Nazai leaned down and kissed me. "Can't a man rent a restaurant out to spend time with his wife?"

My eyes widened and my mouth parted. "What do you want?" I asked.

His grin broadened. "You always think I'm up to something." He bent his neck and pecked my nose, then my lips.

"Sit down." Releasing me, Nazai pulled the chair out and I watched him as I slowly took a seat. He rounded the table and took his original seat back.

On the table was a single rose in a vase between us. A bottle of apple juice and a glass of water with a lemon inside were in front of me while Nazai had water and a glass of brown liquid.

"Go ahead and look at the menu, the server should be back soon." Still confused on what this was, I wasn't going to argue with him. This baby had already begun increasing my appetite and it had only been a few hours since my last meal, yet I felt like it had been days.

"This baby has me wanting damn near everything," I mumbled as I eyed the entrees.

"Then get everything. Whatever you want." I diverted my attention up, gazing at him over my menu.

"Do you want me to blow up like a balloon?"

Nazai flashed me a crooked grin. "Wouldn't matter to me either way."

Rolling my eyes, I went back to the menu. I was stuck between the barbeque baked chicken and NY strip. The server came to the table. "Mr. Tavarez, here are the appetizers you requested. Are you two ready to order?"

I lifted my eyes and watched him drop jumbo shrimp, calamari, potato skins, and some kind of dip.

"Give us a few minutes," Nazai said, barely giving the middle aged man a glance.

"Yes, sir." He nodded, turning and walking off.

I eyed the food. Everything looked good and my mouth watered. "Why did you order so much?"

"You need to keep my baby fed."

I pressed my lips together tightly. Nazai was a helicopter dad already and I was still in the beginning stages. He made sure I ate three times a day and didn't allow me to do anything strenuous. We even argued about me going to the gun range. Some might have seen it as sweet, but I found it worrisome most days.

Rolling my eyes, I reached for my water and took a sip. I set the glass down and grabbed a shrimp, already tasting it before I bit into it.

We didn't speak at first. By the time the server came back, I had finished the shrimp and was working on a potato skin. I ended up ordering the garlic NY strip with loaded mashed potatoes and steamed lemon broccoli. Nazai got the T-bone steak and lobster mac and cheese with a loaded sweet potato.

"This is nice, huh? Just the two of us together. I don't think we've had a moment like this since our wedding night," Nazai said once it was just the two of us.

"I don't get why we're here though."

"Can't a man just take his wife on a date. Since we've been married, our lives have constantly been on the go. Now we can enjoy married life." He lifted his glass of liquor and took a sip.

A date? My brows scrunched. It was the first time I had ever been on one. When it came to Nazai, I was learning to trust him more, but I wasn't raised to be domestic. So all of this was foreign.

"I've never been on a date before." I shifted in my seat.

"I know. My mom informed me that since you're carrying my child, I should be more accommodating to you and show you that I appreciate the changes your body is about to go through." He paused and laughed to himself while shaking his head. "So consider this my appreciation."

My heart did an erratic dance inside me and my stomach flooded with heat. It still took me some time to accept when Nazai spit nice things my way.

"Thanks," I muttered, tugging on the corner of my bottom lip with my teeth. "Me and the baby appreciate it."

Sometimes I still resented Nazai for forcing me to get pregnant when I made my stance on it clear, other times I pictured myself as a mother and how my baby would look. I was starting to come to terms with things. Carson now knew about the baby and was excited to become an uncle. Nazai's parents were on board, as well as his brothers, including Emmet. He still rarely spoke to me but he did congratulate us.

"You look to be deep in thought. What's going through that wicked little mind?" Nazai asked. Another thing about him was he watched me a lot. Sometimes it felt like I never had a thought to myself when he was around. Oddly, I didn't mind it. No one had ever paid this much attention to me before without having ill intentions.

"Just thinking about how different the baby will grow up compared to how I did. Your family already seems to be in love with it and I'm still early on."

For a second, my stomach knotted. I didn't have anyone but Carson in my corner to celebrate this with and it was bittersweet at times. Nazai's family was so close and I'd never experienced that before.

"*Our* family," he stressed. "Our family is excited about this baby. You're carrying the next generation of greatness, Wildfire. A legacy is growing within you and that's something to be excited about." When I didn't respond, he continued. "Are you excited too?"

My head snapped back as if I had been struck. "What?"

"When you first learned about the pregnancy you weren't happy."

"I wonder why?" My eyes narrowed, but he smiled.

"It needed to be done." He shrugged. "But do you still feel the same?"

I bit the inside of my cheek, thinking about his question. "It's starting to grow on me," I started. "Knowing I'm about to be a mom is still unsettling, but I guess there's nothing I can do about it now, is there?"

"Damn right about that. Once that positive word popped on the screen, your fate was sealed." I frowned and this time reached for the apple juice.

"I never saw myself as a mother. My only goal was to take care of my brother and keep him safe. Knowing I'm about to have to do that again, but this time with someone I birthed, scares me and that's not easy to do, but I'm terrified I'm going to fuck this up." Maybe the baby was causing me to be more open than I was used to, but for the past few weeks I'd been internally battling whether or not I was meant for this.

"You didn't run when Neil and Maddox were taken care of, why?"

I balled my face up. "Because you threatened to track me down and kill my brother."

"I believed that was the case at first, but now I think it's more than that."

Something appeared on Nazai's face that made the knot in my stomach grow. Casting my eyes down at my plate, I poked the half-eaten potato skin with my fork. "And what's that supposed to mean?"

"Well, wife, I believe you finally realized I'm not your enemy. At times some of my actions may be questionable, but it's only because I know you can handle it. You're not some soft woman that needs to be handled with kid gloves, yet at the same time you are."

Lifting my eyes back to face him, I started to argue, but he held his hand up. "I don't mean that you're weak, but simply that you still have a lot to learn when it comes to allowing people to get close to you. Sometimes I see that wall breaking and you let me in, but then there's still times where you're guarded and ready to attack. Yet, I believe you're starting to trust your husband and see that I *am* on your side. You didn't feel the need to run like you did in the beginning because now you're more comfortable with bringing *our baby* into the world knowing you're not in this fight alone, but you have someone to fight alongside or even for you."

My stomach ended up doing flips as the room suddenly became too hot. I tried not to be so open. I had been groomed to not wear my emotions on my sleeve but it seemed I had grown too comfortable around my husband, causing me to expose my feelings without any actions.

"Tell me I'm right?" He pressed, staring at me over the rim of his glass.

Swallowing hard, I jutted my chin upward as my heart pounded inside of me viciously. I had reservations about opening up to Nazai after what he did to me at the barn that day, but since then Nazai had shown me that I could be open with him and it wouldn't be used against me. When I openly revealed what I did to my parents and why, he comforted me and brought me a security I hadn't felt, ever.

Scraping my bottom lip with my teeth, I balled my fists on the table. My lungs threatened to fail as they took in air.

"In a way, I guess you are," I finally admitted. "You helped me take care of Maddox and Neil. Your dad is helping me gain custody of my brother. You went to bat for me when it was clear your whole family didn't approve of us." My eyes lowered and my throat tightened. "I never had anyone do that for me before." My words came out in a whisper. "No one ever defended me or stood up for me. I always had to be strong and the protector and I…" I inhaled a deep breath and closed my eyes, suddenly feeling pressure building behind my eyelids. "I didn't want to go back to that. I *can't* go back to that. I'll never be the perfect submissive housewife, nor will I ever just bow down and do what I'm told." That brought a smirk on Nazai's face. "But you said that we were in this together, that you would take on my burdens, and I'm trying to believe that."

My skin felt itchy and my muscles twitched. It felt like I had been cracked open for all to see as I spoke the truth. I had never experienced a relationship before Nazai and I didn't even know how to have one but he didn't seem to care. It was clear he liked how things between us were going. It wasn't easy for me not to worry because growing up that was all I ever experienced. But being with Nazai showed me that maybe, just *maybe*, those times were behind me.

The server came with our meals, halting the conversation, which I was grateful for. I didn't like being so seen. My nerves were racing and my mind ran a million miles a minute. I needed something to distract me and help me stay grounded for the time being.

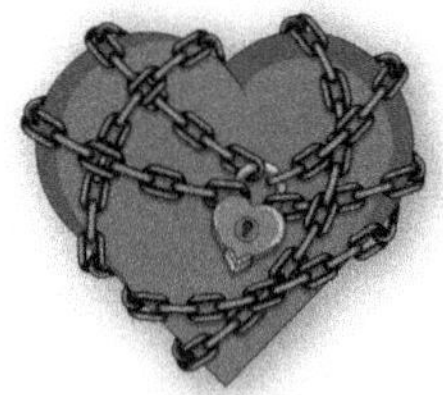

Nazai

I tabled the conversation when the food came, saying a quick prayer so the two of us could eat. I watched my wife, possibly more than most would deem normal, but I had learned things about her that gave her away in ways I wouldn't have in the beginning. Right now it was clear she was uncomfortable. She hadn't glanced toward me since the food had come out. Her body and movements were tense.

Renting out this restaurant and bringing her was mostly selfish. I didn't want anyone else to have my wife's attention but me. We had made major breakthroughs in the months we'd been married, but I still found there were some walls we still needed to climb, like her inability to express her love. Since being with her, I had heard her express it to Carson once and it was late at night when she went into his room to turn his TV down after he'd fallen asleep.

I wanted to tell her when we found out she was pregnant weeks back, but she wasn't ready to hear it. What I felt for Cashlynn might surpass love, it was like I craved her, everything about her, from her smile, to her curses and anger. The crazy and impulsive side to the withering mess she became when my dick was buried deep inside her. I wanted it all to the point where I didn't want her thoughts to be her own without me knowing them. My goal when we got married was to break and tame her, now it was to keep her. She still fought me. The pregnancy seemed to intensify that burning inside her, causing her to be more impatient than normal. She was also more sensitive than I'd even seen her too. I never knew which mood I would get nowadays.

"Cashlynn," I called out toward the end of our meal.

Unhurriedly, her eyes lifted to meet mine. They were guarded and distant.

"Do you believe me when I say I don't ever want to change you?"

Stiffly, she nodded, blinking slowly.

"And do you believe that no matter how much you fight it, I'm going to always push back to make you follow my lead?"

Again, she nodded, this time her eyes cut into slits, causing one corner of my mouth to rise.

"Then also believe that as long as there's breath in my body, I will never allow you to fight any battle alone again. I don't want a soft, compliant wife because there's no fun in that. One of the main reasons I can't get enough of you is because you challenge me and I *never* want that to change. Any threat toward you? We're handling that shit together because you know it turns me on to you see do your thing, baby." I licked my lips and her cheeks flushed. "I know you're not ready to say it, but I'm ready to tell you. I love you, probably fell in love with you the night of our wedding when I saw your blood coating my—"

"Okay, I get it!" She cut me off with a flustered expression on her face, causing me to chortle. "And no one besides Carson ever told me they love me before, how do I know…" Her words trailed off and her eyes averted from mine.

"That it's true?" Still, without looking, she nodded.

My heart tugged as I thought about the trauma my wife had experienced. It made me want to dig up her parents and kill them all over again, but this time slowly so they suffered.

"Because… even if you discount my words, then look at my actions. You know I don't tell you shit I don't mean, but if that's not enough, then just watch me, baby. You think I be ready to go toe to toe with my family over just anyone?"

A smile tugged at her lips but she still refused to meet my eyes. "I don't know when I'll be able to say it back. What if I'm not even able to tell our child?" This time she did face me and fire burned in her orbs. Her mouth turned upside down and her nostrils flared.

"I don't think that'll be an issue. You're stubborn as shit so I know you'll be able to push past your hang-ups eventually, and until then, if hearing it from me is what you need to help, then I gotchu."

Cashlynn released a heavy breath and fidgeted with her hands.

"Are we doing dessert this evening?" the server asked.

I looked toward Cashlynn for an answer but she shook her head. "Nah, we're good. Just bring the check."

"Yessir." He nodded, turning to leave.

I licked my lips and glanced at the black box that had been sitting next to me all night. Pushing back from the table, I picked it up and went around to the other side.

"What are you doing?"

"Just trust me." I set the box down and her eyes went to it. Confusion was plastered all over her face. Digging into my dress pants pocket, I grabbed the key to her collar and reached for it.

"What are you doing?" Her hand went to my wrist in a panic when I placed the key inside. Ignoring her, I unlocked and removed the collar for the first time in over three months. There was a slight tan mark from where it used to be, making the area lighter than the surrounding skin.

"Nazai." She rubbed the now empty area. I watched her to see how she would react to the gesture.

"Why?" Her voice shaky and airy as she squinted.

"When I first put that on you, it was a sense of entrapment. While I still want you and everyone to know that you're mine, I think the meaning of the collar has changed." I reached for the black box and opened it.

Cashlynn's mouth dropped and her brows shot to her hairline seeing the diamond collar. The base was made of white gold and diamonds covered it. Hanging from it was a charm that had NT just like the nipple rings I had pierced her with.

"Did you have to include your initials?"

I smirked and brought it to her neck.

"Of course, wife. Everyone has to know who you belong to."

"I'm not your property," she muttered, bringing her hands to the collar and brushing it lightly.

My dick filled with blood seeing my initials hanging from her throat.

After securing the collar, I moved my hand up and cuffed her hair. I gripped it tightly, forcing her head back. Leaning over, I inhaled her heavy breathing, loving the blazing passion now in her eyes.

"And that's where you're wrong, Wildfire. Everything about you, from the baby growing inside you to the air you breathe to the fight inside you belongs to me. There will *never* be another who will ever say they have ties to you."

"Same goes for you," she breathed out. Her chest rose and fell quickly.

I grinned. "Of course."

"Because you know what will happen if you ever tried to be with another woman."

My dick grew harder and my pulse raced.

"Tell me… tell me what would happen." My mouth was now inches from hers.

Cashlynn reached up and gripped my beard. "I'll kill both of you, slowly and painfully, using my knife."

Smiling harder, I crashed my mouth into hers. She moaned and slanted her face a tad to give me better access when she opened her mouth for me.

Cashlynn might have felt love wasn't for her or that she wasn't capable of handling it, but she was wrong. Her actions proved to me every day that she loved me more than she allowed herself to see.

The end!

Enjoyed the Taverez family? Please don't forget to leave a review/ rating!

Although Cashlynn and Nazai's story has ended, the main background plot isn't over. If you want more don't worry, Ezra's story is coming spring 2025.

More By Tay Mo'Nae

Standalones:
4 Ever Down With Him
He Ain't Your Ordinary Bae
Overdosed off a Hood Boys Love
These H*es Ain't Loyal
These H*es Doin' Too Much
These H*es Actin' Up
When Love Becomes A Need
When Love Becomes A Reason
When Love Becomes A Purpose
This Heart Plays No Games
This Heart Still Holds You Down
Riskin' It All For A Bad Boy
Rescued By His Love
Tempted Off His Love
DND: Caught Up In His Love
Imperfect Love
Got It Bad For An Atlanta Boss

Novellas:
Let Me Be Your Motivation
Xmas With A Real One
Valentine's Day With A Real One
Switch'd Up
Please Me
Still 4 Ever Down With Him
The Way You Make Me Feel
Who I Used To Be

Series:
His Love Got Me On Lock
My Love Is Still On Lock
Addicted To My Hitta

Serenity and Jax: A Houston Hood Tale
A Houston Love Ain't Never Been So Good: Yung & Parker
A Bad Boy Captured My Heart
Down To Ride For An ATL Goon
Still Down To Ride For An ATL Goon
In Love With A Heartless Menace
Turned A Good Girl Savage
Finessed His Love
She Got A Thing For A Dope Boy
& Then There Was You 1-2

Maple Hills:
The Sweet Spot
Strokin' The Flame Within' Her Heart
A Blind Encounter
A Second Swing At Love

Butter Ridge Falls:
Remember The Time
Can't Help But Love You
Chocolate Kisses
Tattoo Your Name On My Heart
Capture My Love
Aisha & Gage: Wedding Special
It's Always Been You
Trust Me With You
A Girl Like Me

New Haven:
Drunk in Love
All He Ever Needed
All He Ever Wanted

Pikemoore Falls:
When A Bad Boy Steals Your Heart series
Ariah & Lucian: A Pikemoore Novel

<u>West Pier:</u>
<u>Wrapped Up In His Ruggish Ways</u>
<u>Love In The Studio</u>
<u>Inflamed In His Love</u>

<u>The Parker Sisters:</u>
<u>The Parker Sisters: Gianna</u>
<u>The Parker Sisters: Aurora</u>
<u>The Parker Sisters: Sloane</u>

<u>Dark Romance:</u>
<u>Captured Beauty</u>